Alva

Rose Doyle graduated in English from Trinity College, Dublin, and went on to become a successful journalist. She is the author of three best-selling children's books, written following the first broadcast of her radio play, and two previous adult novels. The first of these, *Images*, was published in Ireland in 1993, and was followed by *Kimbay*, her debut novel in the UK. Rose lives in Dublin with her two sons.

Also by Rose Doyle

Kimbay

ROSE DOYLE

Alva

PAN BOOKS

First published 1996 by Macmillan

This edition published in 1997 by Pan Books
an imprint of Macmillan Publishers Ltd
25 Eccleston Place, London SW1W 9NF
and Basingstoke

Associated companies throughout the world

ISBN 0 330 34845 0

1 3 5 7 9 8 6 4 2

A CIP catalogue record for this book is available from
the British Library

Typeset by CentraCet Limited, Cambridge
Printed by Mackays of Chatham plc, Chatham, Kent

For my family and friends

Acknowledgements

I was very lucky to have the ear of friends who are independent film-makers. They gave me time, advice, plenty of low-down and, between the jokes and gossip, encouragement. I am indebted – and wish them all the luck they wished me.

A hundred thousand thanks too to my friends, generous and supportive to a fault. And to my family, always there when I need them.

A special thanks to Simon for his inspirational advice and to Uriel for his practical help.

Prologue

As Constance Moore she stood, rigid and controlled, inside the long front window. When the brass knocker on the front door echoed for the second time she took a deep breath and looked across the garden. Without expression she took in the late, late roses of autumn, the leafy walks and distant summerhouse. Beyond it all the deep, calm indigo of Dublin Bay lay languid in the distance.

'Come!' she called and watched in the rococo-style mirror over the mantel as the door opened.

It was there, in its reflection, that Constance Moore met the eyes of the brother she had not seen for twenty-two years. 'Hello, Jimmy.' There was no welcome in her voice.

'Adye,' he nodded. 'So you made a woman, in the end. A well got-up woman too. Not dead at all, like we thought.'

She stood, still as stone and silent.

'We lost our father to the same influenza plague as took your husband, Adye . . .' His eyes were mean and unblinking.

'Our father was dead to me long before I left.' Constance, interrupting him, was harsh. Jimmy O'Brien's face reddened.

'You've made a cold, hard woman.' He paused. 'And from the sound of things you were a worse than cold wife to the man who died while you were nursing him through the influenza ... It was thought you poisoned him ...'

'You know nothing of what happened, Jimmy, nor of what I am.'

'I know that Adye O'Brien's well and truly dead, anyway.'

'I had hoped so.' Constance's voice was low, and flat. 'What do you want, Jimmy? What have they asked you to—?'

'Cut! For fuck's sake, cut it!'

The cry was harsh and sudden and female. It coincided with the appearance in the bay outside of a high-speed catamaran. Filming stopped and all hell broke loose.

In the mêlée a young woman who'd been watching slipped out of the room. Tall, with black hair and blue eyes, she was almost, but not quite, beautiful. Too striking for that convention. She made her way across the garden to where an old man was cleaning a pond.

'They're working on the last scenes.' She trailed her hand in the water. 'They'll be gone in days.' She smiled. 'We've survived.'

'We have?' He slopped greeny sludge into a bucket.

'Of course we have. More than.'

'They've brought a lot of changes and they're not gone yet.'

'Could be that some of the changes were needed.' When the old man grunted and began to fill another bucket she stood impatiently. 'We'll be back to being a hotel in a week's time – and we'll be doing better business than we ever did before.'

'*That,*' the old man was decisive, 'remains to be seen.'

Chapter One

The phone call came on the day of a crisis at De Novo House Hotel. So much followed it so quickly that Alva, looking back, wondered if there had been some sort of cosmic design at work on that glorious sunny day in May. But that was when she was in a place so removed from the old hotel that anything seemed possible.

Whether cosmic design or chance, the call was definitely where it all began. The crisis wasn't really important – things at De Novo had reached a point where every day produced an upset of some kind. That day's problem simply meant that, when the call came, Alva was more susceptible than she might otherwise have been. It primed her, made her ready to jump at any opportunity to make money, grab at any novelty which would bring people to the hotel.

Thomas was the cause of the problem, and not for the first time. Alva's first indication that he'd been interfering with the hotel's only guest came when, thin and twitching and dressed in a yellow tracksuit, the man came to her to complain. She was at the davenport in the hallway which served as a reception desk.

'Miss Joyce.' She'd noticed the reedy voice when he checked in. 'There is a cat asleep on my bed.'

'Oh, that'll be Thomas. I *am* sorry.' Alva, straightening

up, sounded as if she meant it. 'I'll have him removed at once—'

'At once won't be soon enough.' He sniffed noisily. 'Creature shouldn't be there in the first place. I'm allergic to cats and I'd like my bill.' His eyes were red-rimmed and runny.

'Mr Webb, isn't it?' Alva smiled brightly and checked the single name in the ledger. She'd been right in thinking, when he arrived, that he had fuss-pot potential. 'I can give you another room . . .'

'Thank you, but no thank you.' The twitch became quite violent. He produced a large hanky. 'I came here for the peace your advertisement promised, and had hoped to lie down after my jog. The cat has put that out of the question.'

'I can only apologize again . . .'

'You could also do your business a favour by getting rid of that animal.' He blew his nose in the hanky. 'It's been all over the place since I arrived. To say it's unhygienic would be stating the—'

'Thomas lives here. This is his home.'

The imperious, interrupting voice was elderly. It belonged to a straight-backed woman dressed in mauve. She stood at the bottom of the oak staircase, smelling vigorously of musk perfume and aniseed fumes and holding a bushy-looking, indolent tabby in her arms. George Webb sneezed loudly and took several backward steps to the open door.

'I would appreciate your keeping that animal at a distance, madam,' he said through the hanky. The

6

cat's tail uncurled and moved in a slow, grey arc against the woman's dress.

'Poor Thomas.' She stroked him, a languorous movement with a hand wearing a clutter of rings. 'He's used to being loved, you know.' Her faded grey eyes, energetically daubed with mauve eyeshadow, looked with dislike at George Webb.

'Mr Webb is allergic to cats, Ellen,' Alva said.

'Explains why he looks like a canary, doesn't it, Thomas?' Ellen Donovan stroked the cat again. 'You should try to conquer your allergy, Mr Webb.' She took a step closer and for a moment it looked as if she might hand George Webb the cat. He blinked, then swallowed.

'Ellen! Please take Thomas out of here.' Alva's voice was sharp and exasperated. The older woman sighed and made a cooing noise to the cat before, without warning and with a shrug, she opened her arms and dropped him to the ground.

'Go catch a rat, Thomas,' she urged, 'earn your keep.' When the tabby stood there, back arched and stiffly stretching, she encouraged him on his way with a swift toe in the tail. George Webb's twitch became a series of shudders as the cat streaked across the quarry-tiled hallway to the back of the house. 'You're quite safe now, Mr Webb,' Ellen said, 'but what a *terrible* pity you're leaving us.' Yawning, she jiggled beringed fingers in a farewell wave and headed back up the wide staircase.

'You've been with us two nights, I think?' Alva,

businesslike, pulled a ledger across the writing slab of the old desk.

'Two nights, yes,' George Webb agreed reluctantly. 'And I must say, Miss Joyce, that while it is one thing to find a dumb animal strayed onto my bed, it is quite another to be insulted by a vulgar old woman who behaves as if she owns the place . . .'

'Ellen grew up here. It was her family home. I think she can be forgiven a little oddity of behaviour, don't you?'

George Webb sniffed into his hanky without answering. Alva, looking at his sparse red hair and yellow tracksuit, thought that vulgar exactly described his appearance. Ellen, in her odd way, had style. She also had an attitude problem with guests.

'Your bill will take a few minutes,' Alva said. 'Perhaps you'd like to stroll in the garden while I make it up?'

'I would not. Your gardener is a surly, unwelcoming type. And in any event I am not a stroller. I am a jogger. I will pack.'

'As you like.' Alva was brisk.

His sneakers echoed squelchily in the oak-panelled hallway as he went up the stairs. It was a large hallway with the wide part of the staircase rising from the back and climbing to a lurid, church-like stained-glass window. From a landing under the window two narrower sets of stairs led to the semicircular gallery around the hallway. The bedrooms, eight of them, opened off the gallery landing. Light from the window, that sunny day, shone blameless and gaudy through the window and caught the tracksuit in its beams. A canary, Alva thought, was a charitable description of George Webb.

Half an hour later she stood in the door and watched him drive away, carefully and slowly, between the trees of the avenue. She was a tall young woman, and slender, but even so was dwarfed by the grandiose proportions of the door. Framed there she looked deceptively delicate, even ethereal. Physically, she was neither of those things.

Alva Joyce was striking. She had a wealth of black, curling hair which, for now, was caught severely at the nape of her neck. Her eyes, under diamond-shaped brows, were a cool, uncompromising blue. She bit her full bottom lip.

'Good riddance,' she muttered, 'and don't send your friends.'

Which would have been all very well if there had been even the promise of another guest to take George Webb's place. But the summer season was under way and De Novo House Hotel's three guest bedrooms lay empty and unspoken for. If it weren't for the restaurant (small and with a wine licence only), and for the straggling lunchtime clientele and regular, modest numbers of evening diners attracted by cook Bernie Brennan's excellent fare, things would have been desperate. As it was, things in De Novo were merely approaching that state.

Alva sat on the first of the granite steps and turned towards the garden, squinting into the afternoon sun. There hadn't been many days like this recently and she'd hoped the sun would be an omen for good. Large, grey, old and imposing, De Novo soaked the heat into its wintry stone. The gardens were coming to life, making the move into summer with splashes of colour by the pond and in the rose garden. Only a joyless nerd like George Webb could have resisted the light on the clematis-draped bower, the romance of the old summerhouse in the distance. All *he'd* seen, most likely, was the wilderness aspect, the rampaging growth. And, of course, De Novo's 'surly gardener'.

Theo Donovan was not, unfortunately, getting any younger and Alva didn't at all doubt that he had been less than welcoming to George Webb. But what seventy-five-year-old Theo lacked in social graces towards the George Webbs of this world, he more than compensated for in his ministering, productive care of the garden. He refused all help, and there was a lot of garden for him to be productive in. Where it sloped down the hillside and around the house his obsession ensured that the willow oak and fuchsia, delphiniums, lupins, old roses and phlox of De Novo's Victorian heyday flourished, but with a lot more abandon.

De Novo House was Theo Donovan's family home; with his sister, the cat-loving Ellen, he'd grown up there. These days, he was its joint owner with Alva, her ostensible partner in the running of it as a hotel. His care of the garden was his sole contribution. Alva searched for him now, eyes lazily covering the pathways and bushes, and saw him almost at once. His mane of silvery-white hair was half-buried in the dark green of the old desfontainea bush he was working on and, even sitting on the steps, she could sense his contentment.

She stretched her legs in front of her, absently and from habit frowning at their length, slipped off her shoes and allowed herself to enjoy the cooling heat of the granite under her feet.

'George R. Webb may not have been the dream guest.' She spoke aloud, swearing a little. Talking to herself was something she'd been doing since the times, as a child, she'd had no one else to talk to. 'But he was a full-paying one until Thomas went catnapping . . .'

'Talking to ourselves again, are we? Such a lovely day for it, too.' Ellen, appearing on the step behind her, lifted her face to the sun. She had put on the dark, bluish-brown sable she wore for even the briefest of outings from the house. 'Mmm. Some heat at last. Enjoy it while you may, my dear, the next onslaught of guests could happen any minute.' She gave a short snigger.

'I wish you'd stop creeping up behind people,' Alva sighed.

'You need a sunhat, my girl,' Ellen said. 'Nothing ages the skin quite like ultraviolet rays. And of course you're not getting any younger, are you?'

'I'm twenty-seven,' Alva said. But Ellen knew that, was horribly aware that Alva was forty years younger than she was. Ellen could not accept growing old. Ignoring her, Alva raised her creamy, pale face to the sun. She wasn't unaware of her looks but was more conscious of their drawbacks than advantages. She would have preferred her skin without its pepper-dusting of freckles, a smaller mouth, and eyes a warmer colour than the cobalt blue she'd inherited from her mother. She also fancied cutting her height down to size. Five-ten was a fearsome height for a woman.

'Might as well go with a bang as a whimper.' She grinned and brushed an escaped curl clear of her upturned face.

'Nothing like living dangerously, it's true.' Ellen, sailing down the steps in a waft of musk, was waspish.

Alva opened her eyes and watched her make her way surefooted over the cobbled frontage of the house, the lynx swinging loose to the calves of what were still an excellent pair of legs. In the distance Ellen had the vigour and slender appeal of her beautiful youth. Her tragedy lay in her ability to convince herself that this was still the reality.

Unlike George Webb's, Ellen's journey would end in the nearest pub. In the dark of McNally's snug she would sip Pernod through the afternoon before returning for a dinner which she would not eat and a bottle of Chablis which she would efficiently demolish. This diet, which as far as Alva could see was one she'd followed for a lifetime, had no apparent physical ill effects. The effects on her mercurial disposition and terminal boredom were harder to discern.

Alva dabbled briefly with the idea of joining her but decided against it. Ellen wouldn't welcome company and, as far as exercise went, Alva'd already had her daily run. Not a George R. Webb-type job either, but a

proper, burning streak along the winding roads outside the ivy-clad walls of the garden.

The roads around that hilly part of the coast were
narrow, some of them leading to the sea, some to the
village and other houses on the wooded slopes. The
widest and straightest of them followed the coast into
Dublin. Below it an electrified rail line, successor to
the earlier railway which had made the place a haven
for the nineteenth-century commuter, followed a par-
allel route. On fine, or even reasonably fine days, the
train brought people to the strand below to picnic and
swim, exercise their dogs and their children. Some of
them, sometimes, climbed the wooded hillside to De
Novo House for drinks or to eat. Most went to one of
the two large hotels lower down.

A small breeze had blown up, chilly against Alva's
bare legs. She slipped her shoes back on and was
standing when the phone rang, strident in the empty
hallway.

'Hello. De Novo House Hotel.' Alva was cheerful
but not effusive. No point advertising their
desperation.

'Alva?' The voice on the other end was doubtful. 'Is
that you?' Alva had no such doubts. She knew instantly
who the voice on the phone belonged to. There was
no mistaking Seona Daly's high, girlish tones. She
tightened her hold on the handset and felt her anxiety
rise. She did *not* want to talk to Seona Daly, not now,
nor at any other time she could think of in the future.
Seona must know that – so why was she ringing? The

thought kept her holding the phone until the voice sounded in her ear again. 'Alva? Please don't hang up . . .' it was breathless and pleading.

'Hello, Seona,' Alva said. 'What can I do for you?' Apart from dropping you over a cliff somewhere, she thought, and cursed the curiosity which had prevented her hanging up.

'You sound so *officious*. Not at all your friendly self.' There was a laugh on the line. 'How *are* you?' The question sounded sincere.

'Fine. How're you?' Alva, polite and discouraging, sounded anything but. Curiosity had, after all, killed the cat.

'Not bad. You know how things are in here, up and down. More down than up at the moment, if you want to know, but I suppose you don't. Mulcahy's still on my case, day and night . . .' Seona was babbling, definitely babbling. Which meant she was uneasy – and so she should be, deserved to be. Alva let her run on a little before cutting her short.

'You didn't ring me to discuss newsroom politics, surely?' she asked.

'No, I didn't.' The voice slowed down. 'I actually want to do you a favour, believe it or not. Only you're not making it easy . . .'

Alva needed a favour from Seona Daly like she needed a hole in the head. 'Why should I?' she was curt.

'Because you should be big enough to forgive and forget. Oh, come on, Alva, surely to God what happened is history now? We all make mistakes—'

'I make that three platitudes in as many sentences. You should try editing yourself, Seona. But yes, I agree, we all make mistakes. Mine was trusting you.'

'I'll concede you that one.' Seona sounded humbled. 'What I did was definitely among the less forgivable of mistakes. *Mea culpa, mea culpa.* I'd have said it before but you never did give me a chance to apologize.'

'You knew where to find me. You could have contacted me here any time in the last seventeen months.' Alva took a deep breath. She wished most profoundly that she wasn't having this conversation. Seona Daly was a good journalist, when she wanted to be. But she'd been a lousy friend and colleague. Alva didn't want to talk to her but didn't want to maintain hostilities either. 'I don't know that an apology is what's called for, anyway,' she said.

'What is then? What can I do?'

'Nothing. Look, let's forget it. You're right. It's over, in the past.' Seona must want something. She would never put herself through this kind of humiliating call unless she did.

'I could explain if you want—'

'No!' The interruption was sharp. 'I really don't want to talk about it, Seona. What's the favour?' Alva allowed herself to be mildly encouraging.

'Well, something came up the other day that reminded me of you. To do with your having moved on to bigger and better things, become an hotel owner . . .'

'Half owner.'

'Same difference.' Seona's voice, now she'd got Alva listening, had become more confident. 'Thing is, in my own continuing position as a poor journeywoman hack I was attending a press conference. More of a drinks thing really, to announce another film being made here. Hardly news any more, is it? I mean, the hills and valleys are falling down with creative souls with cameras these days, aren't they?'

'If you say so.'

'Well, this movie's more interesting than most.' Seona dropped her voice to a low rumble. 'It's the true story of an unsolved Dublin murder. Period piece about a woman who murdered her husband at the turn of the century and got away with it.' Her voice resumed its normal tone. 'Nice one, huh? It's being made as part of a multi-film deal called the Millennium Project. Seems someone in filmland came up with the idea of celebrating the end of the century by filming hundred-year-old unsolved murders in six European capitals. Dublin got in on the act through the director, fellow called Luke O'Hanlon, who seems to have a personal stake in it. But the big thing is that it's going to star Clara Butler. Remember her?'

'Clara Butler?' Alva, waiting to hear how any of this involved her, was caught on the hop. 'Don't think so. Should I?'

'You should. Though growing up the way you did I suppose you missed out on trivia like stars of the seventies . . .'

Alva could see her ex-colleague shrug, pity and impatience a likely mixture on her round face. There would be the inevitable cup of cold black coffee on her desk and her small, berry-brown eyes would be on a constant rove around the newsroom. 'Is there any reason why I should know about Clara Butler now?' she asked.

'You should know because she's going to star in this film. And if you play your cards right you just might get some money out of the people making it . . .'

'I hate mysteries.' Alva, doodling idly on a pad, sat up straight. 'What exactly are you talking about?'

Seona laughed. 'Thought that would get your full attention,' she said. 'I'm going to put a proposal to you, one that should bring in a few bob for that hotel of yours. And don't pretend you don't need it. I *know* you do, and how badly you need it too. I'm an investigative journalist, remember?'

Her laugh this time was short. Seona Daly had long lost her once biting enthusiasm for truth and a good story, and for years had been coasting along with an eye on the main chance and next junket. Alva's years working with her had been an eye-opener on how to operate the system. Any system. That there was something in this film business for Seona she had no doubt. That she needed something from Alva was also a growing certainty.

'What's the proposal?'

'First you must hear me out on Clara Butler and the film. Things will come together when you've got the whole picture.' She laughed. 'Picture. Get it?'

'I get it.'

'Same old bundle of laughs, Alva.' Alva heard a

deeply drawn breath, the unmistakable sound of Seona succumbing to the cigarettes she was constantly giving up. 'First the dope on Clara Butler. She was one of Hollywood's unoriginal, green-eyed temptresses, made a lot of junk films and a few goodish ones. She was touted about as wild and Irish but her exact connection with the auld sod was shrouded in PR hype. In the early eighties she disappeared from the scene and the world was told she'd tired of the celebrity life. Euphemism for drug-abuse, most likely. Then, a few years ago, she resurfaced on the New York stage. I got very little on her from the people handling the press conference, so her Irish heritage may not even exist.'

'You want to interview her.'

'Bingo. I want to have first whack at getting not only her but the director and others involved, too. It's looking like Justine O'Dea and a ravingly sexy young English actor called Nick Hunt will have parts. I want to follow it up with a few little trips around Europe to visit the sets of the other films being made. It'll make a very nice series . . .'

'And bring a few nice trips your way, too.' Alva was dry.

'Why not?' Seona enjoyed an enormous and satisfactory-sounding drag on her cigarette. In the background Alva heard the familiar, raucous newsroom buzz with its rush, tension, camaraderie, cynicism and laughs. She felt not a whit of nostalgia.

'So, now you know where I stand and what I want,' Seona went on. 'The rest is for you, so listen carefully, Alva my pet.' She became coaxingly businesslike. 'This is the voice of the real world and it's making you an offer. Have I got your full attention?'

'Yes.'

'Great. Thing is, the crowd who're making this film badly need an old house to make it in. Seems they had a place all lined up and it fell through. I got the word from Oscar Duggan – you know Oscar, don't you? Gay and fat and forty and works in films when he's not interior-designing houses? Says he knows *you*, anyway. He's location manager for this film so when he told me all this I immediately thought of my old colleague Alva and her Victorian pile by the sea. Ideal, just what you're looking for, I told Oscar . . .'

'You've never been here, never even seen the place . . .'

'A technicality. I have my spies and I've heard. Glorious and dingy was the word I got back. Sorry about that, Alva, but it does sound as if you could do with a few bob. Look, just consider the pragmatics of it. The big money circulating in this country at the moment is in the film industry. And there's a *lot* of dosh behind this project, European Union as well as American. This is your chance to grab some. You'd be a fool not to.'

'Yes . . .' Alva was thinking. 'What would I have to do for the money?'

'Nothing much. Let them use the hotel for filming, is all. From what Oscar says they'd take it over for about six weeks, pay you a large cheque and be off again. More than that, though, it would put your De Novo House on the map, make it known. I'll mention

19

it in my articles and the production company, obviously, would include it in their promotional guff. Your hotel will be all over the place, Alva. People will gallop out there in droves to eat in the room where Clara Butler murdered her husband . . .'

'You're very persuasive, Seona.' Alva's cool tone belied a mounting excitement. Seona was right. Everything she said *could* happen. This could mean money and publicity, exactly what the place needed. On the other hand it could mean disaster. Marauding camera people and technicians could wreck the place and the film could be a dud and make a joke of De Novo.

But it was a commerical joke at the moment, and the repairs needed were like a running sore.

'What do I do?' she asked.

'Meet with Oscar Duggan. Let him have a look at the place. I've practically sold him the idea already so there shouldn't be any problem. It's up to you to work out a deal which gives you what you want.'

'Providing I decide to go for it.'

'You'd be crazy not to. Believe me, Alva, I'm doing you a favour. Buying into De Novo House was a good shot on your part but, let's face it, it's the hotel nobody knows. You've blown your job in journalism and you've blown your money. This is a chance to recoup . . .' An exhaled breath came heavily down the line. 'Another thing you might consider, Alva, is that my intentions *could* be for the best. I might even be trying to make amends.'

'You might.' And pigs might fly and fish sing, Alva

thought. Aloud she said, 'You do know I'm only half owner of De Novo . . .'

'So you said. But the other half belongs to the old man whose family owned the place for years, right?'

God, but she could investigate when she wanted to.

'Right,' Alva said. 'Theo Donovan. He'll have to agree too.'

'That's your problem.' And if you can't deal with it, her tone implied, then you shouldn't be in business. 'You do know Alva,' she was crisp, 'that Kevin was a rat in his heart? Still is. Anyway, be seeing you. Have fun with Oscar.'

She was gone, the phone dead in Alva's hand and a wildly probable proposition in her head to consider. She would ignore Seona's last remark, concentrate on the real content of the call. De Novo would make a perfect film set. It was eccentric, authentic and quiet. What more could a film company want?

Theo would hate the idea, but would hate the alternative even more. As things stood, the chances that they would have to sell within a year were good. If she stopped working in the hotel, pulled out her effort, the chances were rather more than good.

And that was the alternative she would put to Theo if he didn't go along with having the film company at De Novo. He wouldn't dare call her bluff.

Chapter Two

Oscar Duggan had grown fatter, and altogether more flaccid, since Alva had last seen him. His increased girth rolled in soft folds from under an embroidered waistcoat and an additional chin folded itself uncomfortably into a cravat at the collar of his prim-rose shirt. The rest of him was draped in the floppy folds of a brick-coloured linen suit. For a man of not much more than forty he did not look one bit healthy.

It wasn't until he swept into the hall, beaming and too friendly for someone she'd met only twice before, that Alva was struck by his increased sense of import-ance, too. She reminded herself that he was a known and notorious gossip and that gossips, in her experi-ence, invariably presumed friendship when it suited them. Oscar Duggan, she had no doubt, knew a lot more about her business than she did about his. He went on to prove her right immediately.

'Alva, sweetheart! You look wonderful! As always.'

As always. The man hardly knew her. Mildly irritated by his effusive familiarity Alva sidestepped his hug and gave him her hand. 'Hello, Oscar,' she said, 'nice to see you again.' His fingers felt spongy.

'The role of chatelaine suits you, dear girl.' His

sepia eyes slid from under her gaze to wander around the hallway and up the stairs. 'You were never an authentic part of the media mob. Now, this,' he beamed and displayed a rather endearing dimple, 'is *much* more you. Dignified and handsome. Don't you think she's dignified and handsome, Jack?'

Alva, smile fixed and wearing a little thin, turned to greet the man who'd sauntered in after him. He was the antithesis of Oscar Duggan; fit-looking, urbanely and perfectly besuited, fiftyish. His dark hair was shot through with silvery grey and his face, probably the rest of him too, was tanned.

Meeting his eyes, Alva reckoned he was about an inch shorter than she. They were nice eyes, cool grey but friendly.

'Ms Joyce.' He enunciated her name slowly and gave her a frankly observing look as he extended his hand. *Touché*, she thought. She'd certainly taken him in.

'Dignified and *lovely*,' he corrected Oscar. He held her hand firmly and for seconds only. A once-broken nose made his smile crooked. 'I'm Jack Kelly, executive producer of the movie we're here to discuss.' His accent was American, New York it sounded like, and his voice deep. She liked it. 'Hope you don't mind me appearing like this. Our director is tied up this morning and since I was in town I thought I'd come along with Oscar here . . .' He gave a small, apologetic shrug and smiled his crooked smile. A much-practised smile, Alva guessed, but likable. 'I sure hope you can help us with this location problem we're having.'

'Let's hope we can accommodate one another.'

Alva, always slightly unnerved by charm, was crisp. 'And please call me Alva.'

'Jack. Mind if I slip off my jacket?'

'Of course not, please do.'

'I'm told this weather isn't typical.' He hung the jacket over his arm and loosened the neck of his stone-coloured silk shirt. He had broad shoulders, a narrow waist and, unless he was wearing a corset, a flat stomach. 'Everyone had me geared up for rain and wind.'

'Everyone was right,' Alva said. Since the day of Seona's phone call the weather had grown progressively warmer. Already, at ten in the morning, there was an unnatural humidity in the air. 'We've had three days of this heat and the city's gone into minor shock. But don't worry, it won't last. Why don't we sit in the drawing room? It's cooler.'

Leading them across the hall she wished she'd gone for something more exciting than the prim formality of her beige suit. With these two men it made her feel like a schoolgirl. In the drawing room, suffused with bright sunlight and at its best at that hour, she shook her hair loose and felt a lot better.

Oscar Duggan sank immediately into an armchair by the window. He took in the garden and sea views and gave Jack Kelly a raised-eyebrow look which the other, standing in the centre of the room, ignored. Alva, given the hour, decided against an offer of alcohol. 'Tea? Coffee? Fruit juice?' she asked.

'Could you manage a gin and tonic?' Oscar Duggan gave a small groan. 'Hair of the dog, you know.

Consequences of the excellent company and hospitality afforded by Jack here last night.' He stretched his short legs in front of him and mopped his forehead with a primrose-coloured handkerchief. 'Make it a tall glass, Alva, there's a sweetie.'

'Same for you?' Alva looked at Jack Kelly.

'Coffee. Black.' He was terse, adding a 'please' as she left the room.

Oscar Duggan had phoned within hours of Seona's call. He had been brief and businesslike and had arranged today's appointment in minutes. The two days since then had given Alva just enough time to figure out exactly what she wanted from the film company.

She hadn't told anyone at De Novo House about the proposal to film there. Time enough when the deal was done. By keeping things to herself she'd eliminated the possibility of a glowering Theo, mischievous Ellen and insecure Bernie on hand while she negotiated. This way Ellen and Theo were, thankfully, keeping their usual distance from what they supposed to be potential guests and Bernie hadn't yet arrived for work.

Even so, she couldn't rely on them ignoring things indefinitely. She had about an hour, at most, to wrap up a deal.

The coffee had begun to perk and she was slicing a lemon for the gin and tonic when Jack Kelly spoke from behind her in the kitchen door. Leaning against the jamb he looked tanned and travelled.

'Sorry to hassle you, Alva, but a call to the car,' he

jerked his head toward the front of the house, 'says I have to get out of here faster than I'd thought. Think you could show us over the place right away?'

'No drinks?'

'Later, if we move fast.' He stepped into the kitchen. 'Script doesn't call for a kitchen. We'll only need a few rooms,' he spoke quickly, rubbing the side of his face reflectively, 'three, if I remember correctly. Staircase could be useful, especially with that coloured window, and definitely the gardens and the room we just visited to the front. Why don't we join Oscar and take a look at the rest?'

'Suits me.' Alva turned on the coffee maker. 'I'm fairly pushed for time myself.'

'I appreciate that, Alva.' He looked around the room while she dried her hands. She knew he must be taking in its excellent cooking and storing facilities, it's barely adequate everything else. His scrutiny unnerved her, made her hate herself for subjecting the old house – and herself – to examination. She straightened up, perversely for once glad of the advantage of her height. But even this seemed more apparent than real as Jack Kelly elegantly bowed, smiled and gestured for her to lead the way.

The tour didn't take long. The executive producer took quick stock of rooms as they came to them, a man in a hurry with bigger fish to fry. Alva obliged by not dawdling, matching her long stride to his speedy one. Oscar Duggan puffed protestingly behind them, jotting copiously into a notebook.

Neither said anything but Alva could not, for the

life of her, see how they could fail to love De Novo. When she'd bought into the house she'd found most of her money immediately swallowed by fundamental repairs to the roof, plumbing, electrics and kitchen. What she'd been left with, and been able to borrow, she'd put into refurbishment. The result, with corners cut and economies everywhere, wasn't perfect. But it at least had a certain Victorian authenticity that was faithful to the house's origins. Some things, like the evil smiles of the carved wooden monkeys on the staircase banisters, gave it a validity beyond price.

From choice, and not just because it was cheaper, she'd cut right back to the original plasterwork and wood. The result – wood-panelled walls, polished floorboards, pale corniced ceilings and cast-iron fireplaces in almost every room – pleased the aesthetic in her soul. It did nothing to heat the rooms.

Rejecting the Victorian clutter and opulence De Novo had been designed for, she'd gone for pale colours and hung light-revealing muslin at the huge sash windows. Weakening after all that, and as a concession to that same Victoriana, she'd found and hung lots of ornate gilded mirrors on the walls. She still, looking at it critically as the tour went on, thought she'd done the right thing.

But then none of De Novo's problems were apparent at that hour and on that day. These men weren't to know that the plumbing was anything but foolproof, that the inordinately expensive heating had to rationed and that, apart from very occasional part-time staff, De Novo was run entirely by Alva and Bernie

Brennan. And why should they care, even if they knew? Of no practical interest to them either was the fact that the attitudes of Theo and Ellen, running the gamut of indifference to, to resentment of, guests, made managing a hotel more than ordinarily difficult.

The De Novo show was a two-hander; the players, Alva as manageress and Bernie Brennan as cook supreme. De Novo, the film, would be run the same way. Or not at all. That one fact, at least, the men would know soon enough.

Back in the hallway, crossing her fingers and hoping they'd say no, Alva asked if they would like to see the gardens. Theo, in a certain mood, was liable to swoop with explanations of his gardening philosophy. In another he could ask them to leave.

'Gardens looked fine as we drove up.' Jack Kelly gave an affectionate rub to one of the carved monkeys. 'Maybe you could give Oscar a close-up after I leave?' He hesitated. 'If necessary. All right if we talk a deal now?'

'Fine. I'll bring our drinks to the drawing room.'

Oscar, wearing wire-framed bifocals, had spread timesheets and schedules across one of the long low tables when she arrived with the tray. Jack Kelly was talking into a mobile phone by the window. They both, immediately she appeared, turned and smiled. They wanted the house. She knew it.

'What you've got here, Alva,' Jack smiled, 'is a location waiting to become a film set. Question is, can we deal?'

'Give me a few details and we'll see.' Alva, sipping a

coffee, cursed her mouth for being dry and her heart for thumping too loudly. She wanted this deal to work but wished it could happen without the preliminaries of bargaining, talking money, putting her needs on the line. 'I'd like to know when you would intend moving in and what exactly is involved.' She consulted, at speed, the list she'd made. 'Also how long your people, and how many of them, would be here; if it will be necessary for us to stop functioning as a hotel for the duration and how much you're willing to pay . . .' She looked up, fixing what she hoped was a bright smile on her face. 'I've got a couple of other things, but they'll keep for the moment.'

'It's all fairly straightforward.' Oscar was blandly reassuring. Jack Kelly, sitting opposite Alva and studying the toecaps of his Italian loafers, seemed content to allow the location manager to do the explaining. 'Filming of the earlier street scenes, tenement life and all of that, begins in August and goes on until mid-September. Which is when we'd like to move in here.' He worried the sheets of paper on the table. 'Ideally, we'd like to use De Novo more or less as a headquarters and finish up here in mid-October. That would mean us spending a month in total. The hotel couldn't really function while the company is here but, as you'll see from the dates, we're not cutting into your high-season time anyway.'

'That's true,' Alva said. 'How many people, and what about the equipment?'

'Don't worry about damage.' Oscar spoke quickly, jotting notes and not looking at her. 'There won't be any. And if perchance an accident should happen your contract will ensure that all will be restored exactly as was. There are up to a hundred and twenty people involved but rarely, if ever, would everyone be here at the same time. We would use, and dress or make over for filming, this room and the dining room as well as one of the upstairs bedrooms. The trailers and trucks would park in that courtyard we saw at the back, maybe use the old stables for storage. The gardens,' he paused, cautiously, 'look fine. I'll need to see them.'

'Of course.' Alva took a deep breath. 'Sounds like an awful lot of people . . .'

'You won't be aware of eighty per cent of them.' Jack Kelly silenced Oscar with a small frown. 'They'll spend most of their time in the courtyard with the trailers and equipment.'

'Can you guarantee the privacy of their rooms and sitting room to Theo and Ellen Donovan, who live here?' Alva paused. 'My privacy too. This is my home . . .'

'No question.' Jack Kelly was brisk. 'We'll have it written in and everyone will be told. I'll be frank, Alva,' he was watching her closely, 'we need this place. The other location falling through has given us a major headache.' His cool look at Oscar left the other unperturbed. 'We'd be willing to agree any reasonable terms you come up with.'

'Good.' Alva's heartbeat had become more or less normal. Having the upper hand was a relaxing experience. 'Because there are a couple of things I'd like as part of a contract . . .'

Oscar had finished his gin. He clinked the ice and focused on her through his bifocals. Alva didn't offer him another.

Jack Kelly took a quick look at his watch. He hadn't touched his coffee. 'Shoot,' he said.

Standing with her back to the window, Alva told them what she wanted by way of a deal for De Novo. 'Firstly, I'd like this hotel to provide the catering.' She ignored Oscar's loud groan and incredulous look. 'In the circumstances I think it's a reasonable, not to say logical, request. We have an excellent cook whom I intend keeping and who would not be at all pleased by a month's unemployment. I don't fancy a month with nothing to do myself, so I'll run the catering service with her. I'll get seating and tables for the old basement kitchen and it will serve as a dining hall. Our rates will be well within your budget.' She looked from one to the other. Jack Kelly was cracking his knuckles. Oscar was sitting forward, notebook balanced on bunched knees. He was literally wringing his hands.

'Jesus, Alva! You can't . . . you don't understand how these things work. There are the unions to deal with, conditions laid down about coffee and tea on demand, meals and sandwiches needed day and sometimes through the night, not to mention,' an hysterical note had crept into his voice, 'the catering company we've already hired . . .'

'Keep them on.' Alva was crisp. 'We'll compete. Can't see any of your people objecting if you tell them they're going to have better food and a second choice for the last month of filming. Think of the goodwill and other benefits.' She leaned against the side of the window and folded her arms. Jack Kelly was watching her again. He had stopped cracking his knuckles and she returned his look with a small smile. When she went on she spoke to him, not Oscar.

'Where do you intend having people eat? In a trailer?'

'In a converted bus,' Oscar answered her question.

'Mmm, OK in the summer, I suppose. Less wonderful in September and October. We can provide a lot better than that.'

'Alva, it's just not on. There'll be nothing but trouble. You don't want the pain an arrangement like that will bring, believe me . . .'

'Cut it, Oscar! I'll deal with this.' Jack Kelly's voice was a precisely slicing instrument. He stood, smiling, leaving no doubt that he was the money and real power talking. 'Let's be straight here. We both want this deal. Give us two bedrooms to use for dressing rooms and you've got your catering contract. Deal?'

'Deal,' Alva said.

'That everything?' He collected his jacket from a chair back. Slipping it on he checked his watch again.

'Not quite.' Alva was cool. 'I'd like it written into the contract that in publicity about the film De Novo catering and hotel will be mentioned. I'd like there to be a mention in the film credits too.' Her smile was friendly, reasonable. 'If we're going to be closed for a month we'll need to remind people we still exist.'

'You got it. Oscar will draw up your contract. You got things clear this time, Oscar?'

Calm gone, Duggan's face had become roundly aggrieved. 'Of course. And the cock-up last time wasn't my fault—'

'It sure as hell wasn't mine.' Jack Kelly stopped as his chauffeur's head appeared round the door.

'Phone, Mr Kelly. New York.' The man coughed. 'Caller says he wants a word in private.' He held up a mobile and moved back into the hall. Jack, frowning, followed him from the room.

'I prefer to look on the other deal falling through as an act of God,' Oscar tittered, 'and so should you, Alva my pet. You're the beneficiary, after all.'

'Oh, I think the benefits are mutual.' Alva was off-hand. 'Your film people are getting a very good deal in De Novo.'

'Well, of course we are . . .' Oscar was huffing a little as Jack Kelly came back into the room, fingers drumming impatiently on the mobile in his hand.

'Sorry about this, Alva.' He raised his shoulders hopelessly. 'And I really mean sorry. I gotta go, right away. Oscar will have to talk money to you.' The room seemed all at once too small for his impatience. 'We'll give you what we'd offered the other place. Can't bend the budget on that. Oscar will answer any further questions you may have. Right, Oscar?'

'Right.'

Alva, at a walk which by his side became a quick stride, went with the executive producer to the front door. The engine of the waiting limousine was already humming as he briefly took her hand.

'I'm glad we could deal, Alva. Things are going to

work fine, I can feel it. I'll look you up in a month, when I get back.'

'I'll look forward to that,' Alva said.

The long black limousine made the least noise she'd ever heard a car make on the avenue's stony surface.

Oscar Duggan, when she went back inside, had vanished from the drawing room. A trail of open doors led her to the kitchen. He was helping himself to another gin.

'Didn't like to bother you.' He poured the tonic sparingly.

Standing beside him she noticed that his hair was sprayed and going thin.

'Want me to mix you one too?' he asked.

'I'll stick with coffee . . .'

Ellen's footsteps sounded on the upstairs gallery, distinctive because she was the only person who wore heels which brutalized its polished wood. Alva swooped, took the glass from Oscar's shocked grasp.

'Why don't we take a look at the garden right away? I'll carry this across the cobbles for you.' She held it away as he reached for it. 'You can sip as we walk in the garden.'

They'd almost made it through the front door when Ellen's voice came piercingly from the stairs.

'What *have* you got there, Alva Joyce? Is it human, or merely rolling flesh?'

''Morning, Ellen, talk to you later.' Alva didn't turn. 'Mr Duggan has come to see the gardens . . .' Even as he tried to look back she propelled Oscar firmly forward.

'That jungle. No accounting for taste.' Ellen's heels reached the hall tiles and faded as she headed for the kitchen.

'Who was *that*?' Oscar was peevish as he fumbled down the steps after Alva. They crossed the cobbles side by side.

'That', Alva sighed, 'was Eleanor Donovan, one of the two people I mentioned who live here. Ellen,' she paused, 'is a woman with a past and no interest in either the present or future. Her brother Theodore lives here too. The Donovan family owned De Novo for several generations. Theo is responsible for the gardens, and what he does with them, when you consider that he's seventy-five, is little short of miraculous. What he did with them in the past *was* miraculous. You'll see . . .'

They stepped off the cobbles onto the first of the garden paths and Alva handed Oscar his drink. He sipped, sighed and tottered after her on his short legs as she began walking again.

'What does that woman do?'

'Gets through each day. Drinks. Maintains an interest in life by insulting all and sundry. Don't pay any attention to what she says . . .'

'Will she be a problem? When the company gets here, I mean?'

'Probably.' Alva nodded. 'But for me; nothing your film people need worry about.'

The path grew wider and paved. They walked side by side, slower than before, heading for the rose garden and, beyond it, the summerhouse. Oscar looked around avidly as they went. Either the fresh air or second drink had perked him up.

'What about the brother?'

'I'll handle Theo, too.' Alva frowned down at him. 'Everyone will be . . . pleasant and accommodating.'

'Good. Because pleasant is how Jack Kelly likes things.' He finished the drink, slipped the empty glass into his pocket and jotted briefly in a notebook. 'Gardens are fine. We can go back inside now and talk money . . .'

'I'd prefer to talk out here. Air's better.' They would also be away from Ellen and, hopefully, not joined by Theo. 'We'll sit in the summerhouse.'

Oscar grumbled along beside her past the terracotta urns of the rose garden to where the path divided by a cluster of pink and red peony trees. Alva plucked a showy, pink bloom. 'This one's the Sarah Bernhardt.' She slipped it through his buttonhole. 'For luck,' she said.

The summerhouse was side on to the sea. They sat quietly for a while until, faintly in the distance, a car backfired. Oscar, revealing a flash of red braces, took his notebook from an inside pocket.

'They'll pay you twenty-five thousand for the month.' He ran a finger over some figures. 'The catering's different. Jack will work that out and pay you from a separate budget. Lucky for you he came along today. You wouldn't have got an OK on the catering from anyone else. This is going to mean trouble, big trouble. The director won't like it, the unions won't like it . . .'

'We're talking about a month's work, Oscar.' Alva patted his knee consolingly. 'Not a lifetime's commitment.' She paused, followed a seagull's path for a few seconds. 'I'll take the twenty-five thousand,' she said.

'Magnanimous of you,' he muttered sniffily.

'Oh, come on, Oscar,' Alva's laugh was impatient, 'am I supposed to get down on my knees?'

'Not at all.' He sniffed again and gave a small cough. 'Especially since you've been there already.' When Alva swivelled to stare at him he squirmed, but only slightly. She'd been right. He knew more about her business than she did about his. He'd obviously informed himself – most likely through Seona. His tone became confidential and he put a hand on her arm. 'We both know what I meant by that. I was appalled and disgusted when I heard about your ... difficulties. But the past is another country and I must tell you, my sweet, how glad I am to see you looking so well.'

Alva counted to thirty before she said, 'Thank you, Oscar. You have a delicate way of putting things. And you're absolutely right about the past. Now,' she removed his hand from her arm, 'tell me about this film, the actors and the director and all that. Does it have a name yet?'

'They're calling it *Death Diminishes*, as in "Any man's death diminishes me, because I am involved in Mankind" – Donne. Nonsensical sentiment, of course, but a nicely commercial title for a murder mystery.'

'I like Donne,' Alva said.

'He doesn't have an awful lot else to do with the

story, I'm afraid. That I can see, anyway. But you'll be able to judge for yourself. Now, to begin at the beginning . . .' he swept the hanky from his pocket and wiped his lips. The peony blossom fell to the ground and he left it there. 'How much do you know about the Millennium Project?'

'Not much. Never heard of it until Seona phoned. She mentioned something about European and American interests coming together to make films of a number of unsolved murder mysteries dating from the turn of the century. Seems a strange way to celebrate coming up to the year 2000 . . .'

'Ours is not to reason why.' Oscar waved a lofty hand. 'We have thrown in our lot with commercial greed and must be grateful for the money and benefits which will be ours in the fullness of time. What *you* need, my sweet innocent, is a little background information to put you in the picture.' He crossed his legs at the ankles and leaned back. His face became very slightly pink. He was about to impart gossip and was, momentarily, a happy man.

'The director is one Luke O'Hanlon. A film-maker of the worthy kind but not the choice of Executive Producer Kelly.' Oscar chortled. 'Not by a long shot. No two people could be more different and no two people could disagree more on the kind of film to be made from the script – quite a decent one, according to those who've read it. O'Hanlon, who has his reputation to think about, wants to go for social realism and woman triumphant. Our friend Jack is having none of it. He wants a box-office hit and reckons the story needs sexy stars and plenty of good triumphant over evil. He could be right. But then again Luke O'Hanlon could put bums on seats with his very PC angle. I've heard the Germans are keen on a social-conscience pic too and the French are working on some twist in the tale . . .'

Alva, impatient with this digression into the wider scheme, cut him short. 'Who decides, in the end, how it's going to be?'

'Depends on a lot of things. In this instance it's looking like the director will have his way. And there you have the nub of our little conflict, really. Seems the whole project originated with O'Hanlon. He was the one who came up with the script, oh, about two years ago now. He has his own independent production company, Silver Apple it's called, and had gone a long way towards getting the thing off the ground on his own when the big boys stepped in. One of his backers had the bright idea of expanding, saw the money to be made from developing half a dozen scripts on the unsolved murder theme of *Death Diminishes* and making one in each of six European countries. The Millennium thing, quite simply, is a gimmick which seems to have worked. It caught the imagination of the money men, backers popped up on both sides of the Atlantic and Luke O'Hanlon's film became part of a multinational business deal.'

'But he came with the film, as its director? Is that it?'

'You're catching on.' Oscar nodded. 'Not only that. He'd already persuaded Clara Butler to star and she came as part of the deal too. They're thick as thieves, that pair, or as lovers. Who knows?' He took the empty gin glass from his pocket and looked at it regretfully. Alva took it from him.

'Later,' she said, 'when you've told me the rest.'

'Well, to even things up, Jack's been busy getting a few of his own people onto the cast,' Oscar spoke quickly, 'Justine O'Dea is part of Jack's stable, so's Nick Hunt. Both of them are young, demonically ambitious and into the flesh 'n' sex school of acting. Should add to the excitement.' He shivered slightly and pulled the lapels of his suit together. 'There's a chill come into the air. It's not exactly mint julep weather any more, is it? Why don't we toddle back to the house and replenish my drink? I'll tell you anything else you need to know while we're retracing our steps to the bottle.' He stood. 'Imparting all this information's bloody thirsty work.'

Oscar was not a fast walker. But if his movements by Alva's side could be described as an ambling crawl his sharp, capricious mind more than compensated. On their way back he filled Alva with gossip and anecdote, most of it of questionable veracity, and in between managed to jot garden details into his notebook.

'Do you think, if we have to, that your Theo will let us cut things back a bit? It's all *very* wild and wonderful out here, isn't it?' He stopped to sniff the perfumed leaves of a sweet briar. '*Rosa rubiginosa.*' He shot a sly look Alva's way. 'Surprised you with that, didn't I? I'm not just a pretty face, you know.' He laughed, a cheerless sound, and looked around.

'Luke O'Hanlon's going to have a field day with this place. If it's all right with you I'll bring him out for a viewing some day next week. I'll bring your contract and cheque at the same time. Oh, my dear God, just look at this . . .'

Awkwardly, he hunkered down by a patch of fern, pudgy hands reverently parting the feathery leaves as he inhaled their musty odour. 'The Victorians grew ferns, you know, lots of them.' He straightened up, slowly. 'Very atmospheric plant for a film like this . . .'

'A film like *what*?' Alva asked. 'All anyone's told me so far is that it's the true story of an unsolved murder and that the villain was a woman. Who was she? Whom did she kill?'

Oscar pushed his belly forward and hooked his thumbs around the red braces. The stance seemed to improve his balance and he rolled a little faster by her side as Alva guided him back to the house. 'Constance Moore was our villain-lady's name by the time she came to live here,' he peered up at the looming house, 'at what will be called Myrtle House in the film. She was born Adye O'Brien, in or around 1862, into a large family and worse than dirt-poor conditions in Irishtown, close to the docks. The location certainly suited her father – he put her on the streets and on the game on her fifteenth birthday.' He stopped and looked around. 'This is not the way we came. You're force-walking me, Alva. I'll not have it . . .'

'Relax. I want to show you something. It's relevant and it'll only add a couple of hundred yards to the journey.' She smiled and took his arm. Grumbling, he moved along with her. 'Go on with the story,' she urged, 'it's fascinating.'

'I doubt our Adye thought so, at the time.' Oscar was primly indignant. 'Fascinating is hardly the word for the life lived by a fifteen-year-old prostitute in a city notorious for its filth. We're talking here about a Dublin in which the sewers were defective and the water supply inadequate, where pollution was rampant from slaughterhouses and dairy yards.'

'Point taken.' Alva was calming. Oscar righteous was a swollen, agitated sight. 'So, what happened? How did she escape all that?'

'James Moore happened to her, poor bitch. He picked her up in a whorehouse and decided to mould her for his wife. He was in his forties, wealthy, unmarried. He was also, by all accounts, a sadist. He sent her to a school outside Paris to be groomed for Dublin's middle-class society. When he in due course produced her as his wife she'd become Constance, an orphan with no family but him. According to the script the marriage was made in hell but produced a daughter ... What now?' He was working at his forehead with the hanky and bumped into Alva when she stopped. '*This* is what you wanted me to see?'

Together they gazed into the murky depths of a small pond.

'Well, the flowers as well as the pond.' She poked at the curl-edged leaves with her foot. 'You want atmospheric menace for the film? This is it ...' She dropped a pebble into the still water.

'Don't get involved, Alva.' Oscar looked morosely

into the pond. 'Do the food and take the money and keep your distance. It's not your scene.' He looked at her with surprising seriousness. 'Believe me, I know what I'm talking about.'

'I'll try to remember.' Alva spoke lightly. She felt discomfited, not a little gauche. 'Tell me the rest of Constance's story.' She speeded up, forcing Oscar into a trot to keep pace. 'They had a daughter,' she prompted.

'Called her Julia. When she was ten her father died, an apparent victim of the flu epidemic raging at the time. But circumstances were suspicious and Constance was arrested for his murder, accused of giving him poison along with the sweating draughts and antiperiodics she'd been treating him with for the flu. Nothing was ever proven, though, and within months she'd sold the family home in Dublin and moved with the daughter to a lonely house on the coast outside the city. Just like this one . . .'

They'd reached the edge of the garden and stepped again onto the cobbles. The house stood grey and quiet and old in front of them. A location, as Jack Kelly had said, waiting to become a film set. They walked slowly toward the front steps.

'Constance established herself as a respectable recluse and reared the child with all the middle-class trimmings she'd been taught in Paris. She obviously did a good job, because when Julia reached eighteen she met and became engaged to the son of a wealthy and socially well-got merchant family. And that, alas, was what eventually undid Constance.'

'The boy's family didn't approve?'

'Bingo. They acted on their disapproval, too; set a private detective on Mrs Constance Moore and came up with her past. The daughter lost her man, blamed her mam and left home. Constance sold the house, packed her bags and left for the New World. At least that's what she does in the script. I'm told that it's not actually known where the real Constance disappeared to.' They had reached the steps and Oscar took several deep breaths before starting to climb. He was by now permanently mopping with the hanky. 'And it's anything but clear', he puffed, 'what's going to happen at the end of the film.'

'But if it's already written into a script . . .'

'God, Alva, you are frighteningly naïve for such a big, grown-up-looking girl.' He joined her on the top step and caught his breath. 'Didn't you learn anything—?' He caught her glare and felt her stiffen. 'Scripts are written to be ignored, by and large. But in this instance we've got a director who actually wants to stick to the written word and an executive producer who wants to change to having a rejected murderess alone and suicidal in an empty house.' He shrugged. 'For my money, the suicide has it. Send 'em home weeping and you're onto a winner. O'Hanlon, though, doesn't feel she's the kind of woman would give up and neither, apparently, does Clara Butler. So there you have it. A good old predictable row about commercial viability versus the integrity of the story. Now can I have my drink?' His sepia eyes pleaded with her.

Ellen was waiting for them in the drawing room.

44

She was wearing silver mules and a lot of make-up. Her humour didn't look good.

'You brought the toad back with you, I see.' She didn't look at Oscar, standing frozen in the doorway. 'Is he a paying guest?'

'I have business to discuss with Mr Duggan.' Alva kept her voice level. 'Please, Ellen, be good and leave us alone.'

'Something's going on.' Ellen didn't budge. 'Saw another one earlier on.' Her eyes flicked over Oscar. 'Better-looking, monied type.'

Oscar, still in the doorway, cleared his throat loudly.

'Come on in.' Ellen leaned forward in her chair. 'I don't bite.' She chortled and turned to Alva. 'Man looks as if he could do with a drink. His colour's bad.'

'Ellen!' Alva's tone was seriously warning.

'Oh, all right.' Ellen, with some grace and a flash of slim leg, eased herself out of the chair. 'You could at least introduce me,' she said. Alva did so, briskly. Oscar nodded, keeping his distance, as Ellen held out a hand.

'How do you do?' she said. He moved a cautious inch towards her, touched her hand and quickly let it go again. Alva, watching as Ellen arched her eyebrows and swept past him into the hallway, realized something. Oscar Duggan, urbane, cynical and a hedonist, was terrified of Ellen Donovan.

She got him a drink, measuring into it equal quantities of gin and tonic. 'Don't let her get to you.' She was quite gentle talking to him. 'She's old and she's bored. She needles people all the time. It amuses her.'

'I know.' He took the gin. For a moment, holding it without drinking, he was an overweight, pitiful sight. 'I've got blood pressure.' He took a long drink. 'She frightens me.'

'I could see that. But why?'

'She sets herself no boundaries.' Oscar pursed his lips. 'She's destructive and she doesn't give a damn about anything.' He sank into an armchair. 'I hate that. I prefer people to observe the social niceties. Otherwise all's a state of chassis.'

'What bullshit.' Alva shook her head in wonder. '*You* set your own social limits, exactly as she does. And *that's* what frightens you about her. The bits of yourself you see in a cantankerous, not very likable old woman. You're afraid of ending up like her.'

Oscar looked deflated, his chins more saggy. For quiet, endless seconds Alva feared he was preparing to reveal his life's story to her. To her infinite relief he shrugged, resumed his normal, mordant expression and said, 'You're a kindly, naïve creature, Alva, and you might be right. But keep her out of my way whenever I'm here, there's a good girl. Now, call me a taxi. I must be going.'

Alva rang for the taxi. Her voice, when she came back into the room and sat opposite, startled Oscar out of a doze.

'One last thing before you go.' Alva smiled coaxingly. 'Tell me a little about how these people will be. Will it be champagne and fresh figs for breakfast every morning?'

46

'Oh, lord, lord, you really did come down with the last shower.' Oscar closed his eyes wearily and leaned back. 'Breakfast menu's more often a case of cold water on tantrums and rampant egos. Film-making's a *mélange* of conflicting interests. Take the advice I've already given you and don't allow yourself to be sucked into the ego-tripping and insecurities and sheer greed of it all. Not unless you can deal with it.' He opened his eyes and fixed her with a bleary look. 'And frankly, my dear . . .'

'You don't think I can?' Alva smiled. 'I might surprise you.'

'Listen and try to understand.' He shifted his glance upward, to the sky beyond the window. 'Making a film is a hazardous business and *everyone* involved comes in for a share of hassle. If you imagine it's only the stars behave like prima donnas, then wait till you see the crew and minor players in action. The less talented, by and large, the greater the histrionics and tantrums.

'Try and see it as it is. There's a director, and gathered around him there's a motley crew. From these he's stuck with extracting talent, and non-talent in many cases, and putting it together so a decent film results. All of this makes for a strong interdependence between the director and everyone working on the film.'

A taxi appeared through the trees of the avenue. It stopped in front of the house and the driver gave a short, impatient blast on the horn.

'Cheeky sod.' Oscar glowered. 'The company's

paying so he can wait. Before I go I should mention the producer too, in this case a decent enough fellow by the name of Felim Gray.'

'He's the *real* boss?'

'God, no.' Oscar began the process of heaving himself out of the chair. 'Your problem, Alva, is that you're too bloody simplistic.' He stood and so did she. He wagged a fat finger. 'Everyone's dancing to someone else's tune in films. The producer is a sort of bridge between the creative process and the financiers. A friend at court, if you like. He organizes the money, allocates resources. He's there to facilitate the company but held on a leash by the backers – all of whom want the film to make money while spending as little on production as possible.'

The taxi horn blasted again, louder and longer this time. 'Nasty little twerp.' Oscar made a grumbling way to the window and gave a rude signal to the waiting driver. 'He's paid to sit there ... knows he'll get his money ... Oh, and talking of money, the executive producer is the major financier.'

'Jack Kelly, in this case.'

'The very man.' Oscar, preparing to go, picked a fern leaf from his lapel and rearranged his jacket into further creases. He looked thoughtfully at Alva. 'You'll be seeing a lot more of Jack, unless my intuition's faulty. Stay cool, my sweet.' He blew her a kiss. 'Ta ta for now.'

As she watched him ease himself into the taxi Ellen joined Alva in the doorway. 'Poor man,' she said, 'he'll have killed himself before he's fifty.'

Chapter Three

With unerring, self-protective instinct, Ellen and Theo avoided Alva all that afternoon. Theo, when she told him she had something to discuss with everyone, pleaded a plague of greenfly. Ellen simply said it would have to wait. Both then disappeared.

Bernie Brennan was different. Bernie, thirty-one years old and the mother of Sam, twelve and by any standards a brat, was devoid absolutely of the instinct to self-protect. If she'd had any, even a shred, she'd have kept clear of involvement with Sam's father, a trainee butcher who'd deserted her the day her pregnancy test proved positive. It had taught her not to trust butchers. All other men she trusted implicitly.

Alva ambushed her immediately she arrived for work. It was midday. Oscar Duggan had been gone a scarce fifteen minutes.

'I've got something to talk to you about.' Alva pounced as Bernie climbed out of her ten-year-old Renault. 'A plan for the hotel. It's going to put De Novo on the tourist map and it's going to make you a world-renowned cook.'

'Alva?' Bernie's eyes, behind the heavy lenses of her spectacles, betrayed alarm. 'Have you been helping Ellen demolish the Pernod?' She touched Alva's forehead. 'No temperature, anyway. Thank God for that. Maybe a couple of hours' sleep will cure it . . .' She stood with her head to one side, a large, shapely young woman, slightly awkward and with heavy golden hair.

'Come inside,' Alva ordered, 'you nasty, cynical creature. I'll talk while you prepare the lunches.'

Bernie, muttering, went to the back of the car and threw open the boot. 'If it's not the Pernod then it has to be the noonday sun. Help me with these vegetables,' she said. 'Maybe carrying a crate of carrots will bring you down to earth.'

De Novo's lunchtime customers began arriving, as a rule, around one o'clock. By three o'clock the last would have left. Bernie, fastidious about fresh vegetables, cooked from scratch every day. And every day she managed, within the limits of De Novo's tight budget, to produce innovative as well as basically good food. For Bernie was creative, an artist in the kitchen. She had also become, in the thirteen months since starting work in the hotel, a friend to Alva. And Alva had no intention of losing her in either role.

'Heat will keep some of them away today.' Bernie vigorously chopped a cucumber. Her cold cucumber and tarragon soup had been going down well. 'They'll take sandwiches to the beach.'

'Listen carefully.' Alva began on a salad. 'Because what I have to say could affect the rest of your life.'

'Rest of my life! World-famous cook!' Bernie stopped chopping and sighed. 'All right. If you've something to tell me then tell. I can't stand this over-the-top stuff. You know I can't.'

'Sorry,' Alva grinned, 'thought I'd build you up, get you as keen as I am. We're going to have to work as a team on this.'

'On *what?*' Bernie, all at once, was unsure. And therein lay the reason she was available to work at De Novo, why her brilliance as a cook went unsung. Bernie Brennan lacked confidence. The world beyond the kitchen was for her beset with traps and pitfalls and a competitive striving she wouldn't, or couldn't, take part in. No one was more aware of her insecurity than Alva. She faced her now, putting as much up-beat confidence into her voice as she could manage.

'You and I, Bernie, are going to become caterers to a film company.' She held Bernie's gaze as she spoke. Bernie's creamy pink skin darkened and her eyes became worried. She adjusted her glasses on her nose. She said nothing. 'It'll all happen here, Bernie, at De Novo,' Alva said, 'and it'll only be for a month. Sit down. We'll take five and a glass of white each and I'll tell you all.'

She didn't tell Bernie quite all; just what she felt she needed to know. She told her about the money and about the publicity the hotel would get and about the promise of catering credits on the film. She spoke not at all of Oscar Duggan's warnings about tantrums and trouble ahead and kept the *coup de grâce* until last.

'There will be a hundred and twenty people to feed, every day for a month.' She took a deep breath. 'And a huge percentage of them, Bernie, will be *men*. Purely on the law of averages . . .' She shrugged, letting the endless possibilities speak for themselves. Bernie hated going alone through life and her search for the right man was ongoing and forever hopeful.

Sammy was her love, her joy. But Sammy was getting older and more self-sufficient by the day and Bernie saw herself bleak and lonely in a few short years. Unless she found a man. She craved 'hugs and a bit of hot sex', but men willing to take on a woman with a twelve-year-old son were thin on the ground. A few bouts with Sammy tended to rout even the most promising.

'Fellas! Hordes of 'em! Hungry, every day ...' Bernie sat down. This was different. The ideal come true. The prospect of meeting men on her own turf, the place in the world she felt sure and confident, the one place she could strut her stuff and not feel outdone by thinner, younger, more beautiful women. She would be meeting men in her kitchen ... 'Tell me more. No, tell me all.'

Lunchers that day amounted to five in total. Which was just as well because Bernie's head, spinning with recipes and feeding plans, was for once not on the job. De Novo Catering would provide *real* food, she declared. None of the fast-food stuff usual in such situations. They would out-gourmet anything the other catering crowd supplied.

'I'll just do as I'm told,' Alva grinned. 'I'll chop and clean and do the shopping. I'll lay the tables and serve the meals. We'll be perfect together.'

Theo and Ellen had to eat. And when they did so that evening, at the small table in the sitting room, Alva joined them. Across the hall from the drawing room, the sitting room was large, and furnished to cater to the varied needs of those who used it. In a far corner was a roll-top writing desk, used by both Alva and Theo. A television, rarely used by anyone, occupied a niche in a wall lined with book-filled hardwood shelves. A piano, which both Ellen and Alva played, stood at right angles to the window.

Alva eating with them was not usual and the Donovans were resignedly courteous. Thomas, as *was* usual, lay asleep on Ellen's lap.

'No one booked to eat in the restaurant tonight, then?' Theo asked. Alva hoped he had his hearing aid turned on. He often didn't bother.

'Two couples, actually. But they're not due until nineish.' Assured by Theo's nod that his aid was on, she helped herself to salad and said, 'I've something to tell you both.'

This produced silence. Theo cut diligently into his lamb chop, Ellen pushed hers aside and topped up her wineglass. She stroked the cat absently. Alva took a deep breath, let it out and told them about the film company. Neither interrupted but she knew, as she came to the end of explaining, that what she'd expected to happen had happened. Ellen was looking perky, anticipating a diversion and some glamour about the place. Theo was looking furiously opposed.

'A month, you say? It'll help kill some time, I suppose.' Ellen's look at her brother was gleeful. 'Think of it, Theo, your garden overrun by marauding, made-up hordes of philistines with cameras. Think of the break in the monotony—'

'I won't permit it.' Theo glowered at Alva and

ignored his sister. 'Neither this house nor the gardens is suited to that sort of thing. Simian creatures, film people. I've met a few of them in my time, all of them vulgarians and ignoramuses, given to a lot of posturing about their "art form", but then you find there's damn little substance to any of it. I don't know what in hell you were thinking about, Alva, encouraging those people to sell you the idea.' He pushed his plate to one side and drummed his large-knuckled fingers on the table. Alva suspected he had arthritis but he never complained so she couldn't be sure.

'I was thinking about how badly the hotel is doing and how we desperately need a way of attracting more customers,' she explained. 'I was also giving consideration to the state of our finances and the fact that £25,000 for a month's use of De Novo is more than we're going to make all summer. And I was thinking, Theo,' she leaned across the table so that he couldn't avoid her eye, nor fail to see that she meant what she said, 'about the amount of work I put into this place without any return. And without support from you.'

'Bravo!' Ellen clapped her hands delightedly. 'That was a really pretty speech, Alva. And very well delivered too. Very convincing indeed. Don't you think so, Theo?'

Theo ignored her. 'You'd no right to negotiate with those people without first talking to me.' There was hurt in his aggrieved expression. 'We're partners after all, you and I.'

'You wouldn't have entertained the idea, not even for a second.' Alva disliked doing it, but she was whiplash sharp with him. 'You don't help me, Theo, and you've gone ostrich on our financial situation for almost nine months now. I was offered a chance to do something about things and I took it. It's as simple as that.'

She sat back, poking at the food on her plate with a fork. She'd eaten very little. When she looked up Theo's eyes were on her, inscrutable and serious.

'The timing couldn't be better.' She didn't try to use a coaxing tone. He'd have hated it. 'We'll reopen at Hallowe'en and people will come in their droves to eat and sleep in the house which starred in a murder film and where Clara Butler and company ate and slept.'

'You said nothing about them sleeping here.' Ellen raised a laconic eyebrow. 'Now *that* could give rise to all sorts of possibilities.'

'Well, I don't think anyone actually *will* be sleeping here,' Alva admitted. 'Just indulging myself in a little publicity hype. Point is, people will come, if only out of curiosity. We'll establish a name for ourselves, earn some money and be able to raise more on the strength of it.'

'Should be interesting,' Ellen yawned, 'providing they're not all like that pasty-faced little poof who was here today.'

'Oh, be quiet Ellen.' Theo sounded tired. 'Man can't help his complexion.' So, Alva thought, he'd seen her with Oscar in the garden and avoided them. Typical.

'What he can't help is his sexual predilection,' Ellen

snapped. 'He most certainly *can* do something about his skin. Some of my very best friends have been faggots and none of them have ever been pasty-faced.'

'Oh, be quiet, you silly, psychotic old woman.' Theo's tired voice had none of the anger of the words, but Ellen's reaction was livid.

'I am *not* psychotic,' she shrieked. 'I'm not the one who's spent a lifetime buried in the garden of this house, avoiding reality and people. I'm the one who has *lived*. And neither am I the one who's afraid to have Alva's film people come here.'

'Fear is not what I feel.' Theo was cold and curt as he fiddled with his hearing aid. Turning it down, Alva reckoned. 'My misgivings about the proposed venture are based on something else altogether.'

'Rot!' Ellen jabbed a vermilion-tipped finger his way. 'You resist everything, Theo Donovan, always have. God, but you're predictable, and boring as hell.'

Alva brought a hand down, hard, onto the table. 'Act your ages, both of you,' she snapped.

'Mental or physical?' Theo's tone was conversational. 'Because if it's mental you mean, then that woman's about twelve years old.'

Before Ellen could gather her breath to reply Alva asked him, loudly, to make sure he heard her, 'What are your exact objections to the film company, Theo?'

He sat quite still as he answered, long snowy hair shining in the light from the desk lamp behind them. 'The entire project seems to me altogether alien to this house and gardens,' he said. 'The change to a hotel was one thing, and I agree I haven't been supportive enough ...' He paused. 'But this film business is entirely different. Different ethos at work, different culture ...' He sighed deeply, shaking his head. 'It'll bring changes to the life and expectations of the house which won't be sustainable after they're gone. And that's my fear.'

Alva was quiet. And puzzled. There was something here she didn't fully understand. 'I appreciate your worry about the gardens.' She spoke slowly. 'And I'll get a clause in the contract restricting access. But I'm not at all sure what you mean about the house, Theo.'

'No, I suppose you don't.' Theo looked past her reflectively, through the window at the yard and stables, pleasant in their old-stone-with-creeping-ivy way. 'You're young. You still believe change is good and that times change and we with them. It's not so. We merely adapt, or try to. Some of us don't and when that happens change can be destructive.' He paused. 'It is my belief that this venture would bring destructive change to De Novo.' He looked down at his hands. Blunt, strong hands for a blunt, strong man. 'I can't explain any better, or any more, than that.'

There was silence around the table. Ellen seemed to have fallen asleep in a sitting position but Alva was simply puzzled into silence. This mood of Theo's was a funny one. He didn't seem, any longer, to be saying a categorical no to the plan. It was more like he was saying he had a fatalistic feeling, a premonition that the film company would somehow bring harm to De Novo – or to those who lived there. Yet he wasn't a superstitious man. Certainly he wasn't a stupid one.

'Theo,' she spoke gently, 'I don't really understand what you're telling me. You must see that this could make us as a hotel. I'm really not asking you to *do* anything. Except sign the contract, of course.' She tried a smile, which he ignored.

'I'm merely telling you that I feel this proposal isn't right for De Novo.' He looked vexed. 'There must be some other way you can make money and encourage guests.'

'None that I've been able to make work and none as good as this. Do *you* have any suggestions?'

'Of course he doesn't.' Ellen came suddenly to life. 'It'll be entirely his fault if the place goes to the dogs. Sorry Thomas, nasty analogy.' She rubbed the cat behind the ears and looked balefully at her brother. 'Perhaps he's worried his manageress/partner will be taken with the charms of some technician, or even an actor. Of course she won't,' Ellen shrugged. 'All of that is beneath her. Our Ms Joyce is Hera waiting for her Zeus. What's far more likely is that developers and the like will build a road through the gardens. They'll pour cement over every bit of it if you don't face reality and agree. Not that it would be any harm to eliminate that wilderness.'

Theo returned his sister's look with one of his own which was both weary and resigned. 'All right,' he said, 'I'll sign to allow these people come here.'

Bernie, in the kitchen preparing dinner for the

nine o'clock bookings, gave an ungainly skip at the news of Theo's agreement. 'I'd started to worry,' she admitted. 'Begun to think it was all too good to be true.'

'O, ye of little faith.' Alva moved back into the kitchen from the pantry where she'd been checking the wines for the evening. 'There must have been some cosmic force at work because Ellen came on side with a pushy argument about developers pouring cement over the garden.'

'Huh. You can be sure she wants the film crowd here for reasons of her own.' Bernie tasted a sauce and added a little milk. 'She couldn't care less if the sea rose up and swallowed the gardens in the morning. She's just a sad, bitter, bored old doxy who wants everyone to be as unhappy as she is herself.'

'I don't think she does.' Alva shook her head. Bernie's feelings about Ellen were influenced more than a little by the old woman's animosity towards Sammy. The fact that Sammy, on his rare visits, was more than able to deal with Ellen in no way placated Bernie's protective instincts. 'I don't think Ellen can help herself.' Alva put some house white into the fridge. 'The only solution would have been for her to die dramatically in her prime, killed in a speedboat crash in Monte Carlo waters or murdered by a jealous lover in a Roman bedroom. Old age is the ultimate cruelty for a woman like Ellen.'

'You'd think all that love and all those men would have left her with enough memories to keep her warm till she's a hundred, at least.' Bernie looked dreamy.

'Wish I could lay my hands on even an eighth of the number of men she boasts about.'

'Ellen doesn't want memories,' Alva said, 'she wants the love and adoration back again. She never wanted it to stop.'

Bernie, still dreamy-looking, put her hands on her ample hips and then moved them over her stomach. 'I'm going on a diet. Tomorrow. God, but I'd adore a nice fella. Someone half decent-looking to have a laugh with and a bit of old sex. And don't look at me like that, Alva Joyce. It's only natural. You'd adore it yourself only you won't admit it.'

The house was still when Alva climbed the stairs to bed. Without the sound and movement of people it was a very quiet house, prone to none of the usual creakings and groanings of old houses. Its history too was a calm one, with no recorded tragedies or disasters. It had been built in the 1840s and had thereafter passed from the ownership of one safe, middle-class family to another. The eminently respectable Bartholomew Donovan had bought it in 1890. It was only when it came into the ownership of his squabbling descendants that its fate, for the first time in its more than 150 years, became doubtful.

Alva sat in the window of her room for a long time before going to bed, looking over the bay without seeing it, thinking about the film and its story and about John Donne's poem.

Donne was right, she supposed, when he wrote that death diminished. But misguided if he imagined that people were aware or cared. Both her mother and father were dead. She rarely thought of them and, when she did, felt more guiltily relieved than diminished.

One thing she did know, and which Donne hadn't written about at all, was that if death diminished, then so too did love.

Chapter Four

Alva had been brought up without affection or gentleness. The only child of elderly, reclusive parents, her conception and birth had been a shock from which they'd never recovered. Before marrying, Bernard Joyce had been a Jesuit priest and Dorothy Leonard, after she married him, became his most ardent acolyte. They were stoically dutiful towards their unexpected offspring, good people with emotional deficiencies who had, as she changed from baby to child to teenager, grown used to and fond of Alva.

The tragedy for Alva was that the growth of their affection took too long, and by the time she became aware of it it was too late. The smothering, consuming, demanding love of old age and illness was a burden she did not want. And in any event, she had by then found love, or something very like it, elsewhere.

She was a little more than five years old when she began to realize that life in the big dark house she knew as home was in every way different to life as it was lived by other families in other houses in the locality. She had started school by then and was allowed to make the occasional visit to the home of an approved schoolfriend.

The first of these visits, for tea with the large family of

an unremarkable child, she would always remember as a light being turned on in the dark. She'd been dazzled by the exuberance and noise, the jostling body contact, argumentative talk and teasing laughter. But more than all of that it was at tea in the O'Malley household that Alva had experienced the first, confused stirrings of a rejection of the stifling life with her parents.

This glimpse of another way of living hadn't changed things in any practical way, but from that day on she had known that she did not want to live as her parents did and that she would escape them as soon as she could.

There was a photograph of Alva with her parents in the room her mother called the parlour. It was taken when Alva was four, and as she grew older she studied it often, hoping to find in their posed faces some revelation about her parents. The camera had caught the habitual stern expression on her father's long, bony face. Her mother, handsome and austere, looked resigned and was half-smiling. In her case too this was how she usually looked.

Alva, between them on a chair, was round and staring. Her curly dark hair, whose provenance was a mystery, made her seem like a wanton, trespassing gypsy child. All three were posed with spaces between them, no one touched anyone else. As a photograph it was a statement of how they were as a family. It didn't tell Alva a single thing she didn't already know about her parents. Or herself.

Small intimacies became milestones: like the day her mother revealed why she'd chosen the name Alva for her daughter. Alva had asked why, more out of a desire to create sound between them while they prepared tea than from any real desire to know. She'd been surprised when her mother had answered.

'I liked the name.' She scoured the teapot thoughtfully. 'And your father had no objections. Alva was the name of the nurse who attended your birth. It was a difficult time for me and she was a fine girl, fair-haired and with soft hands. She seemed to me a happy person and the name a joyful one.' She smiled her half-smile. 'I hoped for happiness for you, too.'

Alva took refuge in books and discovered a talent for languages. By the time she was fourteen she could speak more than reasonable French and Spanish. This became a comfort to her. She could, she told herself, use her fluency to escape home. In this way, planning and dreaming, her entire childhood was spent waiting for her life to begin.

When Alva finished school at eighteen her father decided what she should do. 'You will study law,' he said. Alva was appalled.

'But I've no feeling for law,' she said.

'Feelings don't come into it. Feelings negate reason. The law is a fine discipline.' He'd looked away, ending the conversation.

But the prospect of the acid company of her father's legal friends had emboldened Alva.

'I intend doing an arts degree.' She hadn't until then.

'A waste of time, the resort of the idle and undisciplined. I'm not throwing good money into useless study.'

Nor had he. But Dorothy, surprisingly, stubbornly, and to the annoyance of her husband, had funded their daughter for the three years it took to do the arts degree.

Alva defied her father again when it came to a choice of career. Her years at college left her relatively untouched. The turbulent lives and emotions of her student colleagues seemed to her absurd, and frivolity touched her not at all. She emerged with a good degree, but having failed absolutely to learn what she needed to know about human relationships.

She did, however, discover what she wanted to do with herself. Roped into helping with the college magazine she decided, largely because it was her sole work experience, that she would become a journalist.

'Jackals.' Her father's contempt for her choice had been harsher than she'd anticipated. 'Living off the misery of others, invading privacy and exposing it without justification or benefit to anyone.'

It was a Sunday, early, and they were breakfasting. Alva cracked open her boiled egg as her father finished his and wiped his mouth.

'I don't agree,' she said. She hadn't thought about it. Her father threw down his napkin.

'Journalism is a case of the ill-informed leading the ignorant. The so-called freedom of the press is no more than a corrupt way of making money. If the public—'

'I'm going to become a journalist, Father.' Alva stood.

Her father went quite still. He spoke without looking at her. 'You defied me on the matter of your degree. You will not—'

'Let her be, Bernard.' Her mother's voice was precise, icy in a way Alva hadn't heard it before. 'Let her discover for herself. We are all entitled to at least one mistake in our lives.'

It was the first, and last, time Alva ever heard her mother refer to her father's leaving the priesthood as a mistake: it had always until then been spoken of with pride. He had stiffened into silence.

Dorothy Joyce had spoken out because she was dying. Within weeks she had become too ill to hide the reality of her cancer's creeping speed. On the day she collapsed, and the doctor gave her husband and daughter the news, she called Alva to her bedside.

'There is no good my having treatment.' She aligned the edges of the turned-down sheet with white, twig-like fingers. Her face was grey as her hair. 'I know this disease and I know its inevitability. I watched my mother before me try to live with it and I am not going to do that to myself.' Her hands lay still. She wasn't wearing her wedding band and Alva supposed she'd become too thin for it to stay on. 'I will die here, in this room. It won't take long. I want you to stay with me, Alva. Your father . . .' She sighed and looked her daughter in the eye and the truth lay between them. Her husband would not look after her. It wasn't in him. 'Promise me, Alva. Promise me you'll stay.'

'I promise.'

It took six months for her mother to die. Alva studied in the sick room.

Her mother was a quiet, long-suffering patient, her dying as subdued as her living had been. When death became imminent Alva hired a cheerful, fair-haired nurse to help administer the morphine. Dorothy Joyce never said whether the woman was anything like the nurse after whom she'd named her only child. She died quietly and alone in the night. Alva felt only release.

And she came quickly to a decision. She hired a housekeeper and found herself a flat. When she told her father, he laid the book he was reading across his knees and looked past her at the rain falling outside.

'I don't want you to go,' he said. 'I won't pay a housekeeper.'

'You don't have to. I will.' Alva had money her mother had left her. There would be an ironic justice in using it to pay someone to take the dead woman's place.

'This is your home. I am your father.'

'It was,' Alva said, 'and you are.'

Her Rathmines flat had a bedroom and kitchen. The bathroom was shared and Alva thought it the most excellent accommodation in the city of Dublin. She visited her father and found him much more bearable now she wasn't living with him.

And she found herself a job in journalism, lowly and junior but a job. She was nearly twenty-two years old and she was free, as the wind and as everyone else her age. She was filled with a craving for wild friends and reckless living, for loud music and dancing. She wanted to drink too much and be held by tall, handsome, laughing men who would kiss her until her lips ached and were swollen with the pleasure of it.

She wanted to live.

But for now, shopping and cooking and learning to be alone, there was still the old feeling of waiting for life to begin. A lifetime's habit would not disappear overnight, but she was willing to give it time. Only not too much time.

Chapter Five

Four months after leaving home Alva was living in a state of controlled desperation. Nothing was easy. Not the job, not making friends, not life in the flat – which turned out to be less than the excellent accommodation she'd thought. With the hedonistic eighties raging in the streets outside, and clubs all around, she found that she was still, somehow, apart from it all.

At the paper she felt excluded from journalism's iconoclastic camaraderie. The harder she tried to match her colleagues' robust cynicism the less she seemed to fit in. There were problems with her work, also – she wrote too slowly, her articles were too long, too short, had too many facts or not enough of them.

A comfortable flat would have helped. Beyond telling her that her room would always be available, her father took no interest in her living arrangements. Through it all Alva never once thought of retreating to the grim comforts of the house in Churchtown.

Shaking off the spectre of her father wasn't easy. In the early months she would feel his hard, disapproving gaze on her as she shopped, hear his measured tones questioning every word she wrote. As the months went by, though, there came days when she didn't think about him at all. By December he occupied her thoughts only on those days when she went home to see him.

It was two weeks before Christmas when she first saw Kevin Carlyle. She'd been sent to a press reception where details of a seasonal scheme to get the homeless off the streets were to be announced. Midway through she spotted him standing at the edge of the crowd. He was tall and blond and, from where she stood taking notes, completely and perfectly handsome.

'*Who* is that?' She nudged and whispered the question into the ear of Seona Daly. Seona was a colleague, and if anyone knew who the Adonis was she would. She was a tireless hunter of contacts and information, knew everyone in town and could supply versions of most of their personal histories. Her own story was as obscure as the original colour of her hair, at that moment an impossibly bright auburn. She shared a desk with Alva and treated her with equal measures of contempt, caution and envy. Very occasionally another side of her nature surfaced and she could be well-meaning, benign even. It happened now.

'*That* is Kevin Carlyle.' She knew immediately whom Alva meant and eyed him coolly, not bothering to keep her voice down. 'He's best and most kindly described as a getting-on boyo about town. Thirty-eight if he's a day and with a hammer-man reputation as long as your arm.'

It would have taken someone a lot braver than Alva to remind Seona Daly that she had passed the mid-thirty mark herself. Seona was short and round, extremely pretty in an elaborate, made-up way, a child of nature only in her appetites for food, drink and, it was rumoured, sex. Free drink was the reason she'd come along that night, as well as a desire to see who she might see. Concern for the homeless had not been a consideration. She sipped wine, more than happy to go on about Kevin Carlyle.

'Stories are legion about the women who've fallen for him and lost. Can't understand it myself, wouldn't be my type at all. Too *obvious*, if you know what I mean. I prefer my men subtler, a bit off-centre.' She grinned and displayed lipstick-stained teeth. 'Mind you, I doubt I'm his type either. The leggy model brigade seem more to his taste.' She made a rueful pout of her magenta lips. Seona was five-foot-two, max, her voluptuousness in danger of turning to fat.

'What does he do?' Alva asked. At that moment, loudly and infectiously, Kevin Carlyle was laughing at a poor joke made by the speechmaker. Sign of a generous nature, Alva decided. He really knew how to laugh, too. Funny thing was, she didn't usually fancy good-looking men. She found their brash confidence off-putting. But the face across the room had mobility and humour, didn't seem brash at all.

'God alone knows *everything* he does,' Seona shrugged. 'Bit of this, bit of that, wheels and deals and makes a lot of money, by all accounts. Property investments have been mentioned. But mainly and for the record he's a PR consultant. He does well at that too. Got government contacts, so he's probably helping sell this plan to clear the unsightly homeless off the streets for Christmas.'

'Not bad looking, is he?'

'Definitely a honcho, but used to be even more so. Up close his age shows . . .' She turned the full voltage of one of her shrewd looks on Alva. 'Take a word of advice from Aunty Seona and keep away from him. He's nothing but trouble and you wouldn't have a clue how to handle him.'

'You think not?' Alva's look was more coolly diminishing than she realized.

'Please yourself,' Seona snapped, 'but don't come whingeing to me when your knickers are in a knot and he's dumped you.'

She moved off, eyes searching the crowd, her everyday, restless self again. Alva was barely aware of her going, certain she was wrong about Kevin Carlyle. Seona was wrong, or at least half-cocked, about a lot of people. She was noted for it. The only facts she checked were those she had to put in writing. The rest of the time her information on people was embellished, or otherwise, to suit her mood. Naturally someone who looked like Kevin Carlyle would have lots of women. God, he probably had to fight them off. Alva was even willing to bet he'd rejected an advance of Seona's. It would explain her attitude.

The speeches ended and people began to mingle. Alva made her way slowly round the room. Kevin Carlyle's head disappeared from view, then reappeared. She had no idea what she would say when she got to where he was. Wish him a happy Christmas perhaps, ask him what he . . .

He was gone when she got to the spot where he'd

been standing. She let out a breath she hadn't realized she'd been holding and grabbed a glass from a passing tray. Just as well, she told herself, you'd probably have made an ass of yourself. No way a man like that's available.

Time anyway to get back to the office, write up what was basically a government PR exercise. The homeless would be back on the streets by the New Year.

The absurdity of her manoeuvring struck her again when she hit the street and walked into a blistering, sleet-filled east wind. She broke into a trot, partly to keep warm but mostly to distance herself from what was fast becoming a cringe-making incident.

'You were like a loony adolescent, Alva, panting around that room after a man who didn't even know you were there.' With the cold stinging her muttering lips she pulled her scarf over them and put her head down. She collided with Kevin Carlyle as he stepped back from the kerb to avoid being splashed.

'Whoa, there! Take it easy.' He caught her arm, laughing, saving them both from falling over. 'There's always another bus.'

'Sorry – very sorry—' It was all she could manage. He did, as Seona had claimed, look older close up. Older as in mature. She searched for something to say but it was he who spoke next.

'My fault entirely.' He smiled. His teeth were every bit as perfect as they'd seemed across the room. What was extra was that she could now see his eyes. They were blue, light and teasing, with nothing of the dark seriousness of her own about them.

'I should look where I'm going.' She smiled and he shook his head.

'You were fairly moving there. Not being chased, were you?' Still holding her arm he looked over her shoulder. His voice was surprisingly accentless and flat, but definitely Dublin.

'Only by the cold.' Alva shivered. 'I was running to keep warm.'

'You were at the Safe Haven reception.' He dropped her arm but held her gaze. 'I saw you there. Work or partying?'

'Working. I'm still working. I'll have to go . . .' She didn't really. She could write the damn thing up in five minutes. Much better to stay here, chatting and shivering in the freezing wind . . .

'Forgive me,' he said, 'I didn't mean to hold you up.' He nodded and smiled and stepped away, back to the kerb, onto the road. Alva stood petrified and silently swearing. She'd been given a golden second opportunity and she'd blown it. Or maybe she hadn't. The pedestrian light was still green.

'We seem to be going in the same direction.' Her voice, as she fell into step beside him, was light, friendly. Not nervous at all.

She would wonder later, when they were living together and she was dizzy with happiness, at how sure she'd been of her feelings for Kevin that first night. She who had been so cautious with men up until then, who had never felt her virginity even slightly threatened. It was more than his immodest good looks and the pleasure of standing shoulder to shoulder with a man who was her own height; more than being made to laugh by him and feeling herself melt at his teasing looks.

It was the differences: the things about him which were alien to everything she'd grown up with had been the hook. He was so completely unlike the thin, retreating asceticism of her parents. Where they had merely hung on to life, Kevin, from that very first night, had seemed to her to take it by the throat and shake it. Much later still, when she could see things even more clearly, she added to this the ruthless desire she'd felt, but not acknowledged, that night. He'd oozed energy and a confident, knowing sexuality. She had sensed instantly that he was nothing at all like the hesitant boys and young men who had until then been the ones to proposition her.

Kevin Carlyle had loved before, she hadn't, and that too had a powerful appeal. She wanted to be taken and moulded and taught all about loving by a man who knew. By a man like Kevin Carlyle. *By* Kevin Carlyle.

They made love the second time they met. She had known it would happen when she agreed to them going back to his place. She had wanted it to happen.

'I like it. Very designer.'

Standing between the open, stone-coloured curtains of his living room, the lights of Dublin behind and below her, she'd instantly loved his apartment. It was high and spacious, part of a Ballsbridge complex.

White walls met dark grey carpeting and black leather seating sat at all the right angles. A dining area had an art deco-style table and chairs.

'It should be "very designer".' He pulled a rueful face and handed her the white wine she'd asked for. 'I paid a very designer woman enough money to come up with this minimalist sort of thing.' He shrugged. 'It's easy to live with. I'm not here a lot of the time.'

'I can see that,' Alva said. The impression was of a furniture-filled space which was passed through but not touched. She wondered about the rooms she couldn't see. How lived in they were. How lived in the bedroom was . . .

'Here's looking at you, kid.' Kevin raised his glass. They drank and he took her hand, leading her away from the window. 'You're sweet,' he said.

'Sweet?'

'And beautiful.' Hesitantly, as if afraid she might not want him to, he stroked the back of his fingers across her cheek. 'And you have no idea, have you?'

'No idea?' She wanted to stop echoing him but nothing original came to mind. Nothing at all came to mind. In that cool, cool room she felt hot and flustered and tongue-tied.

'How lovely you are. You're unique, Alva, like something just emerged from a chrysalis . . .'

'A rare bird on this earth, like nothing so much as a black swan.' She laughed, to hide her embarrassment and escape his intense gaze. 'Juvenal,' she muttered, 'meant to be a joke . . .'

He put his glass down carefully on a glass-topped

table. He moved closer and touched her hair. His thigh was against hers, his mouth an inch away. Just as she thought her nerveless fingers would drop the glass he took it from her and, without creating space between them, put it beside his own. She wondered how many times before he'd made the same smooth move, but then put the thought away. It didn't matter. Tonight he was making all his moves with her. That was all she cared about.

'It's late.' Her mouth was dry.

'Very late,' he agreed and put his hand on her neck, under her hair, and massaged gently. His other hand fell to the small of her back, holding her against him. Alva yielded, her breasts, stomach, thighs all pressing into him. His mouth brushed hers with a light, experimental touch and she pulled away, but only slightly. She was breathing very fast.

'I . . .' she stopped and he waited. Her eyes felt heavy, slumbrous.

'I want to . . .' she said.

'I know,' he said.

He kissed her and the game-playing ended. Alva's last coherent thought, before passion took over, was that she at last understood what was meant by white heat.

Slow and devouring, the kiss went on. Between groans and whimpers, and not half fast enough, they tore at one another's clothes, pulled apart for greedy, famished looks as bodies were revealed.

His was beautiful, muscled and broad. The Adonis she'd seen across the room was hers. She touched him quickly, his chest, his stomach, the hard swollen heaviness of his penis. Like something famished she circled him with her arms, clinging to him and bringing their bodies together again. She heard herself whimper, felt herself hot and wet between her legs and knew, God, oh God, knew exactly what she wanted him to do to her. She was alive, alive and out of control – didn't want to know about control, about anything except these explosive sensations, this glorious pleasure. She wanted her body's need gratified, to be filled with him, here, now, standing as they were in the middle of the room. The briefest of thoughts about safe sex vanished as his mouth covered hers again and his fingers held and caressed a nipple. She thrust her gyrating hips against his, wrapping a long leg around him, letting him feel the heat burning between her thighs. His hand went down and he buried his fingers in her wetness.

'Jesus God,' he breathed and pushed into her, hard and then harder, slow and then quicker, on and on for ever, his hands cupping her behind, holding her to him until her moans and initial pain turned to cries of loud, howling pleasure and she came in a great, blinding purge of awareness, a burst of sheer, spinning, abandoned sensation.

Kevin came immediately after, or maybe it was with her, she couldn't tell, and they sank together slowly onto the soft grey pile of the carpet and lay there, quietly, barely touching one another.

'Thank you,' she said and blinked to stop slow tears as they began to fall. 'That was nice.' She felt drowsy, unreal. She had no idea why she was crying. He turned his head and saw the tears.

'What is it?' Lazily puzzled, he ran a hand lightly across her belly, down her thigh. Another tear fell and he caught it with his tongue. 'Didn't think you were the type to go all weepy,' he said.

'I'm not.' Alva stared at the ceiling. 'Reactive tears, I suppose.' She paused and then told him, not at all sure how he would take it. 'That was my first time,' she said.

He was silent. She knew he had turned his head and was watching her but couldn't bring herself to meet his gaze. Not until she heard him give a low chuckle. She did turn then and he pulled her to him.

'You're a fucking natural,' he said and it was the most treasured compliment of her life. He nibbled her ear, then put his tongue in it. She quivered.

'Time to go to bed,' he said.

It wasn't all sex between them but sex was a huge part of it.

'I'm going to take you and make you,' Kevin said to her later on that first night. And he did.

In the weeks which followed he took her whenever and wherever they could find the time and place, made her crave and enjoy pleasures of sex she'd only dimly imagined possible. He was protective and demanding, possessive and caring and she felt, for the very first time in her life, utterly and completely loved.

Three months after meeting him Alva moved in with Kevin Carlyle, exchanging the Rathmines flat with its oozing damp and disastrous electrical system for the order of his designer efficiency in Ballsbridge. Giving her father the new address she told him only that it was more convenient for work (not a lie) and a lot more comfortable (the absolute truth). Kevin was amused by her furtiveness – and not keen anyway to know her father.

'Outside of you, my love, I doubt we'd have much in common,' he grinned. 'It's probably best for everyone if we don't meet.' Alva agreed.

Seona, calling it an act of friendship and saying she was marking Alva's cards, voiced the general, gossip-about-town view of the relationship.

'Word is our Kev has fallen at last,' she said. They were sharing a break by the coffee machine. 'The begrudgers are saying it's because he sees the big four-O approaching and wants youth by his side. But they don't know you like I do so I tell them it's your mind he's after.'

'Thanks.' Alva decided on hot chocolate. 'With a friend like you, Seona . . .' She sipped. The chocolate was over-sweet.

'Don't bother to thank me.' Seona waved a hand. 'Just tell me, what's his place like?'

'Comfortable,' Alva said, 'great panorama over town . . .'

'So I've heard.' Seona fluffed her hair. She'd had it permed. With the magenta lipstick and the frown on her face it made her look like a cross peacock. 'Though I'm not, of course, one of the legions who've been privy to a viewing.'

'OK, Seona.' Alva was curt. 'You've made your point. I ignored your warning about Kevin and you're convinced I'm making a mistake. But it's my mistake and my life. I know you mean well,' she knew no such thing, 'but, please, let's drop the subject.'

'Fine by me. It's become boring anyway.'

Seona rarely referred to Kevin after that – and when she did she was only mildly snide.

All her life, except for the time spent in Rathmines, Alva had lived with two people who'd guarded themselves from her. Kevin was the opposite, there in every corner of her life, guiding, moulding her socially, giving her confidence. If she depended on him too much, that was simply the other side of the coin, an inevitability of the way they were. His protective possessiveness was reassuring proof of his love, the sheltered intimacy in which he preferred them to live part of his desire to safeguard what they had. Alva grew to dislike going places without him, happy only when in his company. When Seona questioned the wisdom of her turning down invitations, Alva was laughingly dismissive. There was nothing stifling about the relationship, she assured, everything was as *she* wanted it to be. Reluctant to be away from Kevin she even cut visits to her father down to one a week. She was in love and happy and had come to anchor.

And she never tired of the intimate sharing of space, of shopping for two, planning meals for two, of thinking about someone else. She'd never been domesticated but now she loved even the small things. Kevin was amused and surprised, and humoured her. And beneath the order there was their sex life, voracious, ever hungry and always needing to be fed.

In the warm early autumn of their first year together they went to a garden party. It was a lavish, showy affair, held in the dense, sporadically lit gardens of a house in the foothills of the Dublin mountains. Alva wore blue, a Chinese-style silk jacket and narrow pants. She wore jade earrings and caught her hair behind her ears.

'You look great.' Kevin, as they left the apartment, was abstracted. 'But I'll have to leave you to your own devices. I'm wrapping up a deal at this thing.'

'Fine.' Alva took his arm. 'I'll try to behave.'

He put his arm around her shoulders. 'You'd better,' he said.

The party was noisy and oddly uptight. Alva circled and spotted faces – a captain of industry, an hotelier, a wealthy ex-footballer. She came to a halt in the brightest corner, by an acacia tree, and watched a couple of sulky models in identical white crochet Prada dresses display their spectacular bodies to an award-winning interior designer and to a short, stout man she recognized as having met before. When the models and designer moved off she placed herself, smiling, in front of him.

'Hello, Oscar,' she said.

'Hello there.' He nodded vaguely.

'Alva Joyce,' she supplied helpfully. 'We met briefly at that film première last month. You were there with Seona Daly . . .'

'Ah! Well, if you say so I'm sure we did ...' He saluted her with his glass. 'Why don't we take a pew?'

They sat on a long wooden garden seat and he began to roll a cigarette. 'Godawful boring party,' he said, 'don't know what I'm doing here.'

He sprinkled some fine white powder into the half-rolled spliff and offered Alva the first smoke. She declined and he dragged deeply himself, a satisfied grin spreading across his round face as the distinctive aroma of cocaine drifted in the air.

'Amazing how much better this evening's become.' He leaned back and looked at her. 'You're not a Seona type of person, but maybe her taste's improving.' He giggled.

'We work together,' Alva said.

'Ah! That explains it. Explains why your face is familiar too. But not what you're doing here.' He eyed her critically. 'You don't look like an *arriviste* – but then it's getting harder to tell by the day.' He sighed mightily and looked around the garden. 'Most of this crowd came down with the eighties money shower and are already burnt out and ulcer-ridden for their pains.' He giggled again. 'Whose arm did you arrive on?'

'Maybe I came on my own.'

'Did you?'

'No.' Alva shrugged and, without really wanting to, gave him Kevin's name. He yawned.

'I've met him but he's not someone I know. Be a darling and grab me a glass, will you?'

He waggled a short finger and a passing waiter stopped. Alva stood, relieved the tray of two of its sparkling flutes and handed one to Oscar Duggan. She didn't sit down again. There had to be less acid company around.

'I'll tell Seona I met you—'

He interrupted her with a burst of fruity yodelling at a short, blonde woman in a sheath of white fabric. 'You haven't met your hostess, have you?' Oscar stood.

'No.'

'Thought not. No *savoir faire*, these people. Not a bloody clue.' He was smiling as the woman approached. 'With any luck she'll be indiscreet about someone . . .'

'Oscar! You old reprobate!' The woman kissed him roundly on both cheeks, without strain since they were of a height. 'I didn't actually believe you'd venture this far into the wilderness.'

'Don't know why you invited me so. And less of the old, if you don't mind.' Oscar suffered the kisses before turning the woman towards Alva. 'Here's somebody else you invited. Alva, meet your hostess, Trudi McDonald.'

'Lovely of you to come.' Trudi McDonald, to her credit, didn't pretend to know Alva. She was made-up and pretty and had the voluptuous, corseted figure of a fifties pin-up.

'I'm the "friend" part of your invitation to Kevin Carlyle,' Alva said helpfully.

'You are?' The woman's tone dropped from party-polite to plain curious. 'So you're the lucky girl. Handsome devil, isn't he?' With a swift, practised eye she took Alva in from head to toe.

'Yes.'

'We were delighted when we heard he'd ... met someone.' Her eyes lingered on Alva's midriff. 'Life's more fun if you share it, I always say.'

'Much more fun.' Alva considered announcing that she wasn't pregnant, didn't want to be, and that she and Kevin were together because they cared about one another. She sipped her champagne instead.

'Have you known our gorgeous Kevin long?' Trudi McDonald did not seem about to drop the subject and Oscar Duggan, his eyes moving avidly from one woman to the other, seemed to encourage her.

'A while.' Alva was cool. 'Have *you* known him long?'

'For ever.' Trudi McDonald gave a deep throat laugh. 'Kevin is a *very* old and very dear friend. Which is why I'm so very glad to meet you, my pet.' She paused, put a hand on Alva's arm and became confidential. 'You're young, so a word of advice. Make the most of it, hay while the sun shines and all that. What I'm saying is, the very best of luck to you.'

'Thank you.' Alva smiled and seethed and moved out of range of the woman's hand. 'I think I'll take your advice straight away and mingle, make the most of the party . . .'

Kevin was nowhere to be found. Alva had two drinks in quick succession as she searched, growing increasingly fed up and impatient to leave. She was standing at the French windows of the house, undecided about where to look next, when a hand took her elbow and a hot-breathed voice spoke in her ear.

'This is supposed to be a fun party. Can I do anything to put a smile on that beautiful face?'

Alva, turning, found there was less than an inch of air-space between her mouth and that of the dark-eyed man now holding her arm quite tightly.

'You can let my arm go.' She was icy.

'Mmm. Suppose I could.' He smiled. His breath smelled of beer. 'But you're the juiciest looking thing I've seen all night so I'm not inclined to. Why don't you and I . . .' he moved quickly and brushed her lips with his, 'go someplace quiet and . . . talk?'

'Hands off. Lady's with me.' Kevin's voice, from close behind Alva, was low, controlled and menacing. It was the voice of a stranger.

'Didn't seem to me to be with anyone.' The dark-eyed man looked lazily and drunkenly over Alva's shoulder. His grip on her arm tightened even more and made it impossible for her to turn around. 'Alone and lonely is how I'd have described her.'

'I'll tell you once more, and once more only. Let her arm go and fuck off.' Kevin moved to Alva's side. By just slightly turning her head she could see how white his face was and how a muscle throbbed in his neck. She shivered.

'Please . . .' she said.

'I warned you,' Kevin's new, thick voice was barely audible as his body jerked back and his fist, tightly bunched, smacked off the side of the other man's face. The hand let go of her arm. 'Now get out of here,' Kevin said.

'Jesus, head, are you mad or what?' The dark-eyed

man, hand to his cheek, looked groggily at Kevin. 'There was no need for that. No need at all.'

Someone pulled forward a straight-backed chair and pushed him down into it. A silent crowd had gathered. The man sat, shaking his head in disbelief. 'Fucking ridiculous,' he said.

'We're leaving.' Kevin turned on his heel and Alva, caught between an apology and a desire not to make things worse, followed after a small hesitation.

Kevin drove too fast.

'Please slow down,' Alva said as the Alfa Romeo whipped past cars and changed lanes on the Stillorgan dual carriageway. 'I'm frightened.'

He said nothing and he didn't slow down. His anger, as much as the speed of the car, frightened her. She had never seen him in this icily furious mood and didn't know how to handle it. She shouldn't have got into the car until he'd calmed down, shouldn't have . . .

'He's lucky I didn't break his neck.' The words, the first Kevin had spoken since leaving the party, came between closed teeth.

'*You're* lucky he was too drunk to feel anything and that he was a peaceful type.' Alva knew immediately she'd said the wrong thing. She closed her eyes and clutched at the seatbelt as she felt his fury accelerate with the car.

'Wrong. Wrong, because I'd have killed him if he tried anything and he knew it. And wrong to think that he, or you, could make a fool of me publicly and get away with it.'

'That's not the way it was, Kevin.' They'd stopped at the Nutley Lane traffic lights. With cars on either side and a garda on the footpath opposite, Alva felt safe enough making her point. 'He thought I was alone and, anyway, I was dealing with the situation.'

'Yes. I could see how you were dealing with the situation.' The lights turned green and the car shot forward. There was a garda car to their right now and Kevin drove less wildly. But his voice was harsh, somehow more intimidating because it was calmer. 'Don't ever try to make a fool of me again, Alva. Ever. You're mine, for as long as I say so, and don't ever forget it.'

'I wasn't—'

'Shut up! Subject's closed.'

Outside the flat he drew up and left the engine running. She shrank instinctively against the seat when he leaned across her to open the door.

'Out,' he said.

'Aren't you coming . . .?'

'Out.'

She lay alone that night, the first time in the seven months since she'd moved into the apartment. She didn't sleep and, in the morning when Kevin still hadn't returned, found herself unable to face work or the outside world. She phoned in sick and at eight thirty began pacing with black coffee. At ten she wrapped herself in a blanket and, huddled on the settee in the living room, fell into exhausted sleep. When she awoke Kevin was standing in the doorway.

'How long have you been there?' she asked.

'Long enough,' he said. He looked terrible, sleepless bruises under his eyes and lines she'd never seen before dragging his mouth down. He hadn't shaved. 'I'm sorry, Alva. Jesus Christ, I'm sorry. I don't know why it happened.' He shrugged, put a shoulder against the door jamb, looking as if he would collapse without its support. 'The deal I was there to wrap up fell through. I went looking for you, saw that animal with his hands all over ... Won't happen again.' He straightened and walked down the corridor, closing the bedroom door quietly when he went inside.

After that they didn't party much together, tacitly agreeing that parties weren't for them, that they didn't need them. Kevin still went, because parties were where he met contacts and more often than not worked out deals. Alva was happy to stay at home. For a life outside of Kevin she had her job, and her visits to her father. It was enough.

Then, on a day in March when spring was looking hopeful and Alva had been living with Kevin a little over two years, something she'd quietly dreaded happened. She picked up the intercom and heard her father's voice on the other end.

In the apartment he sat, stiffly, in one of the harder chairs. He looked terrible and terribly out of place, stooped and dark-clothed and seeming to Alva like nothing so much as a hunchbacked, waiting crow.

'Tea or coffee?'

He ignored the question. 'Your companion is not here, I take it?'

Companion – did that mean he knew about Kevin?
'Not at the moment,' Alva said.

'Good,' he said. 'I had hoped to avoid him.'

In the silence which followed Alva felt the room close around her. She was fourteen years old and she was in the parlour in Churchtown. The years between had never happened.

'How long have you known?' Her voice too had changed. Sitting in the armchair opposite him even her voice was faint and unsure.

'That's of no matter,' he said. 'Has he offered to marry you?'

'Offered . . .? No, Father. He has not offered to marry me. And nor have I offered to marry him. We are happy together as we are. I love him.'

'Love. Love is no more than gratification of the senses. You confuse lust with love and fornication with happiness. Love between a man and a woman brings with it responsibilities . . .' *This* was her father speaking. He would never change.

'You're damn right it does,' Alva interrupted him harshly, 'for you as well as everyone else. It is a father's responsibility to show love to his child. When did you ever do that?'

'You had everything you wanted.' Stiffly.

'No. No, I did not have everything I wanted.'

'I provided you with moral guidance, a good home, an education—'

'Self-righteous shit!' Her father winced. 'When it came to college, Mother paid. You refused because I wouldn't study what *you* wanted me to. Is *that* morally

90

right? Is that the moral guidance I'm supposed to emulate?'

Her father was like a waxen figure, his eyes faded to the same slush grey as his skin. 'I was wrong.' One shoulder moved in a shrug. 'You would not be in this situation if you had studied the law.' There was resignation in his face, nothing else. 'And I would be reneging on my present responsibility if I did not tell you that what you are doing is wrong. Morally and socially wrong.'

He paused and Alva breathed a sigh of relief. He'd come to fulfil his moral duty, said what he had to say. Surely he would go now . . .

'I would like you to come home with me, Alva,' her father said.

She stared at him. 'I can't do that,' she said and was pleased how firm and calm her voice sounded.

'I am dying,' her father said.

So that was it. She stood and backed away from him, towards the door, panic rising in a tide of nausea to her throat. Of course he was dying. He was dying and he needed her and *that* was why he was here. He had no one else.

'I have always cared for you, Alva,' her father said.

Standing with her back to the door she knew, with bitter resignation, that she would go back to the bleak, shadowy house in Churchtown and stay with him until he died. The thought made her want to cry, for herself. She had no tears in her for her father.

Three days after his visit she moved. By then she'd learned that her father, as her mother, had cancer. He would live, the doctor said, three months at most, and the pain should be controllable. A nurse was hired. This time Alva found a thin, efficient woman who spoke little. Cheerfulness wouldn't be a factor with her father.

Kevin had been frightening in his anger. 'I won't let you do it. That selfish old fucker is exploiting you. This' – they were in the kitchen and he'd thumped hard on the table top – 'is where you belong. *I* made you, not that loony father of yours.'

Alva stood away from the table and faced him. 'I don't need this, Kevin. He may well be all that you say he is but he's dying and he's my father. I have to live with myself after he dies. It'll only be for a few months. Please try to understand.'

'Understand what? That you're betraying me?' Kevin's voice was ragged, going out of control. He made a fist of his hand and punched the wall behind him. Alva closed her eyes and tried to still the shaking.

'Please stop it,' she whispered.

'He doesn't own you, Alva.' He'd stopped shouting but the effect was the same. 'The nurse will look after him. You can visit. This is going to endanger our relationship, have you thought about that? Or about *my* need?' He moved quickly, catching her off guard and holding her tightly by both arms. He shook her. 'I want you here.'

'Don't you think I'd prefer to be here? Do you think I *want* to do this?'

'Then why? Why are you doing it?' He was calmer, genuinely puzzled. 'Is it the house? It was your mother's. You'll get it whether you take care of him or not . . .'

'The house isn't the issue, Kevin.' She felt anger herself now. She understood how *he* felt, why couldn't he make the same leap for her? His grip on her arms was painful and she tried to pull away.

He shook his head and tightened his grip. 'I don't like what happens in my life being decided by other people.' He spoke softly. 'I don't like anything you've ever told me about your father and I certainly don't like the way he thinks he can walk in and take over your life. Look, I'm sorry,' he loosened his hold and circled her with his arms, holding her against him. 'I'm a possessive bastard, Alva, you know that. You're mine. Not his. I found you and I opened you up and I don't want anyone else to have you. Especially not him.'

Alva got extended leave from work and moved back to Churchtown while Kevin was at work. The loneliness of old settled over her within days, like a damp, familiar blanket.

Her father weakened immediately she moved in and made it almost impossible to get away for nights with Kevin. The house was overheated and he was constantly cold, his knees jutting like mountain peaks beneath the rugs on his bed as he complained about draughts. His skin swiftly took on the yellowed appearance of paper dried in the sun and his eyes the inward stare of someone facing death.

She'd seen it all in her mother before. This time she was able to distance herself.

She missed Kevin, day and night, and as if there was some great void in her centre. The first couple of months she managed to see him four times. The third and fourth months she saw him only twice.

Her father lived for four months, dying on a bright sunshiny day in July. Alva opened the windows and took down the curtains which had all her life kept the daylight out.

'Enough,' she told herself, 'is enough. It's over.'

A week later she moved back to life with Kevin.

Chapter Six

The change was disorientating. Alva spent several weeks in fitful sleep, still alert for her father's frequent, fretful calls, lying wakeful when they didn't come and waiting for feelings of peace and freedom to wash over her.

When they did she grieved for her father *and* her mother, feeling an immeasurable sadness for lives so miserably lived. This changed, slowly, to an acceptance that her parents had lived as they had from choice. She would not spend her own life regretting theirs. She too *would* accept, and move on.

She had deliberately put dealing with things between her and Kevin on a back boiler. He had been happy to have her back, and loving. But things weren't the same and she didn't, at first, feel equipped to deal with whatever had changed. They made love as passionately as ever, and as often. They quickly slipped into the old routine of laughter and gossip and shared meals late at night. Kevin wasn't any different. That he was happy with things, and for them to go on as they were, she had no doubt.

And yet, and yet. She couldn't shake off the feeling. It was as if a crisis had happened, and been ignored, and they were now heading for the inevitable crash.

She had changed, of course; she knew she had. Though she had Kevin, she was aware of feeling quite alone in the world. And of wanting to push back the frontiers a bit, explore life's possibilities in some way.

In the autumn Kevin helped her sell the house. The price, together with the savings her father left, meant Alva had quite a lot of money.

On a wintry October day, when half the city was down with flu, Alva was stricken with the bug and reeled home early from work. She crawled into bed, sniffling and shivering and dosed with lemon, hot whiskey and Disprin.

She knew instantly that something was different, foreign about the bed. It looked, but wasn't, how she'd left it that morning. The duvet had been arranged the same way and the pillows plumped up. The smell was what gave them away. The bed was pungent with a perfume Alva knew was not hers, and with an odour of recent sex so strong it infiltrated even her blocked membranes. She closed her eyes and tried to believe she was imagining things. All that happened was that the sickly sweet perfume and sex smell threatened to smother and overpower her.

She staggered from the bed and searched the rest of the apartment. Evidence she could have seen any time if she'd been looking jumped out at her: her dressing gown in the living room where she was certain she hadn't left it; a broken earring clip on the bathroom window – Alva's own ears were pierced; an empty wine bottle by the waste disposal in the kitchen which hadn't been there that morning.

Such carelessness had to be deliberate. One or both of them wanted to be found out. It was either that, or contempt for Alva's ignorance. She felt sure that afternoon wasn't the first time Kevin had brought the woman to the apartment. God alone knew how long it had been going on, or how many women. All the time she'd been away, probably; certainly all the time since she'd got back. This was the crash she'd subconsciously been waiting for.

Alva had prepared herself, long ago, for the reality of Kevin having the odd sexual fling in the night. Incidents but never episodes. But she had never ever thought he would bring anyone here, to their bed. She felt as if she'd been cut open, every part of her exposed to a raw, merciless wind.

She changed the linen, making the bed smooth and perfect and wrinkle-free. Then she grabbed some blankets, dosed herself again with hot whiskey and Disprin and, weak, shrivelled, shaking with a despairing sickness of the heart, curled herself into a blanketed ball on the settee. Thoughts whirled, unfocused; when at last her distracted mind gave up she lay for a long time blessedly insensate.

At some point she slept and was awoken by church bells, ringing in nearby Haddington Road. Their message was clear and their voice was her father's: 'Punished, punished ... you will be punished ...' After a while she slept again, fitfully and to dreams in which crows swung on bells and stared at her with unblinking, washed-out grey eyes.

When she woke again it was dark and the digital

clock on the video said eight o'clock. She was sweat-drenched but her temperature had fallen. Her head had cleared too. At some point in her nightmare-riddled sleep, things had fallen into place and the confusion of the past months had gone. She was filled with a cold, strength-restoring anger as she showered, changed and climbed into bed. On the settee she left a note, and the blankets, for Kevin. 'Got an awful flu,' she wrote. 'You'd better sleep here and avoid the bugs.' He didn't disturb her. She hadn't expected that he would. He was very careful about his health.

She pretended sleep through his dressing and departure next morning. When he'd gone she turned over and really slept, exhaustedly, until midday. For part of the afternoon she walked briskly in Herbert Park. Then she packed a suitcase and waited for Kevin to come home.

'Flu better?' He looked tired.

'Much better,' Alva said.

'I need a drink,' he said. He smelled as if he'd already had several.

'Pour one for me too,' Alva said. He poured and handed her the same large whiskey measure he'd given himself. Standing by the window he loosened his tie and downed the drink in two gulps. Alva swirled hers and let the silence stretch. When Kevin went to pour himself another drink she spoke.

'I'm leaving.' She didn't look up. She heard Kevin put down the whiskey bottle.

'You're *what*?'

'I'm leaving.' Alva looked up this time. 'I can't stay.

You shouldn't have brought her here, Kevin, whoever she is, into our bed. I can't take that . . .' She paused. He was staring at her, his face in shadow from the light behind him. She felt quite calm. All things considered she really had no choice but to leave. 'I'll get in touch in a few weeks and we can talk things out. I don't think now is the time, for either of us, to decide what we're going to do.'

'God, but you're a self-righteous bitch.'

He didn't move and she slipped from the armchair and went towards the door. 'I didn't want an argument about this, Kevin, and I'm not staying for one.'

'But *I* think you should explain yourself, Alva. What exactly are you running away from?' He stepped closer.

'Several things. I'm getting away from existing just for you, Kevin, from the kind of relationship you wanted and I've allowed this to become. I've been the perfect background companion, always here when you wanted me—'

'You wanted it that way. I didn't force you to do anything.'

'Not overtly, no. And I really do blame myself as much as you. You could never have made me so dependent if I hadn't allowed it happen. I was a willing victim, Kevin, but I'm not any longer.'

'What do you want, for Chrissake?'

'I don't know. I really don't have a clue. But I *am* leaving. This affair of yours, here,' she jerked her head towards the bedroom, 'is simply the spur. How long has it been going on, Kevin, in our bed?'

'A while. You shouldn't have left me alone, Alva.

I'm not the fucking priest your father was. Why don't you go back to bed? Sleep off the effects of whatever you're taking for the flu. We'll talk things over tomorrow . . .'

Alva picked up her coat. 'I need distance. And time. I'm going.'

'You're not going anywhere.' He moved closer, into the middle of the room. 'I'm the one who does the leaving, Alva, when the time comes. And our time hasn't come. I'm not ready to let you go just yet.'

Alva opened the door and slipped through into the hallway. She picked up the packed suitcase. 'We'll talk next week,' she said.

What happened then happened so quickly she didn't see it coming. She was aware of the glass Kevin had been holding hitting the wall close to her head, then of the suitcase being yanked out of her hand. By the time she'd screamed a protest she was against the wall and Kevin was pulling at her coat, holding one of her arms behind her in an agonizingly tight grip.

'Stop it, stop it, Kevin! You can't do this—'

'Can't I? Who says so?' He turned her so that she was facing him, close enough to feel hot breath on her face. He was white and perspiring, his voice thin and high. 'I can do what I like, Alva, and no one, especially you, is going to tell me otherwise. You will *not* leave and we *will* sort this jealous pique of yours out tomorrow. She was nothing anyway, just an amusement.' He pushed her away from him, though not far, and stood blocking her way out.

'Very amusing,' Alva said, 'to use our bed . . .' If she

could keep him talking until she got hold of the suitcase again, got through the outer door . . .

'It was stupid to bring her here, I'll grant you that.' He shrugged, and seemed to have relaxed. 'She insisted, but I shouldn't have indulged her. She said being in your bed gave her a buzz. Certainly it improved her performance, silly little slut. It won't happen again, I promise. She's passed her sell-by date anyway. Christ, the woman must be nearly forty.'

'She's someone I know?' Alva asked. Kevin looked at her in genuine astonishment.

'You said you – I thought you knew.' His mouth twisted in thin, rueful irritation. 'You might as well know, anyway. Teach you to trust people like her.' His eyes were coolly amused. 'My love-in-the-afternoons friend was your colleague Seona Daly. She was there for me when you weren't, and extremely obliging she was too.'

'Seona.' Alva felt oddly lightheaded. 'Seona.' She picked up the suitcase. 'You deserve one another.'

She had straightened up when Kevin's fist, rock hard and tight, punched her in the stomach. The breath left her body as pain and nausea doubled her over. She made a mewing sound, like a lost cat.

'And you deserved that.' Kevin, standing over her, was breathing quickly. 'Now get back into the bedroom and stay there.'

Alva straightened up and closed her eyes to stop the dizzy feeling. The sound of his breathing filled the hallway. Dear God, she prayed, calm him down, please. Please don't let him hit me again.

Out loud she said, 'I'm going now,' and turned for the door.

He was there before her. She could see the muscles in his neck, taut and stretched. She was looking at them when his fist came up again, smashing into the side of her face, viciously jolting her head sideways. 'Go,' he said, 'but you'll be back. On your knees.'

The young doctor in St Vincent's Hospital casualty was kindly but irritated. 'Report him. Before he does it to someone else.' He examined the tiny stitch she'd needed at the corner of her eye.

'It wasn't like that. I walked—'

'Be a fool if you want to,' he sighed and touched her cheek, 'but don't expect me to be one too. You're damn lucky the fist which damaged your eye didn't break your cheekbone. Report him.'

'Yes,' Alva said, and the doctor shook his head.

'I do not understand women like you. I see it all the time. Taking abuse and allowing the animal responsible to go free to do it again, and again. Because, believe me, they do.'

'I've nowhere to go at the moment,' Alva interrupted him. 'You don't know of a quiet, out of town hotel I could go for a few days, do you?' She tried a smile which didn't seem to work. The doctor turned away too quickly.

'As it happens, I do know a place.' He scribbled hastily on a prescription pad. 'It's in Bray. I'll give you the name of a good local man too, you'll want to have that face looked at again soon. It'll take a couple of weeks to heal so I presume you'll need a cert for your job?'

Mutely, Alva took the pieces of paper as he handed them to her. He pulled the cubicle curtain open and she picked up the suitcase.

'Thank you,' she said, 'I really do appreciate—'

'Report him.'

'Yes,' Alva said, 'and thanks again.'

'Good luck,' he shrugged.

She hired a taxi to take her out of Dublin and along the coast road to Bray.

On the way she stopped, bought a stamp, shoved the medical cert into an envelope and posted it to the paper. It would show a Dublin postmark; she did not want to talk to, or be tracked down by anyone, until she was good and ready.

Bray was a good choice of town, its burgeoning population making it a relatively easy place in which to be anonymous. The hotel was small and near the seafront, the elderly woman who booked her in, and who appeared to own it, friendly but weary. Too weary, or perhaps too polite, to ask about her guest's facial injuries. She gave Alva a room to the front of the house, with a bay window and view of a dark, unfriendly sea. When she left, Alva closed the curtains on it, took one of the sleeping tablets the doctor had given her and slept for ten hours.

In the summer months Bray's sand and shingle beach, its esplanade and granite promontory, brought day-trippers and spending money to the town. During that end-of-October week, bitter and inclement by any standards, Alva had the lot to herself. She walked the beach, esplanade and headland relentlessly, often after darkness had fallen and always when she was sure of meeting no one. The hotel owner, whose name was Mamie Mulcahy, was casually kind and genuinely incurious. When Alva booked for a second week she added extra blankets to the bed. When the local doctor gave Alva a cert for a third week and Alva decided to stay on she put a desk in the room and a small supply of detective novels.

By then Alva had decided she was not going back to anything in her life before. Not once, on all of her walks and climbs about Bray, had she been able to come up with a good reason why she should.

Kevin was over; there was only the taste of love gone sour to deal with.

The job was over; as a career it had been going nowhere, and as far as friendships went she was probably the only person on the paper who hadn't known about Seona and Kevin. Not one person had seen fit to tell her.

She wrote giving notice, saying she wouldn't be back and that they could work out her notice against days and holidays due. It was a lousy thing to do but she felt not a qualm.

She was alone and free and she had money. She could do anything she wanted with her life and the thought terrified her.

Mamie Mulcahy gave her the local newspaper each morning with breakfast and Alva read it to be polite.

The detective novels offered far better escapism. During the third week in November she took to reading the back-page ads. The one which decided the rest of her life was discreet to the point of disappearing.

It was headed *Investment Opportunity*, and read simply: 'Small hotel seeks investor willing to become involved in running same.' There was a PO box number.

After nearly a month in Mamie Mulcahy's comfortable small hotel the idea of running one had a certain appeal. Alva answered the ad.

An original and lovely hand-drawn card from a Mr Theodore Donovan arrived by return of post. In perfect copperplate he suggested they meet, 'without obligation on either side', in the tearooms of an elderly Wicklow hotel the following afternoon.

The drawing on the card was of a flowering shrub called *Camellias japonica*, otherwise known as Tomorrow's Dawn.

Chapter Seven

'You got yourself tea. Very wise.'

The man standing in front of her was tall, bespectacled and old. Difficult to say how old; difficult, too, to imagine him any younger. He had a great amount of silvery-white hair with eyebrows and moustache to match. The latter was of the sweeping-brush variety, sitting over a long, smiling upper lip. He had one gold tooth, the rest looked to be his own, and perfect. When Alva attempted to get out of the squashy armchair to greet him he held up a large, knotty-jointed hand.

'Stay where you are,' he said, 'the girls' seating is not designed for jumping up and down. No indeed. In this instance the mountain must come to Muhammad . . .'

With slow, methodical movements he pushed another squashy armchair into position opposite her. He placed a tall standard lamp behind it and put a brown folder and glass of whiskey on the cane table between them. He checked the arrangement, then sat on the edge of the armchair and offered his hand. It felt like a piece of tree bark, ridged and hard and about as pliable. He did not apologize for being late.

'Theodore Donovan.' He had a voice like heavy gravel. 'Good of you to answer my advertisement.' He paused, took a clay pipe and pouch from his pocket and raised a questioning eyebrow.

'Please go ahead,' Alva said and he began to pack the bowl with tobacco.

'You were the only one who did.' When he frowned the white eyebrows met over the heavy frames of his glasses. The frames were exactly the same black as the eyes which regarded her closely and, she thought, doubtfully.

'The only one who answered?' Alva wasn't sure whether this should have pleased or dismayed her. She went for a cool tone that betrayed neither feeling. She hoped. You couldn't be sure with this man.

'The only one.' He nodded, lit the pipe and puffed vigorously. Smoke, spicily sweet-smelling, circled his head. 'Didn't expect *any*, to tell the truth. You being here puts you into the unique and courageous category. Are you?'

'Am I what?'

He sighed. 'Unique and courageous.' He'd obviously discounted intelligence.

'Why don't we find out?' Alva, with difficulty, sat forward and poured hot tea into her cup. 'Why don't you tell me a bit more about your ad, what it is you're looking for?' She smiled. 'Without obligation.'

She was glad they'd been given privacy in this small sitting room. The Rose Briar Tearooms, fifteen feet away along the corridor, had been a family bedlam. The hotel part of the long stone house no longer functioned but the tearooms, with their treacherously uneven floors and ceiling beams low enough to be a

concussion hazard, were so cosy as to be claustropho-
bic. There were two of them, identical and on either
side of a corridor hung with unlikely sporting prints.
Both were noisy, warmed by roaring log fires and the
place to go for the very best tea and scones. They were
an intensely popular Sunday afternoon venue with
parents seeking peace and tea after exercising their
young on Wicklow's hills and plateaux.

Alva had been expected. The sisters who owned the
place, combined age a conservative 150, had flurried
over to her as soon as she sat down.

'You're Miss Joyce, Theo's guest,' the plump, bossy
one declared. 'He said you'd be here at three.' It was
five past. Alva was the only person without children or
dogs in tow. The woman might look like but didn't
have to be Miss Marple to figure out who she was.

'You can't wait here,' the thin sister said, 'too
crowded.' She wrinkled a beaky nose at their paying
guests. 'Come along to the drawing room and wait for
him there. We'll bring you tea, won't we, Lucille?'

Lucille nodded and hurried Alva along by helpfully
picking up her gloves. She was directing a family to
Alva's table as the three of them left the room.

'You'll be much better able to have your little chat
with Theo in here.' The thin sister guided Alva to an
armchair. They hovered as she was swallowed into a
sponge of cushions.

'We should introduce ourselves.' The thin sister
smiled and looked like a small chirpy bird. 'I'm
Angeline and this is my sister, Lucille Fogarty. We've
known Theo all our lives, haven't we, Lucille?'

'All our lives,' Lucille echoed and placed a cane table within Alva's reach. She had pinkly unlined skin and a square jaw. 'Scones with the tea?' she asked.

'That would be lovely,' Alva said. 'I've never met Mr Donovan myself. What's he like?'

The sisters exchanged a look and Angeline giggled. Both, when they'd been young and dewy fresh, must have been extremely pretty. They had the air of women unselfconsciously feminine, happy with themselves and their tearooms.

'You'll find him interesting,' Lucille said briskly.

'A wonderful man,' Angeline added.

'He's *lived*,' Lucille was quietly rapturous, 'and he knows what's what. Just you be straight with him and you'll do all right.'

'We all had such ... fun when we were young people together.' Angeline giggled again. 'It's a great bond to have as you grow older, to have shared ... adventures when you were younger. Of course, you're a bit young to understand but I'm sure you already have your own friends, exciting young men.'

'Things are different nowadays,' Lucille shook her head, 'altogether different. We lived our youth just after the war, a special time to be young in the world. Theo was such a man of that world ...'

'... And Ellen. Ellen was beautiful.'

'She was indeed.' Lucille became brisk again. 'Now, Miss Joyce, you just prepare yourself for Theo, and Angeline will bring you tea.'

Angeline patted her on the shoulder and they left. Prepare herself, they'd said, but for what? For someone who was obviously no spring chicken if he'd been the Lothario the Fogarty sisters had adored in the forties. Not someone whose virtues included punctuality, either. It was fifteen minutes after their appointed meeting time of three o'clock.

No one had taken her parka and she slipped out of it and dropped it alongside the armchair. The jeans and jumper underneath weren't business-discussion clothes, but they were the sort of thing she'd been wearing since moving into Mamie Mulcahy's hotel. She'd purchased an entire alternative wardrobe of woollies, boots, jeans and leggings in Bray and hadn't bothered to unpack the suitcase. She'd been damned if she was going to haul out the glad rags for a deepest wintertime trip into the Wicklow countryside.

One thing she *had* decided, though, in the taxi on the way here. She would buy a car and learn to drive. Maybe not in that order but she would do it, join the ranks of the car-owning, air-polluting public. Even today, with the countryside in the grip of mid-winter at its most dour, a scrubby brown predominant on the hills and everywhere else a faded beige, moving through it had been liberating. A car would free her.

The sitting room wasn't at all like the tearooms. It was bright, furnished to overflowing with armchairs and small tables. There were paperback novels everywhere, on shelves and stacked on the floor and mantelpiece.

The light came from a wide, low bay window jutting into a chaotic, brambly garden. The roses of the name, Alva guessed, pretty seedy-looking now, and old.

Theo Donovan had arrived at half past three.

Watching him now, as he leaned back and prepared to tell her what his ad was all about, he struck her as a man who made his own rules and kept his own timetables. She would remember, if anything came of their talk.

'You're younger than I'd expected,' he stretched his legs in front of him to avoid hitting the table. He took up a lot of the room.

'You're older than I expected,' Alva said.

'I suppose I am.' He looked surprised and fidgeted with the red-spotted cravat in the neck of his bulky green jumper. He cleared his throat. 'I'll be brief as I can and I will not embroider. I am the owner of a large old house, Victorian, which I have been attempting, without success, to run as an hotel. It needs money and it needs time. I have neither. I am a gardener, gardening is what I am best at—'

Alva interrupted. 'Where is your hotel?'

'Not a million miles from here, on the south Dublin coast at Keelmore. It's called De Novo House. De Novo as in new beginnings. The name was given it when it was built, in the 1830s.'

'I see,' Alva said.

'I've taken on different people to run the place for me over the last few years but none of them has worked out.' He paused. 'They've all been male, which may or may not be a factor. In any case, I've come to the conclusion that what De Novo needs is an owner-manager. Someone to put their money where their mouth is so as they'll have an interest in making it go.

De Novo is authentic but no longer unique. Every jackass who can't make an honest living is running a country-house hotel these days. It will need energy and hard work . . .' He looked at her hard and she tried to straighten her slouch. 'Here's what I propose,' he said.

With a long arm he reached for the folder on the table. He drew up his knees, lay it open across them and shuffled through the papers. Alva thought how incongruous he looked in the low, chintzy sitting room, sunk in the armchair with his knees jutting up almost to meet his chin. He was studying a sheet of figures and looking irritated.

'To hell with these figures.' He shoved the sheet into the folder and tapped it with his pipe. 'You can read them afterwards if you're interested. The basics are these: with an investment of, say, £100,000, De Novo House can be refurbished and made viable. As it stands, the house is worth about £200,000. Refurbished and as a going concern it would sell for half a million. In return for his or her £100,000 the investor in De Novo would become co-owner. He or she would then control and manage the hotel while I continue to keep the gardens. Written into all of this would be the option to sell should everything not work out. It's a cast-iron investment. You cannot lose.'

'I can if the hotel doesn't work and the house doesn't make it on the property market.'

'Of course De Novo would sell.' His eyebrows came together again. 'I've had offer upon offer over the years. It's not at all an ordinary house, you know.' She was glad when he stretched his legs in front of him again. He looked less ridiculous.

'I don't know.' She pointed out, 'I've neither seen nor heard of it. How many rooms?'

'Eight bedrooms, five of them viable as guest rooms. Drawing and dining rooms, of course, private sitting room, wine licence . . .'

'Why is it that only five of the bedrooms are viable?'

'I have to sleep somewhere, Miss Joyce, and so does my sister Ellen who lives at De Novo with me. I presume that the investor would be keen to live in also.'

'I see. You've a sister . . .'

'Miss Joyce, do you have any money?'

'I have money, yes.'

'Do you have the amount we're talking about?'

'I do.'

'So we are not wasting one another's time?'

'You're not wasting mine, anyway.' Alva smiled without any idea how rueful the expression was. 'I'm interested.'

She couldn't lose, he'd said, and maybe he was right. At the very worst she would get her money back if they had to sell the house. And what else had she to do with the money, anyway? What else had she to do with her life?

It was after four now and already darkening outside. Theo Donovan flicked the switch on the standard lamp and the room was filled with a hundred-watt glare. Alva blinked.

'The better to see the novels,' he explained. 'Tea

and trashy novels are what the Fogartys have been reduced to.' He looked out of the window, sighing. 'Garden has great potential too ... However, you'll have to come and see De Novo, naturally. If you decide to go ahead the details can be thrashed out between solicitors. You can do what you like with the house, I won't interfere. If the venture fails, we sell and you double your money.'

'You don't know a thing about me ...'

'I'm seventy-five, Miss Joyce. What have I got to lose?'

'Your home,' Alva spoke slowly.

'I'm on the way to losing that anyway. I'm a gardener, as I've already told you. I make things grow. I was a painter once but came to find landscaping gardens more fruitful.' He tugged, smiling, at his moustache. The pipe had long gone out. 'I have designed gardens in Jerusalem and in Kuala Lumpur as well as in Britain and the Americas. For twenty years now I've looked after my own garden. I would like to die doing so.' He shrugged. 'Maybe you and I can both get what we want from this venture.'

'Maybe.' Alva pulled herself out of the armchair and walked to the window. In the distance the Sugar Loaf mountain was a violent purple against the dusky winter sky. 'And what is it you think I want, Mr Donovan?' she asked.

'Time,' Theo Donovan said and she turned, nodding at his accuracy.

'You're right,' she said. 'I want time.'

*

Two days later Alva went to see De Novo House and gardens. She had the taxi driver drop her at the wrought-iron gates at the bottom of the avenue. These, Theo Donovan had assured her, would be open. She stood between them, getting her bearings and an initial feel of the place.

The gates were open because they could no longer be closed. Rust and broken hinges had seen to that. She pulled a wry face at herself, her circumstances and the gates and started walking. Things could only, she hoped, get better.

They did. The avenue was a joy to walk. The early part took her through a sentinel row of high old trees, some beech and what she knew was an ailanthus because there had been one in the Churchtown garden. The tree of heaven, her mother had called it and as a small child Alva had always expected to see angels on its branches. She touched it as she passed, older and so much wiser, and knowing that the most she could expect to see on its dark, bare branches at this time of year would be the remains of its reddish-brown fruit.

The trees thinned as she went, the avenue meandering past bushes and winding walks, a summerhouse and the end of a path. Deeper into the garden she could see a pond and pergola, the latter wound with the thick stems of clinging creepers.

Apple trees, old and gnarled and worthy-looking, had crows sitting on their branches; small, black vultures waiting on their stripped perches for prey. She put a memory of her father out of her head and looked away, across a rose garden with large, terracotta urns, towards the house.

She liked it immediately. Grey and solid, it had dignity and a still peace. But it looked tired too, and empty, the long windows all unlit and the deep, arched porch in shadow as she climbed the steps. The peeling paint on the door filled her with a protective urge. This was a house which deserved to be sorted out and taken care of.

Waiting for someone to answer her ring on the doorbell she decided that De Novo's enchantment was the kind she could deal with. Bricks and mortar were manageable. Even before Theo opened the door she knew she was going to buy into De Novo House. She had probably, if she were honest, decided to involve herself with whatever the ad was about on the day she sat down and answered it. It had all, quite simply, been a question of timing.

Theo that day had been charm itself and Ellen, haughtily and wisely, had minded her own business. The gloom in the house was a shock but the original features, screaming to be revealed or cleaned up – flagged stonework and panelled walls, cornices and brass handles, a glass-and-metal lantern in the hallway – compensated.

Alva, feeling herself to be an immediate and possess-ive part of the place, made tea in the kitchen. She and Theo sat there and worked out, in less than an hour, an arrangement to which their solicitors would give legal language and status.

Christmas intervened, slowing things up a bit. But by the early new year everything was tied up and Alva moved in. The necessary repairs were more than she'd bargained for and the refurbishment needed all the inventive and imaginative resources she could call on. But the isolation, ferocious concentration and sheer physical energy needed to get De Novo back in business were therapeutic. She was left with very little time to think, no time at all to feel.

Theo's promise of non-interference held good. The flip-side was that she got absolutely no help from him. The gardens, subdued by wintry decay for the first few months, began in the spring to take on a ferocious life. It became clear that they needed huge amounts of attention and energy and that Theo was not up to it. He just couldn't keep pace with the rampant growth his care and planting over the years had encouraged.

Easter was in mid-April that year. Three weeks before, with as much as was possible done by way of refurbishment, Alva began looking for staff. It proved the easiest part of the venture. An ad in the small village supermarket produced several people willing to work part-time.

And it produced Bernie Brennan. Alva knew immediately Bernie rang who she was. She'd heard her voice, only days before, furiously protesting in the kitchen of the small Italian quick-food joint next to the supermarket. She'd been there herself because the food was so good and she needed a break from eating with Ellen and Theo.

'Who turned off the oven?' The female yell from the kitchen had been disbelieving and anguished. 'The focaccia wasn't cooked . . .'

'I turned it off. It shouldn't have been in there.' The restaurant owner, a good-looking thirtyish male, left off clearing a table to stand, yelling too, in the kitchen doorway. 'We don't need it. I don't want you making whatever you fancy. I've told you and told you – cook what's on the menu and leave it at that.'

'Focaccia's *bread*, for God's sake. A few loaves of sage bread is all I had in there. If customers were given a nibble they'd love it and we could add it to the menu.' As the voice in the kitchen became muffled the owner's rose by a shrieking decibel or two.

'Keep away from that oven! Don't you dare turn it on again.'

Both of them seemed to have forgotten about Alva and the two other late-afternoon diners in the restaurant. Either that or too much Italian food and wine had given them a penchant for volatile rows. The owner, hand-waving now as well as screeching, had certainly got inside the role.

'I'm in business to *make a profit*, Miss Brennan. I can't do that if you've got ovens going full blast all the time, experimental food extras running up my electricity bill. I pay you good money to cook what I want, not what you—'

'You pay me damn all of your good money.' The woman's voice became tearfully angry. 'You're a miserable bloody sod, Derek. You're cold and mean, do you know that? Mean, mean, mean. You've no feeling for food. For anything else either. All you have feelings about is money and if I didn't need this stinking job I'd be out of here in the morning.'

'Why don't you leave *now*?'

The owner's voice had been taunting, not at all that of a man who expected his bluff to be called. Seconds later, when a big, fair-haired young woman, red-faced and boiling with resolution, came marching through the door and right out of the restaurant, he looked aghast.

'Hey, Bernie, come back—' There was panic and a new, pathetic squeak in his voice as he ran into the street after his cook. Alva left the restaurant and the other diners to rabid speculation about the outcome. Would the cook return? Had her mean boss learned a lesson?

In the days since, she'd wondered idly if the pair had made up. Bernie's reply to her ad for a cook answered the question.

The Easter they opened the hotel did well. It wasn't until some time in the midsummer that Alva began to feel they were in trouble. Circumstances – the dollar was down, the weather bad, the tourist season lousy – went only so far as excuses. De Novo just didn't have the luxuries, nor did it have the cachet, to bring customers in the numbers they needed.

When a campaign offering an authentic Victorian Christmas fell flat, Alva knew they were headed for serious trouble. Things had failed to get better. It was now seventeen months since she'd bought into De Novo and she'd gone through a terrifying amount of her money.

To say that the film business had arrived in just the nick of time was tempting fate with a tired cliché. But the phrase struck Alva as appropriate in a way that no other did. An end-of-October Hallowe'en reopening offering good food, a brush with film glamour and the long-dead spooks of a Dublin murder mystery, couldn't, surely, fail to revamp the hotel's fortunes.

Chapter Eight

On a day when Alva was least expecting it, and when the hotel was freakishly busy, Jack Kelly came back to De Novo. In the three weeks since his first visit, apart from a contract and cheque in the post, she had heard not a peep from anyone connected with the film. She'd signed the contract and lodged the cheque and since then she'd been waiting.

It was early June, a breezy, fresh day, much more invigorating than the day of his first visit. A minibus full of the Actively Retired had arrived in the mid-afternoon and its passengers, all fifteen of them, had appropriated Theo for a garden walk and talk. Passionate, critical gardeners, they'd been told about Theo and sent to De Novo by Angeline and Lucille Fogarty. Theo bore up gallantly.

When they got back to the house they declared themselves famished and set about demanding great quantities of sandwiches, tea, coffee, sweet sherry and, for one group of four, 'a decent claret'. Alva, hair in a severe coil, and loose cotton dress flapping, was with Bernie's help coping valiantly. The claret-drinking group was on its second bottle when, tray in hand, she looked up and saw the urbane figure of Jack Kelly in the drawing-room doorway.

In contrast with the actively retired, in their walking shoes and summer blouses, he appeared quite dandified. He was wearing a beige suit which accentuated his tan and a dark green, raffish-looking silk shirt. A definite example, she thought, of what was meant by culture clash. It was her first inkling of how things were going to be when the film company took over De Novo.

'We weren't expecting you.' She held the tray in front of her and resisted an urge to loosen her hair. The coil, useful when she was working with food, seemed all at once like a burdensome yoke at the back of her neck. 'It's good to see you,' she said.

The platitude was the literal truth. Jack Kelly's tanned, worldly, rich and sudden appearance was reassuring. It brought the reality of the filming closer.

'Sorry to arrive unannounced . . .' He didn't look sorry, smiling lopsidedly at her, hands in his pockets as he leaned against the door. More than half the room's occupants had stopped what they were doing to look at him. The rest were pretending to ignore the fact that an attractive male had entered their exclusively female company. He turned and included them in his smile, every inch the executive. Amused, Alva studied him. He couldn't help himself. He was just one of those men who had to be in charge.

'Ladies,' he nodded, and turned back to Alva. 'I'm not alone.' He held the door open, waiting for her to pass through. 'I've got the producer and director with me. They wanted to see the place, so I came along to make the introductions. Looks like we picked the worst

of times. My apologies, ladies, for the disturbance . . .'
He flashed another smile at the assembled gardeners.
A few rewarded him with chilly looks but most beamed
and a few giggled and announced that they weren't at
all disturbed. They were of an age to take life's
pleasantries at face value.

'Everything's under control,' Alva assured him. 'But
it *would* help if you showed your colleagues around
while I finish up here.'

His eyebrows shot up, then immediately down again.
'Yeah. Why not?' he said. 'Good idea, in fact. But why
don't I just introduce you first?'

'Fine. Be right with you,' Alva said. She took an
order for more tea and two sherries and followed him
into the hallway.

One of the waiting men was examining the banister
monkeys. The other, the taller, younger-looking one,
was halfway up the stairs with his head at an angle as
he scrutinized the stained-glass window. They turned,
together, as Alva and Jack Kelly crossed the hallway.

'Alva,' Jack Kelly put an arm around her shoulders
as he effected the introductions, 'this here,' he indicated the man on the stairs, 'is Luke O'Hanlon, our
esteemed director. And this,' he gave the smaller man
a light, friendly punch on the shoulder, 'is Felim Gray,
our producer. They're gonna see to it that we get one
helluva picture made here.' He tightened his grip on
Alva's shoulder, drawing her slightly to him. 'This lady,
fellas, is Alva Joyce,' he grinned, 'to whom we are
much indebted for the use of this hotel as a location.'

Alva, uncomfortable about her hair, the tray and

Jack Kelly's arm about her shoulders, smiled stiffly. 'Glad to meet you,' she said, 'really I am, and I'll help in any way I can. But just at the moment I'm . . .'

'. . . up to your neck in it.' The director, Luke O'Hanlon, came slowly down the stairs. 'Pleased to meet you.'

The greeting was entirely perfunctory, saved from rudeness by the natural warmth of his Dublin-accented baritone. His looks were of the lean-and-hungry variety, attractive in a restless, dark-eyed way. He had untidy brown hair, that way because of a habit, indulged even as he spoke to Alva, of combing it with his fingers. 'We'll just take a look around, if that's all right with you.' He gave a fleeting, busy man's smile.

'Of course. I'd suggested to Jack—'

'I'll take the tour.' Smiling, Jack Kelly cut her short. 'I'm kinda familiar with the place.'

'Pleased to meet you, Ms Joyce.' Felim Gray, laconically extending a courteous hand, struck Alva as almost comically different to the other two men. Where their energy had an obvious, itchily extroverted quality, his was contained, reflective. He was slighter too than either of them and fine-boned. His hair, emphasizing the sculpted quality of his face, was closely cut. Alva knew instinctively that he was gay. She also immediately liked him.

'Please call me Alva.' She shook his hand. 'And I'm sorry I can't come with you.'

She saw them on their way up the stairs, a friendly trio exhibiting none of the ravaging tensions Oscar Duggan had claimed existed between them.

Bernie groaned and panicked when Alva arrived in the kitchen with another order. 'Is there no satisfying those old biddies? *When* are they going to have enough? I wasn't prepared for this and I didn't give Sammy a key and my mother's not at home today. There is positively no God of justice for working mothers.'

But there was, that day anyway. He manifested Himself minutes later in the form of an impatient minibus driver, tapping the window and his watch as he harried his passengers into leaving. They gathered themselves together in an agitated flurry and in less then seven minutes had paid and gone, driving too fast down the avenue.

'What're these film guys like? What'm I missing?' Bernie stacked dishes, made a threatening face at Thomas, loitering with intent by the fridge, and grabbed her car keys. She waited briefly in the doorway for an answer.

'Worldly types, all three of them.' Alva was thoughtful. 'Fit. Busy. None of them the swollen, cigar-chewing sort of mogul you read about. Jack Kelly is definitely the type who works out, probably the producer fellow Felim Gray is too. Not so sure about the director, Luke O'Hanlon, though. Cool customer. Touch of the breed of the greyhound about him. Probably lives on his nerves and couldn't put on weight if he was paid to . . .'

'Fascinating,' Bernie interrupted. 'You're trying to tell me I won't get to them through their stomachs, right? Why don't you tell me instead what they look like?'

'Presentable, all of them. And before you ask me I haven't a clue about their marital status. Felim Gray, who seems all gentle courtesy but is probably steel magnolia since he's a producer, is gay. I'd stake my life on it.'

'With my luck *he'll* be the one who's a foodie.'

After Bernie left Alva loosened her hair, lip-glossed her mouth and went to the drawing room to wait for the men to finish looking around. Some of the gardening women had wanted the curtains half-closed against the sun and she opened them again. They were heavy, the colour of over-ripened plums, and pulling them back immediately filled the room with light. She opened the window too and treated herself to some long, deep breaths of sea air.

Faint, reassuring sounds floated up the hill; children playing somewhere, a car accelerating along the coast road, a seagull's cry. She felt at peace. She also felt expectant. It was a not unpleasant combination.

She was still at the window when she saw the director and producer go down the front steps, alone. She pushed it higher and leaned out. They couldn't, surely, be leaving without some word to her about the house; even a question or two? She waved and called to them. 'I'm free now. We can talk if you like.'

'Great.' They both turned, but Felim Gray it was who called back. 'We're going to have a look at the garden. Please don't feel you have to come . . .'

'Stay.' Jack Kelly's voice spoke behind her in the room. 'Luke likes the place. Just wants to suss out some garden shots.' He touched her on the shoulder and she turned. 'Talk to me, Alva. How've you been?' He was standing close enough for her to see clearly the laughter lines around his eyes. 'Everything working out OK? You happy with the deal we got?'

She smiled, sidestepped to put a more comfortable space between them. 'The deal we got seems fine,' she said, 'though I was getting a little panicky about not hearing from any of you. Result of reading too often about film projects collapsing, the millions of dollars lost . . .'

'This one's not going to collapse.' He was brisk. 'Don't even think about it. I don't want you to worry about a thing. Here.' He produced a card, black with white lettering. 'You got numbers there can get me any time, anywhere, day or night. Use them. Doesn't matter what for, just call me. I don't want any of this,' he nodded in the direction taken by the producer and director, 'to be a hassle for you. You just keep in touch with me and I'll sort out any problems.'

Alva took and looked at the card. There were eight or nine phone numbers on it, some on both sides of the Atlantic. This was a solicitude beyond the needs of the contract. She was grateful. Cautious too. She looked at him and saw friendly reassurance, nothing more, in his face. 'Let's hope there won't be any,' she said. 'Problems, I mean.'

Voices from outside made them turn – and made Alva wish she hadn't spoken so soon. Ellen was a problem Jack Kelly could do nothing about. Didn't even know about.

She was walking towards the house now between

the producer and director, voluble and expansive, thanks to an afternoon in McNally's. Theo, looking hugely indifferent, followed a few feet behind.

'Lively old dame,' Jack Kelly said and Alva shot him a quick look. His expression was amused, nothing more.

'Yes,' she said and prepared for battle as the four-some mounted the steps to the house.

Ellen, though, chose for the most part to be charm itself that afternoon. She sat regal in a straight-backed chair, allowing everyone to talk. She even, Alva could have sworn, dimpled at Jack Kelly at one point.

'The house and gardens will do us fine, Alva.' Luke O'Hanlon was sang-froid itself as he sat down. 'Sorry not to get here before this. I was away and had to trust Oscar on this one. He's good on old houses . . .' He paused, seemed about to say something but thought better of it, and ran a thoughtful hand through his hair. 'Did Oscar give you an idea of how we'll need to use the place?' he asked. The baritone voice was cool, his eyes were cool. Altogether, Alva thought, Mr Cool Hand Luke. The thought amused her and she smiled.

'Is that smile a yes or a no?' O'Hanlon looked at his watch and Alva, with a fixed smile, waited until she had his full attention, and had irritated him a little, before answering.

'Oscar explained quite a lot,' she said.

'Good. Maybe I should fill you in on a few things anyway. Stop me if I'm telling you what you already know.' He was leaning forward, hands dangling between his knees, speaking very quickly. 'Right. The early inner-city stuff will be shot before we get here. This place will be doubling for interiors of the town house Constance lived in when she was married and for the country house she retreated to when her husband died.'

Alva noticed he didn't say was killed. It said a lot about his thinking on Constance. She didn't interrupt when he went on, repeating some of the things Oscar had told her. Nothing wrong with having two versions.

He was facing the window and in the light she could see that he was tired and in need of a shave. Fine lines about his mouth and eyes suggested that he laughed, or at least smiled, quite often. He looked in his early thirties and was wearing jeans with a T-shirt under a jacket which was too heavy for the day. Tiredness apart, he continued to talk at speed, without seeming for whole sentences to draw breath, giving clear, perfunctory details of how he expected to operate at De Novo.

'. . . And we'll need a room we can set aside to look at daily footage of the film as we're going along. What about the small back bedroom up there? That free?' Alva nodded and he went on. 'We'll have our own resident nurse so you don't have to worry about the smelling salts. Oh, and some of our people will be coming and going over the next while.' He ticked these off on his fingers. 'The designer will drop by to look the place over, help her decide on the look of the film, that kind of thing. In fact the heads of all departments – art, photography, wardrobe, production, a few technicians – will all be dropping by over the next couple of months. They won't interfere, bother you with questions unless they need to.'

'Oh, I'm sure I can manage . . .' Alva began. He went on as if she hadn't spoken.

'It's good that you're closing for business while we'll be here. I appreciate that. This catering business though . . .' He shrugged, a one-shoulder, impatient movement. 'That'll have to be delicately handled. Don't get me wrong, Alva, quality of food isn't the issue. The sensitivities of the catering company we've already booked will be, and so will union tempers if everyone doesn't get fed when they want to be fed. Incongruous as it may seem, stomachs and what goes into them . . .' he caught Ellen's eye staring at him and stopped, smiling at her as he went on, 'can become as big an issue as the star's salary.'

'Quite right too,' Ellen said staunchly. 'An army marches on its stomach, after all.'

'Aha! Fat lot of good that piece of wisdom did Napoleon and *his* army.' Theo, until then smoking his pipe in silence by the window, came rumbling to life. 'You'd be better off remembering that hunger is the best sauce. Hunger,' he stabbed his pipe at the director, 'drives the wolf out of the wood. Just you remember that when they're all screaming for *foie gras.*'

'Don't see you depriving yourself much of food.' Ellen's restraint snapped into waspishness. 'Or of anything else either.'

Alva jumped in before a row blew up. 'Bernie and myself are hoping to work out an arrangement with the other caterers—'

'Forget it.' Luke O'Hanlon was curt. 'Might as well prepare yourselves for cutthroat competition.'

'No point crossing that bridge until we come to it.' Jack Kelly, who had been watching benignly from a corner armchair, smiled at Alva. 'Two catering companies may just spice things up a little.'

'That's what I'm afraid of.' The director was abrupt and Felim Gray, standing by the mantelpiece, was the one who this time diverted a snappy exchange. He looked Theo's way.

'I was fascinated, Mr Donovan, by what you were starting to tell us in the garden. About how the Victorians went for a return to nature in their gardens, managed the happy cohabitation of all sorts of plants . . .'

This one's a diplomat, Alva thought. Got us neatly out of what could have become a sparring match. Oscar could very well be right about the tensions between director and executive producer.

'Hmm. All true.' Theo had perked up again. He packed down his pipe, his beaky nose, sunburned along the ridge, casting a shadow over the white of his moustache. Two audiences in one day willing to listen while he extolled the virtues of garden and plant life was something to be savoured. And he did, clearing his throat and speaking directly to the producer.

'I'd begun, if I remember rightly and before my sister arrived, to tell you of the extraordinary mystery which exists in the world of plants, and of the garden. Everything that grows has its own character, just as everything that breathes is unique. There is no end to

131

what one can discover, no end to the enchantment of growth . . .'

He had a captive audience. Alva, who'd heard it all before, looked around the room. Ellen was stiff and hard-eyed, suffering the momentary attention on her brother with obvious irritation. Jack Kelly appeared deep in thought, hands a steeple in front of his face, and Luke O'Hanlon was studying the floor between his knees. Felim Gray, of them all, was the one who seemed genuinely interested. Maybe he was, too; maybe the question hadn't been the diversionary tactic she'd supposed.

'. . . Plants teach us, you know, or would if we paid heed to how they interrelate, live together.' Theo's voice, compelling in its rumbly way, seemed unstoppable. 'But of course we pay no heed, the majority of us, only go on destroying in the name of progress and pure greed . . .'

'You've created a perfect corner in a savage world, that's for sure Mr Donovan.' Jack Kelly stood. The movement, though Alva wasn't sure how, gave him charge of the room. Theo had stopped. 'I congratulate you, Mr Donovan. Thing is, we'd like, now we've got your agreement, to expose it a little, so to speak, to that savage world. Maybe your garden, on film, will teach the rest of us something.'

'Doubt it.' Theo stood, shrugging. 'I'll bid you gentlemen good day.'

Jack Kelly's standing had the effect of an alarm going off. Within minutes the visitors had followed Theo from the room and out to their cars. The producer and director left first, in a fairly abused-looking hatchback, Luke O'Hanlon at the wheel. Jack Kelly, before slipping into his chauffeur-driven limo, promised to be in touch.

'I'll look forward to that,' Alva said.

Ellen, sulkily following Alva about as, for the second time that day, she cleared up in the drawing room, had lost her good humour. 'There was a time,' she sniffed, 'when finer men than any of those three would have sat at my feet instead of just putting up with me.'

'They weren't just putting up with you,' Alva soothed.

'Of course they were,' Ellen snapped, 'and I put up with them because maybe, just maybe, their wretched film will break the monotony around here. Talking of which, what's for dinner?'

'Chicken,' Alva said.

The rush of business that day wasn't repeated and the summer drifted along, weather and custom as sporadic as one another. Alva was glad of the diversion caused by the film people as they came and went over the months, some of them fun, others aloof, all involved to obsession with the film they were working on.

There were going to be more pluses, too, than she'd reckoned on. Dado rails were to be remoulded and cornices she hadn't been able to get repaired would be fixed up for the film. The old radiators and pipes would be ripped out, but new ones would be replaced when filming finished.

Oscar Duggan called by a couple of times, though

Alva failed to fathom exactly what he did or why he came. When Alva asked a tiny, waif-like woman called Juno about him she shrugged.

'God knows,' she said. 'I'm first assistant director and *I* don't know what he does. I doubt Oscar himself knows. He made a right balls-up of the first location so he's just about saved his skin by coming up with this one. He *did* turn up a couple of good locations in town. But he's a lazy sod so he probably thinks that's his job done.'

'Nice work if you can get it,' Alva said and Juno grinned.

'He does. Get it and get away with it,' she said.

It was mid-August before Alva saw Jack Kelly again. This time he phoned before calling, giving her time to do something with her hair as well as slip into the comfortable elegance of a rice-coloured cotton rib tunic and Capri pants. She told herself it was because she was representing De Novo. It was partly true.

'I was hoping I could take you away from here for a couple of hours.' He stood, refusing to move beyond the hallway.

Alva, caught off-guard, looked down at the desktop, shuffled things about so as he wouldn't see her face. Away from here meant personal. Making an effort with her appearance was one thing. It didn't mean she was ready for personal.

On the other hand ... There was nobody booked for dinner. She'd just finished laying a breakfast table for the young couple who'd booked in for the weekend. It was nine o'clock and the dusk was turning dark, the days of summer shortening. There was no practical reason she couldn't go.

'I don't know . . .' She looked up, hesitating.

'Give yourself a night off.' He was amused. 'Anyone turns up this time of night, it's tough shit. What'll you lose? The profit on a cup of tea? Come on, Alva, I could do with the company. I don't know anyone in Dublin outside of the picture people and I need a break from them. Boy, do I need a break from them . . .' He moved and stood between her and the door. His face was in shadow but his teeth glistened, white and lopsided in a smile.

'OK,' Alva said, 'since you put your case so touchingly we'll go for a walk along the beach.' She looked down at his Italian loafers. 'I'll borrow a pair of Theo's boots for you. Afterwards we can go to a pub for a pint. I guarantee it'll all be quite removed from your picture world.'

She'd thought she was calling his bluff. A walk along a shingle beach, beer in a local pub. Manhattan it wasn't. Jack Kelly it wasn't. Surely he'd settle for a quiet drink at De Novo . . .

He didn't. 'Done,' he said, 'bring out the boots.'

They walked along the edge of the water. Dusk had turned to dark in the twenty minutes it had taken to put on the boots and get down to the beach. Alva and Jack Kelly were among the last of the day's walkers.

A dog, retrieving a stick, ran out of the water in front of them and shook himself. His owner whistled and he charged after her. When dog and woman disappeared Alva and Jack Kelly really were the last people on the beach.

'This was a good idea,' said Jack. He was taking in the circle of the bay as they walked. It was a bright enough night to see the great hump of Bray head in the near distance, some sailing boats making their way back to Dun Laoghaire. The waves broke over the shingle at their feet, then dragged it back with a rippling sigh.

'We're gonna have to slow down, Alva.' He pulled at her arm. 'Boots are a bit big.' They slowed to a slip-sliding stroll and he slipped a companionable arm through hers. 'There's something I should tell you about myself.' His face when she looked sideways was very serious and Alva stiffened. She fought an immediate instinct to pull away, distance herself from whatever intimacy he felt they should share. He noticed.

'Jeez, Alva,' he stopped and turned her gently to face him, 'you're one defensive female. I'm not about to tell you I raped my mother, you know. Though it is a fact,' he looked thoughtful, 'that my mother's responsible for what I want to tell you.' He looked over his shoulder, cautiously. 'It's my name.' He paused. 'My mother did it, to please my father ... Not many people know and I wouldn't want them to.' He took a deep breath. 'Alva, my mother called me John Fitzgerald Kelly. JFK.'

He laughed and Alva, ridiculously relieved, laughed with him. They walked on.

'I don't suppose you're the first, or last, Irish-

American brat to be labelled with the Kennedy initials,' she grinned. 'Do you think your mother was being superstitious? Hoping some of the Kennedy mythology would reach out and touch you? The millions and the glamour, of course, not the deaths and sickness.'

'I doubt it.' He was dry. 'She was Czech, my old mother. It was like I said – she did it to please my Irish father. He was one cantankerous son-of-a-bitch who never forgave her for not producing an Irish brood. I was their only child. He never forgave me either, for being more her child than his.'

'She spoiled you?'

'Reckon she did. Don't think he gave a damn about that though. What he cared about was my not reaching his six-foot-two and never winning a fight in my life. He was a New York fireman. They're a tough breed.' A small bank of shingle gave under him and he flailed about and grabbed Alva to regain his balance. 'Why don't we head back for that pub?' he said.

A breeze had come in off the sea and they walked more quickly. More unsteadily too, as the incoming tide forced them onto higher piled stones. The conversation became sporadic.

'Is he still alive?' Alva asked.

'My father? Sure. He's eighty-one and still at war with the world.'

After a while, when they were nearly at the steps to the road, Alva asked, 'Is he still at war with you?'

'Nope. Reckons he's lost that one so he mostly ignores me. And my mother has learned to ignore him, so they get along fine these days.'

They had driven halfway up the hill, in Alva's Citroën because she'd insisted, when he asked about her parents.

'Dead,' she said. 'I was an only child too.'

'Guess that makes us a pair of spoilt brats,' he said.

She drove on, up and along a back road, enjoying the comfortable quality of his silence beside her. She envied him the ease with which he'd spoken of his parents, his clear and critical acceptance of the way he'd grown up.

The pub was just off the road and among some trees.

'I love it.' Jack Kelly sat with his back to the stone wall and looked around inside. It was dark and low, old and self-consciously kept that way with blackened pots on a hob beside the fire and elderly artefacts hung on the smoke-blackened walls. Alva wasn't crazy about the place but it was convenient and served a good pint. Jack Kelly refused a pint, however, and ordered a heavily iced gin and tonic.

'JFK and I've never been to Ireland before this summer.' He shook his head, turning the drink on the low table between them. 'I need to know things, Alva. I need someone like you to wise me up. Someone who knows the real places. Like this one . . .'

'*This* is a tourist trap,' Alva interrupted absently. She'd no real objections to tourist traps, wished she could make one of De Novo herself. Jack Kelly didn't seem to hear her.

'I want this film to work, Alva,' he leaned forward, over the table. 'It's important to me, and *not* just because of the money side of things.' He pulled a rueful face. 'I've broken my own rules on this one and gotten personally involved. The Irish in me, I guess. I've always, until now, felt more influenced by my Czech roots. Reckon what we've got here is a case of my Celtic past asserting itself.' He looked down at Theo's boots. The ends of his trousers were splashed and wet. 'Has to be that,' he said, 'no other explanation.'

'Oh, I don't know.' Alva grinned and sat back. She arched a cool eyebrow. 'You're moving in at a time when it's fashionable and profitable to be involved in Irish film. The government here is offering generous tax shelters; companies coming to Ireland get bonuses paid for with Irish taxpayers' money. People here are still impressed by the whole business of film-making, still willing to allow film people loose in the land to do what they will, more or less. I'd say sound business instincts are what's behind your sudden conversion.'

Jack had been staring bemused as she spoke. He clapped his hands together, twice and softly, when she stopped. 'Well now, Alva Joyce, you could be right.' He shook his head, as if clearing it. 'Guess I've got out of the habit of dealing with straight shooters. Too long dealing in a world where bets are hedged and things half said.' He laughed shortly. 'God knows there's very little romance left in my soul.' He shrugged. 'You're right about Ireland being the place to make pictures in Europe today. But they'll be showing off their castles in Czechoslovakia in a few years and then that'll be the place to be.' He looked thoughtfully into the empty fire grate. 'None of this changes today's truth. I want this picture to work and my feelings for this country are part of the reason why.' He looked up suddenly and his expression was a sombre one she hadn't seen before. 'Will you help me?'

'Me?' Alva was startled. 'I know nothing about films. Really nothing. An extra on *The Ten Commandments* would have known more about the business than I do.'

'You'll learn.' He didn't smile. 'You're bright and you're sharp and, like I said, you're a straight shooter. I need someone on the ground here, a sort of aide-de-camp, a detached person who can tell me how things are going. You're ideal because you're not involved directly yet you will, of necessity, be here all the time, which means you'll be aware of the mood of the crew and how they're getting along. The nature of what I do means I'm on the move too much of the time. When I *do* hit base I get ten goddam versions of everything. One I could rely on – yours – would be just great.'

'Sounds a bit like you want me to spy,' Alva interrupted him uneasily.

'For Chrissake, Alva,' he was impatient, 'I need a spy, I got plenty people owe me I can lean on. What I want is an objective viewpoint, one that'll help me make decisions. I don't know Ireland. I don't know how things work here or even what's authentic in terms of this picture.' He pulled a wry face. 'Executive producers, by and large, aren't trusted. Too far removed from the coalface, I reckon. Will you do it for me?'

'Why not?' Alva touched her glass to his. 'If you feel it'll help.'

He made sense. She *was* ideal, from his point of view. Involved yet not involved, she could give him an independent view of things. Watching him as he ordered second drinks she thought with some irony that there was, indeed, no such thing as a free lunch. Jack Kelly had done her the favour of insisting she and Bernie be given the catering deal. This was life's natural quid pro quo asserting itself, nothing more.

Apart from all of which she was finding that she quite liked Jack Kelly.

'Here's getting to know you.' He raised his glass.

'To the honesty of quid pro quo,' Alva said and he laughed. They both did.

When he left her an hour later, in a car whose driver had waited a patient three hours at De Novo, he kissed her lightly on the forehead. He had to reach slightly to do it and the effect was vaguely avuncular. Alva wasn't sure whether or not he meant it to be. She hoped not.

Later, getting ready for bed, she picked up his card from her dressing table. So many telephone numbers, so very little revealed about the man. She didn't even know if one of them was his home. Even if he had a home, a wife, children. Notwithstanding all that he had said that evening, and he had talked a great deal, Jack Kelly could live out of a shoebox between airline flights for all she really knew about him.

*

Even if designers and other set workers hadn't continued to appear at De Novo from time to time with news, and even if Oscar Duggan hadn't visited simply for the purposes of a gossip, Alva would have known when the filming of *Death Diminishes* began on the streets of Dublin.

By the third week in August the papers and television were full of it. There were pictures everywhere, even a few of De Novo. Alva had been long enough in journalism to know that such lavish coverage had little to do with the film itself and everything to do with the time of year. Mid-August, with government, judiciary, industry and most criminals on holiday, was a notoriously slack time for news. It was the silly season, and glam pictures of the stars of a several-million-dollar-budget film were welcome fodder.

Clara Butler was interviewed, and provoked a small controversy. She'd grown up in Dublin, she revealed, but left in her mid-teens. Stories that she had spent her childhood in a mountainy farm on the Atlantic coast were a romantic fabrication. She was a Dubliner, proud of it, glad to be back and especially glad to be working with Luke O'Hanlon. She was going to give the 'performance of her life' in what would be a 'truly remarkable film'.

Pictures showed her wandering the streets she claimed were those of her youth, changed utterly over the nearly thirty years since then. She was slim and elegant, red-haired and with a handsome, high-boned face. Easy to see how and why Hollywood had taken and made of her a latter-day Maureen O'Hara.

Local people gave testimony to remembering Clara Devlin, as she was then. Others as adamantly denied she was the same person. Her family, Ms Butler said, did not want to become involved – and she did not want to involve them. She was accused of gimmickry, of inventing a Dublin past to suit her present film role. Worse, she was accused of doing it to revive a flagging career.

The actress denied all charges. She challenged her accusers to find even one interview, one statement, in which she claimed to be either a country girl or denied her nationality. None was produced.

Alva, reading it all, felt mightily amused. Seona, without doubt and in her own time, would get to the bottom of the real story. But for now, as August came to an end, it was enough to send curious day-trippers De Novo's way. The beginnings, Alva assured Bernie, of what would be a flood once the film was finished.

Chapter Nine

Sod's Law saw to it that a week of glorious sunshine ended the day the film company moved in on De Novo. Rain began before dawn and continued with relentless and growing ferocity through the morning. By ten o'clock, when the first of the cavalcade of trucks and trailers and cars came crawling up the avenue, it was at its worst.

'Oh God, wherever you are, please calm me down! I can't stand the excitement.' Bernie, watching from one of the sitting room's long front windows, was half serious, wholly nervous. 'Just look at them! They're like one of those eastern caravans crossing the desert. You know, full of promise . . .'

'Full of neurotic technicians and would-be artistes, more likely.' Ellen, with Thomas in her arms, watched from the other window. Her hair was loose and on her feet she wore a pair of high, silver mules. It was very early for her to be up.

'Oh, Ellen, don't be such an old killjoy. Use your imagination, think of—'

'Imagination's one thing, stupidity's another. Desert caravan,' Ellen sniffed at the spilling rain, 'is stupidity. And so, I might add, is your attempt to look like a chorister. What, or who, are you attempting to attract to yourself, you silly woman? Not, I hope, love?'

'Yes, I hope, love.' Bernie was impregnable. It was, she'd decided, do or die time as far as getting a man in her life was concerned. She was not going to be put off either by the rain or by bitter, twisted old Ellen Donovan. She felt good in the oversized white shirt and long red skirt. She'd had some doubts about threading the red chiffon through her plait but had gone ahead anyway and now she felt strong, in the best position she'd ever been in to change the course of her life. Feeding people was her forte and Alva had given her *carte blanche* to express herself in the month ahead. If she didn't get a man and some decent loving out of this film affair then it wouldn't be for want of trying.

'Love. Hope.' Ellen cleared the patch on the window her breath had clouded up. 'You'll give yourself a coronary believing in such nonsense. And if you think the itinerant types who make films believe in *anything* then you should think again. They don't, and I know what I'm talking about. I've been there.'

Bernie laughed, magnanimous in her buoyant mood. ''Course you have. Been-there-done-that Ellen, that's you. Well, thing is, I haven't and I'm willing to put my head in the noose. You know, Ellen, you might even enjoy all of this.'

Ellen shrugged. 'One of the few compensations of old age is that you cease to hope. You will know that yourself, soon enough.'

'They've stopped.' Alva, beside Bernie at the

window, spoke for the first time since the procession had begun up the avenue. 'Why've they stopped? They can't stay there . . .'

The lead trailer had drawn up on the wet and streaming cobbled frontage. Behind it everything else pulled up in a long, straggling line which stretched to a vanishing point between the avenue trees.

'Ha!' Ellen rubbed her hands together. 'Looks to me as if that's exactly what they intend doing. You took their money, you're going to have to pay the price in inconvenience.'

'Maybe not,' Alva said.

A long male body, draped in a large oiled cape, slipped down from the cab of the leading trailer. At a doubled-over run he made for the front steps. When the bell sounded Thomas bristled and Alva went to answer it.

The man on the doorstep had streeling, blue-white hair. He was weather-beaten and tanned and the oiled cape gave him the air of a highwayman.

'Come on in.' Alva stepped aside and he passed her into the hallway, cowboy boots with silver tips clunking on the flags. Under the oiled cloth he was dressed entirely in denim. He was one of the boniest individuals Alva had ever seen.

'Leo Cullen,' he faced her, 'Production manager. Need to go through the house to your back yard. Need to guide the vehicles into their positions. OK?' He took a few steps towards the back of the hall. 'Straight through?'

'Yes,' Alva said, 'I'll show you.'

'No need. Find my own way.' He was gone, leaving only a trail of water from the rain cape.

The convoy moved from the front of the house, round the side and slowly into the yard at the back.

'They'll be wanting something hot.' Bernie, in the kitchen, fussed with kettles and a couple of army-sized thermos flasks. She'd already that morning baked scones.

'Relax,' Alva soothed, 'they're not exactly time travellers. They've only come out from town.'

The rain got heavier. Great pools of water gathered across the yard and drops large as pennies drummed on the roofs of the corralled vehicles. The company remained locked in their vehicles.

'If they're waiting for the sun they could be waiting a long time,' Bernie giggled nervously. 'Surely to God they're expected to work in rain as well as shine? The rest of us are. Maybe I should go down with coffee? What do you think?'

Alva, with a sigh, pulled out a kitchen chair and forced her gently into it. 'I think, Bernie, that you're over-anxious and getting yourself into a state before we even begin. If they're prepared to wait out the rain, then why shouldn't we?' She put a couple of mugs on the table. 'You and I are going to sit here and have some of those scones while they're still hot. We're going to have coffee, too, and we're going to relax and wait for the picture show to begin. We're ready, the house is ready. Next move is theirs.'

De Novo was indeed dressed and ready. In the week gone by designers and set workers had descended in scurrying troops and had with meteoric speed remade the rooms which would be used for filming. They'd taken over far more of De Novo than Alva had bargained for and the ruthlessness of the metamorphosis had stunned her. She'd taken to following painters and carpenters and props people around, biting her lip and frowning, until the set designer, a thin, busy woman called Freda Ryan, had in exasperation taken her aside.

'You're making everyone nervous.' She had short, wiry grey hair and pale, no-nonsense eyes. 'Not to mention what you're doing to yourself. Look, I've been doing this sort of thing for a lifetime and I've never yet failed to put a place back exactly as we found it.'

Alva looked around. 'It's just that . . .'

'I know, I know. You love the place, love it as it is, slaved to get it looking like this. But look at it this way: De Novo House is getting a chance to be young again, be as it was a hundred or more years ago, when it was in its prime. Which of us wouldn't like to turn back the clock?'

She grinned, showing enough creases and furrows to make her point eloquently, and went back to supervising the coats of dark green paint being applied to the drawing-room walls. The effect was totally to annihilate Alva's primrose and create an overpowering gloom. The dining room was already a dark red and filled with foreboding. The hallway and stairs had been left much as they were, the carved wooden monkeys and stained-glass window causing near ecstasy in the art department.

The props department had had a wildly successful time, and a great clutter of embroidered cushions, painted plates, heavy candlesticks and porcelain filled every available surface. Walls were hung with prints and dark, important-looking oils. Windows were hung with heavy velvet drapes which were in turn ringed with tasselled fringes. The same fringes ringed cushions, mantelpieces and tablecloths. Armrests and chairbacks were covered in linen antimacassars and occasional tables in rich-coloured chenille. When they had finished, a large part of De Novo House had been made opulent, oppressive and murkily, authentically Victorian.

'There now.' Freda Ryan was brisk and pleased with herself. 'You're seeing it as it originally was, or pretty damn near what it originally was, anyway. What do you think?'

'It's incredible,' Alva hesitated, 'it reminds me of the house I grew up in.' The drapes did, in the way they kept out the light, and the heavy furniture smothering the rooms . . .

'Good,' Freda Ryan said, 'you'll feel at home then.'

The rain stopped just after eleven. Clouds rolled back and a small patch of blue sky grew quickly to free a sun warm enough to dry the pools in the yard. Like citizens after a siege the occupants of the various vehicles began cautiously to emerge.

'Looks like we got lift-off,' Alva grinned.

'Lordy, lord,' Bernie sighed with satisfaction, 'what a grand, big crowd of hungry-looking people.'

The front doorbell rang.

'That'll be the actors,' Bernie said with certainty, 'using the front entrance.' She tied on an apron which read 'Cook in Charge', and relieved Alva of her coffee mug. 'Better let them in,' she said.

Luke O'Hanlon, looking distinctly damp, was about to ring again when Alva opened the door. A small truck, motor running, stood on the cobbles.

'Sorry I couldn't be here this morning.' He shook himself like a dog and stepped into the hallway. 'Few street details had to be wrapped up. Oscar looked after things for you, I hope . . .?'

'Oscar? Well, mm, he . . .'

'Didn't arrive. Jees-us!' The director's eyes flickered with a quick, impatient anger. He shook his head as if clearing it and looked around. 'Everything all right here?' he asked.

'Everything's fine . . .'

'Good. We'll set up as quietly as we can. Talk to you later.'

Over the next couple of hours Alva would remember, as if in a dream, the peace of the morning's thunder shower. The tumult of bodies and equipment spilling from trucks and filling the yard spread quickly into the house. Cables and tracks appeared, snaking treacherously all over the place. Cameras, sound and lighting equipment were polished and fondled and put into position. An upstairs bedroom was turned into a mini-cinema for showing daily rushes of the film and

in the yard the company's own electricity generator –
a necessary precaution against power failure – began a
persistent, dull hum. Babble was constant and the
entire company, from lowliest gofer to the taciturn
Leo Cullen, appeared to communicate solely via
walkie-talkie and mobile phone.

Food's Up, the on-set catering company, proved that
being there first was nine-tenths of any business deal.

Lunchtime was one o'clock. Everyone, as if an
invisible cord had been pulled, slumped to a standstill
and then began, in small groups, to make for a double-
decker bus parked in a quiet, far corner.

'This is it,' Bernie breathed, 'the beginning or the
end. What do we do now, Alva? Go and have lunch in
the bus, make friends with the enemy? Or do we march
over there with placards showing the day's alternative
menu?'

'We keep the food hot and we wait. The company's
been told they've a choice of caterers for the while
they're here. There's bound to be a certain loyalty to
Food's Up but people will be curious, too. Once we
get a few customers word'll get around.' She grinned.
'A Bernie Brennan lasagne's not something to keep
quiet about.'

They waited, and the precious hour-and-a-half alloc-
ated for lunch moved on. The yard was mostly empty,
the few people who *did* cross it from time to time
heading straight for the bus-canteen. Luke O'Hanlon
appeared and for breathtaking seconds, until he was
stopped by his diminutive first assistant, seemed to be
heading their way.

Watching the small drama between director and assistant Alva thought it like a silent film. Juno handed Luke O'Hanlon a mobile which he took, spoke into briefly and handed back. Juno stuffed it into the back of her jeans. He walked off. Juno tripped after him, hands waving and agitated. He stopped and smiled, shook his head and disappeared into a trailer marked Production Office.

Alva cursed under her breath. 'Looks like God has decided to sit this one out,' she said. 'The director's gone for a working lunch. Now if *he'd* come to eat here . . .'

'Someone's coming.' A flush began at Bernie's neck. 'See him? Fella with glasses crossing the yard? Quick, get down to the dining hall.'

De Novo Catering's first customer was one Jasper Clarke, square to plumpish, red-haired, good-natured and a cameraman with sensitivity and a shining talent. He ordered the soup, which was minestrone, and Bernie's *plat du jour*, which was lasagne. He ate alone and in obvious contentment. When he was almost finished Alva sat opposite him at the table and smiled. (They'd gone for green gingham cloths with a fresh rose, discreetly plucked from under Theo's nose, in a vase on every table.)

'Food all right?' she asked and he nodded.

'Better than all right.' His accent sounded Liverpudlian.

'We've got enough made to feed the entire company,' Alva said.

'That's good.' He gave her a gentle, vague smile

and stood up. Alva groaned. They'd got themselves a solid, man-of-few-words type when what they needed was a bigmouth, someone who would blab about the fabulous good food to be had from the new caterers. She took a deep breath and went for broke. This was not a man to be subtle with.

'You're our first customer,' she said. 'In fact you're our only customer.'

'Thought I might be,' he said.

'What my partner is telling you is that we need more.' Bernie, framed in the archway at the bottom of the steps leading from the modern, cooking part of the kitchen, held a bottle of wine in one hand and three glasses by the stem in the other. 'But since you're all we've got we're going to spoil you a little.' Face flushed and eyes bright she put the glasses and wine on the table and sat down. Strands of hair had come loose and she blew at them impatiently and tossed her head.

'It's a Riserva Chianti and I'm not going to drink alone.' She waved Jasper Clarke back into his seat and began to pour. To anyone else it would have seemed as if she had already been drinking a lot and alone. But Alva recognized Bernie's rare determination when she saw it and sat on, taking one of the filled glasses and waiting for Bernie's next move. Jasper Clarke, bemused but willing, sat between them.

'To a brave man and our first customer.' Bernie raised her glass.

'To the man who crossed the yard.' Alva raised hers.

'Well, to be honest, it weren't really like that.' Jasper

Clarke sniffed the wine. 'Ah, that's good.' He sipped, sipped again, then looked from one woman to the other. 'I came in here for a bit of peace, is all,' he said, 'bloody bus gives me a headache. Cigarette smoke's choking. Food's rubbish. Noise is terrible.'

'Ah,' Alva said. 'But the important thing is, you're here.'

Bernie looked genuinely puzzled. 'Why would anyone want to eat bad food in lousy conditions?'

'Hunger, habit . . .' Jasper Clarke stared as if seeing her for the first time, 'and no choice . . .' He went on staring.

'Well, they've got a choice now,' Alva said.

Bernie, aglow and aware now of Jasper Clarke's adoring look, nodded. Alva doubted she'd heard a word she'd said.

'Maybe you could tell your hungry colleagues about the choice.' Alva spoke into Japser Clarke's ear.

'I'll do that,' he said and touched Bernie's glass with his. 'You're the cook?' he asked and Bernie nodded. 'I'm Jasper.' He held out his hand.

'Bernie.' She took it. Smiling, they touched glasses gently and drank.

'I'm off,' Alva said loudly, 'to salvage what's left of the lasagne. We just *might* get another customer when Jasper spreads the word.'

The afternoon was well under way, and Bernie had departed to collect Sammy from school, when Juno dropped in on Alva.

'Sorry not to have bid you the time of day before now.' She swung onto a worktop and sat, hugging

154

herself and looking like a small berry-eyed monkey. 'How about a cup of *real* coffee? Setting up's always a bit of a shit and everyone's cranky because of the rain. We'd planned to squeeze in a scene, too, and Luke's like an anti-Christ because we've lost a half day thanks to Nick Hunt's picking up a bit of a sniffle. Nothing much, but our Nick worries about himself, has himself in constant fear of AIDS.' She grinned and slapped her thigh. 'He should be, the way he puts himself about. Mind you, so would I be if I put myself about as much, and as carelessly, as he does . . .'

'Sounds as if he *should* worry.' Alva, grinning, handed Juno the coffee.

'He won't.' Juno sounded happy for the actor. 'He'll continue to be a horny, undisciplined devil and not so discriminating as he might be about his partners. So – things all right here? I like the dining hall you've made up down below. Sorry I didn't get across for lunch. Didn't have lunch at all, as a matter of fact. Those scones, are they . . .?'

Alva gave her one. 'We did have one lunchtime customer.' She grinned. 'Don't know which he appreciated more, Bernie or her lasagne.'

'Jasper Clarke,' Juno nodded, 'saw him. One of the good guys but not one of life's impulsive doers. Likes his grub, though.' She wrinkled her nose and looked more monkeylike than ever. 'You telling me he gave Bernie the eye? Doesn't sound like him. Our Jasper's engaged to be married. Has been for four years now, by all accounts.'

'Well, it looked like he was giving her the eye to

me.' Alva sighed. 'Typical of Bernie's luck that he's spoken for.'

'Oh, oh, the boss man cometh.' Juno slipped from the worktop. 'Listen, Alva. There's a bit of a panic on and he wants you to do him a favour. Say yes, please?' She put her head to one side, impish, pleading, and ruthless about getting what she wanted. Alva could see how, in a work sense, Juno was the perfect foil to Luke O'Hanlon's itchy diffidence.

'Depends,' she said and Juno sighed despairingly.

Luke O'Hanlon wasn't at all comfortable about asking Alva to do something for him. He paced for several minutes after coming into the kitchen, refused coffee and, when he at last got round to asking, stood looking at a comic print on the wall.

'Look, I don't like taking up your time like this . . .' He straightened the picture. 'Thing is, Oscar can't be located and I need someone to show the lead actresses around when they arrive. I'd do it myself if I didn't have to get to a meeting.' He faced her. 'Will you do it? Give them a look at the house and show them which rooms will be their dressing rooms? Whole thing shouldn't take longer than half an hour.'

'Be glad to.' Alva looked at him a little curiously. Why should he imagine she would mind? Did she really come across as so very cold and unobliging? 'We're talking here about Clara Butler and Justine O'Dea, I presume?'

'That's right.' He looked relieved. 'And I appreciate your help.'

'Look, it's no big thing,' Alva said, 'please don't—'

Juno roared her huge laugh. 'It's a big thing, Alva, believe me. But you're just the person to carry it off. Isn't she, Luke?'

'Hope so.' The director grinned and finger-combed his hair. 'Day's been a bitch. Ideally Clara and Justine should've seen the place before now, at the very least this morning. Schedule's rather behind though. You might find them a bit ... frazzled.' He caught sight of the wall clock, muttered a heartfelt 'Christ!' and turned to Juno. 'Get Leo, will you? That bloody meeting's in less than an hour. Last I saw of him he was hanging around in props.'

'Yessir.' Juno touched a curly dark forelock and disappeared down the steps.

'And bring my car keys back here,' he called after her. When she yelled an acknowledgement he dropped into a chair by the table. 'That gives me six or seven minutes, with luck. Any chance of a bite of the lasagne Jasper was telling me about?'

'I think I can manage that. And good for Jasper, didn't take him long to get the word around. Six or seven minutes ...' Alva sliced and popped a portion into the microwave. 'Two to heat and five to eat. Hope you've a good digestive system.' She poured him a glass of the Chianti. 'We're treating our first few customers well,' she said. 'Catch is, you're expected to pass the word around about Bernie's cooking.'

'Done.' He tasted the wine. 'You should know that Mel O'Sullivan of Food's Up is not pleased. No doubt he'll make his feelings known to you himself. He's been in the business a long time and he's made an art of the production of quick fodder. He'll tell you he's got a staff to support, but don't be too taken in. Mel's never been known to put all his eggs in one basket. And don't for Christ's sake involve me unless the battle becomes nuclear. Get Juno to help. She's good with him.' The oven pinged and Alva put the food in front of him. 'Looks good,' he said.

'It *is* good,' Alva said.

He ate quickly, talking between mouthfuls, feeding a hunger that had nothing to do with enjoying the food. 'Juno's a useful go-between. Talk to her if things get rough. She's a good head and likely to be the one to keep a lot of things together before filming ends.'

'You make her sound like a war nurse, ministering in the field of battle.'

'Not a bad analogy.' He drained the wine. 'Juno's sound. If there's anything you need to know about all of this,' he jerked his head towards the yard outside, 'just ask her. She'll be glad to explain.'

'How do *you* see this film?' Alva asked the question abruptly, and he stiffened before looking at her thoughtfully, considering his answer.

After too long a pause, and with a smile she didn't understand, he said, 'As a commercial proposition and a moral tract. Your hotel, Alva, is hosting what will be the first film to deal with justifiable murder and its effect on the Victorian whalebone.'

Alva laughed, matching his ironic tone. 'I can see it's engaging your emotions,' she said.

'I'll give it my best,' he shrugged.

'Speaking of whalebones, when should I expect your leading ladies to arrive?'

He checked the wall clock again. 'In about an hour. I should warn you that they . . .' he paused . . .'don't get on all that well.' He grinned. 'Keep one on either side of you and you should be safe enough.'

After he'd left, and after Theo, very civilized and suspiciously benign, had helped himself to something to eat and gone into the garden, Alva spotted Juno sitting on the steps of a trailer with a newspaper. She went down and sat beside her.

'You look like someone with time on their hands,' she said.

'How can you tell?' Juno yawned.

'That's yesterday's paper. And you're twitching. What do you do to relax?'

'I work.' Juno grinned. 'Not working makes me *most* unrelaxed. So – what can I do you for? You didn't pop down to enquire about my nervous disposition.'

'That's true. I was hoping you'd give me a rundown on all of this.' Alva tapped the side of the trailer. 'If I'm going to be living with it for a month it would be nice to know something of the practicalities . . .'

'The practicalities, indeed.' Juno looked at her sideways, her quick, sharp face mocking. 'God, but you can be stuffy sometimes, Alva. Is it cause or effect? What I mean is, are you stuffy because you live here, in this old house, or do you live in this old house because you're stuffy?' Something in Alva's face made her stop. Gently, her face genuinely distressed, she took Alva's hands in hers. 'Christ, I'm sorry. Really sorry. That was way out of line. You're not stuffy. You're beautiful and I'm a jealous bitch. Ignore me. Don't ever talk to me again. Don't feed me, don't—'

'Stop it, you idiot.' Alva, laughing, shook her head and freed her hands. 'To answer your question, the stuffiness came before the house. I'll work on it, I promise.'

'I can't figure you,' Juno said. 'I like you – but what's a nice girl like you doing with Jack Kelly?'

'*Doing* with Jack Kelly?' Alva froze, but Juno, aware and watching her, merely shrugged.

'Doing as in involved. Rumour on the set has you two an item. But since I'm the only one's bothered to talk to you, I say they're wrong . . .'

'They're wrong.' Alva was curt. 'Jack Kelly worked out the deal for De Novo when the rest of you were still, I gather, looking for a place. He's been back a few times. And that's it.'

'Glad to hear it.' Juno was on her feet, picking up a leather jacket from the steps, slinging it around her shoulders. 'Come on, I'll give you a quick run around. Thing you want to remember about JK is that executive producers, given the nature and perversity of this business, are deeply suspected of just about anything by the lower orders. We're not always wrong. JK, in this instance,' she grinned, 'is seen as wanting to make this a low-concept, high-emotion picture.' Alva looked blank and Juno laughed outright. 'Think about it, because that, my dear lady of the house, is my piece

said and my nose out of your business. Come on, I'll
trot you around this playground.'

Alva, peeved but determined not to show it, followed the bobbing Juno as, quick and good-natured,
she dispensed information.

'Don't know how technical you want to get, but
this,' she laid an affectionate hand on a platform-like
contraption moving past them, 'is the ubiquitous dolly.
Used to transport cameras for tracking shots and the
like. Under your feet you will see sets of the even more
ubiquitous tracks themselves. In here,' she punched
the side of a truck, 'you'll find our gaffer and his
beloved lighting. Not recommended that we stop to
inspect. Next truck is wardrobe and the following two
are make-up and dressing. The bus over there you're
familiar with . . .' She looked around. 'That there,' she
indicated a large trailer, 'is the production office.
Nerve centre. Place to keep away from. Now, anything
else you want to know?'

'What does a first assistant director *do*?' Alva asked.
She liked Juno, but warily. Her insouciance and cheerfully blunt non-conformity made her in a way untouch-
able. What she actually *did* was the biggest mystery of
all.

'Well, now.' Juno thought for a moment. 'What I do
depends on the director. In this instance I'm a devoted
lap dog. A privileged slave to Luke's needs. Basically, I
organize things for the set, get people to do what I
want.' She wrinkled her nose. 'Put another way, I get
what Luke wants done, done. I'm a born organizer.

161

Not, it is true and has been said, the world's greatest thinker. But I am very, very good at getting things done.

'I'm a background person and every director, good or bad, needs one of me. I like what I do and there are, of course,' she gave a sly, secret smile, 'the perks that go with the job. We won't discuss those. Basically, it's a hard, twenty-four-hour-a-day slog and I love it.'

'Well, that's all clear as mud.' Alva gave a rueful laugh. 'Glad I asked.'

'One last thing, and this is my final word, I promise.' Juno put her arm through Alva's and steered her out of any earshot, back towards the house. 'All you really need to know to survive the next month is that the different departments in the unit: art, props, lighting, cameras, wardrobe, actors – especially the actors – are interdependent and hate one another for it. And we're talking real, red-hot and smoking hate in some cases. Everyone works on contract, which makes their positions precarious and means it's every man and woman for themselves around here. If you're keen on the peaceful life,' she looked momentarily gloomy, 'then you should think about taking a holiday, heading into the west for the next four weeks.'

'Thanks, but no thanks.' Alva was curt. 'I think I can handle the excitement.' She would handle it a lot better if people, notably Oscar Duggan and Juno, stopped advising her as if she was some unworldly sub-species.

'Atta girl,' Juno said blithely, 'and mind how you

handle our divas too. We are very, very happy to have them aboard. Both of them.'

The limo bringing Clara Butler and Justine O'Dea to De Novo sloped up to the front steps in the getting-on-for-late afternoon. Alva, watching from the open door as they got out, thought it interesting that one of the women opened her own door while the other waited for the chauffeur to open hers.

She waved, called hello and began down the steps as Juno, as if on telepathic link, appeared from the side of the house and shooed the car around the back. Bereft of the limo as prop, the women stood there, a good ten feet apart, watching Alva draw near.

One wore a hat, straw and with a froth of something pink falling from the brim and down her back. The other, taller and older, preferred to display a tumult of unnatural, but stunningly effective, russet-coloured hair. Both wore sunglasses and both were slim to wispy-looking in the honey-pale sunlight. Alva reminded herself that these two women would be playing mother and daughter in the film. It would be interesting to see how it worked out.

Neither attempted to bridge the gap between them; both stood quite still, in fact, as Alva introduced herself. The woman with the hair, Clara Butler, nodded slightly, smiled as she looked up at the house and said, in a throaty, dark malt voice, 'Very impressive, very Victorian,' before turning with a swirl of mauve silk to survey the garden.

'Where's Lukey?' The voice from under the hat was entirely different, high and sweetly peevish. 'He *promised* he'd be here.'

'Bidden away by the money men.' Juno bounced to Alva's side. 'He's really, really sorry. But you know how it is, the old dollar calling the tune as always.' She lowered her voice. 'It's about additional production finance. He was sure you'd understand.'

'What a shit! I wouldn't have come if I'd known.' Justine O'Dea's voice was high to shrill, the peevishness not so sweet any more.

'I've been delegated to show you around.' Alva, aware she sounded chill and unwelcoming, smiled a little desperately. 'I'm the owner so I actually know the place better than Luke. Would you like to come inside?'

''Course we would, honey.' Clara Butler removed the sunglasses with a flourish. 'Nice of you to invite us.' She had wide green eyes, made luminous by the sunlight and their contrast with the russet hair. As eyes went they were lovely and very obviously a much-used part of her sexual arsenal. Around them her flawless skin was thinning a little, and tightly drawn over her high cheekbones. Her accent was low and neutered, bits of America as well as what could be hints of Irish. 'I'm Clara Butler. Hope they're making it worth your while our being here.' Her hand was long and white and held Alva's briefly.

'You must be Justine O'Dea.' Alva smiled at the other actress. 'We've been looking forward to having you here.' How easily the lie came, she thought. Either

I'm learning diplomacy or becoming immune to the truth. If there's a difference . . .

'That's nice.' Justine O'Dea flashed a shining smile from under the hat and sunglasses. 'Sorry to be a cow just now. I haven't seen Lukey boy for *two* days and this film means such a *tremendous* amount to me.'

'Must be nerve-racking.' Alva followed up the steps after Clara Butler and Juno.

'You'd better believe it.' Justine's voice had become hard-edged and brittle. Not, Alva reckoned, a play-acting voice any more. This was the real Justine speaking. Or at least an aspect of her.

On the top step they stood together, the four of them, Alva smiling uneasily. Juno broke the silence.

'I'm off,' she said. She was deadpan as she handed Alva a walkie-talkie. 'Call me if you need me.' She waggled her fingers at the actresses. 'See you later, girls.' She took the steps two at a time as she went down.

'How very beautiful.' Justine's voice shifted to sweet and breathless as she gazed over the gardens and presented Alva with a perfect profile. In a short, floral dress and no jewellery she was fine-boned and ethereal looking. 'And the gardener! Is he for real or is he one of us?'

'Very real.' Alva waved to Theo who immediately disappeared.

'Theo *is* the garden. He—'

'I just hope it doesn't play havoc with my sinuses.' Justine put a hand to her nose. 'I need to be around a low allergen garden. Is it low allergen?'

'I'm afraid I don't know,' Alva said truthfully, 'that's something you'll have to check out with Theo.'

'Maybe we could check out the house first.' Clara Butler suppressed a yawn.

The hallway, after the light outside, made them all blink. Justine removed her hat and sunglasses, shook a mane of heavy, pale gold hair back over her shoulders. Clara Butler, gliding across to the bottom of the stairs, was straight-backed and elegant in a way that came with knowing her body. Strands of Indian beads hung heavily between her bra-less breasts. A certain worn weariness apart, she was stunning, the ultimate example of how a woman can grow into her looks and become interesting. Alva, between them in jeans and blue shirt, felt like a slob.

The actresses were mostly silent as they followed Alva through the rooms which would be used for filming. Clara Butler asked a few desultory questions about De Novo's age and history but Justine O'Dea drifted quietly along, her thoughts, if she had any, a guarded secret. They'd reached the bedroom which was to be her dressing room before she found her voice, faintly.

'Oh, dear, and everything was going so well . . .' She leaned against the wall inside the door. 'I couldn't possibly use this room. At least not without changes.'

'Take mine.' Clara Butler was crisp. 'We'll swap.'

'That's sweet of you, Clara, but it wouldn't make any difference. They're both all wrong, energy-wise. They're full of negativity.' She gave a small shiver. 'Such a pity because the house *could* be perfect.'

'What sort of changes do you want?' Alva, with

controlled impatience, looked from the high ceiling to the polished floorboards and woollen throw-rugs.

'You don't want to know, honey.' Clara Butler toyed languidly with her beads. 'Believe me, you don't want to know.'

'The mirror can't stay opposite the bed.' Justine ignored her. 'The spirit should *never* see itself when it rises from sleep. But I *would* like a mirror on the desk. A round one, to magnify energy. And the flowers are a lovely touch – but could I have red next time? Red magnifies fame.' She looked apologetic. 'They're just small things but they would help *so* much. Vibes are *so* important and feng shui is the only way to make sure you've got things right.'

'Feng shui?'

'It's an oriental science about the effects of the environment on our inner selves,' Justine parroted. 'It's—'

'I did warn you, Alva,' Clara Butler, cutting Justine short, drawled sardonically. 'If you must encourage her, then I'm going downstairs. I want to see that drawing room again, get the feel of it. In the present script I spend a lot of time there.'

'There's another script?' Alva's surprise brought a pitying expression to Clara's face.

'There's always another script, honey, in life and in the movies. Hasn't running a hotel taught you anything? Nothing's absolute.'

She was humming a raggedy version of 'Claire de Lune' as she went down the stairs. Slowly, Alva and Justine started after her.

'Clara's wonderful, considering.' Justine's eyes, following the other actress, had become soft with understanding.

'Considering?' I'm like a damn mayfly, Alva thought, rising to the bait every time.

'Well, her age and the rotten time she's been having career-wise.' Justine became confidential. 'Her husband dying was a blow, too. He propped her up, you know. But she *has* brought a lot of her troubles on herself, poor old thing. Still,' she gave a long, shuddering sigh, 'she really needs the part of Constance to work for her. I hope she can swing it. We all do, especially Luke. He got her the part, you know.'

'I'm sure she'll be fine,' Alva said. 'With you and everyone else behind her she can hardly go wrong. She's certainly got that tragic heroine look about her.'

'You think so?' Justine snapped, then shrugged. 'I'm glad you think so. Most people think she's too old to play my mother. But when they say that I say to them, not at all, with make-up and decent lighting she'll be fine . . .'

Alva thought briefly about shoving the actress down the stairs. But Clara, she'd no doubt, could fight her own battles with an equal armoury of bitchiness.

'Oh, dear!' Justine stopped dramatically at the return on the stairs. 'This really *is* a fatal situation.' Alva kept on down, faster now, but Justine, following, didn't miss a beat. 'You should *never* have a staircase directly opposite a front door. It allows energy to fly right out of the house. Surely you can see that?'

'The logic escapes me, I'm afraid,' Alva said.

'Take my word for it, it happens.' Justine was reassuring. 'All you need to do is move the reception desk to the centre of the hallway. That way there will be something between to stop it. Simple, isn't it?'

'Yes.'

'You'll do it then?'

Alva, at the end of the stairs and crossing the hall, grunted noncommittally. If Justine wasn't careful she would set Ellen on her. Hotel furniture was not up for grabs. She was damned if she was going to move it around on foot of the obsession of a neurotic actress.

Clara Butler was circling the drawing room. She ignored them when they came in and continued, murmuring to herself, slowly around, frowning when she came to the window. She raised her chin and looked out. It was a movement made for the proud, trapped Constance Moore.

Yawning, Justine O'Dea fell into an armchair, holding her head at an angle which swung her hair in a silken arc behind one ear. She stifled another yawn and curled into the chair. 'Don't suppose Nicky Hunt's deigned to visit yet?' She was lazily irritable. 'He's becoming a bloody liability.' She sighed. 'God, but I could kill for a glass of water. Any chance you could rustle one up, Alva?'

'I'll have a coffee.' Clara Butler didn't turn. 'Black.'

In the hallway Alva met Thomas. He miaowed and gave a slow swish of his tail when he saw her. Alva bent down and looked him in the eye. He didn't flinch.

'You, my lad,' she spoke softly, 'are facing real competition in the catty stakes around here. And believe me, Thomas, these newcomers are not amateurs.' Thomas licked a lazy paw and began to clean himself.

Bernie was waiting for her, an arsenal of food prepared for the six o'clock tea-break, when Alva at last got back to the kitchen.

'Don't apologize,' she said, 'I know where you've been. Jasper popped in for a bite and told me. Are they beautiful and wonderful and all that?'

'They're beautiful and all that,' Alva said. 'How've things been here? Mad rush of diners?'

'Jasper brought three mates with him,' Bernie beamed, 'and Juno's been and so have eight hungry, curious types who all say they'll be back. It's going to build up, Alva, I know it is.'

'Never doubted it,' Alva said, 'not for a minute.'

In all, over the tea-break hour, they served twenty-one people, a good twenty-five per cent of those working late that evening. It was enough to bring Mel O'Sullivan of Food's Up storming into the dining hall at exactly ten past seven.

'Miss Joyce, you have exceeded your remit.' Wavy-haired and beetle-browed, he confronted Bernie. 'The terms of—'

'*I'm* Alva Joyce.' Quietly, without moving from where she was clearing a table, Alva spoke to him from across the room. 'And I'm very clear about the terms of the contract. You're Mr O'Sullivan, I take it?'

'Mel O'Sullivan, official caterer to this company.' He turned but didn't move from where he was. Behind his back Bernie made a throat-cutting gesture with her index finger. Alva kept a straight face. Mel O'Sullivan did not look like a humorous man.

'My understanding, Miss Joyce,' his voice was high and tight, 'is that you have a contract to supply back-up meals, nothing more. Regardless of this you've been operating a full service here all day—'

'Your understanding is altogether wrong.' Alva shook her head. 'My contract allows us to operate as a full catering service as we wish for as long as the company is based here at De Novo. We'll be in direct competition, Mr O'Sullivan, for the next month. May the best food win.'

For several minutes it seemed as if apoplexy would do for Mel O'Sullivan. His colour turned a nasty puce and his breathing stopped entirely. Bernie, concerned, went to him and hesitantly rubbed his back. Alva stayed firm, and cool, where she was. Bullies, in her experience, always found their second wind. Mel O'Sullivan did.

'Food's Up has been catering to film and shift-working companies for eight years. There's a helluva lot more to it than just supplying food.' His face remained puce while his breathing became heavily bad-tempered. 'You have neither the experience nor the ability to meet demands. I give you three days!' On the way out he collided with a laughing group of last-minute diners.

'There goes a man', Alva declared, 'who had a money-making situation all sewn up and is watching it come under threat for the first time.'

'He might be watching it come apart altogether,' Bernie said hopefully.

They had cleared and shut up for the night when Theo appeared in the kitchen, petulant and trying not to be.

'Any food for those of us who live here?' he asked. 'Or has the old order yielded place completely to the new?'

It was ten hours exactly since the film company had arrived at De Novo House.

Chapter Ten

Filming began with a languid intensity. From the outside looking on, there seemed to be a stop-go mechanism at work. Long, wearisome hours were spent setting up scenes which were then shot, and re-shot, with dead time and more delays between each one as lighting and sound and angles were changed and adjusted.

'Sweet God, I could *not* earn my living like that. Not for all the glory and money in the world. Not for Liz Taylor's diamonds.' Bernie stood with Alva in the door of the dining room. It was mid-morning and they'd come into the hall with the hot drinks after a third take of a scene between Constance and her husband James. The scene called for the throwing of a glass of wine which, because Clara, as Constance, had each time to change her dress, made for long and nerve-stretching breaks.

'Very little chance of you being asked to,' Ellen, Thomas in her arms, stopped to chortle in Bernie's ear. Unlike Thomas, who was in open warfare with the newcomers, Ellen had been in rare good humour since their arrival. She dressed to kill and spent a large part of each day hovering, with the hostile Thomas, about the set. Her arch remarks and air of ladylike superiority were a source of amusement. So far.

'I wouldn't have believed that man could become more awful.' Bernie, ignoring Ellen, scowled at the actor playing James Moore. 'But he does, doesn't he, when he becomes James Moore? I suppose it's just a case of stretching himself a bit.'

'It's called acting, you silly girl,' Ellen told her. 'Which is of course the lowest form of the arts, if it's an art at all. They're trained performers, these people; nothing more. Dogs and parrots can be made to perform too. But not cats. Isn't that so, Thomas?'

'That David Blake needed very little training for *his* part.' Bernie, with a sniff and a shrug, went back to dispensing tea, coffee and scones from the trolley at the end of the hall. Her scones, freshly baked each morning, were proving an everyday, day-long hit.

Her aversion to David Blake, the actor playing Constance's husband, had its origins in a drunken pass made at her in the kitchen. When she'd rebuffed him the actor had huffed that she should be grateful, and when she'd assured him she wasn't he'd beaten an ill-tempered retreat.

And there things should have ended. But the actor, spotting Jasper Clarke and Bernie laughing together, had taken exception to the cameraman's apparent success where he had failed and had since been making life difficult for Jasper on the set. It was this which had aroused the dozing giant of Bernie's motherly instincts. Jasper, apparently unaware of the fiercely protective passions he'd inspired, continued to eat exclusively at De Novo while Alva worried about Bernie's heart and Jasper's fiancée, in that order.

The lights came back on and Juno's voice, like her laugh altogether too big for her frame, yelled for 'Qui-et!' and then, more threateningly, demanded 'Sil-ence!' Alva slipped inside the door as she bellowed 'Ac-shon!'

Constance Moore was sitting with her husband at a candlelit dinner table in the centre of the room. She did not look well. Her eyes were darkly circled and her face a smooth, deathly white. Her hair was in ringlets to her shoulders and she wore a high-necked, cream-coloured girlish dress. She could have been any age. Certainly she looked a lot younger than the thin, peevish man sitting across the table from her.

'I am told that you left this house again today, my dear.' His voice was low and sibilant, his face narrowing as he spoke. 'You were seen walking, alone, without our child, at three in the afternoon. Explain yourself!'

'I . . .' Contance's knife fell from her shaking hand onto the floor.

'Leave it!' The command was a hiss. It was followed by the staccato drumming of the little man's fingers on the tabletop. Constance sat still where she was, staring straight ahead, her eyes huge and dull.

'You have eaten enough, whore.' The man picked up his cutlery and began to cut the meat on his plate. 'You will have no more food from my table tonight.' He looked up briefly, smiling. 'Go to your bed and wait for me.'

Constance swayed in her seat and for several seconds it seemed as if she would faint. Then, slowly, her entire body trembling, she began to get up. She was not speedy enough for her husband. With a quick, careless flick of his wrist he lifted a glass of wine from in front of him and threw its contents into his wife's face. An instinctive closing of the eyes was her only protective action, her only movement. She didn't attempt to wipe away the wine and, as it dripped from her face, its red stain spread across the bodice of her pale dress.

'I will never again eat at this table with you, James.' She said the words without expression. Her eyes on his face held loathing. Her husband shrugged, turned away and refilled his glass, slowly.

'You will eat where you are told to eat, whore.' He looked up and across the table. His wife had gone, the room was silent.

'Cut! It's a take!' Luke O'Hanlon's call brought an immediate sighing buzz and darkening of lights.

'Thank God for that. I don't think I could have taken another glass of that muck in my face.' Clara Butler, wrapped in a towel and with a dresser hovering, mopped at her face and chest. Her make-up had run amok, giving her the appearance of a clown. The director put an arm around her, kissed her gently on the forehead.

'You don't have to. You were great. Couldn't have been better. Get out of here now and change. Go on, go.' He gave her a small shove in the direction of the door and turned to David Blake. 'You got him, David, you really got the little bastard there. Great stuff.'

'Don't I get a kiss too?' The actor was simpering, pleased and half serious. The director grinned.

'Just keep this up, David, and you never know your luck. Now come on, everyone, we need to move things along faster than this . . .'

He was, Alva thought, like God, feeding titbits to egos, dispensing confidence, wheeling in the returns. She wondered how much he meant of anything he said. How much he enjoyed controlling people.

Theo refused to fraternize with what he was calling 'the squatters' and kept himself busy in the furthest reaches of the garden.

'Haven't the time. Autumn tasks need doing if we're to get the benefit of next spring's growth,' he muttered when Alva asked if he would meet Clara. The actress had said she'd like to know a little about the garden before beginning to film there.

'They're going to be shooting out here next week.' Alva poked at the dead heads in a wheelbarrow with a pruner. 'It would help if you met Clara at least beforehand . . .'

'I intend absenting myself when they descend – which means I must work now, while I can. I'll be cutting back and tying the shoots of the climbing plants as well as staking and securing everything from the winter gales. I'm intending to sow some sweet pea and a few antirrhinum and I need to thin the shoots of the dahlias . . .'

'All right, Theo, all right. I'll tell her you're busy.'

Oscar Duggan turned up for lunch that day, his third appearance – each one at lunchtime – since the company had moved to De Novo. Seeing him reminded Alva that she hadn't heard from Seona. No doubt she would be in touch in her own good time; nearer to the end of filming, most likely. Chances were she was busy researching Clara Butler's, and everyone else's, background, rattling out what skeletons she could find.

Oscar joined Juno and Jasper Clarke at the table they'd made theirs by the window.

'The discerning place to be, obviously.' He was jovial. 'What's Bernie got for us today?'

'Fish casserole. Very good too. Your timing, Oscar, is impeccable. As ever.' Juno grinned at him.

'Thank you, Juno, for your always kind word.'

Oscar ordered the casserole and also, with ostentatious magnanimity, a bottle of house white for the table.

'You'll have a glass with us?' he said to Alva.

'Thanks but no,' she smiled, 'not while I'm working.'

'You're taking all of this far too seriously, my pet.' Oscar eyed the respectable crowd at the tables. 'Now they've discovered an alternative to burger-chips-and-tepid-tea there'll be no keeping this lot away. Relax. You two've got it made.'

'Some of us have consciences.' Juno was unusually sharp. 'We believe in actually doing the work we're paid to do.'

There was a small silence. Alva, aware of other, waiting tables, knew she should leave but felt rooted.

'Glad to hear that, Juno.' Oscar was cool. 'Your country needs more people like you.'

'This *company* needs more of *you*, Oscar,' Juno said.

'Or are you doing the honourable thing and taking half pay while you double job on that TV mini-series?'

'That's all a vicious, jealous rumour.' Oscar was loftily unperturbed. 'I was visiting a friend on the set there, that's all.' He gave Juno's hand a reassuring pat. 'It's a lovely day, my dear. Enjoy and don't be argumentative.'

'Nice one, Oscar.' Juno beamed her monkey-smile at him. 'I'd want to change the subject too if I was working on something called *Death in Ennis*. Are they serious about the name?'

'Absolutely.' Oscar shrugged and looked at his watch. 'Oh, dearie dear me. I *must* make a call. Can I borrow your mobile, Juno? My batteries are down.'

Jasper, quietly eating until now, allowed himself a smile and a few words. 'You want to have that mobile of yours checked, Oscar,' he said. 'People are complaining your batteries don't last any length of time.'

'Things are in a sorrier state than I thought around here if I'm begrudged the odd phone call.' Oscar picked up Juno's phone and turned his back while he dialled.

'Some people,' Juno shrugged, 'get away with murder.'

'People like Constance Moore?' Jasper smiled.

'Her too.' Juno stood. 'I'm off to see Nick Hunt. He's in wardrobe – we're hoping to start on his part next week. Prepare yourself, Alva,' she grinned, 'the Hunt bod is something worth feasting your eyes on.'

By the end of the first week, and despite a mood which seemed constantly fraught, word on the daily rushes was good. Film, once shot, was couriered to London to be developed and brought back next day. Delays were causing chaos, and bitter recriminations about Zippo, the courier company hired by Jack Kelly. Hysteria reached epidemic proportions when a Zippo minion managed temporarily to lose the stock shot of the scene in the dining room. When it turned up the angry calm was almost as awesome.

Three nights after she'd watched the shooting of the scene Alva slipped quietly into the back of the converted bedroom and viewed the rushes. In all there were some half-dozen people in the room, including, together in a row, the director, producer and David Blake. Clara sat in front of them, wrapped in a woolly jumper and playing an unconvincingly laconic role for all she was worth. Leo Cullen sat behind them and apart. No one spoke while the footage, raw, unedited, but clearly more than good, rolled on the screen in front of them.

'Well, thank God we didn't lose *that*.' David Blake mopped his brow as the lights came on. Leo Cullen moved and stood by the door, obviously intent on giving his views briefly from there. Alva decided to wait, offer congratulations too.

'Amen,' Felim Gray agreed quietly. 'It's looking OK, Luke.' He put an arm, briefly, around the director's shoulder. 'You're doing the boy proud. It's really shaping up into the film he wrote.'

'There's a bit to go yet,' the director said, 'but with less interference and a bit more give on the budget we'll make it. Good work, you two.' He nodded, smiling, at David Blake and Clara.

'I need a brandy.' The actor got up. 'For my heart.' Sighing, settling a Paisley scarf about his neck, he left the room. Along with everyone else he seemed to have forgotten Alva was present.

'He's pleased,' Clara smiled, 'it's just his way of showing it.' She turned to Luke, smile replaced with a concern which created a deep furrow on her high forehead. 'I've heard talk of budget cuts. I *could* ask, I suppose, but really I prefer to keep things between us three. What's the problem? Will these cuts be deep?'

'It's not your problem.' As the director put a hand on her shoulder and spoke quietly Alva was struck by the easy intimacy between them and surprised to find herself wondering just *how* intimate they were. Looking from one to the other as they stood there she became uncomfortably aware that in fact her surprise was at her own, very real, feeling of jealousy. It was a disease. The turbulent emotions all round were getting to her.

'I don't want you thinking or worrying about anything but Constance Moore and what we're doing here.' Luke kept his hand on the actress's shoulder. 'We're going to make a damn good film from this script, Clara, for the sake of a lot of people . . .'

'Hopefully, I'm one of them.' Felim Gray spoke lightly. 'Why don't we move off? I'll buy you both a drink on the way back to town.'

'You're on.' O'Hanlon pushed back his chair and the others stood with him.

Alva, as they turned towards the door, found herself facing them alone. Leo Cullen had slipped through the door. She had the awful sensation of being caught out of bounds, of being an intruder in her own house.

'I . . . wanted to tell you how good I thought the scene was . . .'

Clara smiled. 'Thank you, Alva. You should have joined us, not stayed back there with that chatterbox Leo.'

'I came in late . . .' Alva heard herself making excuses and stopped, all at once annoyed at them for their exclusivity, for making her feel like an intruder. Annoyed at herself too for feeling annoyed.

'Let me know the next time you want to view.' Luke O'Hanlon was cool. 'Independent comment is always welcome.'

Alva stared at him. His sarcasm was palpable, so thinly disguised it was almost physical. O'Hanlon did *not* think her view was an independent one. Just who or what interests did he imagine she was representing here?

'I would certainly like to view again,' she held his gaze, 'and my views are *always* my own.' She nodded to all three in turn and left the room quickly.

She thought about the director's attitude as she got ready for bed. She was beginning to see, all too clearly, what Oscar had meant when he said that film companies thrived on division, cliques and intrigue. Since nothing, obviously, was sacred or secret it was likely

182

that Luke O'Hanlon knew she'd had meetings with Jack Kelly – and completely misunderstood. It was clear he saw her as someone whose view of things was influenced by the executive producer. A righteous anger kept her awake for quite some time.

She had a headache next morning and looked sourly at Bernie, kneading dough in a chambray dress with scooped neck. Since the film unit's arrival Bernie had taken to wearing something different every day, a habit in stark contrast to the granny-print overalls she'd invariably worn before. The lavishness of her wardrobe stunned Alva.

'Nice dress.' Alva ground out the words between taking a couple of Disprin.

'Thanks.' Bernie knew a bad humour when she saw one. 'Same old T-shirt, I see. We *did* get out of bed on the wrong side this morning, didn't we?'

'Got *in* on the wrong side, more like.' Alva began making the coffee. Breakfast was important to the unit but she and Bernie had decided it was not an area in which they could profitably compete with Food's Up, who provided a traditional fry. Even so, there were usually a half-dozen stalwarts for Bernie's scones when hot. As she worked she told Bernie about the viewing and Luke O'Hanlon's attitude afterwards.

'Hmmn.' Bernie looked thoughtful. 'Jasper seems to think Luke has a *very* personal interest in the film . . .'

'He's right,' Alva said. 'Apparently it originated with him but was subsequently swallowed into the whole wider project of a half-dozen Euro films.'

'I know that,' Bernie put scones onto an oven tray, 'but Jasper says there's a complication, that Luke has an agenda of his own, something personal.' She put a first tray into the oven. 'Anyway, who cares? The whole lot of them are divided into factions. It's a pain in the ass, if you want my opinion. Jasper agrees with me. He says not to get involved. He doesn't.' She straightened up.

Juno was right about Nick Hunt. He was ridiculously handsome, just over six feet tall and with broad shoulders over which he constantly draped a white tennis jumper. He had gold-blond hair and had trained a lock to fall over his blue, blue eyes. His self-assurance was so awesome as to be comical. It was as if he genuinely believed the world had been created to revolve around him. He was also naïve and likable and believed that looking as he did would get him everything and everyone he wanted in life. So far it had. Nick Hunt was twenty-two.

Watching him with Justine was like looking at an example of the perfect human pairing. Getting closer gave the lie to it all. Nick Hunt and Justine O'Dea did not get on. They did not like each other and there was absolutely no sexual chemistry between them. They had yet to do a scene together but if the negative vibes, not to say antipathy, between them were anything to go by, their screen coupling was going to be lukewarm, if not disastrous.

It was not until the day before they were due to do their first scene together that Alva realized that Justine, at least, was aware of and worried about the pitfalls ahead.

Filming had begun in the garden and most of the unit were concentrated there when Alva decided to go for a run. It was a warm day with light breezes, and the restrictions of De Novo were getting to her. Her body screamed for the liberation of a quick burn and she knew, belting down the avenue, that she was overdoing it but pushed herself, down the hill and up again, panting and paining and wanting to become tired and sweaty and revitalized. To feel alive again.

Jack Kelly's limo pulled alongside her as she gasped back up the avenue, the window rolling down without a breath of sound.

'Can I give you a lift somewhere?' His look was amused and Alva, in her loose white T-shirt and cycling shorts, felt ludicrously exposed. She rubbed her sticky palms on the end of the T-shirt.

'I started so I'll finish,' she said.

'I'll walk with you.' He got out of the car and they walked, Alva setting a brisk pace, back to the house. She towelled, changed her T-shirt and brought him the coffee he wanted in the sitting room.

'I was kinda hoping you'd call.' He pulled a rueful, good-natured face when she handed it to him. 'But I guess things are working out OK for you here.' He took the coffee to an armchair by the window. 'What's your feeling on the mood on the set?' He asked the question abruptly, legs crossed and balancing the mug on the peak of his knee.

'Difficult to say,' Alva spoke slowly, 'since I've no experience of how a film set works. There are what everyone takes for granted as everyday ups and downs, fits of temperament, that sort of thing.' She grinned. 'I've seen as bad, even worse, working on newspapers. Seems to me to be jogging along fine and what I've seen of the film looks good.'

'But at a cost.' Jack shrugged. 'Budget's gone way over and the director doesn't seem able or willing to rein in. I tell you, Alva, this one's getting to me. We're going right along the line to meet O'Hanlon and he's not giving an inch. He's got Clara Butler, great draw and a Dubliner—'

'Is she? Only there seem to be some doubts about her background . . .'

'She's a Dubliner. We'll produce the family and proof in time. We don't need to yet. Clara apart, I got him two of the sexiest young actors around for the lovers. And I'm paying them, by God am I paying them. He's got David Blake, a fine cameo actor, but he costs money too. And now, when I ask for a few, reasonable cuts in the script he goes ape about contracts and interference.' He let out a deep breath. 'Sorry to load you with this, Alva. But I reckoned I owed it to you to tell you where things are really at. Great coffee.' He took a gulp.

'Explain to me about the script,' Alva said slowly. 'Surely a decision to make changes is the scriptwriter's, not the director's?'

Jack shook his head. 'Not necessarily and not with this one. O'Hanlon's got himself a watertight contract on the issue of the script. He came up with it in the first place.'

'Luke wrote it?'

'Nope, O'Hanlon didn't write it.' The exec-producer uncrossed his legs and studied the coffee in its mug. 'Just acquired the rights to it. Fact is, I went up front with my own money on this one because I believe in the Irish film industry. The other backers came along because I put myself out on a limb. Now I find myself with not enough control . . .' He left the chair and began to pace. Alva could sense his frustration, see it in the whiteness of the knuckles holding the coffee mug. For whatever reason Jack Kelly needed control – probably he was one of those people who felt things would never work out unless done his way. The phrase divide and conquer came to her and she mentally shook her head. If Jack thought she had insider information on O'Hanlon's thinking and plans he was wrong. Even if she had she didn't want to become involved in the film-makers' intrigues and machinations. What she could do was listen. She owed Jack that much at least.

She crossed her legs and leaned back, deliberately relaxed. 'Look, Jack, I really don't know anything about budgets. Would it help if you told me what's worrying you about the script?'

'Might do.' He looked at her briefly before standing with his back to her by the window. 'What we're looking for here, Alva, and what we're paying for, is a good, commercial movie. One that'll bring the punters in their millions to the box office. Problem with the script is it's too wordy. Way O'Hanlon's dealing with it we could end up with a half-cocked, half-assed, feminist statement and no story.' He turned and faced her. With the light behind him she couldn't see his eyes but she'd have bet money against them smiling.

'Don't get me wrong. I'm not saying there isn't a place for feminist philosophy in film today. Makes commercial sense to have some of it in there. A sympathetic treatment of women is part of the times we live in.' He shoved his hands into his pockets. 'But this is *not* that kind of film and I'm worried about the distortion of a good story.' He sat down again and loosened his tie, grey silk on a darker grey shirt. He opened the collar and top buttons on a thatch of black-grey chest hairs. 'Wish like hell I could be here more often than every ten days . . .'

'You're here now.' Alva stood, touched him on the shoulder and smiled. 'So why don't we take a look at the filming? They're in the garden . . .'

'Good idea.' He stood and pulled her to her feet beside him. He was close enough for her to get the faint, clean smell of him and to feel self-conscious, again, about her cycling shorts, the dead sweat lingering from her run.

He dropped her hand and touched her cheek. 'You're very lovely,' he said. 'Maybe, when I get back, we could have dinner?'

'Sounds good,' Alva said and was surprised at how pleased he looked. They smiled at one another, friendly, acknowledging a liking. Maybe even something more.

'Jack? Jaa-ck, where are you?'

They'd reached the sitting-room door when Justine's voice, high and pleading, sounded in the hallway. Kelly lifted Alva's hand and kissed the finger-tips lightly. 'Until the next time,' he said and stepped into the hallway.

Justine O'Dea was standing in the main doorway. She was wearing pink, a floating slip-dress which, against the light, revealed her long, slim legs and the way the filmy stuff balanced on her nipples. A gossa-mer, fantasy creature, she raised a hand and looped a lock of sun-dazzled hair behind an ear. As a graceful, flirtatious gesture it was perfect.

'Jack!' She held out her hands and he took them, drawing her to him and kissing her on both cheeks. She had on thin high heels and they made her taller than he was.

'You look wonderful, Justine, just wonderful.' He dropped her hands and stood back admiringly. Justine played with a lock of hair. She ignored Alva.

'Jack,' she sighed breathily, 'I *have* to talk to you about Nicky. I can't see how ...' Her voice rose. 'There's nothing *there*, Jack. It's not going to work.'

'It had better work, Justine.' Jack Kelly was brusque. 'I got you the rawest sex-fiend around and you just better make sure the audience knows why Julia doesn't want to give him up ...'

'But I don't have any decent scenes.' In one swift movement Justine slipped out of the high heels and clasped them to her breast. Barefooted and smaller than him now she looked up at Kelly. 'The whole film's being made around Clara. Luke seems to think she's the only one who matters. She and Felim Gray and Luke are like a holy bloody trinity. No one else gets a look in.' She took a long, trembly breath. 'I can't seem to get it through to Luke that Julia is *pivotal*, and getting to talk to Felim is like getting an interview with the dead. You have to do something, Jack, before we begin shooting my scenes.'

'Trust me, Justine baby.' Jack put an arm about her shoulder. He was avuncular, reassuring. 'Everything'll be sorted out. You're not to worry about a thing. Give the part your best shot and leave the rest to me. Now,' without taking his arm from about Justine he reached and drew Alva to them, 'why don't the three of us take a look at what's happening outside?'

In the garden they stood with Theo, well back from the business of getting a close-up of Clara, as Constance, pruning roses. From Theo's relatively calm expression it was obvious she knew what she was doing.

She was wearing navy-blue and her hair had been coiled and put into a net. She looked a much older woman than the one who'd suffered her husband's insults at the dining-room table. They did the close-up three times, Constance's look of melancholy distress increasing each time.

When it was over Luke called for a break and strolled to where Jack Kelly stood with Alva and Justine.

'If the weather holds we'll get the outdoor stuff wrapped up in a few days.' He smiled at Justine. 'We're changing your garden stroll with Nick from Monday morning to the late afternoon.'

'Why?' Justine stared at him, managing to inject both a tear and a drop of ice into the one word.

'Because the light will be softer around four o'clock, more romantic.' The director spoke as if to a recalcitrant child. It was not, Alva thought, the right tone at all. 'And because I want to do a follow-up sequence with Clara in the morning, where she finds a bird in pain and kills it.'

'There, I told you!' Justine turned a tearfully triumphant face to Jack Kelly. 'Extra scenes for Clara – there's nothing in the script about a dead bird – while my part is shifted around and delayed. At this rate it'll be a miracle if Julia makes more than a two-minute appearance . . .'

'Can we talk, Luke?' Jack Kelly asked.

'Sure, Jack.' The director's voice was neutral. 'Production office trailer OK with you? I need to collect some stuff there.'

'Wait! Before you go I've a proposition I want to put to you guys. Alva too.' Clara, pruning knife still in her hand, blocked their way. 'A money-saving proposition.' She smiled at Jack.

'You're going to agree to a few less scenes, then? Let us get on with the rest of the film?' Justine, flushed and flint-eyed, swung her magnificent hair.

'Oh dear, oh dear, jealousy is not a pretty emotion.' Clara yawned and handed the knife to a hovering gofer. 'It distorts even the most appealing of faces. You really should watch it, my dear.'

'You're the one should watch it,' Justine's teeth were clenched, 'though it's probably too late since everything's behind you. On reflection, you're right to make the most of this part, Clara darling. It's likely to be your last.'

'So young and yet so far-seeing,' Clara laughed. 'Let's hope my demise sells a few seats.' She threw a merry look the way of the assembled crew, inviting them to share the joke. There were a few feeble titters and a honk from an overhead seagull. Clara sighed. 'The reality, my dear Justine, as you will realize when you come to my age, is that only time can tell. And some advice: a bit of work on your part *now* might ensure that you actually *have* a career when you reach my age. Well,' she turned to the two men, 'my proposition. Can we step into the bushes?'

Bluntly conversational, out of earshot of the crew and behind the covering of hydrangea and *aralia elata*, Clara put her proposal.

'I'd like to move into the De Novo for the rest of the shoot,' she said. 'It makes sense, if you think about it. I've already got a bedroom at my disposal for dressing, I'll simply sleep there nights too. Meals won't be a problem.' She flashed Alva a smile. 'Damn costumes allow me barely a scratch of food.' She turned the full effect of her green-grey eyes on the exec-producer. 'You must see the benefits, Jack. It'll save money, be a hell of a lot cheaper than the chrome and cement tower of Babel you've got me staying in at the moment. And with the night scenes coming up it'll be handier too – plus I'll have more time with my lines and be a damn sight better rehearsed, living here with the role, so to speak.'

'Sounds like a smart move.' Jack appeared to be thinking out loud. 'And I take your point about the rehearsal advantages. Could even save us a day or two. OK with you, Alva?' He ignored Luke O'Hanlon. Alva, after the briefest hesitation, told them what they wanted to hear.

'Fine,' she said. 'I'll root out fresh linen for the bed.'

What difference, she thought, can one more person in the house make?

The difference, had she really thought about it, would be that Clara would now be a part of De Novo. And that would change everything.

Chapter Eleven

Clara Butler, aka Clara Devlin, disagreed with John Donne. In her opinion the poet had been quite wrong when he'd pronounced that 'no man is an island'. As far as she was concerned every man and every woman was exactly that: an island, ultimately alone in the world and capable of surviving its lunacy only when they recognized their aloneness.

Since discovering this truth for herself, in her young teens, she had tried always to live by it, to be sufficient unto herself and not lean on others. With a few notable exceptions she'd managed.

The night she moved her bags and chattels into the big, high-ceilinged room at De Novo she felt relief. She also felt in touch with herself in a way she hadn't managed since coming back to Dublin. She would be alone here, wrapped in the peace of the old house, once the unit packed up each day. The modern hotel had been a nightmare, a hive of gossip, grievance and plot. Here she could think, get inside the head of the woman Constance Moore had become while she lived with her secret in this house. Or, at least, one very like it.

She could also think about and try to put the past into perspective. It was time.

The weeks filming in the streets, the stupidity of

allowing herself to be pushed into publicity before family things were sorted out – it had all been a mistake. Here, in this house, she could be in Dublin without being a part of it.

The people who lived in De Novo would not bother her.

Now *there* was a trio of islands, if ever there was. Together but alone, each of them, in their own, self-contained world. Clara wondered about them, but not for long. She had her thoughts on her own world to sort out.

But for a long time, the afternoon she moved in, Clara sat and thought of nothing. The day's shoot had ended early and she wouldn't be needed until the afternoon of the following day. It was the first time, since filming had begun, that she'd had time alone. Twilight became dusk and then a dark, starless evening, and still she sat with the curtains open, watching the night deepen, feeling her mind empty itself.

When she was good and ready she let the memories come. They'd been there all the time anyway, crouched in waiting, ready to pounce once she gave the nod. She lit a cigarette, and that too was part of the plan. She'd given up cigarettes when she'd given up drink but the ritual of lighting up, dragging in, holding the cigarette gave life to the memories.

When Clara Devlin was six years old she decided her parents hated one another. It had taken another three years, and the birth of her twin brothers, before she realized that life, and the relationship between Ronnie and Dolores Devlin, was more complicated than that. Her parents hated each other all right, but not all of the time. Sometimes they fought out of love and sometimes out of hate. Her father drank and her mother hated him for that. Her mother nagged and followed him to the pub and her father hated *her* for that. But in the rare in-between times they were gentle with one another and it was then their daughter could see how things had been with them and why they'd married in the first place.

Ronnie Devlin was handsome, after a heavy, square fashion, with a head of dark red hair which he passed on to his only daughter. His wife Dolores had, as a young woman, been too pretty for her own good. An only child, whose mother had died when she was two, she'd lived with her arthritic father over his newsagent's shop. She'd never seen why she should refuse the advances of the oversexed and under-employed young men of the inner-city neighbourhood.

She and Ronnie Devlin met when she was seventeen, and on her eighteenth birthday they married. He was nineteen, she was six months' pregnant, and they moved into the rooms over the shop with her father. Ronnie, unskilled and unwilling, worked only sporadically. Dolores worked with her father in the shop and dreamed of what might have been.

Dolores and Ronnie went on to have four children. Clara was their second, born two years after the baby they'd married to legitimize, a boy they called Danny. After Clara there was a welcome gap of seven years before the birth of the twins, Joseph and John.

Of all her children Dolores Devlin loved Danny the

best. She was not a naturally maternal woman and her daughter interested her not at all. Clara was a pretty child, and as she grew and was admired, Dolores's lack of interest turned to a jealous resentment and mindless punishments. Clara, as a result, spent a large part of her early childhood confined to the small dark room she shared with the twins, denied friends or toys. The much younger twins created their own self-preserving, enclosed little world and were no company.

Ronnie Devlin tried fathering as sporadically as he experimented with work, and with the same impatience. By the time he was thirty years old he had a son of eleven whom he knew hardly at all, a daughter of nine who was a stranger to him and twin sons of two years old who could have belonged to anybody.

Clara, old for her age, saw quite clearly that it was possible for love and hate to live together, for a mother not to love a child and for a father to be indifferent to his children.

She knew too that it was possible to pray on your knees to God every night that things might change, and for God not to listen.

Clara's grandfather died when she was nine. His passing created extra room for the family over the shop. It also released curbs on Ronnie Devlin's bullying tendencies. Rows with his wife became noisier, and a lot more violent.

When Clara was ten she saw her father hit her mother. The row was the same as all the others and her parents had forgotten she was there, eating cereal on a winter's afternoon at the kitchen table.

'You're a poison in my life.' His voice was low and venomous. 'I could've done things with my life if it wasn't for you. You got me to marry you with the oldest trick in the book . . .'

'Nobody forced you.' Her mother was immediately irate. She had grown thin and brittle over the years. 'You were the one did all the running.'

'It was you. You couldn't get enough of it. Like a bitch in heat, you were—'

'It was love!' Her mother gave a piercing shriek. 'I gave myself to you out of love.' She began to cry. 'Why can't you let us have a bit of peace, instead of always bringing up the past.'

'The past is what we are, Dolores; the past is the reason I'm here.' He caught and shook her by the shoulders. 'Danny, bloody Danny, the spoiled brat. He's the cause of it all. And a right fucking sissy boy you've made out of him too.'

'Someone has to care for him. You don't. All you think about is getting your face into your next pint—'

One of his hands left her mother's shoulder and, closed in a quick, merciless fist, smashed into the side of her jaw. 'Shut up,' he roared, 'just shut your bloody mouth and leave me alone.' Clara screamed as he pushed her reeling mother away from him and turned for the door – to meet the silently watchful gaze of his firstborn.

She would always remember her father and brother eyeing one another in terrible silence. Remember too how she prayed her father would not hit Danny. He didn't. What he did was, in retrospect, worse.

'Out of my way, nancy boy,' he snarled in disgust and brushed past the boy in the doorway.

By the time Danny Devlin was fourteen he'd been in court three times. By the time he was fifteen he was part of a tough, joy-riding fraternity. No one in their right mind would have accused Danny Devlin of being a sissy.

When he was killed, in a joy-riding crash when he was just sixteen, it was Clara, not her mother, who went to identify the body.

The morgue was an icy sepulchre. When they pulled back the sheet it was all she could do not to grab her brother's body, pull him from the ghoulish, white-draped trolley and run with him, away, anywhere. Death, as well as taking Danny from her, had shrivelled him. But his face, his thin, boy's face, was the same as it had been when he was nine or ten, pinched and small and sad. He had never ever been so still.

It was that, the terrible stillness, which confirmed for the fourteen-year-old Clara that her brother, the only person ever to look out for her, was dead.

'That's him?' The guard by her side was as gentle as a hulking man of over six feet could be. 'That's your brother?'

'That's Danny,' she said and touched his poor, cold, dead face. Tragedy, it is said, never comes single-handed. Two weeks after laying his eldest son in his grave, Ronnie Devlin, drunker than he'd ever been in his life, walked out of a pub and into the path of an oncoming car. He was killed instantly.

His wife and daughter and twin sons buried him

next to his firstborn. Their combined age was fifty-one.

They were like ghosts for a long while after that, Clara and the twins and her mother, silently inhabiting the space over the shop, living without really seeing one another. The twins became closer than ever and Clara's mother found God.

'I have sinned,' she told her children, 'I must mortify my flesh, pray to God for forgiveness. And you must all pray too, lest you fall into the ways of sin as I did.'

Clara had no difficulty ignoring all of this. Her mother's eyes reminded her of the icy, blue-painted eyes of the Madonna in the church where they went to mass. Our Lady of the Sorrows, the church was called, and its statue had a constant retinue of hollow-eyed women kneeling at her feet. Clara vowed never to become one of their number.

When she was sixteen she left home for London. The twins sat on her bed and watched her pack and her mother gave her a rosary. None of them suggested she stay.

London in the sixties was where Clara came to life. She looked older than she was, and was growing beautiful, and it would have been hard to find someone more willing to embrace the free-wheeling, exuberant spirit of the decade.

Mark Preston was an actor making a living mostly out of voice-overs. Clara met him when she'd been two years in London and was working in a Hampstead pub called the Blake Inn. She saw him notice her the minute he came in. Her skirt was micro, her tank-top tight, and when she reckoned he'd seen enough she served him, giving him the wayward smile she'd perfected, and tossing her long red hair.

'What'll it be?' she asked.

'You'll do,' he said. 'Come away with me, now.'

She looked at him. He had straight fair hair falling into grey eyes and a clean-cut, likable English face.

'I don't finish here for another hour,' she said.

'I'll wait,' he said and he did and that night they became lovers.

Mark Preston wasn't the first. There had been two before him. But he was the first man she really cared for and he was the one who would be responsible for changing the course of her entire life.

Three months into their relationship she was spending as much time in his attic apartment in Highgate as she was in her bedsit in humbler Holloway.

'You are wonderful and beautiful and I'm crazy about you,' he told her one night, 'but we must do something about your accent.'

'My accent?' she said sleepily, unprepared.

'Your accent, my darling. Nothing wrong with a regional accent, but your supersonic Dublin is *too* regional by far. We'll have to get you toned down.'

'We will . . .?' Clara moved away from his hand on her back. He played with her hair where it spread across the pillow.

'Hey, Clarakins, it's just a suggestion. You're wasted

behind that pub counter. You need to get out, use your assets. Become a receptionist or something. You've a lovely *voice*, nice timbre, all of that. It's just that your accent is ... well, too *strong*, frankly.' He tried to turn her to face him but she shook her head and lay there, aware of his growing erection and for once unmoved. 'Don't be mad at me ...' He buried his face in her hair and muttered apologies. Mark Preston was very well-mannered.

Clara wasn't angry with him. She simply wanted to think. See, maybe, if he had a point. Her accent had never bothered her. She even used it in the pub to get laughs. She hadn't given it a lot of thought, but was aware of all she had going for her and knew she didn't want to grow old pulling pints of bitter. She knew too that London was full of girls as pretty as she was and that an awful lot of them were receptionists, smiling dolls in psychedelic-coloured offices. Apart from not becoming one of them she hadn't the slightest idea what she wanted to do. Maybe changing her accent would help her decide. Also, if toning down her accent shook off another layer of where she'd come from, then what the hell – why should she hang on to it?

Mark had stopped apologizing but his body language had become more insistent. Clara, turning to his large and glorious erection, laughed.

'How do I go about getting voice classes?' she asked.

'I'll show you,' he grinned.

The voice teacher was American, an elderly Anglophile who lived at the top of the high old house he owned in Regent's Park. His name was Lewis Cleveland

Wilson, known to his pupils as LCW, and it amused him that as a Bostonian he should be a sought-after teacher of standard English speech in England.

In Clara, Lewis Cleveland Wilson saw a challenge. He was old enough and wealthy enough to allow himself the indulgence of following up such interest in a pupil. Ten minutes into their first class he told her she had a 'glorious resonance' and promised to eliminate her 'shudderingly harsh vowels'.

'I will give you a voice, Miss Devlin, of such melting appeal that people will pay to listen to it.' His long face was wryly humorous. 'I will be 'Enry 'Iggins to your Eliza. Fitting enough, since it was a countryman of yours who dreamed up the fiction in the first place.' He brought his grey eyebrows together and blew his nose in a spotted handkerchief. LCW was full of cultivated mannerisms. 'But you will *work*, Miss Devlin, or I will discontinue our classes. *My* efforts will not be sufficient. *You* must work every day.'

Clara worked and heard her voice change and realized that with effort and concentration she could do many, many things for herself. She spent less time in Mark Preston's flat, which wasn't what he'd had in mind when he suggested the classes, and a lot of time pacing her own small room, throwing her voice into its corners, hearing for herself what she could do with it.

The idea that she might act wasn't her own. It was LCW's and he mentioned it to her first by his cheerfully blazing fire on a dreary wintry night.

'Stage or screen?' She grinned at him.

'The choice would be yours.' He didn't smile. 'Your natural advantages suggest you would make an impact on the screen. Stage training, on the other hand, is in my opinion the equivalent to learning to ride a bike before entering the Tour de France.'

'I was joking, LCW.' Clara shifted uncomfortably under his gaze. It was assessing, the way he might size up one of his antique pieces before buying. 'I've never thought about acting . . .'

'Nor did you think about having your voice trained until it was suggested to you.' LCW took the one cigar he allowed himself each day, rolled it between his fingers and snipped the end. 'You've got the bones and the colouring to photograph well. You're bright and you're able to take direction. Look what we've accomplished, you and I, in three months. There's no reason why you shouldn't try for work in films.' He gave a small cough and watched the smoke spiral between them.

'I'm listening,' Clara said.

'Good. I am, as a rule, cautious about pushing my pupils towards what is a notoriously insecure profession. But in your case I have observed certain strong points . . .' He smiled a little. 'You don't so much listen as *absorb*, Miss Devlin. You *become* a piece of poetry when you say it. You even, instinctively, move to the different rhythms. In summary, you are a young woman of unusual, if not perfect, beauty, able to take direction and get into the mood of a piece of writing. Added to that, now that I've worked on it,' he positively beamed at her, 'is an extraordinarily pleasing voice.

So. If you want to take your chances in the world of film I can be of help to you.'

She thought about little else, but didn't say anything to Mark. No point, she thought, until LCW came up with something. She would surprise him then.

Things did not, however, go according to plan.

The first premonition, quickly dismissed, came with a missed period. But within days she was filled with a strange, limp exhaustion. She was three weeks overdue before she went to the doctor. It was only when her pregnancy was confirmed that she allowed herself to face the reality.

She was repeating her mother's life. The life she'd made for herself, the person she'd become, the life she was *going* to make – it would all be ruined if she had this baby. She would certainly lose Mark. He was a million years away from being ready to become a father. He would dump her and she would be on her own. There would be no acting, no screen test, not for an unmarried mother of nearly nineteen.

The thought of ending the pregnancy terrified her at first and she put it out of her mind. But it crept back, insidious, relieving, telling her it was the only way her new life could go on. She wished she could pray but she'd given that up too long ago to start now.

She told Mark because she didn't see how she could keep it from him. They were in bed and, when he reached for her, she found herself shivering.

'Are you ill?' his concern was so innocent.

'No. Yes.' Her teeth were rattling like a klaxon. 'I'm pregnant.'

The rattling stopped. She lay frozen stiff, on her back and not looking at him.

'You're joking.'

'I wish I was.'

'How long?'

Sensible question. She turned her head to look at him. He was lying on his back too, staring at the ceiling. She knew that at that moment she repelled him.

'Seven or eight weeks,' she said.

'Have you thought what you want to do?'

'Yes.'

She turned and slid from the bed. Her nakedness seemed inappropriate, disgusting, now that she knew he did not want her. She found and slipped into her jeans and sweater.

'I'm frightened.' She sat on the floor pulling on her boots. She didn't look up when she heard Mark leave the bed and pad her way. When he stood in front of her she kept her head down, studying his bare feet, the long toes on them.

'I'm in shock,' he said. 'I thought you were looking after that side of things. The Pill and all that . . .'

She said nothing and he hunkered in front of her. His nakedness didn't seem to bother him the way hers had minutes before.

'Seven weeks,' he repeated and stopped before he said, slowly, 'I can't marry you, Clarakins. It wouldn't work.'

'I haven't asked you to marry me.' She looked up at

him then, into his decent, worried face: 'And I don't want to marry you myself.'

It was true. In all of her dreams and schemes marriage had not been a factor. A glorious, endless, carelessly free love affair had been.

'I'll make some coffee,' he said and got up.

As soon as he left she gathered her things and slipped, silently and swiftly, out of the flat.

For two days she didn't answer either the phone or doorbell in the bedsit. She'd taken time off work and knew the persistent ringing had to be Mark. She needed time alone to psych herself up, make herself ready.

Mark, relieved and helpful when she called him at the end of two days, gave her the money for the abortion and booked her into a clinic. There was, he assured, nothing to it. He went with her the morning she signed in. It was a bright, clear October day and Clara felt absolutely calm, prepared. She smiled at the Jamaican nurse when she came for her.

Only she hadn't been prepared at all. Not for the floods of grief and tears, the agonizing sense of loss when it hit her a week later.

'It's the old RC guilt thing in you.' Mark, sitting with her in the bedsit, tried hearty cheer.

'No, it's not.' She was flat. 'It's nothing to do with being Catholic. It's hormonal. It'll pass. Maybe you should go now.'

Relieved, he went. What they'd had was gone and they both knew it. Clara crawled into bed and lay there, hopelessly sad and hopelessly crying. She felt as if she were falling apart and could do nothing about it.

But the despair and grief did pass, and when it happened she moved quickly to repossess her life. LCW, when she turned up after having missed two weeks' classes, was understanding.

'Don't explain,' he said, 'don't tell me.'

'I want to go to America,' Clara said, 'to Los Angeles. I want to take my chances there. Can you help me? Please, LCW . . .?'

'Give me a week,' he said, 'to call in some favours.'

The favours must have been large because what he got for her amounted to a whole new life. There was a place to stay and a place in an acting class. There were introductions, no strings attached, to two film-makers, the promise of a screen test from one.

'Thank you.' Clara, hugging him, was shocked at his frailty. He had always seemed so able and strong. 'I'll miss you,' she said, 'but I'll be back.'

'You won't, on either count,' he smiled.

It wasn't until years later, when she'd made a name and career for herself, that she realized how formidable his contacts had been and how ruthlessly he'd exploited them on her behalf. But by then LCW was dead, from a heart attack brought on, she was sure, climbing the steps to his top-floor room.

She went home to Dublin for two days before flying to California. It was the first time she'd been there since leaving three years before and she couldn't wait to get away again. At twelve years old the twins were inseparable and uneasy with her. Her mother was obsessed still with God and was, Clara decided, quite mad. None of the three of them seemed to take in what she told them about America and she really didn't care.

She left Heathrow for Los Angeles with one suitcase. Packing it she'd realized she would miss LCW more than anyone else she knew. He'd been, for a while, like a father to her.

Airborne, she looked down on the city she was already thinking of as a stepping stone. It was grey, a wintry pall everywhere. But she would miss London too, along with LCW.

Chapter Twelve

The Hollywood years had all the wild glitz of Clara's fantasies. They brought adoration, money, parties and fun, fun, fun. She bought a house in Long Beach, small, very Spanish-style and with a patio to breakfast on in the sun to the sound of the Pacific whenever she felt like it.

Not that she often did. Parties in Los Angeles began late and ended early and she went to a lot of them. And she worked. From the very beginning she worked.

It all happened relatively easily. As with swinging London, Clara merged seamlessly into the Los Angeles movie scene. The trick, she found, was to go with the tide. The difference in LA was the extra effort needed to keep from drowning. This she managed to do, for quite a while.

The brash informality and free-wheeling paranoia of LA life had her reeling a little at first, but luck and timing were with her even then. LCW's introductions gave her an entrée, she was seen by people who mattered, invited where it was useful to be seen, given a screen test and put on an agent's list. The drama classes cost money, and so did accommodation. But she'd never been work-shy, and waitressing came easy and tipped well.

She didn't have to do it for long. Riding on the coat-tails of a vogue for British and Irish actresses she got bit parts, a few lines here, a few there, the odd commercial. Nothing much but it put her name around. And LCW was proven right. Clara had screen presence and knew how to take direction.

When a small role was created for her in a period drama the studio suggested she change her name. They came up with the name too and she became Clara Butler. The film, mediocre though it was and small though her part, launched her career. Clara Devlin ceased to exist.

In the early years she made a lot of commercials, a few goodish films and some which were downright bad. Survival instincts sharply honed she refused to refuse work, took everything she was offered and put it down to experience.

She was right about the experience. By the time she was twenty-three she knew more about the technique of performing in front of cameras than many who'd been around a decade longer. She'd also made enough money to buy herself the Long Beach house and gained enough ambition and confidence to fire her agent, who was a friend of LCW's, and hire another.

She needed, she told Max Bliss, a terrier and not a pussycat. Max became her terrier, and he made her. He also, in the end, unmade her. The Hollywood years became divided for Clara into before and after Max periods.

'I'm going to make them pant for you,' he promised

at their first meeting. 'From now on you start saying no, except when I tell you to say yes. Got that?'

'Sounds clear enough. What if I disagree?'

'Then you disagree. But you still say no.' When he grinned his wizened face showed pure cunning. He was a tiny man, saved from absurdity by the sheer elegance of his hand-made clothes and the perfection of the little body on which they hung. He had been married four times and was heartily mourned by each of his ex-wives. He was ruthless and he was rich – the latter because he was so very, very good at representing those he worked for.

Clara looked at him thoughtfully. She had become used to, and grown to like, having her own way. 'But we are agreed that *you* will be working for *me?*' she asked.

He looked immediately bored. 'Of course. For fifteen per cent of everything you earn. Which is why I'm going to see to it that you earn a helluva lot.'

Clara made fewer pictures but, since they all had bigger budgets, a lot more money. Max worked for her, and himself, tirelessly. He created and pushed a new-look Clara Butler. Before Max she had been a second-string actress, in demand but not a big name. After Max she became the tempestuous, red-haired Irish star of several box-office hits.

'You *look* Irish, for Chrissakes,' he'd put down her initial misgivings about his publicity campaign, 'and looking Irish is commercial right now. So what if you weren't happy as a kid and don't want to go back to the Emerald Isle? That's got nothing to do with anything. Make an opportunity out of disaster, that's my motto. Use what you got.'

'Fine. Only we don't need to be specific, do we? I mean, bring my mother or brothers into this?' The idea of Dolores, or the gormless twins, popping up to claim her made Clara feel sick.

'They don't sound like they'd be an advantage.' Max shrugged.

'The appeal of the wild Celt is more what we're after. Barefoot in the mountains, back to nature, that sort of thing.' He laughed his hoarse laugh and lit another cigar. 'Trick is to swing with the times, sweetheart, and that's the sort of broad the times want.'

He was right. Her wildcat, earthy image took off and parts became bigger and better. Max managed everything. Clara didn't even have to do the lying herself. He sat in on all interviews and with skilful innuendo and adroit sidestepping managed to tell not a word of truth about her background. Clara, smitten by conscience, sent occasional cheques to the twins. They acknowledged them with the barest slivers of information about themselves and their mother. Clara didn't want to know anyway.

And then, slowly, the Hollywood years became a blur. The Clara Butler created by Max Bliss began to believe her own publicity. Bliss had done it, and bliss it was to be adored and loved, by millions for all she knew. Real-life affairs became rare. Clara Butler, rampaging sex-goddess, had little interest in sex and even less in the intimacy of a relationship.

Once introduced to the heady, liberating experience of drink and drugs she found them a lot more satisfying.

It happened quite slowly, and for a long time didn't affect her work. But by the time Clara was twenty-six the extravagant beauty who strode the screen was, for most of her off-camera life, either stoned or drunk. Day became night and night day, and whole weeks, then months, passed in palmy, robotic insensibility. The writing was on the wall and anyone who could read was reading it. It being LA, no one told her. Except Max, and only then when it began seriously to affect her work.

'The industry still likes you, Clara; don't blow it.' They were beside her pool and she was half-asleep. He touched a limp, dangling hand to get her attention and she twitched as if a fly had landed and opened her eyes. 'It won't always need you,' he said. 'Get yourself dried out, detoxed. Whatever it takes.'

'Why? I'm fine.' She felt great, apart from a headache. A longer snooze would get rid of that. She wanted very much to close her eyes again.

Max Bliss stood up. 'There's blood being shed for parts you could still, if you got your act together, walk right into. But things are changing. Fast. And so's your reputation. Don't say I didn't warn you.'

Clara gazed blearily into the pool. 'Needs filtering,' she said. Max Bliss left. His golden goose had stopped laying and Clara Butler's time at the top was ending. It was time to find another goose to cook.

Clara was headed for the scrap heap, oblivion and possible death when her mother died and saved her.

Dolores Devlin was buried while her daughter was on a two-week binge in San Diego. It fell to Max Bliss, a final duty, to find and tell Clara. He did so with blunt impatience, telling her he'd been on the point of having her declared dead along with her mother.

'You made me a lot of money one time, princess.' He was uncharacteristically gentle as he put her on a plane for Dublin. 'So do yourself a favour now. Stay off the booze while you're back in the old country.'

Clara spent two weeks in Dublin, her first visit since going to California. Her mother, after a five-year decline into premature senility, had died quietly in her sleep. The shop had been sold years before, to make way for an up-market apartment complex, and the twins, at twenty-one shy and serious-minded, had bought one. They were close as ever and, though seeming pleased to see her, their cool blue eyes were her mother's eyes.

'She went to see your films whenever they came around,' John, the slightly less shy one, said to her one day.

'You don't have to say things like that to me,' Clara said, 'you know she couldn't stand the cinema.'

They smiled at one another and for brief seconds their mother came to life between them.

Clara didn't drink while in Dublin and when the pills she'd brought ran out she did without. It wasn't so hard. Her mother, in dying, had filled her with a terrifying sense of her own mortality and a raging desire to live.

When she went back to California she sold the

house, crossed the continent and bought another, smaller but also on a beach, on Long Island. It was the furthest she could imagine being from Los Angeles without actually leaving North America. She cut links, finding it frighteningly easy to do, and went into analysis. She found she didn't miss California at all.

'Let me help you.' Clara had seen the man before, walking on the beach in the evenings, when she came there herself. She'd never spoken to him. She didn't speak to any of the people on the beach. Two years after moving to this corner of Long Island she was still apart from the small community. It was how she wanted things. And now this man, with his probably well-meant offer to help with the sticking gate, was interfering. She wasn't having it.

'Thank you. I can manage.' She turned her back and pulled at the gate. It held firm. When she pulled again it moved deeper into the sand. 'Damn thing is supposed to be maintained,' she said. The man was still by her side. 'Perhaps you might, after all, open it for me?' She smiled, briefly so as not to encourage him, and looked properly at his face for the first time.

He was handsome and the other side of middle age, nearing sixty she guessed, with neatly trimmed white hair and openly curious dark eyes.

'Be delighted to.' He smiled easily, put both hands on the gate and lifted it out of its sandy furrow. 'I'll do a job on it tomorrow ...' He paused. 'Jack Darrow died, you know.'

'Jack . . . died?' She hadn't known. Jack Darrow was the maintenance man for the strip of beach guarded by the gate and shared by some half-dozen houses. He kept the sand clean and garbage pails in order. Clara had spoken to him once or twice but hadn't missed him. 'When did he die?'

'Two weeks ago. Heart attack – but then he hadn't been well. It was a small funeral.' The man watched her as he spoke. His expression was kind, and still curious.

'I suppose . . . everyone,' she gestured at the cluster of houses, 'went along?'

'Most of us, yes. He didn't have any family, you see. None that could be traced anyway.'

Us. So he owned one of the houses. Most of us . . . *She* hadn't been there. 'I'm sorry. I didn't know.' A sharp gust of wind blew her coat open and she pulled it tighter. 'I would have gone . . .' She spoke half to herself.

'One of us should have told you.' He was apologetic, sounding as if the fault were entirely his. When he added, 'It's cold, standing here. May I walk with you?' it seemed in the circumstances impossible to say no.

Larry K. Palmer was a widower with three grown children. He was a partner in a corporate law firm in New York and owned the largest house on the beach. He was sixty years old and Clara married him seven months later.

Marriage to Larry brought her a peace she'd only ever dimly imagined. She told him so, over and over.

They loved one another with an unquestioning joy, accepting that they had been meant to meet and share one another. There was no other way to explain their happiness.

They had been married eighteen months when Clara had a son. They called him Danny, after her dead brother. He had Clara's hair and his father's eyes and when he was two years old his brother, Frederick, called after Larry's father, was born.

Clara, an ecstatic mother, decided two children was as much as she could give her best to and called a halt. Larry was relieved.

'Don't know that I've the energy left for an Irish-sized brood,' he said.

'You'd manage,' Clara said, 'but I mightn't.'

They lived, for the most part, in Larry's five-bedroom apartment on the west side of Central Park. Weekends they headed, almost always, out of the city to his Long Island house. The apartment was grand in the real sense, with spacious rooms leading from one to the other in a semicircle which ended in a magnificent, horseshoe-shaped room overlooking Central Park.

Max, for all his faults, had made a few wise investments for Clara and she wasn't penniless. With this, her second bite at the cherry, she had it all and knew it. An occasional, niggling demon of insecurity worried her that it might disappear. It was a tiny discomfort in a world which was never meant to be perfect.

'God, I'd forgotten it was so awful!' Clara, curled in

front of the TV, shuddered. 'Why on earth would they choose to show this one?'

'Because there's a lot of you to see,' Larry, grinning, didn't shift his gaze from the screen, 'and because it's so quintessentially of its time. In the way Clara Butler was a creation of those times.'

Clara fought the urge to smoke. Watching her old films rekindled the urge for a cigarette but not for anything else that had been part of those years. The one they were watching, *Love's Loss*, was cheap hip and cheap flash and Clara's wardrobe ran the gamut of bikini to hot pants to, on one occasion, a towel.

'Do you really want to see the whole thing?' Clara's desperation for a cigarette grew.

'Not if it's going to bother you.' Larry pressed the remote and the screen went dark. 'Let's go to bed.'

In the bedroom Clara paced.

'What bothers me,' she stopped to check in the mirror briefly for Clara Palmer, 'was that I knew that picture was dross and still I made it, happily. For the money.'

'The moral high ground doesn't suit you, Clara.' Larry, waiting for her in bed, was dry. 'You're too much the pragmatist. So you grabbed a chance for money and security – and why the hell shouldn't you have? Now – what's really troubling you?'

Clara plopped onto the bed and took his hand in hers. Lying with her head on his chest she considered the ceiling. 'I know I can act but I've never really proven it. Never even tried to. I learned camera techniques and used what natural assets I had. It's the equivalent,' she turned her head and looked at him, 'of your playing golf without ever even *trying* for a hole in one.'

Larry, an avid golfer, stroked her hair absently and nodded. 'I suppose it is,' he said and she knew his habit of linear thinking would make him ask the obvious question. 'What do you propose to do about it?'

'It's occurred to me,' Clara spoke slowly, 'that I should give the stage a try. The boys are at school most of the day. I've got the time. I'd really like to see if I can do it.'

It wasn't easy; nothing like breaking into the movie scene in seventies Hollywood. She was a mid-thirties 'retired' film actress with no stage experience and an uncertain cv. The New York theatre world was exclusive and competitive.

But her curiosity value, undeniable presence and the fact that she might, just possibly, be a box-office pull, got her an audition. She took to the boards in a modest, off-Broadway production of *After the Fall* and both she and the play got good reviews. It ran for three months and by that time she'd got another off-Broadway offer. She also knew she could act.

The party at which she and Larry met Luke O'Hanlon was large and stylish, given for a visiting Irish theatre company on St Patrick's Day. She'd liked him immediately but it was with Larry, retired now, that Luke had developed the closest friendship. He'd at the time been making a name for himself with cutting edge TV documentaries, dramatic in style and controversial in content. Only weeks after the party he'd enlisted Larry's help on a programme dealing with a legal scam. The result had hit a lot of people where it hurt and been compulsively viewable. They celebrated with a dinner in the apartment.

'Larry tells me your boys have never been to Dublin.' Luke O'Hanlon, opposite Clara, stopped a Roquefort grape halfway to his mouth. 'Why not?'

'When they're older they'll no doubt go on their own. I was very young when I left, Luke. I've no real desire to go back.' Clara was smiling, polite and very firm. What he didn't understand, and she didn't feel like explaining, was that they might have come from different cities for all their backgrounds had in common.

'You can tell me it's none of my business, of course,' Luke was gently sardonic, 'but I think you're denying them the experience of a lifetime. It's the other half of their birthright, and all that.'

'It's none of your business.' Clara, her smile slightly chill, indicated to the waiter that he should refill glasses.

'Dublin's changed,' Luke said, 'and so have you.' He smiled and it occurred to her that maybe he understood more than she gave him credit for.

When he next came to the apartment Luke brought his brother with him. Eric O'Hanlon was everything Luke wasn't – dreamy where Luke was nervily alert, a listener while Luke talked. He was physically different too, shorter and fairer, with a fine-boned poet's face and large brown eyes gazing myopically from behind wire-framed glasses. At twenty-eight he was younger than Luke by five years. Handing him a beer, Clara asked him what he did.

'Hard to put a name on it.' He gulped half the beer and looked at her apologetically. Clara had to strain to hear him. 'I do development work in Latin America. I'm here because I've just finished a three-year stint on an educational project in Peru.'

'You're planning to work in New York, then?' Clara indicated an armchair opposite but, standing awkwardly with the half-finished beer, he didn't seem to notice. She sat herself and he continued to talk to her, staring into the glass.

'Sort of,' he admitted. 'I'm here to do something I hope will raise money for a project in Colombia . . .'

He hesitated and Clara, curious but impatient, made an 'oh?' sound as encouraging as she could. Luke's brother was a strangely diffident soul, a bit of a dreamer, she reckoned. She hoped his money-raising scheme didn't require Eric O'Hanlon to market or hype it up.

'I think you can help me.' He looked at her directly for the first time, and smiled. 'I'd appreciate it very much if you would.' As smiles went it was angelic and totally disarming and made Clara think she was wrong, in part at least, about Eric O'Hanlon. His smile alone probably got him most of the things he wanted in life.

'I asked Luke to bring me here because I wanted to meet you.' He smiled again.

'Oh?' Clara's interrogative sound was a lot more cautious this time. He didn't appear to notice and sounded, for him, quite lively as he went on.

'It's to do with a screenplay I'm writing. I want you to talk to me, help me develop the main character . . .'

'I've never written anything in my life.' Clara's protest was dismissed with a wave of his hand.

'I'm not asking you to *write*. Just to talk. The plot's fine, based on a true story I've known about for a long time, and set in turn-of-the-century Dublin. What I'm having difficulties with are some of the dramatic techniques and the character. She's a murderess.'

'I've never murdered anyone either.'

'You're a woman.' He didn't smile. 'And you've been a screen actress and you grew up in Dublin. I want you to help me understand what might have happened to this woman *after* the murder, how she would have been with her daughter.' He wasn't asking, Clara realized. He was assuming she'd help.

'Where does making money come into this?' she hedged.

'Luke's going to film it. He'll raise as much as possible for the script.' He blinked at her and smiled.

He was so very positive, Clara thought, so very certain. So unreal.

'It's not that easy, Eric.' She was gentle. 'Luke will have to get backing. He won't get that unless the script's really good *and* sure of making money . . .'

223

'It *is* good and it will make money.' Eric sat down at last and pulled a diary from his pocket. 'Luke's already got a promise of some backing from a TV company. I could bring the script over tomorrow.'

'Why not?' Clara gave in.

What Clara hadn't considered was that Eric O'Hanlon could write. The script, when he brought it over to her, was a revelation. The writing was sharp and passionate, the plotting sure and professional. Working with him, having read it, Clara knew she was a sounding board, nothing more. He finished the screenplay for *Death Diminishes* six weeks after she'd first spoken with him and, with a wry grin, attached the pseudonym Oliver O'Casey.

'I prefer anonymity,' he explained. 'I can't deal with the razzmatazz of the film world the way Luke can.'

It was, as he'd promised, very good. Clara had absolutely no doubt that it would make a fine film.

'I'm going to put money into it,' she told Larry on what would be their last weekend in the Long Island house. 'Don't ask me why – I'm working on gut instinct. It's good and . . . I want to be involved.'

'Fine. But why not go a step further?' Larry's arm on her shoulder turned her into the wind and back towards the house. A grey sea sent white-capped waves crashing along the shore. They stopped to watch for a while before Clara, knowing the answer, asked, 'A step further?'

'Play the part,' Larry said. 'You know the character and you know Dublin.' He stopped. 'You'd be going

back there on your own terms, as an actress with a job
to do. It's the way to do it, Clara.'

'I'll think about it,' she said.

'When you decide, I'll put money into the film too,'
Larry said.

Luke, hosting a party in his small apartment to celebrate the launch of his Silver Apple production company, was euphoric.

'We can't lose,' he said. 'We've got a script and
we've got a star and we've got one of the world's best
locations. The aim is to be in Dublin, shooting, before
the end of the year. Here's to *Death Diminishes*.' He
raised his glass and they drank. 'To NYTV9 for its
backing.' They drank again. 'And to Larry and Clara
Palmer,' he was quieter, 'who're putting their money
where their faith is.'

There were more people than the apartment could
hold. Larry disliked crowds and Clara was edging them
both quietly out when Eric caught her arm. He was
wearing his apologetic look again. 'I've a friend wants
to meet you,' he said, 'a fan.'

'Hi.' The woman with him was large, with pale eyes
and a mass of blond hair which needed cutting. 'I'm
Marcia Tulins. I admire your stage work, Ms Butler,
and I sure admire what you're doing here, putting
money into Eric's film.'

'Thank you.' Clara retrieved her hand from the
woman's tight grip. Eric with a woman was a shock.

Eric with this kind of overpowering female was a bigger shock. Could they possibly be an *item?* 'There's nothing to admire. I'm merely backing a winner.' Clara smiled at Eric, her eyes questioning.

'Marcia and I met in Peru,' he said. 'She's just got back.'

'We met in the line of duty, as it were.' Marcia's pale eyes hovered over Eric. Whatever his feelings for her, hers for him were not in doubt. Marcia Tulins was *very* keen on Eric O'Hanlon. 'I work with ANS, the news agency, covering Latin America. I got to write up the work this guy did in the mountains, you know, with those Indians in Peru. It's great he's getting the money to get on with his Colombia project. Colombia needs him. The *world* needs more people like him . . .'

'And that's a fact.' Luke, slightly drunk and with a dark-eyed beauty in tow, put an arm around his brother. 'My little brother, my only brother, the saint. Let us drink to him.'

Eric took part of his money and flew to Colombia. Luke got on with the endless business of the production detail.

And Larry K. Palmer, the man with whom Clara had found more love than she'd ever thought possible, died of a heart attack while alone and boarding up the Long Island house for the winter.

It seemed she would never bear the grief, go on living. She felt alone in a way she'd forgotten and now didn't know how to deal with. Memories of Larry warning her, telling her that marrying an older man would leave her a widow, were bitterest of all. They'd had so little time. Twelve years out of her forty-two. Two-sevenths of her life so far spent with him. A lifetime to go without him.

But that first, pure and awful grief was hers to indulge for only a short time. The boys' loss was as great as hers, their terror of the life ahead without him as numbingly painful as anything she was feeling.

A week after the funeral she took them into her arms and began the building of a life for the three of them without Larry. It took a year, but she did it.

Filming of *Death Diminishes* was delayed and, because a good idea is worth much more than its weight in gold in the movie industry, word of it was leaked by the TV backers. Somewhere, somehow and at some meeting the germ of an idea for a series of like murder mysteries across Europe was born. From being a one-off, *Death Diminishes* became part of an American-European six-film project.

In a complex bit of horse-trading Luke O'Hanlon got himself retained as director and Clara as the star. He also got Eric the rest of his money. Clara backed him all the way, using the threat of withdrawing both her own and Larry's money.

She had decided Larry was right. She should go back to Dublin as the woman her life had made her, an actress doing a job. When filming ended she would be ready to bring the boys over. *Death Diminishes* could very well be a sort of epiphany for her.

*

227

In the darkness of the room in De Novo Clara smiled at the word and got stiffly out of the chair. Larry would have laughed at the fancifulness of it, saying epiphanies were for Joycean scholars and awakenings for the rest of the world. He would, as usual but not always, have been right.

Chapter Thirteen

'That woman's after something.' Ellen, by the window, sucked in her breath. 'And it's hardly that old fool's body.'

'She likes the garden. She finds it peaceful, says Theo's knowledge about it all is a revelation.' Alva, trying to work at the desk in the sitting room, wished Ellen would find a book to read, go for a walk, do anything but carry on with the pacing and bitching of the past week. Clara Butler, walking with Theo in the garden, was the peeve of the moment.

'A revelation?' Ellen snorted. 'There's not much left for life to reveal to Clara Butler. *That*,' she tapped a fingernail against the window, 'is a woman motivated by the main chance. If she's interested in the garden there's a reason.'

'Well, then, maybe she *is* after Theo's body,' Alva said. 'He does have a certain robust charm, you know.'

'So does a goat, or a donkey for that matter. He's seventy-five years old and looks every minute of it. Old fool.'

'Why, Ellen,' Alva grinned, 'I do believe you're jealous.'

And many a true word, she thought, spoken in jest.

Only Ellen wasn't smiling. Her profile was cold and stretched, brittle-looking like the shell of an egg and very unamused. She had been unamused since news of the actress's move into De Novo. Clara had been in the house a week now, courteously keeping to her room most of the time, and Ellen's resistance hadn't softened a whit. Alva suspected it was tied up with the hard-to-ignore fact that the film people increasingly regarded her as an old eccentric.

The amused tolerance of the first week had become brusque impatience and she was getting precious little of the flattering attention she'd expected. Clara, no doubt, represented a glamour and pampering Ellen would have adored. Poor, foolish Ellen.

'They're coming back to the house.' Alva flinched at the rising petulance in the old woman's voice. 'One must suppose that she's had enough revelations for one afternoon. I've heard it said,' Ellen left the window and poured herself a glass of wine from the bottle she'd left on the table, 'that there are money problems with the wretched film and that *she* is the main reason. She's apparently demanding scenes and costumes for herself beyond anything that's decent, bullying the director fellow. He's her lover, you know.'

'No, I didn't know,' Alva, resigned, closed the ledger on the catering accounts. Ellen was not going either to disappear or shut up. 'And I don't see how you can say you know either. Sounds like gossip to me.'

'No smoke without fire.' Ellen drained her glass and poured another. Alva wished she'd eat. She was skin and bone, not eating anything these days.

'And you're going to make a volcano out of whatever you heard, aren't you?' Alva stifled a yawn. She was tired, badly in need of sleep. The company had been filming night scenes two nights in a row and today was a rest day. Food had been a priority, most of it snacks to keep people awake, and she and Bernie had been working flat out.

The tension and raw nerves generated by the whole procedure had drained everyone. Except Ellen. She spent both nights sitting in the dark beyond the blue arc lights, silent and broodingly bad-tempered and refusing to go to bed. She had also, obviously, been listening.

'The facts are there for anyone who cares to see them,' Ellen fluttered a hand towards the window, behind her now. 'Too much money being spent and that woman's at the root of it.' She'd made an attempt to catch her hair up, and the sun through the wispy, falling bits gave her neck a scraggy, vulnerable look. Alva sighed.

'Ellen, I'm too tired for all of this. Please shut up.'

'Put your head in the sand, then. Better, I suppose, than watching as this place becomes the hotel where a film went down the tubes.'

'I didn't know you cared.' Alva was dry.

'I don't. I *am* keen to keep a roof over my head, however.'

'Film-making's hazardous, full of histrionics,' Alva said. 'Most of it means nothing.' She hoped. The activities of the past week had sorely tested her nerve. Not to mention tolerance. The latter had involved finding Juno and Nick Hunt in a state of post-coital bliss in her bedroom. The fact that they'd been on the floor and not in her bed had more to do with their enthusiasm than any consideration for her feelings. She'd almost stepped on them.

'We were just going.' Juno grinned, sat up stretching. She had the body of a twelve-year-old boy, her breasts disappearing completely as her arms reached above her head.

'Please don't go on my account.' Alva, tart and determined not to be shocked, leaned against the wall. She was also trying hard to keep her eyes off Nick Hunt's perfect body. Not easy, with golden flashes of him reaching languidly for his jeans in the corner of her eye. Surprise best described how she felt. They seemed so . . . mismatched.

'So sorry, Alva. We tried Justine's room but it was locked.' He pulled on the jeans. 'Your door was ajar. Our need was great.'

Obviously, Alva thought. They left quickly, Juno giving her a hug as she passed. 'Thanks for being so understanding,' she said.

By evening time Bernie, somehow, had heard about the episode and was able to give Alva the word on Juno.

'She's a class of a nymphomaniac,' Bernie explained, 'everyone knows about her. She has it all the time, on every film she works on. It never affects her work, apparently.'

'What do you mean a *class* of a nymphomaniac? She's either oversexed or she's not.'

'Oh, she is. It's just that she's selective. She only ever has her way with young, beautiful men. She prefers it too if they're blond.'

'Jasper, of course, is your source?'

'Juno's an open secret,' Bernie grinned. 'But he did mention it.'

And Juno, Alva remembered, *had* mentioned there were perks with her job. A perk was one name for what they'd been doing.

If Juno's sexual appetite had tested her tolerance, delays and budget restrictions were what had tested her nerve. Trouble with faulty film stock had been followed by a camera breakdown. Cutbacks meant O'Hanlon had had to cancel a crane he'd hired for special shots. It had all, two days before, led to the director asking her if the company could stay an additional two weeks.

'You'll be paid, of course. An extra week would probably do it, but I'd prefer to cover my ass and go for two. If you can see your way to letting us stay I'll get on the blower to Kelly, get him to agree it.'

'Do you think he will?' Alva asked.

'Can't see him refusing once you agree.'

'OK,' Alva said, 'I agree.'

She'd wondered, when Seona phoned next day, what gossip was saying about events in De Novo and on the film set.

'I hear the craic is mighty out there.' Seona was huffy. 'But hearing is as near as I get. Invitations to visit have been thin on the ground.'

'I was waiting to hear from you.' This was a lie.

Alva had been hoping, for a couple of reasons, not to hear from Seona until the end of filming. In the first place she was sure Clara Butler wouldn't be keen on an interview, and in the second it would suit her better to have the publicity just as the hotel was reopening.

'Has anyone from the other papers been out there?' Seona asked.

'No one.'

'Good. Can you set something up for me? Say next week?'

'I'll try. But don't you think it would be better to wait until nearer the finish? It's looking like they'll be here until the end of the month now . . .'

'Too risky. Someone else might have nipped in by then. Be a love and set it up for me, will you? I'd like to talk to the director as well as to Clara Butler. Tell them whatever you have to, about my brilliance and discretion and all of that.'

'I'll see what I can do.'

Diffidently, Alva had put the request to Luke O'Hanlon. His answer had been more or less what she'd expected – though his obvious embarrassment at telling her no had surprised her.

'I'm sorry, Alva, can't be done. Clara won't do it and I . . .' He hesitated. 'Well, I don't want to do an interview, to be honest. Timing's all wrong . . .' He stopped again and ran a distracted hand through his hair. 'I'm not trying to be awkward – whole situation's too delicate at the moment. One wrong word . . .' He shrugged apologetically.

'It's all right,' Alva reassured quickly, 'really it is. I more or less expected you'd feel this way.'

'I've got good reason to "feel this way", as you put it.' Frowning, flushing a little, he cut her short. 'It's completely the wrong time—'

'I think you've misunderstood me.' Alva kept her tone light. 'I'm agreeing with you, Luke. I asked out of courtesy to Seona, nothing more. I've already told her it was a long shot.'

'Oh. That's all right then.' He grinned self-consciously. 'Sorry to jump at you. Budget problems are making me as touchy as everyone else around here.' He gave a rueful shrug and Alva smiled.

'I hope not,' she said. For a moment it seemed the director would develop the conversation, but with a mocking tip to his forelock he smiled, said, 'Keep the faith,' and walked away.

The conversation, and the glimpse it had afforded of a vulnerable Luke O'Hanlon, stayed with Alva as she worked. She wondered again about him and Clara and surprised in herself a sudden and instinctive conviction that he was a man capable of friendship with women. The thought was a comforting one.

Seona was not pleased. Alva didn't want to think about some of the things she'd said when she phoned to tell her. Any fragile reconciliation between them could definitely be said to be sundered.

Ellen, noisily sighing, brought Alva back to the day's reality. 'Just pretend I'm not here.' Ellen was huffy as she drained her glass, filled another and settled with much plumping of cushions into a chair with the morning paper. 'I'd hate to intrude . . .'

Alva pulled the ledger towards her and began work on the vegetable budget. She'd got as far as onions when the door opened and Clara's head came round, cautiously, before the rest of her and Theo appeared.

'Am I disturbing you?' Smiling, dressed in white jeans and a straw hat, Clara did *not* look like someone who'd been working, hard, two nights in a row. Theo, with a nod to Alva and ignoring Ellen, took several books from the shelves and began to study them on the table.

'You're not disturbing me,' Alva lied. 'Can I get you something? Tea? A glass of wine?'

'Nothing, thanks. I'm on my way to my room. Theo's giving me a couple of books . . .' she beamed at his bent head, 'so I'll just curl up with them. I thought, though, that you'd like to know Luke's got the OK for the extra two weeks. We really are going to need them and it's good of you to put up with us.'

'Glad to,' Alva said.

'Why wasn't I told about this?' Ellen, in the depths of her armchair, was strident. Clara, who clearly hadn't seen her, took a startled step backwards.

'I've only heard it confirmed myself this moment,' Alva soothed.

Clara clasped her long white hands to her bosom. 'We're *deeply* appreciative of your hospitality, Miss Donovan,' she said. 'I'm enjoying this house *so* much . . .'

'I've found you the books I was talking about,' Theo interrupted briskly. 'Look here . . .' He beckoned with a large, knotty finger and Clara, flashing Ellen an apologetic smile, crossed to him at the table. Ellen, with a low curse, pulled herself out of the chair and examined the wine bottle. It was still a quarter full. With a grunt she retrieved her glass and, holding both, swept from the room.

There was no warning about the storm which came that night. The day was close and humid, unseasonally so for early October, but a storm hadn't been expected. Certainly not the battering, raging fury which arrived after midnight and wreaked havoc in the garden, and on its filming plans for days to come.

The two late nights had driven the inhabitants of De Novo to bed early. Alva, waking about one o'clock, felt the sharp drop in the room's temperature before she heard the wind in the trees and then rain as it was blown in sheets against the window. She lay for a while listening, wondering if the film people had secured everything in the yard and waiting for sleep to return. It didn't happen and when lightning lit up the room she got out of bed and went to the window. As she stood there another sheet of lightning revealed the storm's progress.

The garden was awash, trees and shrubs insanely thrashing in the wind. There was a slow, creaking groan and she knew a limb had left a tree. Poor tree. Poor garden. She couldn't bear to see any more so, stepping back from the window, she pulled the curtains against it all. There would be no sleeping until it died down. Might as well read. She flicked the switch on the bedside lamp. Nothing happened.

'Power failure ...' swearing in the dark she found her dressing gown. Time for a hot whiskey, if the range was warm enough to boil a kettle.

As soon as she stepped onto the landing she saw Theo. He was standing by the end window, looking as rooted there as one of the older trees and wearing wellingtons with a coat over his pyjamas. She padded softly along to him and touched his sleeve.

'You're not thinking of going out, are you?'

'Thought about it, all right. No point.' They stood watching as the storm tore pitilessly at the garden. 'It has it in its jaws and no mistake,' Theo said, sadly. 'Might as well go back to my bed and wait for morning.'

Alva went to his room door with him. He went inside without saying goodnight. She *definitely* needed that hot whiskey.

She was halfway down the stairs when she saw someone ahead of her, moving with slow hesitancy in the dark.

'Ellen?'

'Clara, actually.' A roll of thunder coincided with a small yelping sound from the actress. She stopped moving.

'Are you all right?' Alva, moving fast, joined her on the step. Clara, nodding violently, was clinging to the banister. Her eyes were closed. 'I'm fine.' Her voice sounded high and strained. 'Just give me a minute.'

She was wearing a pale wool dressing gown and she was shivering.

'You're anything but fine.' Alva put an arm around her waist and began to ease her away from the banister. She felt fragile as a stick-woman. 'Come on, Clara, you can't stay here all night.'

'No, I suppose I can't.' The actress let go and allowed Alva guide her slowly down. 'Storms scare me.' Her teeth clattered.

'I can see that,' Alva said.

The range was its reliable self and boiled the kettle in minutes. Clara refused hot whiskey but took sweet tea in gulps before exhaling a huge, steadying breath. There was a faint drumming of rain on the roofs of the trailers in the yard below but otherwise, now they were away from the front of the house, the storm's worst battering was deadened.

'Got a cigarette?' Clara pulled a rueful face.

Alva shook her head. 'Sorry.'

'Just as well. I've given them up.' In the candlelight she had large, dull-brown sacks under her eyes. The make-up woman was going to have to work hard tomorrow. 'It's ridiculous. Even when I'm most scared I know how ridiculous it is, that whingeing and wringing my hands won't stop the thunder or turn off the lightning.'

'Fear isn't always rational,' Alva said. 'Everyone suffers from *some* sort of irrational fear.'

'What's *your* irrational fear?' Clara was sitting up straight, a melancholy dignity about her as she stared across the table.

'Mine . . .?' Alva, taken unawares, jerked back a little from the table. 'Certainly not storms,' she hedged.

'Nor being alone.' Clara looked around the kitchen. 'What do you do off-season, when there's only the three of you here? Seems to me it could be pretty lonely.'

'Oh, it's not too bad,' Alva smiled, 'this is a friendly house.'

'Yes. Yes, it is. It's the sort of house I didn't even know existed in Dublin when I was growing up here.'

'What sort of a house *did* you grow up in?' Alva was genuinely curious.

'Not friendly and not big. Not even a house, really. We had rooms over the family shop. There were seven of us, to begin with. By the time I was fourteen we were down to four.' Clara's tone was light, bantering. Alva matched it.

'Not the house's fault, surely?' she asked.

'I'm sure conditions were a contributing factor. My grandfather's time had probably come but not my brother's, nor my father's.'

'They all died?'

'Heart killed my grandfather. My brother was killed in a car he'd stolen. My father effectively killed himself by becoming drunk enough to walk into the path of a speeding car. In a movie such pathos would be considered over the top.'

'Is there anybody left? Your mother?'

'Dead. I've got twin brothers, though. Quiet, reclusive men. One of them's married now and seems happy.' Her tone had softened.

'Coming back must have been hard for you,' Alva said.

'The film made it easier. So does the knowledge that I'm pleasing so many people by coming – my husband, sons, Luke and . . .' She stopped and rubbed her eyes tiredly with her hand. 'I'm sorry. It's a cliché to say I don't usually babble like this but I don't. It's the storm, lack of sleep and· . . .' she finished the tea, 'missing my sons. God, but I miss them. Looking at you I can see you've still got the knack of being alone, Alva honey, but I've lost it.' The wry tone was back. 'A good marriage did for me.'

'I was an only child,' Alva said, 'I've had a lifetime's training.' She couldn't be sure but Clara's eyes were bright enough for tears. 'I'll make us a couple more drinks,' Alva went to the range, 'and you can talk to me about your sons and husband.'

'My husband's dead,' Clara said. 'He's been dead nearly two years now.'

'Oh, God, I *am* sorry. Tell me about him.' Alva touched Clara's hand as she put the sweet, hot tea on the table beside her.

'What's to tell you? He was intelligent and funny. He brought me peace and I loved him very much . . .' She took a deep breath and it was as if a switch had been pulled. Sipping the tea Clara began talking as if she would never be able to tell enough. She kept her eyes on Alva's face, piling up words and building a picture of her life that was accurate and sore and not at all flattering to herself.

Distance gave her clarity and perspective and things

she'd forgotten fell into place as she talked. She was grateful to Alva for listening. And listening well. When the candle guttered down Alva got up, replaced it with another and said, 'Don't stop.' Clara didn't, she wanted to get it all out.

It was only as she came to the end, to the friendship she and Larry had shared with Luke O'Hanlon, and with Eric, to the saga of *Death Diminishes*, that she began to censor. The whole story wasn't hers to tell. Parts of it were Luke's – who wasn't keen on it becoming public knowledge that his brother had written the script. Luke wouldn't have wanted it; and was having a hard enough time making the picture he wanted to make without being seen to defend his brother's script too.

She told Alva what she could and told herself she was allowing discretion be her tutor.

'With my own money in this film, and with Larry's money behind it too, I'm obviously and entirely subjective about *Death Diminishes*,' she smiled. 'Which is not, in my view, a bad thing. I read the script early on. I *know* Constance Moore. And I know too that there are rumours about my interfering but I don't give a damn. The only winner on a film set's the film, if it's any good. And I'm sticking with what I think is right for *this* film.'

'Don't see how you can do anything else, given what you've told me.' Alva was leaning across the table, head in her hands. She'd been like that for a lot of Clara's story. Genuinely interested, non-judgemental.

It had been one of the things which had worked for

her in journalism. People had often, like Clara tonight, told her more about their lives than they meant to. 'I'm glad you told me. It explains an awful lot,' she said, 'because of course I heard the rumours about you interfering. I wondered what it was all about . . .' She stopped. She'd been on the verge of asking Clara if the rumours of her affair with the director were true. It seemed more unlikely than ever, given Clara's story. Or could it be that events had brought them together . . . She told herself it was none of her business – and wished fervently that she could believe it.

'Surely you knew a lot of the background?' Clara looked puzzled. 'I imagined I was just topping things up for you. Didn't Jack explain the situation?'

'I knew the film originated with Luke and had been taken over by this six-film thing. Jack said nothing about your money or involvement.'

'Discreet of him.' Clara pulled a small face. 'It might be better if you carried on as if you didn't know, either. Christ knows what Justine would do if she found out. Probably burn her contract. I'm sure that's why Jack hasn't told her.'

'He'd never tell her,' Alva protested, 'even I can see how lunatic it would be to tell Justine.'

Clara gave her an arch, impatient look. 'Only reason he doesn't tell her, and everyone else, is because he doesn't want to be seen to have less control than he has. Jack likes power,' she shrugged, 'and he likes to use it.' She stopped to listen. 'Do you think the storm's passing?'

The thunder had moved on and the lightning had

stopped. But the electricity hadn't come back and wind still howled around the house. They could hear the rain still drumming on the trailer roofs too. Clara checked the wall clock. Three a.m. She had to be on the set at eight. Christ, but she was going to be a wreck. So, of course, was Alva, but she didn't have to face the cameras.

'It's passing,' Alva assured.

'Tell me how come you're here.' Clara was aware of Alva visibly retreating into her heavy dressing gown. This one's not a talker, she thought, and softened the demand into a question. 'I mean, why're you running this place with just Bernie to help? And living with two old people who don't seem to give a damn?'

'Is that how it seems?'

'That's how it seems. Now tell.'

'I . . .' Alva hesitated. Her life had none of the dramatic tragedy of Clara's. It was a small life really, when she thought about it. But it was her life, the sadnesses had been hers. The joys too.

'I'd like to know,' Clara said and meant it. 'Don't think I won't understand.'

'It's all very dull,' Alva shrugged, 'compared to what you've done.'

She began to talk, very fast, wanting to keep her story brief. It didn't work. Out of nowhere memories came and with them an urge to explain, make things clear to Clara. And to herself.

'. . . Mine was what you could call a restricted upbringing. When I was about eleven or twelve I broke an unwritten family rule and asked my mother a

244

personal question.' She gave a small laugh. 'The poor woman almost went into shock.' She stopped, remembering that winter's day, the dank kitchen made darker by the dense evergreens circling the house, her mother's still, pale face.

'What sort of a personal question?' Clara prompted.

'I asked her if she'd ever loved anyone else before marrying my father. I'd found their marriage certificate, you see, and discovered she was forty-five when she married. My father was even older, in his fifties. I was full of romantic nonsense and wanted my mother to have a past, to have suffered at least the pangs of unrequited love. Anthing that would make her more interesting.' Alva sighed. 'What she told me made me wish I'd kept my mouth shut. Hers was such a sad story, the tale of a lonely, repressed life. She'd spent her entire life in that house, as an only child caring for her parents and then, quite soon after they died, with my father when she married him. She described it as "the most sensible thing to do". So much for romance.'

'They had you,' Clara pointed out. 'That wasn't very sensible at their ages.'

'I was unexpected,' Alva smiled, 'and a terrible shock, especially to my father. He'd been a priest, a Jesuit – a "man of God" according to my mother. She was very much in awe of him.' Alva looked thoughtful. 'He was in many ways an awesome person.'

'Not too many personal conversations with him, then?' Clara asked.

'Not many conversations, full stop.' Alva took a deep breath. 'I remember one, though, just before my

245

fourteenth birthday. We had this ritual, every year, where we went to Wiltons Hotel and had tea, the three of us, on my birthday. At fourteen I thought this most uncool and wanted to do something with a friend from school instead. I suggested this to my mother – who banished me to my room to await my father's word on it when he got home. I waited two hours. I remember him coming slowly up the stairs and standing in front of me. I was sitting on the bed and I kept my head down so that all I could see were his shoes. Black shoes, laced. Priest's shoes. He told me I was being selfish, that my birthday was an occasion to share with those who had given me life. My parents.' She looked ruminatively at the floor, traced a pattern there with her foot. 'I lost my temper, told him he was like Dr Frankenstein and that he didn't own me . . .'

'I imagine that went down like a lead balloon,' Clara smiled.

'It was more like I'd shaken the foundations of western civilization.' Alva gave a short laugh. 'I got a lecture on rights and responsibilities and was then told we would be going to Wiltons, as usual.'

'And did you?'

'Oh, yes. We went.' Alva pressed her lips together and, avoiding Clara's gaze, focused on the storm beyond the window.

'I told him I wouldn't go and he hit me. He used his open palm, several times, across my face. Then he shook me. He was beside himself, white with temper. My mother whimpered and cried and moved away.'

'What did you do?' Clara's question was gentle but

even so Alva hesitated. Then she smiled, turned back and looked the actress full in the face.

'I yelled at him that I needed a brassière and that my periods had started and that neither of them gave a damn about me. My father was disgusted. "Women's matters" were all too basic for him to deal with. He left me to my mother.'

'Was it true? About the bra and periods?'

'Oh, yes. My mother saw to the necessaries and she and I got on a bit better after that. My father said I had "put myself beyond him" – which I had, and which was something of a relief.'

'Sounds like a bundle of laughs,' Clara said and then blinked when, as if a switch had been thrown, the lights came back on. Alva rubbed a hand across her eyes. Across the table from her Clara's face was a blanched white.

'Do you think you'll sleep now?' Alva asked and gave an involuntary yawn. 'Because I really want to myself.'

In the hallway, at the bottom of the stairs, Clara impulsively hugged Alva. 'Thanks for tonight,' she said. 'I won't forget it.'

She linked arms and they went up the stairs together, silenced by exhaustion.

'Alva.' Outside her room, still holding her arm, Clara turned the younger woman to face her. 'I want you to think about something. You may not, you may say it's sweet-eff-all to do with me, and you'd be right.' She shrugged. 'But as far as I can see, from what you told me tonight, there's no one else to say this to you. I want you to think, Alva,' she took a deep breath, 'about what you're really doing here. I can see the appeal of the place but you're much too young to bury yourself . . .'

'I am *not* burying myself. I am running a business which I intend making a success of . . .' Alva was too tired for this. Clara had no right.

'Are you sure that's what you're doing?' Clara seemed to think she had. 'Are you sure all of this,' her gesture taking in the stairs and landing was theatrical, 'is not simply a retreat into the world you've left? Could it be that you've swapped one set of elderly house-companions for another? One old house for another?' She smiled whimsically. 'What I really wanted to say was, don't give up, Alva. There's some-one out there for you. I'd been round the block a dozen times before I met Larry.'

In bed Alva fumed, but gently. She'd found herself liking Clara and had neither the energy nor the will to be seriously angry at her. In retreat from life, indeed. It was insulting and stupid but not, she knew, maliciously meant. More likely Clara was suffering from too great an exposure to the American cult of psychoanalysis. Her diagnosis was quite wrong. Alva hadn't given up on life. A man to love wasn't every-thing. It was nice, when it worked, but it wasn't everything. She was happy with her life, had never been so much in control.

She thought about Clara's story, the things it explained about the film. It left a lot of things unex-plained, too. Alva couldn't think what they were, right now. Too tired. But they would come to her.

Chapter Fourteen

The ailanthus tree was lopsided, branches ripped out by the storm and drooping limp and raw against the bark. Everywhere in the garden things were in the same sorry state.

Alva and Theo, walking through it in the early dawn, looked and were quiet. The pool, and all who lived in it, had become lost under a deposit of torn branches and leaves. Urns from the rose garden were up-ended and late blooms beaten into the ground. The pergola was naked except for the wisteria, clinging still with gnarled, defiant fingers. Smaller bushes had escaped but overnight all colour had been wiped out. It was a mud-brown landscape, all summer gone.

'North wind's the very devil when it gets going.' Theo poked with a boot at a broken branch. 'It had a great bloody time for itself here last night, and no mistake.' He shrugged. 'Nature giveth and she taketh away.'

'You'll have to get help with the clearing up.' Alva put a hand on his arm and was surprised when he covered it with his. 'It won't look so bad when the dead wood's taken away. Maybe it'll pass for a bit of excessive pruning . . .'

'Indeed.' Theo stuffed his hand back into his pocket

and Alva, with no real comfort to offer, waited for him to talk again. When he did so he was philosophical.

'It's a risky old bugger, gardening. Bit like life. Nothing for it but to get back into it.' He rubbed his hands together. They made a sound like sandpaper. 'You can tell your celluloid friends they won't be able to muck about out here for a week, at least.' He made the sandpaper sound with his hands again. 'That'll soften their cough.'

But nature wasn't about to be allowed dictate to the art of picture-making. The faulty film stock meant that an earlier scene, with Justine walking in the garden with a period-garbed Nick Hunt, had to be reshot.

'You'll never guess what they're up to.' Bernie, arriving late to begin lunch, was dazed and disbelieving.

'You're right, I won't.' Alva was tired and she was short. 'We're running late.'

'Sorry.' Bernie didn't look it. 'I was having a few words with Jasper. Do you or don't you want to know what's going on out there?'

'I'd prefer to see a bit more activity in here.' Alva was sharper than she intended. Jasper Clarke featured in everything Bernie said these days and she'd begun to worry. He was a fount of information about all sorts of things but, so far as Alva could tell, he had yet to mention his fiancée to Bernie. He was a nice guy and obviously enjoyed her company as well as her food. Who wouldn't? But his heart was engaged elsewhere and Bernie's was free and looking for love. It was a recipe for hurt, with Bernie the victim.

'You're tired, that's what's wrong with you.' Bernie was good-humouredly consoling. 'I'll have things together in a jiffy.'

'All right then,' Alva gave in, 'tell me. What's happening outside?'

'They're putting leaves back on the trees.' Bernie gave a hearty whack to a chicken's breast. 'Can you believe that? Leaves on the trees.'

Seeing was believing. A maple tree, chosen for filming in the first place because of its purple foliage, had been stripped leafless in the night. The art department was playing God, its workers on ladders and branches slowly attaching plastic leaves. Theo was nowhere to be seen. Alva stood with Bernie and watched for a few minutes.

'Think of the money being spent! And all because Justine threw a tantrum. Amazing how Jack can come up with money when it's for one of his protégés. Ah, well,' Bernie shook her head mournfully, 'life was never meant to be fair. What I couldn't do with even a fraction of whatever they're paying for those leaves . . .' She stopped, sucked in a breath between her teeth and clapped a hand to her forehead. 'It's Saturday and I have just', she announced, 'thought of a way of spreading that money around.'

Within an hour the job of leaf restoring had been handed over to Sammy Brennan and a noisy, willing – at a price – band of twelve-year-olds. By late afternoon the cameras were rolling on a dewily youthful pair of lovers, strolling in the dappled sun which shone between the leaves of an old maple tree.

In the house peace had come after the storm. Ellen spent the entire day in her room and Clara, after an early morning scene, went back to hers. Alva sat in the sitting room alone. De Novo, for the first time since she'd come to it, seemed to her subdued. It was as if the storm had stripped it of all energy. It had certainly taken hers. Bone weary, she put her head back and closed her eyes. Let Food's Up do the feeding for a while. Mel O'Sullivan was more relaxed about things since discovering there was a reliable hard core of people who preferred junk food. She needed a rest.

She woke when a shadow fell over her and blocked the light from the window. At first, groggy and struggling to sit up, she couldn't see clearly who it was. It wasn't until he coughed embarrassedly and moved back that she recognized Luke O'Hanlon.

'Sorry,' he was awkwardly apologetic, 'didn't mean to waken you. We can talk some other time . . .'

'You were looking for me?' Alva shook her head to clear it. She checked her watch and saw she'd been asleep for an hour. God, she must look a sight. 'How long have you been standing there?' The question sounded defensive.

'Not long,' he assured, 'but don't worry, you didn't have your mouth open . . .' He seemed about to add something but changed his mind and instead gave another small cough. Alva flushed and pulled herself out of the armchair.

'That's a relief.' She knew she was being unnecessarily curt, but hated being caught off-guard and vulnerable. Luke knew it too. She couldn't imagine why else he would be wearing that over-friendly smile, treating her to a warm look from those brown eyes. 'Now that you've woken me, what can I do for you?'

He looked away, shrugging a little, suddenly businesslike. 'I got things wrapped up early so I thought we might have a chat. I've got something here for you ...' He leaned against the table and began a search of his pockets. Alva, watching him closely, regained her composure by pinning hair which had come loose. Even with all Clara had told her the night before she still felt wary around him, didn't feel she really knew him. He was a good film-maker and inspired loyalty. But he would never, she felt sure, have come looking for *her* unless he wanted something.

'Here you are.' He placed a cheque, found finally in a shirt pocket, on the table. 'Payment for the two weeks we'll be here over time. Arrived today, couriered from on high ...' He hesitated. 'I don't want you to get what I'm going to say wrong, Alva, because we do appreciate your letting us stay on here. It would be nice, though, if everything could be as agreeably arranged as this.' He tapped the cheque, hesitating again.

'I'm not sure what you're trying to tell me.' Alva raised an eyebrow. 'Is there some problem?' If he was implying that she was getting special treatment, then let him come right out and say it. Then *she* would tell him that rent in advance, which was what the cheque was, was part of the deal she had struck.

'Problems, plural,' his voice was low and even, 'all to do with budget cuts. Let me tell you about some of them.' He shoved his hands in his pockets and studied the carpet. The softness of a minute ago was replaced with a tense tiredness.

'We wanted a period carriage to bring Constance's brother up the avenue, and what were we told? Make him walk. I needed funding for a day's filming in Glasnevin cemetery and what did I get? I got, Alva, the suggestion that I create a graveyard in the corner of the garden here.'

'Sounds as if someone's trying to save money.'

'Goddamn it, Alva, you *know* what's going on,' his voice rose, 'so don't treat me like a bloody fool—'

'And don't you talk to me like that!' Alva took a step backwards. She hated this, wanted no part of rows and disagreements about the filming. 'Your problems are not of my making. I don't know what you expect *me* to do about them.'

'Sorry.' He rubbed his eyes and looked, all at once, flattened. 'I really mean it, I'm sorry.' He looked at her, embarrassed and more awkward than before. Straightened up he was a good three inches taller than she was. 'I shouldn't have yelled at you.' He ran a hand through his hair. 'None of it's your fault. Bit like shooting the messenger, blaming you for Jack Kelly's budget cuts and the fact that it's looking like the cost of the extra weeks are going to be balanced out with more cuts.'

Alva walked to the table and picked up the cheque. It was for £10,000. 'This is fine – but it's hardly going to break a company which can pay to put hundreds of thousands of plastic leaves on a tree.'

'That's part of the trouble,' he groaned and began to pace again.

Alva strolled to the fireplace and leaned against the mantel. She was not going to be made as tense as he was, nor to feel guilty.

He looked at her quickly before going on. 'The leaves were for Justine. I *could* have reshot the whole scene, not just the damaged parts. But Justine wanted it kept – she had a point, too, because it's some of the best stuff she's done. She demanded and we got the leaves.' He stopped pacing and stood by the bookshelves. He was in shadow there and Alva couldn't see his expression. His voice was subdued. 'I've been less than diplomatic in my time – and I think I'm about to be again.' He laughed; a short and not very happy sound.

'Luke,' Alva was reasonable, calm, 'I wish you'd just tell me whatever it is you want to tell me.'

'It's this.' He moved away from the bookcase and stood in front of her. His eyes, Alva noticed, were the colour of freshly turned earth. 'Jack Kelly traded the two weeks for budget cuts. The cemetery and carriage are the first, God knows what others he's going to demand. But, as you rightly point out, your £10,000 payment is not enough to warrant wholesale cutbacks. Two weeks isn't that much over schedule. What I hoped,' the words cost him pain, she could tell, 'was that you might use your influence with our executive producer, see if you can get him to cool things a bit on the budgeting scene.'

Alva took a deep breath before exploding. 'Good

God, Luke, what makes you think he'll listen to me?' She stared at him and it came to her that he was jealous. How else to explain his distorted view of her relationship with Jack Kelly?

No. The idea was outrageous, and she dismissed it. Worry about the film was affecting his judgement. It was as simple as that.

'Oh, I think he'll listen to you.' The director shrugged a shoulder. 'Look, I don't know what your involvement is with Kelly and I don't want to compromise your loyalties. But it would make things a lot easier around here if he stopped pulling strings . . .'

'My relationship with Jack Kelly is a friendly, business one.' Alva was chilly. She was also wishing Luke hadn't used the word loyalty. It made her acutely aware of the mobile phone in her room, of the watching brief the exec-producer had asked her to keep on things. 'You're overestimating my . . . influence,' she said. 'I'll sound Jack out, next time I'm talking to him. But I really do doubt that it'll change anything.'

'Let's hope you're surprised.' He gave a tight smile and Alva gave in to an urge to make him relax.

'I had a long talk with Clara last night,' she said. 'We took refuge from the storm in the kitchen. She told me about her husband dying and about the money they've both put into the film.'

'You didn't know?' his eyebrows shot up.

'I didn't know.' Exasperation threatened her careful calm. 'And I don't know either why everyone imagines I'm the repository of all information around here. I simply knew the film had originated with you.'

'It originated, as a matter of fact, with my brother. Didn't Clara tell you that, too?'

'No.' She looked at him, startled. 'No, she didn't tell me that. Is he a film-maker too?'

'He's a development worker, somewhere in Colombia at the moment. He's also a writer though no one knew that until he wrote the script for *Death Diminishes*. Certainly I didn't. Being Eric he's insisted on a pseudonym.' O'Hanlon watched her face closely as he spoke. 'Jack hasn't explained all of this to you?'

'No, Jack has *not* explained all of this to me. Why should he?' Alva, suddenly furious, had an urge to stamp her feet. 'What *is* all this, Luke? Why do I feel as if I'm in a pillory, that I have to account for myself?'

She was angry and flushed and, staring at him, she knew the answer to her own question. He didn't trust her. He had no right not to and it hurt. Luke O'Hanlon thought she was involved with Jack Kelly, and as such privy to all sorts of information which it would be useful for him, as director, to know. Well, he could think what he liked. She damn well wasn't going to be made to feel guilty just because she had arranged her own deal for De Novo with Jack and because he'd then asked her to be his 'Irish eye' on things when he wasn't around. She hadn't once used his cursed mobile phone. She'd played it right down the middle, taken sides with no one. It was just not on for Luke to treat her as if she was some nasty little office snitch.

'Christ, Alva, this is *not* what I intended.' The director took a step closer and for a moment she thought he was going to reach out and hold her. Then he shrugged, crossed his arms over his chest and rocked a little on his heels. His expression was self-mocking.

'You don't have to account for yourself,' he said. 'I should, but I won't bore you now. Another time, maybe.' He made a late-sixties peace sign. 'Can we forget all of this for now?' When she nodded he turned abruptly and dropped into an armchair. 'I do owe you, at least, an explanation of my personal interest in this film. My too personal interest.' He looked up at her. 'I'd feel better if you sat down. I can't talk to you up there.'

She was angry still, and wary, but something about his face, a mixture of tiredness and pleading in it, stopped her. A feeling she'd had before, that this was a man capable of friendship with women, surfaced again. But first he would have to trust. She wanted him to trust her.

She compromised and sat on the arm of a chair opposite him.

'Thank you,' he said and leaned forward. 'Here's the story. Eric is my only, and younger, brother. He wrote the script for money, from a story he'd had an interest in writing for a long time. The money was to be put into a project he wanted to get off the ground in the Colombian Andes. It was to be paid in two lots, half on acceptance, the rest when the film was ready to go into production. He finished the script, got the first half and took off. That was two years ago, and things went well for him, his project got up and started. He needed the rest of the money, though.'

'It took a while, but I finally got it together and sent it out to him. That was eight months ago and he hasn't been to the bank to collect. He hasn't been anywhere that anyone knows of,' his voice was flat, unnaturally neutral, 'in nine months. To all intents and purposes my brother has disappeared.'

'How could he *disappear*?' Alva found she was whispering. 'Weren't there people with him on the project?'

'Quite a few, by all accounts. But Eric has a way of isolating himself, even in a crowd. He's quite an individual.' He stopped, for a moment looking at some memory in his head. When he went on he was businesslike. 'All I've been able to establish is that he walked out one day, telling the people he was with he'd be gone a while and not to worry.'

'Why are *you* so worried?'

'Because the project and the money for it were so almightily important to him. I can't believe he'd leave it sitting there in a bank for eight months unless he . . .'

'Have you thought about going out there?'

'I think of very little else when I'm not filming. I intend going as soon as everything's in the can.'

'Maybe he'll have turned up by then.'

'Maybe.'

'Thank you for telling me,' Alva said. 'If there's anything I can do . . . I speak Spanish . . .'

'Thank you.' He looked surprised and she wondered wryly if this was because of her offer to help – or at the news that she spoke Spanish. He stood.

'Forget that other stuff,' he grinned, 'it's the product of a feverish anxiety about this picture turning into a Hammer/Michael Winner biopic.'

'It won't,' Alva said, confidently.

There were very few for the six o'clock 'tea' she and Bernie laid on daily. The days were shortening fast and filming had ended with the maple tree scene. Apart from the busy art department setting up a graveyard in a far corner, everyone had left.

Alva served and cleared and thought about her conversation with the director. Not having a brother she could only imagine how he felt about the missing Eric. She wondered if distress was affecting his judgement about the film, and on balance decided no; there was a part of him which filmed and a part of him which got on with the rest of life. This second, hidden part had been more on view than he'd probably intended, or knew. He wasn't, she guessed, a man given to harshness or cruel behaviour. Caring was a word which came to mind. So, she thought, was single-minded. A curious mixture, and not uninteresting.

The storm-washed sky and grey of the following morning might have been custom-made for the shooting of the graveyard scene. In a corner of the garden near the boundary wall, by a holly tree and a small pine, a grave had been dug and a convincing stone cross erected. This was where Constance Moore would bury James with a brief and hurried funeral. Apart from a few business associates, she would be the only one to mourn an ungiving life.

Shortly after nine Alva pulled on wellingtons and trudged off to get to the scene before Food's Up with an offer of on-set coffee and tea.

The mood there was not good. It was damply cold in the corner of the garden, and despite make-up Clara's face above the black taffeta mourning gown looked peaky and drawn. Luke was pushing to get the scene finished before the threatening rains came and even Juno, in an anorak which seemed about to smother her, appeared irritable. The chilled, bone-stomping crew greeted her with near ecstasy.

'Great stuff, Alva,' Luke said. 'With a bit more energy around here we could wrap things up before the rain.'

Bernie didn't come in until lunchtime on Sundays so Alva was alone in the kitchen, filling a couple of giant thermoses, when a fat hand fell on her shoulder and a whiff of sweet-smelling aftershave filled her nostrils.

'Hello, Oscar.' She continued to pour without turning. 'Haven't seen you for an age.'

The hand dropped away. 'Indeed,' Oscar sniffed, 'and you won't see me now either if you don't turn around.'

Alva, with a small laugh, finished filling the flask. 'Don't growl at me.' She turned and kissed him lightly on a spongy soft cheek. 'Come on,' she handed him a thermos, 'walk down to the set with me. It'll be nice for you to meet everyone again.'

'Sarcasm is a low and cheap form of wit.' Oscar held the thermos away from him. 'I am kept to a *very* busy schedule doing untold and unseen work for this film company. I want to talk to you.' He raised shocked eyebrows as Alva plodded to the door. 'You can't be serious about my going out there.' He became plaintive. 'Are you?'

Alva, carrying plastic cups and the other thermos, studied his Gucci-like loafers. 'Would you   e a pair of wellingtons?' she asked.

'Certainly not! I have *never*—'

'Fine. Come as you are, then. You can talk to me on the way. Walk will do you good. Fresh air too, from the look of you.'

'There are gofers for this kind of thing.' Oscar, grumbling, followed her out along the hallway and into the garden. Avoiding the muddier spots in surprisingly nippy fashion he kept abreast of her as they went. 'Tell me how you're getting on with our esteemed, very-PC director and his star. I hear she's running the show. Is she running the household too?'

'Clara's actually the perfect house guest.'

'Compared to living with that old woman, I suppose she is.' Oscar swore as he retrieved his trouser leg from the clutch of a briar. 'And O'Hanlon, how's he behaving himself?'

'Exemplarily.' Alva was curt. 'Look, Oscar, you were the one told me to keep my distance from things. So let's forego the gossip, OK?'

'I must say, I think it's unnecessary and ungrateful

of you to take that bitchy tone with me, Alva. I brought the film to you, after all . . .'

Alva stopped. 'You did and I'm grateful. But we made a deal and everyone, you included, got what they wanted. No debts owed, OK?'

'Oh, all right.' Oscar pursed like a prune and stayed silent until Alva asked him, on the way back to the house, what it was he'd wanted to see her about.

'I'm having drinks, and a bite to eat, *chez moi* tomorrow night. Will you come? There'll be some real people there, change from this lot.'

'It's nice of you, but I—'

'But me no buts.' Oscar put a fat finger to his lips. 'You need have no fear that your ex-lover Carlyle will be among my guests. Jack Kelly will be there, however, and has expressed a wish to see you. I'll expect you at eight for eight-thirty.'

'Put like that—'

'You cannot refuse. I know. That's settled then.'

They approached the steps and Alva asked, half-heartedly, if she could get him a drink. 'Unless it's too early . . .?'

'Certainly it's not too early,' Oscar said. 'I'm up, aren't I?' He stayed an hour during which, over two gin and tonics, he regaled Alva with mostly indecent tales about people they both knew.

Alva had walked with him to his car and was speeding him on his way when Ellen came down the front steps, moving fast and pulling on a pair of gloves. As she reached the bottom a props girl came hurtling after her.

'Cheery 'bye, Alva my pet.' Oscar fumbled for his car keys. 'I'll away before that woman—'

'Hang on, there's something wrong.'

The props girl, very aggrievedly, was demanding that Ellen give her the gloves. Ellen, with an imperious flare of her nostrils, was refusing.

'I saw you take them,' the girl, who was very young, hissed. 'They are antique and they are *borrowed*. If you do not return them I will decapitate your bloody cat.'

'Ha! She's been stealing from props!' Oscar chortled. 'But she's met her match in that young madam!'

Ellen, with enormous dignity, was holding her hands passively in front of her while the props girl removed the gloves. The last finger had been barely eased off before she turned, swung the lynx coat about her and marched their way.

'Oh, God, no!' Oscar moaned and jabbed a frantic key at the car door.

'What is that ridiculous man doing now?' Ellen stopped a few feet away and gave what sounded, for her, like a chuckle. 'You silly old fart, you're trying to get away from me, aren't you?'

Oscar had the key in the door. 'I assure you, Miss Donovan,' he began.

'He was, wasn't he?' Ellen ignored him and spoke to Alva. 'He's afraid of me, and so he should be. What's he doing here? He appears to have no function either in life or in this film business . . .'

'Stop it, Ellen.' Alva was sharp and then relieved as Ellen, without a glance in Oscar's direction, turned suddenly and headed down the avenue.

'That woman spooks me, I admit it.' Oscar, in the car, put his hands on the wheel and his head on his hands. 'I've never been able to deal with that sort of naked, uncontrolled behaviour.' He was mumbling so that Alva found it hard to hear him. 'One must preserve the decencies against chaos.'

'She picks on you because you allow her to get to you.' Alva hunkered down beside him. 'And you're right, she doesn't care about scenes or rudeness.' She straightened up. 'Don't take her to heart, Oscar. And don't run over her as you go down the avenue either.'

Going up the steps, feeling the first drops of rain as they began to fall, it occurred to Alva that Ellen cared less and less about anything with each passing day. What had been mischievous eccentricity was becoming a destructive egocentricity. Question was, who was she going to destroy?

Chapter Fifteen

'You're early,' Oscar said, 'but come in anyway.' Cooking had given him pink, clown-like spots on his cheeks. He was wrapped in a vast apron with the words *Plat du Jour* in navy-blue across his stomach.

'You're quite sure?' Alva stepped inside. 'I can always go away, come on time another night . . .'

'Now, now, Alva my pet, no need to be tiresomely touchy. One always gets into a bit of a lather before these occasions. You'll have to allow for my little foibles.' He ushered her between a pair of huge gilded mirrors on either side of a high, narrow hallway. 'I'm very glad you're here, in fact. I was afraid you might not come.'

'I said I would,' Alva reminded him, stopping to look around as Oscar fussed ahead. The ceiling had *trompe-l'oeil* clouds above a gold border. 'This is all very . . . sumptuous.'

'Yes, yes of course it is.' Oscar took her arm. 'If a thing's worth doing it's worth going over the top, I always say. Come along now, Stephen will take your coat and get you a drink. I must return to my labours.' He clapped his hands and like a genie from a bottle a young, pale-blond man appeared solemnly from the kitchen. He wore a blue silk shirt and black leather

266

jeans and extended a long, silver-ringed hand Alva's way. Oscar's over-the-top taste went further than his decor, apparently.

'Thank you.' Alva slipped off her coat as Oscar's round, flapping figure disappeared in the direction of cooking odours. 'I'd like a glass of white wine.' Stephen hadn't seemed about to ask.

He didn't invite her any further in either, leaving her standing in the hallway while he went off with her coat and, presumably, to get her drink. Charm, Alva thought, was obviously not high on Stephen's list. An open door to her left seemed the most likely place to find herself somewhere to sit so she drifted in there. She'd chosen well. What was apparently Oscar's drawing room was painted ochre and filled with seating of every kind – French Regency, spindle-backed Windsor, a couple of French Empire-style chairs and, his *pièce de résistance*, a four-seater sofa upholstered in creamy, gold-threaded silk damask.

'It's a Rubelli damask.' Stephen coming silently into the room, stood beside the sofa with her drink on a tray. Alva reached and took the wine.

'Do people actually *sit* on any of this?' she asked.

'All of it's functional.' Stephen, speaking with great seriousness, went on holding out the tray. 'Oscar wouldn't have it any other way. He is a true *bon vivant* and believes everything should be enjoyed for what it is.' He was shorter than Alva but, a tribute to his hauteur, managed to give the impression of looking down his nose at her.

'He's right, too.' Alva smiled and Stephen, with a

small nod, left her alone with the chairs. She sat in the spindle-backed Windsor, confident she couldn't do it, at least, any harm. After ten minutes of this, and another five examining a series of English watercolours in gilt frames, she wandered back into the hallway. There was no one about, just discreet lights glowing softly and a boudoir mood. She called but, getting no answer, followed the food smells and pushed open the kitchen door. Oscar was in a tizzy of stirring by the cooker while Stephen, with an obliging finger, tested the results. Two young men in white jackets, presumably waiters, sprawled boredly at the table playing cards. The air was steamy hot and every available surface littered. It was hard to see how a meal would ever materialize.

'Mind if I take myself on a tour of your "restored jewel"?' Alva asked and Oscar, cheeks more pinkly spotted than before, turned to nod briefly.

'Please do,' he giggled. 'Just make sure you don't waken the children.' Stephen made a high, whinnying sound which could also have been a giggle.

The house was in Ranelagh, a part of the city Alva knew well and which was an eclectic mix of family homes and a throbbing flatland. Oscar, talking about his house, had once described it to her as his 'restored jewel'. He'd also told her that it dated from the 1830s, which made it around the age of De Novo House – though his refurbishment and decor ensured that similarities ended there. Alva, walking through the rooms as she sipped the Chardonnay, had to hand it to him. From the drawing-room chairs to the chintzy, luridly welcoming bedrooms and a bathroom with a marbled pillar, his taste was consistently for opulence.

'Talk about putting your money where your mouth is.' Alva, thoughtfully, ran a hand over the wood of an elaborately framed oil. 'This is over the top, in spades. Production managing must pay very well indeed.'

A chime on the front door echoed through the entire house. The stigma of being the lone early guest was about to end.

Oscar's other guests, all seven of them, arrived within ten minutes of that first chime. First on the doorstep was a restaurateur of social significance, or so newspaper gossip had it. He was thin and tall and very pale and announced immediately that, with his own place closed for the night, he could eat a horse. Next came a writer and his wife; small, neat people who said it was wonderful to be here but they couldn't drink. They'd already written off two cars, they said, one of them their own, journeying to and from County Meath. They sipped Ballygowan. The remaining four guests arrived in a bunch, Jack Kelly among them. Two of the men were in PR, the wife of one a bookbinder. They all, displaying great familiarity with things, relaxed back into Oscar's chair collection while Oscar, apron gone and revealing a pale pink overshirt and rust-coloured trousers, effected introductions and spread himself around.

Jack Kelly pulled a Hepplewhite close to Alva and raised his glass. 'To the most gorgeous gal in the room.' He exaggerated his accent. 'And to Oscar's generosity.'

'To Oscar's generosity.' Alva sipped, glad she'd worn the coral silk tunic and trousers she'd once blown half a month's salary on. She liked the way he looked tonight, too; casual in a brown wool jacket and ochre shirt.

'You knew about Oscar's decor, then.' She nodded at the shirt and he laughed.

'Too right,' he said, 'I've been here before. To tell the truth, my earlier visit caused me some worry about the sort of place Oscar might turn up for the film. It needn't have. He really did come up with the goods.' The way he was looking at her made her shift uncomfortably.

'Have you been in town long?' she asked quickly. 'We haven't seen you at De Novo.'

'Been here two days, but I stay until the end of the week. Glad you found yourself able to put up with the unit for the extra time. You got my cheque?'

Alva nodded. 'Prompt and welcome, Jack. Many thanks. It's really no problem having them until the end of the month. I wouldn't have reopened until Hallowe'en anyway.'

'Things going well then?' He said the words slowly, his eyes moving over her face as he spoke, stopping for an instant at her mouth. She felt herself flush and was glad of Oscar's subdued lighting.

'Things are going fine, from mine and Bernie's point of view anyway,' she smiled. 'Filming seems to be going well too, not that I'm an expert. I have seen some of the rushes, though, and they looked really

270

good to me. But then I imagine you've seen most of what's been filmed yourself.'

'I've seen some.' He beckoned one of the hovering waiters and held up his glass for a refill. They were silent until the man left and then Alva, not sure if she was doing the right thing, brought up the subject of the cutbacks.

'There was some upset about a period carriage, I believe.' She spoke lightly, her eyes on his to show friendly interest, nothing more. 'And a bit of a fuss about a graveyard.'

'Upset. Fuss. I guess that about sums it up.' He shrugged and looked away from her. 'It's nothing of any importance. Directorial demands have to be kept in proportion to the needs of the rest of those involved. Don't you agree?'

Alva leaned towards him a little, smiling, willing back the closeness she felt slipping from between them. 'I'm a bit confused about proportions and balance at this stage,' she admitted. 'Comes of being too close to it all, I suppose. Luke's worried there may be more cutbacks . . .'

'He should be. And I can see you've gotten close to things all right. Is Clara living in proving a problem?' He looked at her again, his lopsided smile in place. Alva relaxed, reassured that she'd imagined his chill.

'Clara's no problem,' she admitted. 'It's nice having her around, actually. We've got to know each other a little . . .' It was her turn to look away, making a circle with her glass on the table, unsure about revealing her conversation with Clara and even more unsure about exactly *why* she was unsure.

No. She wasn't being honest with herself. She did know why. Revealing her conversation with Clara could put her, in Jack's eyes, in the director's 'camp'. The whole damn film unit was, exactly as Oscar and Juno had warned, riddled with intrigue, drama and power struggles. Everyone seemed to need real-life drama as well as the film kind, and when it didn't exist they created it. It wasn't in her to be a part of it, but it came to her, sitting there watching Jack's urbane, patiently waiting face, that her involvement with the film unit was, in the oddest way, putting her in touch with parts of herself she'd hardly been aware of. Things like how much she valued straight dealing in people; the knowledge that she had genuine organizational ability and could, when she had to, handle an awful lot more than she'd been able to before. She was, in fact, developing an ability to take life head on. And about time too. She stopped fiddling with her glass and looked at Jack again. He was sitting quietly, watching her and sipping his Bourbon. She felt she had to go on.

'Clara explained to me about her involvement with the film, and about her husband's too. She's in an . . . interesting position.'

'You could say that.' He raised his eyes to the pink rose in the centre of the ceiling. 'Whole set-up's an interesting one . . .'

'This is not good enough.' Oscar, petulant and chiding, stood over them. 'You two will have to share yourselves. We can't have you hugger-muggering together all night. I'm going to put you at different sides of the table. No, Jack,' he held up a hand and shook his head, 'you will not dissuade me. You may sit opposite the lady with the blue eyes, but that's my best offer. And now,' he twirled, an ungainly movement, 'we will eat. All,' he spread his hands, 'has been prepared by my good self.'

Murmuring low, a disordered bunch, they trooped after Oscar into the next-door dining room. Someone had lit the two candelabra on the table since Alva had made her tour, and they provided the only light. Its flickering flow muted the flowers-and-fruit wallpaper and gave the dark rust curtains a regal look. An unlit chandelier hung low over an oval table on which tiered fruit dishes were filled to overflowing.

'As a host, Oscar's way out of line.' Jack touched her hand and spoke low as they separated. 'You're the only woman here I want to talk to.'

'I'm the only woman here you know,' Alva whispered and slipped away and into the seat Oscar held out for her.

Oscar's 'bite to eat' was a repast. From modest beginnings – artichokes vinaigrette – things moved to the grandeur of lobster in a creamy sauce, a dish Oscar called *homard à l'américaine* and which he said he'd made 'to honour the palate of our transatlantic guest'. Things wound down a little with servings of melon stuffed with wild strawberries.

'As always, Oscar, your meals are an occasion of sin.' The writer, who'd long abandoned Ballygowan, looked immensely fed.

'I do make my contribution,' Oscar agreed.

'Which is all any of us can do,' said the restaurateur.

The conversation moved to films and filming. Jack was amusing; patient, too, when a great many silly questions were thrown at him by the two men from PR. They were, Alva reflected, the sort of questions she'd probably have asked herself a month before. She chatted across Stephen with the bookbinding woman and found her fun. Stephen, between them, remained almost entirely mute while Oscar, once the dessert was finished and cheese on the table, proceeded to drink seriously and to become maudlin.

The waiters cleared up, and later brought coffee in the drawing-room. While they hovered with Belgian chocolates the conversation became desultory and Alva, listening to the writer's wife on her problems with a local builder, caught Jack watching her from across the room. His head was bent towards Oscar, who was propounding at length. Alva smiled at him and, very slightly, he raised a questioning eyebrow.

'I do hope it works out for you,' Alva interrupted the writer's wife at a point where the builder had dropped and broken her cistern, 'but I have to leave now. I've got an early start and a busy day tomorrow.' She sauntered over to Oscar. No point in giving the appearance of wanting desperately to leave.

'You can't go.' Oscar looked aghast and Stephen, who'd chosen the floor and not a chair to sit on, patted his knee consolingly.

'Lovely party, Oscar, and I'm sorry,' Alva did her

best to sound it, 'but tomorrow's an early start. Will we see you at De Novo?'

'Hardly.' Oscar was caustic. 'Not after this.' His limpid gesture took in guests and waiters. 'I'll be enjoying my beddy byes until late in the day.' His gaze, for the briefest of seconds, lingered on Stephen.

'And that's my point,' Alva smiled. 'I'm up at cock-crow. Don't come to the door with me . . .'

'I'll come with you.' Jack Kelly stood up. 'I came by cab, so maybe you could drop me back to my hotel, Alva?'

Oscar huffed at this second loss, but half-heartedly, recognizing a situation when he saw one. They took their leave of the other guests and left with, on Alva's part, a feeling of relief mixed with guilt.

'I was beginning to feel I couldn't breathe in there,' Alva admitted as they crunched across the gravelled front to her car.

'Touch of the hothouse about it OK,' Jack agreed. 'But we're out and I have you to myself.' He put an arm around her shoulders and left it there while she manoeuvred the key into the lock.

'It's not that I've anything against hedonism,' Alva, stilling a slight panic at his closeness, spoke quickly, 'but with Oscar there's a touch of the forced feeding about it.' She opened the door and he put his lips into her hair.

'I'm staying near Stephen's Green,' he said and gave her the name of his hotel.

They drove through Ranelagh, the village deserted

but for night owls in the Chinese and fried chicken take-aways. They were crossing the canal bridge minutes later when Jack, absently it seemed, began gently to massage the back of Alva's neck. He had strong, supple fingers.

'You're a distraction.' Alva laughed.

'I mean to be,' he said. 'I wanted to meet you tonight.'

'Are you telling me,' Alva asked, comprehending, 'that I wasn't top of Oscar's guest list? That you asked him to . . .'

'Invite you. Yup. Guilty as charged. Seemed the only way to get you away from your house on the hill.' His fingers kept on massaging. 'I wanted a chance to meet with you on neutral ground.'

'Neutral is the last thing you could call Oscar's place.'

'True.' He laughed and took his hand away. 'My hotel room, on the other hand, is definitely neutral. Let me offer you a nightcap.' He held up his hand as she began a protest. 'One peaceful drink together. We both have early starts.'

Jack's suite was painted palest green with creamy-coloured curtains and furnishings. A desk in the sitting room had a fax machine and what looked like several thousand fax messages piled on it. The phone was ringing as they came through the door.

'Take off your coat and sit.' Jack propelled her gently by the shoulder to a sofa. 'Be with you in a minute.'

While he spoke on the phone in curt business

language Alva sat and regretted not having gone on home. She didn't take off her coat. It was warm, but taking it off would be a commitment to staying. One drink and she was going. She wasn't at all sure what her feelings were for Jack Kelly and she didn't want to find out tonight. She looked up when the phone slammed down and as a fax began to rattle from the machine.

'A peaceful drink?' She gave a small laugh and stood. 'Maybe another night would be better.'

'No. They're all the same. Sit.' He motioned towards the sofa and picked up the phone. 'I'll arrange peace.' Into the phone he said, 'No more calls until I tell you. Take messages. Now,' he walked to the mini-bar, slipping off his jacket as he went, 'what'll it be?'

'Any dry white wine in there? Cube of ice?'

'I can do better than that.' With a flourish, he produced a bottle of Dom Perignon. 'Much too late for anything else.' He popped the cork with practised ease and sat beside her on the sofa with two long glasses.

'Please take your coat off.' He spoke quietly as he began to pour. 'You're an adult, Alva. You leave when you want to. You don't need your coat as protection against me.' He held out her glass. 'You just have to say no. I'm not a goddamn rapist.'

His tone was polite, calm – and obviously offended. Alva, flushing, slipped her coat from her shoulders. She took the champagne.

'I've got out of the way of socializing,' she smiled. 'You'll have to excuse me.'

'Hard to understand a woman like you alone.' He touched her glass and they drank. 'But this is a funny old country.' He crossed his legs and leaned back, closing his eyes. He'd left enough room between them for at least one and a half more people. 'So, Clara told you the score about her backing money, and about Larry's. Did she tell you she originally backed it because of O'Hanlon?'

'Yes. She—'

'Makes things pretty damn awkward.' He opened his eyes and looked at her. He was relaxed, grinning a little. 'I don't like sharing control.'

'You mean with Clara?'

He leaned back again and pulled a face. 'Clara's dollars give her a say, but not a huge one. They became small potatoes when the project grew in size. No, I'm talking about O'Hanlon and the contract he got himself by virtue of this film being the springboard for the whole Millennium concept. Sure, I get to look after the money. But it's no fun being obliged to take on board the fantasies of a guy making his first feature film.'

'His brother *did* write the script,' Alva pointed out.

'Another complication.' Kelly opened his eyes and thoughtfully studied the ceiling. 'And one that makes O'Hanlon less amenable to script changes. The usual reality is that scriptwriters don't count once filming starts. It's better that way.' He draped a hand along the back of the sofa and turned to smile at her. 'They don't count tonight, either.' His voice had become gentler. 'I'm glad you're here. Why don't we forget all those others and concentrate on us. You and me.'

'You and me,' Alva repeated. 'Is there a you and me?'

'Could be.' He moved, closing the gap between them. 'Decision's yours.' He took her hand, turned it over between his own. 'I know what *I* want. I've wanted it for a while now, since that first day at the hotel. You stood there, shook your hair loose and smiled. Have you any idea what you did to me that day?' He stopped, looking at her, face close enough for her to see a tiny scar above his left eyebrow. He seemed to want an answer.

'Jack, I'm not ready for this. I . . .'

'This is *us*, Alva, you and me. We like each other. What's to get ready for?' He reached out and took a strand of her hair, wound it round his finger. He was almost whispering. 'I told you I wasn't a rapist. Well, I'm not even the kind of guy likes to kiss a girl without asking. Why don't you put the glass down, Alva, and let me kiss you?'

Alva, without taking her eyes from his, put down the glass. He put his hand on the back of her neck and drew her face closer. She sat very still and he kissed her forehead, her nose and at last touched her mouth, gently, with his. It was a long kiss, and a testing kiss. It was her first kiss since Kevin, and Alva found she liked it. When it ended he whispered into her hair.

'It was a cheap shot, making it so's you had to give me a ride here. But I'm never around for long enough to get to see you.'

'Shut up,' Alva said and kissed him again.

It was another long, exploratory kiss and she felt an immense gratitude to Jack Kelly. Slowly she put her arms around him, liking the way his compact body felt against hers. She put a hand to his hair and was gently fingering the curls when he abruptly pulled back, ending their kiss.

'We're not kids, Alva.' His voice was hoarse. 'We can do better than this.' He stood and pulled her up with him. They stood motionless for a few seconds, looking at one another.

Alva tried to say something but couldn't find her voice. She coughed. 'I think I should go,' she said. 'It's best not to start something we won't be finishing.'

'Alva.' He held her shoulder and shook her, very gently. 'I don't know your story, or whether it's me or the entire male world you're keeping at bay. But you're making a mistake, we could be great . . .'

Slowly, holding her close, murmuring against her mouth, silencing her with small, teasing kisses, he moved them across the room. It was a controlled, perfectly sensual dance and Alva went with it, uncertain still but not wanting to stop.

'Don't,' she said as they reached the bedroom door and Jack reached behind her to open it.

'Why not?' He pushed the door open with his foot as he breathed the question. 'You want it, I want it . . .'

They were moving again, same dance, same delights, only filled with the first shivers of anticipation now as the bed, large and dimly lit, came nearer. Jack's breathing had become deeper and his kisses more demanding; and then they were by the bed. Alva could feel it against her calves as she gently but definitely freed herself.

'Jack,' she said and stopped. He was smiling at her, lazily expectant. His hair was dishevelled, making him look younger. Sudden and unbidden she had an image of Luke O'Hanlon, of *his* dishevelled hair, his serious brown eyes. Then it went.

'God, you're beautiful,' Jack said and reached for her again. She put a hand on his chest, fending him off, then stepped sideways and out of his arms. Away from the bed. A chill, beginning in her neck, spread down her body.

'Please, Jack. I don't want this to go any further tonight. I'm sorry.'

'Sorry . . .' His expression was dazed, disbelieving.

'I really am. It just wouldn't be . . . right for me at the moment. I hope you won't . . .' she was going to say feel offended, but realizing how appallingly banal this sounded, said nothing.

'Forget it.' His voice was harsh. 'Let's just finish our drinks and forget it.'

'I won't do that either, Jack, if you don't mind.' She gave a wan smile. 'I'm driving.'

'Suit yourself.'

By the lift door she kissed him gently on the mouth. 'I'm sorry,' she said again. She felt no return pressure. The lift doors opened and as she stepped inside he stopped them shutting with his foot.

'This is the real world, Alva, not that little hide-away world you've made for yourself.' His voice was cold and his face still. 'And in the real world things come round and give you a shot at them once and then they go.'

He took his foot away and the doors shut.

Chapter Sixteen

'I've seen you look better, honey. Oscar's party more than you bargained for?'

Clara's sympathy, in the kitchen next morning, didn't make Alva feel any better. By telling the actress where she was going the evening before she had, she supposed, left herself open to comment. But a night spent in a restless state of waking-sleep showed and she could have done without being reminded of the fact. Clara herself looked great – apart, that is, from the bilious effect of a lime-green dressing gown. Alva averted her gaze and put food into a dish for an ungrateful Thomas.

'Party was fine,' she said, 'very Oscar, lots of good food and drink. His house is a bit overwhelming, though, and the guests were a dull enough lot.' She managed a small smile. 'Except of course for Jack Kelly, who always manages to be interesting.'

'Interesting. Funny word for Jack, but I suppose he is.' Clara looked doubtful. 'If you haven't met the type before. I have to say, honey, that I was surprised when you said he'd be there.' She bit into a slice of toast with lemon curd. 'He's got a reputation for all work and no play and two divorces to show for it.'

'Oh?' The divorces were news. No one had

mentioned them before – but then why should they? In the world Jack Kelly inhabited a steady marriage would probably give rise to more comment. Two broken marriages explained too why he hadn't spoken much about his personal life. Such things, even among the worldly wise, didn't exactly make for small talk.

'I've once again,' Alva looked moodily at the now gobbling Thomas as she spoke, 'proven myself less than the world's greatest judge of men.'

'There's none of us infallible when it comes to the opposite sex.' Clara was sympathetic. 'Why do I get the feeling there's a story to tell about last night's party?'

Alva, filling breakfast jugs with milk, chose to take Clara's question literally. 'I suppose because what you know about Jack gives you the edge. I walked myself into a situation that you'd have seen a mile off.'

It was half-past eight and in the yard below filming activity was already under way – Clara wasn't due on the set until later. The bus windows were steamed up with breakfasters, but Alva wanted to have their coffee and tea on tap before Bernie arrived at nine.

'Have yourself a mug of that coffee, why don't you?' Clara suggested. 'You look kind of grey. And talk to me. You'll feel better.'

Alva poured herself a coffee and leaned against the worktop, turning the hot mug between her hands. 'These kitchen chats are becoming a habit.' She knew her voice sounded leaden. Leaden was how she felt. Nothing to do with regrets about not going to bed with Jack Kelly. More to do with a certainty that the night before's incident had ended what could have developed into, at the very least, a friendship.

Clara, about to sip her coffee, paused with the mug in mid-air. 'Let me guess.' Her look was shrewd. 'You're about to tell me that Jack-the-lad put his body on the line and you resisted. Am I right or am I right?'

'Something like that,' Alva muttered.

'Oh, come *on*, Alva honey,' Clara raised an eyebrow in a perfect, questioning arc, 'don't stop now. Tell me everything that happened. You'll feel better.'

Alva hoped so. What was certain was that Clara would feel better for hearing about the night before. She pulled a rueful face and began to tell.

'It happened in his hotel room. To be fair I shouldn't have gone up there unless I intended going to bed with him. It was a bloody stupid thing to do. I've ruined what could have been a nice friendship . . .'

'In a pig's eye you have,' Clara snorted. 'Jack Kelly doesn't *have* friends. He has lovers and people he uses and people he does business with and they're all usually the same people. But, to be fair to him in my turn, it's been clear from day one that he had a thing going for you. Everyone's noticed, including our Luke who hasn't been too happy about it. Even so, Jack only does favours when there's financial or personal gain to be had. Believe me, Alva, giving you the catering contract was both a business and personal favour.'

'Everyone . . .' Alva's leaden feeling increased. 'Everyone except me,' she said, but knew this wasn't strictly true. She'd known Jack Kelly liked her. She just hadn't wanted to face dealing with it.

'Personally, I find Jack a dull boy.' Clara was robust. 'I find him predictable, in the way these moguls are, eye on the main chance, playing people off one another, all of that. You're well rid of him.' She pulled the green dressing gown more tightly about herself and Alva looked away. Clara noticed and gave a wry grin. 'Ill-making, isn't it? The boys gave it to me. I feel I should wear it every so often.' She paused. 'How keen were you on our Jack?'

'I liked him,' Alva admitted. 'Last night was just one of those things, but I feel bad about it. I'll talk to him, sort things out . . .'

'I doubt it'll work like that with Jack.' Clara yawned. 'We're talking ego here. Jack was never in for the long haul, honey. He went for his pay-off last night and you didn't cough up. He won't forgive and he won't forget. That's the way guys like him are. It's all a big ego, power thing with them. He'll be particularly sensitive to the fact that you might talk and that word could get around that he failed to score. *I* think you should be on your guard . . .' She looked musingly at Thomas, cleaning himself after his meal.

'On my guard against what?'

'Against him pulling something nasty to save face. You can bet that Jack saving Jack's face will mean punishing you in some way.' Clara plastered another piece of toast with lemon curd. 'Let's just pray to our various gods that he doesn't take it out on the rest of us too.'

'I'm glad I had this little talk with you.' Alva was caustic. 'It's made me feel much better.'

'Better you hear the reality from me.' Clara was gentle. She touched Alva on the arm. 'At least now you're prepared.'

Bernie was late, which was unusual. At half nine Alva shoved the scones she'd made the night before into the oven and hoped for the best. Just before ten Bernie arrived, bleary-eyed behind her glasses.

'Sammy's got measles.' She shoved her unruly fuzz of hair into a net. 'The spots came out last night and they're *everywhere*. You can't imagine the places I found them.'

'I can,' Alva said, 'so don't tell me. How is he? Maybe you should have stayed at home with him?'

'No point,' Bernie said, 'the worst is over, apart from the discomfort. He looks like a plague victim, though. I spent the night lolloping calamine lotion onto the spots.'

'Talking of the plague – adults don't get measles, do they?' Alva asked.

'No, except in extreme and rare circumstances,' Bernie said, 'so don't worry.'

'I was thinking about you, actually,' Alva said.

Lunch had ended and Alva was clearing up when a message came from Jack Kelly that he wanted a meeting that evening. By that time she had had what amounted to her first serious row with Bernie and begun to have a niggle of serious worry about Ellen.

The row came about midday when Jasper Clarke, during a break in filming, arrived in the dining hall for a coffee. Bernie joined him and as she sat at the table, face propped in her hands, ardently listening, Alva saw that what she'd almost willed not to happen was happening. Bernie, if her expression was anything to go by, was seriously smitten by Jasper. She was going to be hurt.

Alva continued laying table places for lunch, but noisily. For a while it seemed neither of them would notice. Jasper was listening now, Bernie with avid demonstrations telling the story of Sammy's measles.

Alva studied his face. Its appeal was in its very ordinariness, a basic everyday decency and gentleness: the face of the sort of man Bernie wanted, in fact. A regular man with a good appetite who would eat her food and, well fed and happy, make love to her every night. Except that Bernie couldn't have Jasper Clarke. Some other woman was waiting, wearing his ring, arranging their wedding. It was time to talk to Bernie.

'I need you to help me, Bernie.' Alva stood over them. She gave Jasper a cool smile. Bernie blinked.

'Be with you in a minute,' she said.

'Fine.' Alva nodded and walked quickly back to the upstairs kitchen. Bernie, a few minutes later, came slowly up the steps.

'Why did you do that?' she stood by the table, holding Jasper's mug. 'Why were you so rude, Alva?'

'Sorry if I was rude,' Alva said, 'but I *do* want to talk to you. Before everyone arrives for lunch seemed a good time.'

'You could have said so nicely. There was no need to be rude.' Bernie's jaw set rigidly and her eyes glinted behind their spectacles. 'Especially to Jasper. He's a friend. He's been a friend since the beginning. He was our first customer. He—'

'Bernie, stop.' Alva pulled out a chair but Bernie, with a furious shake of her head, stayed where she was.

Alva took a deep breath. 'Do you know that Jasper Clarke's engaged to be married?'

'Yes, I know that.'

Alva waited but Bernie, solid and unmoving, said nothing more.

'It's just that I can see you care for him,' Alva was hesitant, 'and I wasn't sure if you knew, about the fiancée, I mean. I don't want you to be hurt, get yourself into a mess . . .'

'Whether I'm getting myself into a mess,' Bernie cut her short, 'or saving Jasper from getting *himself* into a mess is none of your business, Alva. I don't tell you how to run your love life.'

They stared at one another in bleak silence, both of them hating what was happening. Alva moved first, to trace a heart with her finger in a wet patch on the table. 'My non-existent love life,' she said.

'That's your choice,' Bernie said, but her voice had softened. 'You're alone because you won't let any man near you. That's not what I want. If I get hurt it's *my* hurt. But I don't think it'll be like that, this time. I know what I'm doing.' She paused and grinned; a great big Bernie grin. 'I think.'

'God, I hope you do,' Alva said.

The niggle about Ellen came as Alva was in the

middle of serving lunches. Theo arrived to eat, as he'd been doing every other day that week, at a table in a corner of the dining hall. He did it, he said, to save Bernie the trouble of cooking for him in the evenings. Alva suspected there was another, more fundamental reason. Theo disliked eating alone and Ellen, better company than none, rarely ate with him these days. He was eating in the dining hall for company.

'Ellen's not sick, is she?' Alva asked as she put his meal in front of him. 'Only I haven't seen her today.'

'Doesn't appear to be,' Theo said. 'I looked in on her. Nothing wrong with her tongue, anyway.'

'She's staying in her room a lot, isn't she?'

'She is.'

'Should I bring her up some food?'

'I brought her up bread and cheese. You just get on with things here and don't worry.' He bent over his meal and began to eat methodically.

But Alva did worry. She worried that Ellen, alone in her room, might collapse from too little food and too much drink. And she worried that the old woman might lose her frail hold on reality.

She stopped thinking about Ellen, however, when a sober-faced Juno brought word from the production office that Jack Kelly wanted a meeting, at seven sharp, with Alva and Bernie.

'Just us two?' Alva asked.

'There'll be a few others. Six in all. Christ, he was a real jerk about it. I asked if he'd like me along to make the number seven – lucky number, you understand.

He told me to take a flying fuck.' She turned down her mouth. 'There was no need for that.'

'No, there wasn't,' Alva agreed.

It was arranged that the meeting would happen in the dining room, still 'dressed' for filming but unlikely, barring another disaster with film stock, to be needed again.

Juno, with her usual efficiency, laid pads and pencils by six chairs at the table. She put names on them too and Alva, checking, saw she'd been put between Felim Gray and Leo Cullen. Bernie would be opposite, with Luke on one side and Jack on the other. Juno had been careful to create equality; no one would be sitting at the top of the table.

By a few minutes past seven everyone but Jack Kelly had gathered in the dining room. The sombre mood wasn't helped by the heavy, Victorian look the room had been given for the film. Belatedly, Alva thought about lighting a fire. At a quarter past seven Luke stopped doodling on his pad and stood up.

'I'm off,' he announced. 'I'll be in the production office if Kelly ever makes it.'

Another five minutes went by, and then another. Felim Gray consulted his watch and excused himself to make a phone call. Leo Cullen sat taciturn and indifferent, smoking untipped John Players. Bernie pointedly opened the window and allowed in a chill draught. In the uneasy quiet Alva, with a sense of relief, heard Ellen come clipping down the stairs in her mules. She went out to meet her.

'You all right?' she asked.

'Were you hoping I wasn't?' Ellen snapped.

'I was worried, actually,' Alva said, 'but I can see that I needn't have been.'

'That man you've been throwing yourself at is in a car outside,' Ellen said. 'Been sitting there for five minutes on a phone.'

'Oh?' Alva hesitated, wondering whether she should open the front door by way of a hint or go back to the dining room to tell the others. The decision was made for her when the doorbell rang.

'Jack.' She smiled at the executive producer. 'We've been waiting for you. We're all agog as to what this meeting is about.'

'Good.' Jack Kelly smiled too, familiar and threatening. 'We can get started straight away. Ah, Miss Donovan,' he made a small bow in Ellen's direction, 'how've you been?'

'I have been, and am, old and tired,' Ellen said.

'Tired you may be, Miss Donovan, but old never.' The beaming gallantry was entirely convincing. Ellen glared.

'You think not?' she asked. 'You don't agree then that *la vieillesse est l'enfer des femmes*?'

'With you, Miss Donovan, I would never disagree.'

'Even when it means contradicting yourself, obviously.'

'We've arranged to use the dining room, Jack,' Alva cut in hurriedly.

'Good.' Jack Kelly nodded to Ellen and strode through the open door. It took a further five minutes to recall Gray and O'Hanlon, by which time Jack had moved his pad and was ensconced at the top of the table.

'The object of this brief get together,' he checked his watch, 'is production finance and the amount being overspent on this location. Filming has also', he looked without expression at the director, 'gone over schedule. In a project as big as this one we can't—'

'Why don't you cut the crap, Jack,' Luke beat a tattoo on the table with his pencil, 'and get on with whatever it is you came here to do.'

Jack looked at a point beyond the director's head for several seconds. 'I'm here to implement cuts,' he said finally.

'Cuts.' Luke's pencil broke in his hand. 'More bloody cuts—' He stopped as the door opened and Clara, to a small silence, slipped into the room. With a bright nod she pulled a chair to the table and sat down.

'Good to have you here, Clara.' Jack did not look pleased. He bent over the papers in front of him. 'We need to cut back on the food budget and on time spent on breaks,' he said. 'The bills make it look as if this place is still being run as a hotel. Bernie, Alva,' his swift glance at each was accompanied by a regretful, lopsided smile, 'I'm not renewing your contract for the two additional weeks. Food's Up can more than adequately look after things. I'm sorry,' he spread his hands, 'has to be done.'

Alva's immediate reaction was resignation. This, then, was to be Jack Kelly's revenge. Taken publicly too, a proper demonstration of power. God, but she was a miserable judge of men. She'd liked the man. Found him attractive. Yet here he was, revealed as an egomaniac who couldn't take no for an answer. Was she ever going to like anything but rat-like men? She glanced Bernie's way. The other woman's expression couldn't have been more dazed if she'd been shot with a stun gun.

'You are obviously within your rights, Jack,' Alva was cooler than cool, 'and *we* are obviously disappointed. I imagine the crew will be too.'

'Time spent eating and drinking from now on will be strictly as per agreements.' Kelly ignored her and turned to Luke. 'And we can't rise to that extra scene you wanted with Clara back in town.'

'Don't worry about that, Jack, I've decided not to do it. Is that everything?'

'Yup.' Kelly stood. 'Thank you all for your time.'

'A word, Jack, if I may.' Felim Gray was polite. 'What sort of catering overspending are we talking here? Not vast amounts, surely?'

'Big enough to raise questions elsewhere and to risk cutbacks in post-production. And none of us want that, Felim, do we?'

'Perhaps you'd let me see your figures?' Felim Gray held out a hand and Jack slid a sheaf of papers across to him.

'Look, Gray, you too, O'Hanlon. Neither of you have any idea of the realities involved here. You've never got your heads around the fact that this isn't the neat, one-off little picture you tied up for yourselves in the beginning.'

'The Krauts are on time, they're going out in week three. The Hungarians, who were up against it to begin with, look like they're going to produce the best damn film of the lot and the Portuguese . . .' He stayed standing but with his hands on the table, leaning towards Luke O'Hanlon. 'The Portuguese have totally fucked up and their film is going to be scrapped. Scrapped.' He stopped. He was breathing hard and the angles of his face had sharpened. Anger suited him. In an odd way he seemed smaller, though. Alva had never thought about his size before.

'These figures aren't wildly out,' Felim Gray began but Kelly cut him short.

'If we'd wanted to film in the Ritz we'd have booked the fucking Ritz.' His voice had got louder and his eyes narrower. 'You're in the big world now, boys, time to work, think about *making money*. We want a commercial picture. And I want you to see to it, Gray, that this picture is made within budget and on schedule.'

Luke leaned back and crossed his arms. 'We're in serious danger of making a good film here, as opposed to the dross you've been involved with in the past, Kelly,' he said. 'Why don't you leave things as they are? Get back to Hungary or wherever it is they're feeding the crew on bread and water—'

'What Luke's trying to say,' Felim Gray interrupted with a frowning look at the director, 'is that *Death Diminishes* is working out. Changes in the work routine won't be helpful. They could even cause delays. We're not on opposite sides, Jack. Everyone here wants to make the best film possible. Everyone wants a commercial success too. I don't see the two as being mutually exclusive, do you?' He was looking again at the figures. 'I'll hold on to these, Jack,' he said.

Kelly shrugged. 'Be my guest. Well, that's it, folks, bad news time over. I want less wining and dining and more asses kicked around here. Thanks for coming, Leo, production man should know the score.'

'Before you go, Jack.' Clara stood up and walked around the table. She put her hand on the executive producer's shoulder and pushed him, gently, down into his seat. 'I've had an idea that should keep everybody happy. Why don't *I* finance De Novo Catering for the last two weeks? It surely doesn't amount to mega bucks, does it, Felim?' Felim Gray shook his head and Clara, looking pleased with herself, went on. 'I'll be protecting my own interests by ensuring a happily fed crew up to the end.'

'Generous of you.' Jack pushed his chair out of her range and stood. His face was tight. 'Discuss it with Felim. Everything else I said stands.'

Alva jumped up as he strode to the door and, after a quick, grateful look Clara's way, almost ran after him. He'd reached the outside steps before she caught up with him.

'I was under the impression that what happened last night was private, Jack.' He didn't stop and she had to skip to keep pace with him down the steps. 'That it was between us two, nothing to do with business.' He kept going, to his car. 'But I was wrong, wasn't I?' Alva faced him as the driver opened the door. Kelly frowned, waved the man back to his place behind the wheel.

'Damn right you were wrong.' He smiled, and she saw it now; the false, showbiz smile, teeth bared and shining. 'The personal *is* business, Alva, and don't you ever forget it. I wanted you on my team but you never really played ball, did you? I put time into you, sweetheart, and money. I don't have any more of either. I thought you were smart but you just weren't smart enough and now it's over.' He shrugged. 'It's fine by me if Clara wants to pay for the privilege of eating your food. But remember what I just said – the personal is business. Clara Butler's no exception to the rule. There has to be something in it for her too.' He gave a curt nod and slid inside the car.

In the house Leo Cullen was the only one who'd left the dining room. Bernie, talking excitedly to Clara, pounced as soon as Alva appeared.

'I've had a brilliant idea!' Her laughter was the nervously relieved kind. 'It's for a cookbook. You write up my recipes and we call it *Death Diminishes but Hunger is Good Sauce.* We market it when the film comes out. What do you think?'

Alva blinked. 'I think the title needs a bit of work.' She hesitated, grinning. 'Or maybe not.' She turned to Clara, perched on the props department's precious Victorian table. 'You didn't have to bail us out,' she said, 'and you don't have to go through with it . . .'

'Yes, I do,' Clara nodded, 'and not just for you and Bernie or even the crew.' She grinned. 'I did it to get at that bastard. I'll bet he's sick as a parrot. God, you really must have spiked his guns good last night, Alva. I did warn you hell would have no fury like our Jacko scorned.'

'What's all this about?' Bernie's eyes were like beacons behind her glasses. 'Why wasn't I told there had been a happening last night?'

'Another time, Bernie.' Alva pulled a furious, silencing face as the producer and director, until then in deep conversation by the window, came towards them.

'Oh, right.' Bernie nodded and, not very subtly, changed the subject. 'Remember I told you that Leo Cullen was a creeping Jesus? I knew it from the very beginning.'

'Oh?' Felim Gray raised an interested eyebrow.

'Sticking out a mile. He's a Jack Kelly spy.' Bernie was enjoying herself. 'I suppose because he's not around much he wants someone to keep him filled in. And Oscar wasn't much good to him. Lazy sod never shows his face.'

'You're quite right, of course.' Felim Gray stuffed the accounts Kelly had given him into his pocket. 'Jack likes to divide and conquer, it's the way he operates. But in this instance I suspect his little power playing with personalities is only a smidgen of what he's up to.'

Clara swung her legs off the table and stood beside the producer. She was almost as tall as he was, and all at once formidable. 'What's going on, Felim? I want to know,' she demanded.

'You'll know as soon as I do,' he promised.

'When'll that be? Is the picture in danger?'

'Answer to the first question's a few days, and to the second a most definite no. Relax, Clara. The only person in trouble here is Jack, and possibly Oscar . . .' He paused before adding, very deliberately, 'Could be they're working a scam together.'

'God, I can't stand this!' Clara wailed. 'I want to know now!'

So do I, Alva thought, so do I. But possibilities for putting further pressure on the producer disappeared as the door was thrown open and Justine, eyes terrified in a pale face, burst into the room.

'Luke! Oh, God, I've been looking for you everywhere! The nurse is gone, you'll have to get a doctor out here. Quickly!'

'Take it easy, Justine.' The director put his hands on her shoulders and forced her to look at him. 'Just tell me what the problem is. Slowly now . . .'

'It's *her* child!' Justine jerked her head in Bernie's direction. 'It's got measles, and we're all going to be contaminated. I'll come out in spots, scabs! All over! Worse even, we'll all get shingles. That's how it affects adults—'

'What absolute bloody nonsense!' Bernie was irate. 'Why don't you take a cold shower and calm down, you silly woman. If I were you,' she turned, glowering, to Felim Gray, 'I'd be more worried about a real murder around here than any shenanigans old Jack Kelly might be up to.'

Chapter Seventeen

Ellen got rid of Thomas next day. Without warning and without telling anyone, she carried him in a basket down the avenue and into the village. Alva saw her go and thought the basket curious, but felt huge relief that Ellen had left her room and ventured outside again. She looked very jaunty as she went.

She was gone for an hour and she looked even jauntier coming back up the avenue, a long scarf trailing outside her coat and wearing a cloche hat. She had no basket. Alva met her in the hallway.

'You look like the cat who got the cream,' she said and was taken aback by Ellen's sudden, raucous laugh.

'The cat's got the cream all right,' she said. 'Or at least he will if he plays his cards right.'

'What're you talking about?' Alva remembered the basket and stared. 'You've done something with Thomas, haven't you?'

'I have, as the saying goes, found him a new home.' Ellen raised sceptical eyebrows. 'Don't, please, pretend either sorrow or distress. You disliked the animal.'

'But, why? *You* liked him . . .' Alva could have added that Thomas was the only life form Ellen showed *any* affection for, but stopped herself.

'He was mine, to do with as I liked.' Ellen's smile

was cold. She walked past Alva to the foot of the stairs. Caught in the light from the coloured window she looked like a harlequin in drag. 'I will be down to dine at seven,' she said and swept up the stairs, almost toppling a set worker coming down with an armful of costumes from Justine's room.

Alva stood for several disbelieving minutes. The feeling of chilly shock slowly reverted to the nagging disquiet she'd been having about Ellen for a week or so. Getting rid of Thomas was a symptom of something. The cat was eleven years old. Elderly, but not on his last legs. He'd been the only thing Ellen had related to, the only living thing Alva had ever known her touch.

I should tell Theo, she thought. He might know what's going on. And if he doesn't, he should.

It was one of those late autumn days when close, warm breezes circulated the muggy scents in the garden. On her way to find Theo Alva meandered, taking in the muskiness of the pines and bouquet of the late roses which, storm notwithstanding, had just come into bloom. Theo had conceded to the film company's offer of help to clear up and the garden, though spartan in a way Alva had never seen it before, was more or less its autumn self.

She found Theo in the summerhouse. He didn't hear her coming and for several minutes she observed him unnoticed. There was the look of a rock about him, still and craggy as he sat looking out across the bay, his back very straight and his great hands covering his knees. If she hadn't known him better she'd have said his expression in profile was resigned. But Theo was not a resigning sort of person. And what had he to be resigned about?

'So,' she sank onto the blue-painted seat beside him, 'this is where you do your plotting and planning.'

His moustache moved slightly upwards so that she knew he was smiling. He didn't turn to look at her.

'I did once,' he said, 'I did once. The horizon's a good place to rest the eye.' He looked at her. 'You came to tell me about the cat?' He patted her knee and looked out at the bay again. 'The cat will be all right. Ellen would never have given it to someone who wouldn't care for it.'

'Theo, I'm not really worried about Thomas. I'm worried about Ellen. *Why* would she do a thing like that? Get rid of the only thing she cared about?'

'Who knows?' Theo shrugged. He took off his glasses and rubbed his eyes with the back of his hand. 'Maybe *she's* plotting and planning something. Whatever, there's nothing you or I can do. Too late for that now, I'd say.'

Felim Gray was sitting waiting for Alva on the bottom step of the stairs when she arrived back. The light which had caught Ellen so eerily made Felim Gray seem just cheerfully lit up.

'Can we talk?' his smile was determined. Alva had seen similar expressions on the face of her dentist.

'Of course,' she said. 'Sitting room's probably the most private place at the moment.'

Alva shut the door and leaned against it for a moment while Felim Gray settled himself comfortably into an armchair. He rested an ankle on his knee, his arms elegantly along the armrests. He wore chinos and a dark jacket, and compared to Luke O'Hanlon's restless performance in the same room a few days earlier, he appeared almost comatose.

'I've been busy.' He spoke lightly, still smiling. 'And I've uncovered a bit of a mess I think you should know about.'

Alva moved away from the door, took a chair from around the table and straddled it, leaning her arms along its back as she faced the producer. She wanted to be alert, not comfortable, when she heard what he had to say.

'I should get us coffee or something,' she said, 'but I'd prefer to get this out of the way first. I'm not going to like it, am I?'

'Don't see how you could.' He was wry, his voice when he went on subdued. 'It's about Oscar. Seems he's been working a very nice number for himself since taking up employ with the company. He's been fiddling pretty comprehensively, using his "special relationship" with Jack to protect him from too close a scrutiny from people like myself. He'd probably have sailed clear into the blue if I hadn't noticed something the other day. Thing is,' he smiled, with genuine amusement this time, 'he's been putting one over on Jack too.'

'Proving nothing's sacred.' Alva was fascinated and, she found, not altogether surprised.

'You're getting the picture,' Felim said. 'Unfortunately, you're one of his victims too.' His jaw tightened and he came the closest she'd ever seen him to anger. 'He's done you for ten thousand pounds.'

'You're sure?' Alva sat up straight, gripping the back of the chair. Her voice was croaky. The question was rhetorical. Of course Felim was sure. She needed time to digest this, get used to the idea of Oscar the hyper-eccentric as Oscar the grubby cheat. Felim gave her the time, staying silent while he uncrossed his legs and took a notebook from his pocket. He flicked it open and looked at her.

'Will I go on?' he asked and she nodded, mutely.

'The catering figures given me by Jack yesterday showed up a discrepancy,' he smiled at the euphemism, 'and alerted me to go look for others. Oscar had been paid £300.00 from an account controlled by Kelly for entertaining expenses to do with the deal securing De Novo. What Oscar didn't seem to have told Jack was that he'd billed, and been paid by me, for the same "dinner and drinks". I took my little, er, investigation from there. Juno helped.' He smiled and then, his cool deserting him, laughed gleefully. 'By God that woman's a terrier. I'd hate to have her against me. Don't – ' he put a finger to his lips as Alva started to ask something, 'please don't ask me how or what she did to find out all she did. It involved a visit to Oscar at home in Ranelagh, a chat with his disenchanted friend Stephen, and using her charms on some people working in a TV series Oscar was moonlighting for.'

'Sounds simple,' Alva said. She would, if she died in the attempt, get the whole story later from Juno. 'Tell me how I helped him net ten thousand.'

Felim coughed and spoke quickly. It was as if, by telling it fast, he could make the details less awful.

'The budget okayed Oscar to pay you £35,000 for De Novo. He paid you £25,000, right?' Alva nodded. 'Having got away with that, he went on to fiddle wholesale, charging overtime for weekends he didn't even appear anywhere near De Novo, for petrol and mileage on journeys never taken, for business lunches that were nothing of the sort, books he claimed were needed for research and trousers to replace a pair he claimed were ruined by brambles while working in the garden here . . .'

'He snagged a pair of trousers all right.' Alva tried to laugh but only managed a strangulated gurgle. She coughed and went on, thoughtfully, 'What I don't get, Felim, is how he could be so *blatant*, even for Oscar. He must have been pretty sure he'd get away with it.'

'You have, as the saying goes, hit the nail on the head. Since May last, Oscar's siphoned off twenty thousand or so, tax free, for himself. Not an enormous sum in the overall scheme of things, it's true. But not bad either. What's clear from looking through accounts, and how he did it, is that Jack, who took Oscar on in the first place, in all probability knew what was going on and turned a blind eye. Question is – why?'

'Well then, why?' Alva asked impatiently. Felim was in danger of carrying urbane cool too far.

'I'm convinced, but can't find any proof as yet, that Jack was up to more than just exercising his control-freak tendencies on *Death Diminishes*. I think he was frying bigger fish and dealing in much bigger bucks and that Oscar had wind of it.'

'So it was blackmail?'

'Sort of. More a crooks' agreement I'd say. Can't see why else Kelly paid him virtually on demand.' He stopped and looked momentarily bleak.

'Where does all of this leave you?' Alva asked.

'With egg on my face.' He got up and began to rock on his heels, all pretence at cool gone. 'I'm producer for this one film, Kelly's involvement is with the overall project. Since the beginning everything's worked well on a local level but it's been a bitch getting corporate approval, or even the corporate ear, on things. I just haven't, ever, been given the full picture. With the controlling clause in Luke's contract and Clara's money as part of the package we've managed to keep relative control. But there's something . . .'

'Do you think Jack Kelly's been fiddling funds for himself too?'

'Doubtful. Money isn't Jack's major interest. Power is, and manipulating people. Alva, listen,' he had stopped rocking on his heels and looked almost non-chalant again, 'none of this need concern you. I thought you deserved to know the score, that's all. I'll sort things out, get your ten thou if possible – though there may be a problem. Oscar will be fired, of course, and Kelly's not going to like that. It'll make him look bad, put his judgement in question. But the company will be out of here in ten days or so and you'll have your hotel back,' he grinned, 'in one piece. This place is a survivor.'

'Yes,' Alva said, 'yes, it is.'

The house was very quiet after he left. The unit was filming just outside the gates that day, getting shots of Constance's brother as he approached, stood, looked and finally went through and up the avenue. Bernie was with them, doing snacks. Felim Gray had refused a coffee but Alva had one herself, alone and thoughtful in the kitchen. She wondered what Oscar would do. Brazen it out, she supposed. He'd got what he wanted, which was money. The opulence of the house in Ranelagh was explained. Part of her felt saddened to have him revealed as a cheat. Oscar the eccentric had amused her. It would be harder to laugh at him after this. If they ever met again that was; if he ever came back.

Thomas's bowl, in a corner where Bernie wasn't supposed to see it, still held some of the milk Alva had left for him earlier. She washed it out, surprised by the stab of nostalgia she felt for the departed cat.

If *I* miss him, and I didn't even like him much, then God knows how poor old Ellen is feeling, she thought. Ellen had isolated herself almost completely. Not good. Not something which should be allowed go on. I'll go up to her, Alva decided. The story of Oscar's downfall will cheer her up no end.

Ellen was lying on her bed, fully clothed and propped up by a bank of pink satin cushions. Her eyes were open, staring at the darkening sky beyond the window. She turned her head when Alva came into the room and glared.

'I knocked but you didn't answer,' Alva began.

'Extraordinary that you should then presume you might enter.' The barb lacked Ellen's usual energy.

'I brought you some tea. And a sandwich.' Alva slipped the tray onto the bed beside Ellen and sat at the end herself. 'The film's already got a tragic heroine,' she said, 'and the role doesn't suit you. Have the sandwich and tea.'

'If it'll keep you quiet,' Ellen said and began to eat.

'Oscar's been a bad boy,' Alva said. 'He's been ripping us all off.' Briefly, sparing Oscar not at all, she told the story of his misdoings. Ellen continued to eat, slowly, as if she had no appetite. But she did smile.

'Fat fool,' she said, 'to get caught. Where is he now?'

'God knows,' Alva said. 'Licking his wounds or spending the money. With Oscar it could be either.'

'Not much of a businesswoman, are you?' Ellen discarded the second half of the sandwich and sipped half-heartedly at the tea. 'Letting yourself be taken in by that sort of person. See to it that you get your money.' She sounded sympathetic but then, as if exhausted by the effort of civility, leaned back against the pillows and closed her eyes. 'Duggan is a fool but a lucky one. He'll die before he gets old. His liver will give up, or AIDS will get him. Better than to have the heart grow old.'

'Oh, Ellen,' Alva said, 'please try.'

But Ellen had closed her eyes. When she didn't open them again Alva left the room.

In the kitchen Bernie was subdued. She'd come back from feeding everyone on the set with suspiciously bright eyes, and bustled and banged about with a briskness which was forbidding.

'Sammy OK?' Alva asked.

'Fine. Little bugger won't stop scratching. I've tied gloves on his hands but he keeps taking them off.' Bernie whammed a pot onto the cooker.

'News of the day is that Oscar's a crook.' Briefly, aware that she had a millimetre of Bernie's attention, Alva filled her in.

'Thought he was a bit of a boyo all right.' Bernie tut-tutted and took off her apron. 'I'm leaving early. There's nothing needs doing anyway.'

'Don't you care that a moral outrage has been committed here?' Alva kept her tone light. 'I thought you'd be—'

'I've other things on my mind at the moment.' Bernie reached into the pantry for her coat. 'Talk to me tomorrow, Alva. I might be able to work up some indignation by then.'

Alva sat in on the showing of the rushes again that night. The scenes were between Justine and Nick Hunt, and as lovers they shone, a beautiful, honey-gold, tragic pair. The sexual pull between them was palpable and utterly convincing.

'God, I'm impressed,' Alva said afterwards. 'I've seen them practically spit at one another when they're off screen.'

'Never underestimate the power of the ego in this business.' Luke, sitting beside her, grinned. 'Off screen they're too alike to do anything but loathe one another. On screen it's a battle to upstage. Works fine, in this case.'

Clara, yawning, stood up. 'The director's got a bit to do with it too, Alva. But enough flattery.' She looked from one to the other of them, a theatrically pleading expression on her face. 'Look, I've been hanging around, not a scene to shoot for the last two days. I'm bored and I feel a creative urge coming on. How about if I cook tomorrow – will you two come eat with me?'

There seemed no reason, or way, to say no.

Clara's meal, prepared with some friction during Bernie's working day, turned out to be a snack followed by a couple of desserts with the calorific content of a medieval feast. She served her mocha roulade spread with praline cream along with what she called a chess pie, an American-style pecan and walnut tart. She sat, a beaming overseer, while Alva and Luke dug in. Salad and a thin soup had left them more than willing.

'Good, aren't they?' she said. 'The boys love those two in particular. They're the only things I'm any damn good at.'

They were eating in the dining room. Alva had lit the fire and put candles on the table and the effect obliterated the unfriendly ghosts of Jack Kelly's meeting of days before.

Clara, at the top of the table with Luke and Alva on either side, was dressed entirely in burgundy, her face palely dramatic in contrast. She was also, it was clear, enjoying the hostess role. While Alva and Luke ploughed, in Alva's case willingly, through the sweet delights of chocolate and pie Clara talked about her sons and sipped carrot juice.

'I've decided to bring the boys to Dublin in December,' she announced, at a point where Alva had decided enough was enough and that if Clara didn't stop she was going to introduce Ellen as a subject of conversation.

'Good.' Luke wasn't curt exactly. There was more of an 'about time too' to his tone.

'Yes, well ...' Clara, in the candlelight, flushed. 'I *do* listen, Luke, sometimes. And you were right that night when you said I should bring the boys over here.'

In the odd little silence which followed this exchange Alva felt excluded, forgotten by both of them. The thought that they might be lovers came to her again, disturbing her more than she cared to think about. But think about it she did, while they talked on together in low tones. She was upset, she told herself, because the idea diminished Clara's tragic widow role and made Luke appear a less than loyal friend to the departed Larry. But why, logic and forbearance demanded, shouldn't they share love? However it presented itself? She helped herself to the comfort of another slice of the roulade. It didn't taste as good as it had before.

She looked up at Clara's reflective face and Luke's serious one, and told herself that the notion of them as lovers upset her because it knocked her faith in the purity of their friendship. Even as the idea formed she knew she was fooling herself. If she was honest, the real reason had more to do with her own mixed feelings about Luke O'Hanlon . . .

'You mentioned that you speak Spanish.' Luke's head jerked her way. 'Think you could have a shot at interpreting something for me?'

'Sure,' she smiled, 'do you have it with you?'

Clara leaned forward. 'It's Eric, isn't it?' she demanded. 'You've heard something! What is it? Why didn't you tell me?'

'Chill, Clara,' he put a hand over hers, 'it's news of a kind and I only got it today. Marcia came through with a postcard which looks like it's from him. It's in Spanish and off-the-wall enough to be the sort of thing Eric would send.' He stood. 'I've got it in the car. Be right back.'

Clara closed her eyes and held the ice-filled coolness of the carrot juice against her cheek.

'You know about Eric O'Hanlon, don't you Alva?' she asked.

'Luke told me,' Alva said carefully. Thinking about it she'd felt a childish hurt that Clara hadn't told her quite everything on the night of the storm. But Clara, sensitive to nuance, opened her eyes to slits and looked at her.

'It wasn't for me to tell you about Eric,' she said. 'His brother's story is for Luke to tell. You must see that . . .?'

'Yes, I do,' Alva conceded, 'and he did tell me, so now will you tell me what's going on? What's this about a postcard?'

'I know as much as you do about that. It sounds

good news, though. A postcard means that Eric's . . .' she stopped.

'Alive?' Alva finished for her and Clara nodded, her voice barely audible.

'Yes,' she said, 'it means Eric's alive.'

'Who's Marcia?' Alva asked. 'Luke didn't give me a lot of detail.'

Clara sighed, shifted in her seat and leaned forward, chin on hands. The firelight created a coppery halo around her head.

'Marcia Tulins', she began, 'is a friend of Eric's. She's an agency journalist covering South America, based for the most part in Colombia. I met her once, in New York. Solid type, career journalist who had the hots for Eric. It didn't seem to me that he reciprocated, but then it's hard to tell with Eric. Anyway, Luke got in touch with her when Eric didn't collect the money from the Bogotá bank and she was reassuring, said there was nothing unusual about a *gringo* disappearing into the Andes, that Eric-types have been doing it since the sixties. Basically, what she was saying was that you get used to things like that happening when you live in Colombia, that life there isn't anything like life as we know it here, or anywhere in the West. Luke went along with that for several months and by the time he began to get really worried he was into pre-production and couldn't have gone to Colombia even if he'd wanted. And of course he can't go now.'

'I can see that,' Alva said, 'but even so . . .'

'Quite. Even so. Luke's been doing a lot from here, which I don't suppose he told you about. Ireland doesn't have an embassy in Colombia, unfortunately, so he's been hassling the Colombian authorities and police. But they've more than their own share of problems and someone like Eric, who may just have gone walkabout, is not a priority.' Her voice was subdued. 'This postcard's the first contact.' She twisted her wedding ring and sighed.

'What about the O'Hanlon parents? Aren't they able to do anything?' Alva asked.

'O'Hanlon *père* is dead and the mother is an elderly, gentle soul not able to do much more than pray and worry about her second born.' She shivered. 'I would literally lose my reason if Danny or Frederick were ever to disappear like that.' She twisted her wedding ring again, more agitatedly this time.

'I'm curious about something.' Alva traced a pattern on the table and spoke slowly. 'You may tell me it's none of my business, but,' she looked up with a quick smile, 'you've asked me a few personal questions too. And I've been honest with you.'

'Ask, for God's sake,' Clara said and waited.

Alva hesitated for seconds then went for blunt. 'Are you and Luke lovers?'

Clara stared at her, her expression moving from shock to disbelief to, in the end, a sort of wry amusement. 'Is that what they're saying on the set?'

'Some people. Oscar . . .'

'For Christ's sake, Alva, don't tell me you've been listening to Oscar!'

'Are you telling me no? That you're not having an affair with Luke?' Alva felt the beginnings of relief, a lightening in her heart. Maybe friendship and fidelity did exist, after all.

'Of course I'm not having an affair with Luke.' Clara was tart. 'Not only is he not my type, he's a friend and I still . . .' she hesitated, her eyes too bright. Alva wanted to kick herself. She shouldn't have done this. It had been stupid and insensitive. But she *still* wanted to know and didn't try to stop Clara when she went on, quietly, 'I don't *want* anyone in Larry's place. I had it all, you know, with him. Why should I bother with anything less now?'

After that they sat with their thoughts for a while, a sort of loneliness between them. When a log in the fire crackled and spat out a spark Clara turned a sigh into a small laugh.

'Luke's not spoken for, you know,' she said. 'Not for the moment anyway. Why don't you . . .'

'Thanks, Clara,' Alva was snappier than she meant to be, 'but I'll find my own lovers. When I'm ready.'

'Don't wait for ever,' Clara observed drily. 'The heart grows cold.'

'And old,' Alva kept her tone light, 'as Ellen reminded me yesterday.'

'Have you thought about the older man?' Clara beamed as an idea struck her. 'Theo for instance? He's one of the most interesting of the variety you're likely to meet. Loyal, independent, keeps out of the way for the most part. With a little work he could be taught to be more sociable.'

'I'm working on Theo for Juno,' Alva said, 'he's just the man to settle her down.'

They were laughing, companionable, Clara even risking the calories of a sliver of roulade, when Luke came back into the room. His hair looked in more violent disarray than usual and, even as he sat, he ran an agitated hand through it.

'Sorry about the delay.' He tapped the phone in his pocket. 'Got a call when I was out there. Our executive producer venting a bit of spleen about Oscar's ejection from the scene. Firing his man hasn't done much for Jack's image, makes his judgement look bad. It doesn't look, Alva, as if you'll ever see that ten thou.'

Alva shrugged. 'Since I didn't know I had it, so to speak, I'm not exactly at a loss for it,' she said.

'Very philosophical of you.' He smiled at her and for moments, meeting his earth-brown eyes, she smiled too.

The director pulled a postcard from his pocket and laid it, picture up, on the table. She leaned forward with Clara to have a look. It was an aerial view of the Andes, one of a kind bought by thousands of tourists every year. Devoured by curiosity she picked it up and read the back. There were just two lines of poetry, in Spanish and written in block capitals.

> VERDE QUE TE QUIERO VERDE,
> VERDE VIENTO. VERDE RAMAS.

There was no signature, no postmark because there was no stamp.

'How do you know it's from your brother? How did what's-her-name get it?'

'Marcia. It was waiting in her PO box when she got back from an assignment in Peru. She insists the writing's Eric's. I think she's right, even allowing for the capitals.'

'The lines are from Lorca,' Alva told him, glad for once about the intense reading of her adolescence.

'Yes. And that's another thing – Eric's a Lorca fan. I've translated the lines myself, roughly. I was hoping your Spanish might be good enough to find a . . .' he hesitated, looking slightly embarrassed, '. . . nuance, or a variation on the lines as Lorca wrote them, even a misspelling. Anything that could be a coded message. Eric's a cryptic kind of bugger . . .' He cleared his throat and went quiet.

'Relax.' Alva touched his hand, making circles with his glass on the table. God, he was restless. 'Let me think about it . . .'

She lifted the card and read it again, slowly and carefully translating to herself, thinking about the punctuation, the words as they were put down. Clara had become very still and quiet; Luke went on making circles with his glass, but smaller ones. When she was sure, she read aloud:

'Green I love you green. Green wind. Green branches. That's what it says, and the lines here are exactly as Lorca wrote them. It's from 'Romance sonambulo' but I can't see any significance in that, can you?'

'No.'

'Sounds to me like he's just telling you he's happy in the mountains. They have evergreen tropical rainforests in the Andes, don't they? Green I love you green. He's telling you he loves where he is, Luke.'

'Perhaps.'

'You don't think so, do you? Why not? It makes sense.'

'Yes. It does. Or seems to. Look,' he exhaled a deep breath, 'it just doesn't *feel* right. Eric's a loner but he's not an irresponsible bastard. The opposite in fact. As a kid he was the one would return the other kids' marbles I'd appropriated for my collection. He's conscientious. He cares. He's a pain – and he'd never leave the Indian people of that project without the money he promised them.'

'What does Marcia think?' Clara spoke for the first time.

'She thinks I should wait it out. That there'll be another communication of some kind, a letter or card, fairly soon.'

'What does *she* think about your brother not collecting the money?' Alva asked.

'Says he's fallen into the Colombian way of life. Things happen slowly there, people take their time, he's doing the same.'

'But you don't think so.' Alva was watching him closely.

'No.' His impatience made him drum his fingers. 'Eric's his own person. He's never fallen in with other people's patterns.' He pushed back the chair and got up suddenly. 'I'm off.' He stuffed his hands in his pockets and looked down at them. He was smiling, rueful and apologetic. 'Sorry to be such lousy bloody company.' He bent to kiss Clara on the cheek. 'Lovely desserts,' he said, 'keep me some for tomorrow.'

'Alva, will you be a honey and see my guest out?' Clara was smiling. 'You always seem to be seeing people off, I know, but I call the boys this time each evening and they'll be waiting.'

It was cold outside, the air sharp with the threat of an early frost. It was a modestly starry night, a crescent moon lighting the bay and filling the garden with still shadows. Across by Howth the light from the Baily came and went in its reassuring way, but the summer-house, in between and outlined against the shining bay, seemed to Alva like a mausoleum and she shivered. By Luke's car they stopped and he began a search for his keys.

'Clara's right,' Alva said, 'I spend a lot of time either seeing off or receiving people to this house. It's going to be very quiet when you all leave.'

'Peaceful, too.' The search was failing to produce the keys.

'But busy,' Alva held up crossed fingers, 'once the publicity gets going.' She grinned and pointed: 'The keys, Luke, are in the door.'

He swore and gave a short groan. 'It's the effects of Clara's bloody chocolate cake. I need a ten-mile run to clear my head.'

Alva nodded towards the avenue. 'I'm going for a quick walk to the gate and back. Come with me, why don't you; we can both walk some of it off.'

He surprised her by agreeing without demur and they started off briskly, shoulder to shoulder down the avenue. Behind them the light in Theo's bedroom went out and in the extra darkness Alva shivered again, this time from the cold, and wished she'd thrown something over her shirt and leggings.

'Take this.' Luke took off his jacket and dropped it over her shoulders. Alva pulled it tightly round her, liking its tweedy feel.

'Thanks,' she said and then, 'will you?'

'Will I what?' he was almost trotting and she had to skip to keep up with him.

'Will you go to Colombia?'

'If Eric doesn't make an appearance soon I'll have to. Trouble is,' he kicked a pebble, and then another, 'I won't be free to go for another three, four months. Not unless I can get post-production delayed for a few weeks; unlikely, given my relationship with Jack Kelly.'

'What could he do if you just went?'

'Get someone else in to finish off my film, in every sense. I'm going for a downbeat ending, sticking to the story of the real Constance as we know it. Seems her daughter's marriage plans fell through and she left home. Constance duly sold her house and disappeared – to the US it was thought. Kelly's keen on wedding bells for Julia and an embittered Constance living on in lonely isolation – that would really finish it off, Hollywood style.' They reached the end of the avenue and turned back, walking less quickly now.

'You're in the traditional shitty position, aren't you?' Alva said, 'between a rock and a hard place.' He laughed, impulsively putting an arm around her shoulder and hugging her to him. She stiffened and he let her go immediately, still laughing a little and as if he hadn't noticed.

'Thanks for your help with the postcard,' he said when they got back to the car.

'Any time,' Alva said lightly and took his coat from around her shoulders. He smiled at her as he slipped it on and she wanted to tell him that she would like to help, really help, in any way she could. But what if it came out wrong, awkward and false, instead of warm and gracious and genuine, like Clara when she wasn't acting? She said nothing and he opened the car door.

She stood, uncertainly smiling, as he turned to say goodnight. He smiled too and reached for her, putting both hands on her shoulders and pulling her gently towards him. She stiffened, and regretted it immediately. But immediately was too late. His hands dropped away.

'I'll be off,' he said. 'Thanks again.'

'Drive carefully,' Alva said but didn't move. She couldn't. She felt she must, somehow, make amends, dilute the offence of what he might think was a repulsion when it was simply an automatic defence mechanism.

She touched his face with her hand, lightly, felt the stubble there and how still he had become. He seemed to have stopped breathing as she leaned towards him, telling herself it was part of making amends, and put her mouth to his in a swift, gentle pressure.

'Take care,' she said. For a moment she thought he was going to say something but then he smiled, his eyes on hers, and lowered his head to kiss her again. It was a longer kiss this time, warm and oddly familiar feeling, like a kiss she'd been expecting for a long time. He lifted his head, and his mouth from hers, and she leaned against him, unsure what to say but knowing she wanted his arms around her.

He moved away and for seconds wordlessly studied her face before he said, 'Take care yourself,' traced her lips with a finger and slipped into the car. She thought she saw him wave, once, as he drove down the avenue.

Chapter Eighteen

It was almost over. Four scenes, one of them crucial, a bit of tidying up, and everything, according to Juno, would be in the can. The mood at De Novo was buoyant, the concentrated activity keeping people away from one another's throats. The understanding that the film had worked and was going to be a success contributed to the all round good feeling.

And Bernie's mood, uncharacteristically bad for several days, became worryingly euphoric. Alva, unsure which humour caused her more unease, *was* sure that both had to do with Jasper. But Bernie wasn't talking.

Luke was more forthcoming. Without quite knowing how or when it had happened, Alva had become acutely aware of the director. Maybe it was this, or maybe it was simply the logistics of the work being done that week, but she seemed to meet him more often than before. She liked him. He would be gone soon, of course, off to London and post-production, then Colombia, and after that would be making another film somewhere. He wouldn't be part of her life. It was safe to like him.

'Tell me about Jasper Clarke,' she demanded one day. 'He's engaged to be married and he's trifling with our Bernie's heart.' She folded her arms and leaned, a quizzical smile on her face, against the side of a trailer. She'd just left Bernie openly holding Jasper's hand.

'What exactly do you want to know?' He was grinning.

'All about him. What he's playing at.'

'Well . . .' He hesitated, looking at her. 'I've worked with Jasper before. Salt of the earth.' He hesitated again and smiled. 'I've never seen him so happy. I don't think he's playing at all. I think he's in love with your Bernie.'

'He can't be,' Alva frowned, 'he's got a fiancée.'

'Can't be?' Luke raised a sceptical eyebrow. 'Why not? Engaged isn't married – though Christ knows enough married people fall out of love to make one wonder about the point of *that* institution . . .'

Alva wasn't going to be drawn into a debate on marriage. She interrupted him. 'You think Jasper's fallen out of love with his fiancée, then?' He hadn't shaved that day and Alva, considering the effect, decided the dark shadow gave him a rakish rather than seedy look.

'Didn't ever seem to me to be the greatest passion on earth anyway,' he said. 'They've been engaged for four years.'

'I see,' Alva said.

'Bernie's the most alive woman around here and it's because of Jasper,' Luke observed.

'Didn't think you were such an acute observer of your fellow beings.' Thrown by the turn of the conversation, she was arch.

'It's my stock-in-trade.' He looked genuinely surprised. 'I need to be. Are you going to tell me what exactly the problem is?'

'I was worried about Bernie getting hurt, is all.'

'Or worried about her getting married and leaving here?'

'What? Of course not. It would be wonderful if things worked out for them.'

'Well, maybe things will,' Luke said. 'If they do you'll have to let her go, Alva.'

'Of course I will,' Alva said.

It hadn't been one of her favourite conversations with the director. Acute observation was one thing, trotting out snap judgements was something else. Of course it had occurred to her that Bernie might leave De Novo to go off with Jasper to England, or even into Dublin to live. But if that was what Bernie wanted to do, well, then that's what Bernie must do. Alva soothed herself with the thought that there was Sammy to consider and that he couldn't be moved about like an old carton.

Juno was all over the place that week too, hyped up and yelling into a mobile most of the time. Alva pinned her down to ask about Oscar, since she'd seemed to be the one who knew most about him.

'He'll not be back.' Juno was adamant. 'Not that he spent much time here even when he was on the payroll. I'm told he's rolling around town inventing stories to paper the cracks in his reputation.'

'No one's going to take his place then?'

'We managed without him when he was working for us so we'll manage now.' Juno grinned. 'Luke says the money the bugger would have been paid for his last weeks can go towards the wrap party.'

'Wrap party?'

'Didn't anyone tell you? It'll be here, immediately filming ends. And Christ, are we ever going to have one almighty bash!' She paused, then carelessly said, 'You don't mind, do you? It'll liven this old place up a bit.'

'No, of course I don't mind.'

One of the final, and vital, scenes was shot on a Friday. It would show Constance Moore meeting with the brother she hadn't seen for twenty-two years. In the script Jimmy O'Brien was unearthed by a private detective hired by the family of the Nick Hunt character to uncover the truth about Constance's past. What the scene would not reveal was that this brother would, for a price, betray Constance to the Russell family.

Clara had breakfast in her room, refusing to see anyone but her dresser – a tiny, silent woman who drank herbal tea and fussed with silent intensity about the star's costumes. The morning was bright, none of the misty grey of earlier in the week about it. The omens looked good but the mood, oddly, was anticlimactic.

Alva, crossing the hallway as a remote, controlled, in-character Clara came slowly down the stairs, decided she would sit in on shooting.

The drawing room was lit and ready to go; everywhere save the performance area a jungle of wires and lights and sound equipment. Alva found herself a niche near the door and settled against the wall.

The actor playing the brother had only this and one other scene, so hadn't been around much. He was a jovial sort, much used for cameo roles in TV serials. He stood with Luke who, from the looks of things, was easing him into the part.

'Talk about wiping the grin off someone's face,' Alva thought as the man became earnest, then ill-tempered, and positively sour as he trudged past her out of the room and banged through the front door.

The incident turned her attention to Luke. He looked tired, today's stubble blue-black and almost the beginnings of a beard. But he looked all raw energy too, focusing it on camera and sound people, on the set, the continuity girl, a magazine on the table called *Lady of the House*, even. He demanded, coaxed, praised, joked and talked and, finally, ran Clara through the scene. Just once, and they were ready. Juno yelled, 'Action!' and in absolute silence Clara walked across the room to the window. Mesmerized, in a sort of giddy wonder, Alva was carried into the scene as Clara became the embodiment of the tragic, murdering Victorian heroine.

As Constance Moore she stood, rigid and controlled, inside the long front window. She made no attempt to conceal herself from the man approaching on foot along the avenue. She didn't need to. He didn't look up once as he came steadily forward, shoulders hunched and eyes fixed on the ground. He was a big man, ponderous and roughly dressed, and Constance's back stiffened as he mounted the short flight of granite steps to the front door. She closed her eyes and mouthed what could have been a prayer as the brass knocker echoed through the deep of the old house. She made no other movement.

When it echoed for a second time she took a deep breath and opened her eyes to look across the garden. Her large eyes, green-grey in her pale face, moved without expression over the late, late roses of autumn to the leafy walks and distant summerhouse. Beyond it all the deep, calm indigo of Dublin Bay lay languid in the distance.

'Twenty-two years.' Her voice was cultured, careful. 'Twenty-two years and I would have known him anywhere.' Her expression was cold. 'He is coarse and red-faced from beer, as was his father before him.' She shuddered with infinite distaste. 'Our father.' The shudder emphasized the exquisite fit of her dove-coloured tea-gown. Her long hands, under narrow flounces of white lace, smoothed its lines across her hips as sounds from the hallway indicated a maid had opened the front door. Footsteps approached the door and the hands clenched compulsively. She turned slowly where she stood, took a deep breath and looked quickly around the room. Her gaze lingered briefly on an oil portrait of a delicately lovely young woman, then on a wall covered in prints. She might have been looking at the room for the last time. When the knock came on the door she slowly let the breath out.

'Come!' she called and watched in the rococo-style mirror over the mantel as the door opened.

And it was there, in its reflection, that Constance

Moore met the eyes of the brother she had not seen for half a lifetime.

Neither spoke. For fully twenty seconds the long case clock by the wall ticked in the silence before the man cleared his throat and took a step further into the room. Constance, turning at last to face him, did not ask him either to sit or put down the cap he held in his hand.

'Hello, Jimmy.' There was no welcome in her voice either. Jimmy O'Brien nodded, his face still as her own as he looked with a chilly curiosity around the room.

'Hello, Adye,' he said. 'So you made a woman, in the end. A well got-up woman too. Not dead at all, like we thought.'

He threw his cap onto a small table and himself into a tapestry armchair. From there he considered his sister with small, dark eyes. Apart from a longness of limb there was no family resemblance.

'You made a good job of hiding yourself, Adye.' He laughed, a mirthless sound and flat. 'And a fine job of turning yourself into a lady. I suppose by rights I should be calling you Constance. Mrs Constance Moore, widow lady.' He smiled, showing a set of rotten teeth. 'I'd have condoled about your late husband if I'd known of his sad death. But sure we didn't even know at the time that you were alive yourself. Not to mind married.'

'It was best that way.' Constance's expression didn't change but she was watching him carefully.

'For whom was it best?' he mimicked her accent.

'We worried about you, Adye, after you disappeared. We worried about you and we grieved for you like any family would.' He ignored the briefly flickering look of scepticism on her face and ran an appreciative hand over the tapestry arm of the chair. 'But we didn't need to, did we? You were doing fine for yourself, all the time. Fine and dandy you were.'

He stopped, face taunting, waiting for her to say something. But she stood still as stone, and silent. He shrugged, leaned forward with his hands between his knees, and went on.

'We lost our father to the same influenza plague as took your husband, Adye. You were no doubt too taken up with your own sorrows to think on the hard times of the family you'd left.' His eyes were mean and unblinking. 'Only they tell me now that you might not have been all that sorry to see James Moore go at all. They say you may even have helped him on his way . . .'

'Our father was dead to me long before I left.' Constance, interrupting him, was harsh, a rawness in the cultured tones.

'Aye, I'd say that much is true anyways.' James O'Brien was equally harsh. 'You were a cold, hard daughter to him although, God knows, he did his best by you.'

'Putting me on the streets to sell my body at fifteen was the best he could do for his only daughter?'

'We would have starved. There was no work for him, none for me. Needs must.' Jimmy O'Brien's face reddened. 'You've made a cold, hard woman too . . .' He paused. 'And from the sound of things you were a worse than cold wife to the man who died while you were nursing him through the influenza.'

'If you've something to say, Jimmy, then say it.' Her eyes narrowed and she took a step towards him. Her voice was low, a touch of menace in it. For a moment, as their eyes locked, he looked uncertain. Then he looked away.

'It's not me as says it. The man who brought me news of you told me too that you'd been accused of murdering your husband. It was thought you poisoned him, he said.'

'Did he also take the trouble to tell you that I was cleared of any wrongdoing?'

'He told me there wasn't enough proof to hang you and that you were left to go. That you were left in possession too of the dead man's money and free to buy this grand house. You done well for yourself.' He lifted a journal from the table beside him. *Lady of the House.*' He threw it from him onto the floor. 'Is that what you think you are now, Adye O'Brien?'

'You know nothing of what happened, Jimmy, nor of what I am.'

He kicked at the journal with a booted foot. 'I know that Adye O'Brien's well and truly dead anyway.'

'I had hoped so.' Constance's voice was low, and flat. She sat in an armchair opposite him and folded her long white hands in her lap. Behind her the light from the window haloed her piled, auburn hair. Her face had become still again. 'What do you want, Jimmy? What have they asked you to—?'

'Cut! For fuck's sake, cut it!'

The cry, from the other end of the room, was harsh and sudden and female. It coincided with the appearance in the bay outside of a high-speed catamaran. All hell broke loose.

'Where the bloody hell did *that* come from? Didn't anyone check the sailing times?'

'It's not supposed to be out there.'

'Well, it bloody is. And right in the middle of a perfect take too.'

Clearly, as the camera lights dimmed, the catamaran could be seen passing the hill of Howth, moving swiftly onto the horizon and setting course for Holyhead. The accusations went on, a continuity girl tearfully yelling in the face of Juno's wrath.

'Must have been a change in schedule. Maybe there's a storm coming. I'm not God, you know. I can't be expected to see what the forces of nature are.'

'Oh, shut up. Can't you—'

'Cut it, both of you.' The director's shout silenced them. 'Can't be helped. We'll take five and go for it again. From the top.'

Clara, a make-up girl fussing at her face, pulled fretfully at the lace ruff around the neck of the dove-grey dress. 'Will somebody *please* get me a Panadol?' she demanded. Two people rushed with water and tablets. She took them both. 'Wouldn't be surprised if Ellen arranged to have that thing out there,' she said and got a general, relieved laugh.

Alva slipped away as they began to set up the scene again. In the garden, cleaning the pond, she found Theo.

'They're working on one of the last scenes.' She trailed her hand in the water, dried it on her jeans and watched Theo pull at a fistful of trailing weed. 'They'll be gone in days, Theo. We've survived,' she said.

'We have?' He slopped greeny sludge into a bucket.

'Of course we have. More than.'

'They've brought a lot of change and they're not gone yet.'

'Could be some of the changes were needed.'

'Maybe,' he grunted and began to fill another bucket.

'Oh, come on, Theo!' Alva stood. 'We'll be back to being a hotel in a week's time – *and* we'll be doing better business than we ever did before . . .'

'*That*,' Theo was decisive, 'remains to be seen.'

Chapter Nineteen

David Blake, his role as Constance's husband firmly behind him, was dressed to kill and determined to score. In an off-white suit and black shirt he cruised far-flung groups at the wrap party, piling up rejections with drunken good humour. He came to rest at a table next to where Alva was sitting with Clara, raised his glass in their direction.

'First of the night,' he said, 'though I intend having several more, and stiff ones. Medicinal, you know, good for the heart.' He glared reproachfully at Alva. 'I'm partial to ice in my whiskey but it appears to be running out, my dear. It is not, however, essential,' he shook a sad head, 'any more than happiness is essential for living. Don't you agree?'

'Don't encourage him,' Clara hissed. 'You'll get us landed with the story of his four marriages.'

But David Blake had more immediate things on his mind. He bestowed on both women a dewy-eyed, adoring look and a long sigh. 'You are too beautiful and too wise for me, my darlings.' He wobbled to his feet. 'But in the belief that fortune favours the brave I will away and attempt again to impress some of the younger ladies . . .'

Alva, sipping the night's very good champagne,

giggled as he drifted unevenly out of the room. 'Fortune favours fools, too. Which means that either way he's in with a chance.'

'Nasty one, Alva,' Clara laughed, 'but true. He's amazing, our David. Got a hide like a rhinoceros.' She adjusted a huge hooped earring. 'These end-of-film parties never cease to astonish me. For an entire night the bitterest of enmities are buried and all is love and light and fun. But come tomorrow and post-production and everyone will be spitting and competing again over footage and cuts. There,' she pointed and shook a bemused head, 'is a perfect example of what I'm talking about.'

They were in the basement dining hall, dazzlingly lit and with a dance floor covering the flagstones for the night. The disc jockey had put on a tango and Justine, in minuscule red dress, four-inch heels and a shining tumble of hair, had taken sinuously to its centre with a Nick Hunt dressed in Ray Bans and a black leather waistcoat. To raucous applause they were giving a tormenting, tantalizing show, bodies winding together, unwinding, impossibly sensual.

'And they say the movies are make-believe!' Clara lit a cigarette. 'If you believe that pair are dancing for pleasure you'll believe anything.' She blew a circle of smoke and looked wearily about. Clara was playing her older-and-wiser-woman role tonight, hair severely caught back and her dress formal and black.

'I don't know.' Alva squinted through the smoke. 'They look reasonably pleased with themselves to me.'

'Oh, they are,' Clara yawned, 'but it's nothing to do

with the pleasure of dance and everything to do with having an audience. All the other reasons they're dancing have to do with an audience too.' She pulled mercilessly on the cigarette. 'Now *this* is pleasure.'

'Looks like masochism to me.' Alva took more champagne.

'I'm giving them up tomorrow,' Clara said, 'again.'

De Novo had never seen anything like the wrap party, probably never would again. Champagne apart, it was a lavish affair. The catering staff were to a man and woman nubile and dressed in black lycra. Along with drinks they were dispensing a food selection which included salmon, chicken with tarragon, mussels in spiced rice and enough salads to feed Dublin's vegetarian population for a month. The trailers and trucks had rolled, without ceremony, out of the court-yard the day before and where they'd stood Juno had arranged for a suckling pig to be roasted on a spit. There was music and there was noise and there were hot, hot bodies everywhere. Ellen and Theo had been offered rooms in a nearby hotel for the night but both of them, united for once in their indignation, had declined.

The Justine 'n' Nick performance came to a slow end, the music moved up-tempo, a few rockers drifted onto the floor – and Bernie, tipsy-looking, without her glasses and clutching Jasper, stole the show for the night.

'Hello, hello, hello everyone!' Her voice, through the microphone grabbed from the hapless disc jockey, was happy and loud. 'This is Bernie.' She gazed at the

336

calmly smiling Jasper with a myopically adoring expression. 'Jasper and myself want you all to know we're getting married!'

Alva, as applause and whistles and lewd suggestions flew, felt as if she'd been kicked in the stomach. Bernie hadn't even hinted to her earlier. She'd let her find out like this, in public, part of the crowd, no allowances for their friendship. And no discussion beforehand about what it might mean to her job at De Novo . . .

'Hold it, hold it!' Bernie had begun to wave the mike wildly. 'Apart from wanting to give you the good news, folks, I want to tell you that Jasper and me will be living nearby and De Novo will continue to be the best place to eat in on this hill. So I want every one of you to come and eat here, and to tell your friends, the ones with money to spend—'

The disc jockey relieved her of the mike, slipped Whitney Houston into the CD player and Bernie and Jasper began a back-slapping mooch of the floor.

'Happens all the time.' Clara was watching Alva closely. 'Don't think I've ever made a film where somebody hasn't decided to tie the knot.' She paused. 'You didn't know?'

'No.' Alva couldn't trust herself to say anything more. Hurt and relief threatened to turn the lump in her throat to tears. 'The demon drink,' Clara consoled. 'I'd say that little speech was entirely unplanned and the result of a great deal of champagne.'

'Yes.' Alva stood. 'Think I'll get some fresh air,' she said. By standing she'd made herself visible and Bernie, buried against Jasper's shoulder but wearing her glasses again, gave a sudden whoop and blundered through the noisy, generous goodwill of the crowd. Clara, discreetly, slipped away.

'We decided today.' Bernie was wearing a pink cotton shirt and Alva found her face smothered in its folds. 'I haven't even told Sammy, so don't be annoyed at me.'

'I'm not,' Alva sniffed.

'You are.' Bernie stepped back and glared. She was a lot more than tipsy. 'You haven't even wished us good luck.'

Alva was disgusted to find the lump in her throat still there. She looked at Jasper, standing beside Bernie. His face seemed to have become rubberized and his expression as he gazed at Bernie was as silly as hers was indignant.

'Oh, Bernie,' Alva said and Bernie underwent melt-down and held Alva to her again. They sniffed, shed a few tears together, and Alva assured Bernie she wished her *more* than all the luck in the world. Then, because she couldn't help herself, she blurted out, 'I worried that you were going to pack up and leave. That I'd be left looking for a new cook—'

'How could you even *imagine* that I'd let you down?' Bernie was plaintive, but snappy too. 'You deserved to worry – you should have trusted me.'

'I know,' Alva said. She could have defended herself, explained to Bernie that she'd somehow lost the habit of trusting. She didn't say it though. Instead she gave Jasper a quick hug. 'Where are you going to live?' she looked from one to the other.

'Well, we thought about a tent down on the beach,' Bernie said, 'but we've shelved that one in favour of looking for a small house in Ballybrack, close to my mother. That'll be best for Sammy, and Jasper wants to be near the sea.'

'What about . . .' Alva stopped, fearful of being told that Jasper's now ex-fiancée was none of her business.

'It's all right, you can ask.' Jasper's smile was relaxed. 'My engagement had been staggering to an end for some time.'

Alva could only marvel at the understatement, at the certitude which had made Jasper break the engagement which had bound him for four years and had committed Bernie to a father for her beloved Sammy. They'd only known each other for six weeks and there they stood, beaming and confident, preparing to spend the rest of their lives together.

'You're great, both of you,' Alva said, 'and you're brave.'

'No, we're not,' Bernie giggled, 'we're foolhardy. Go on, Alva, say it, that's what you really feel, isn't it?'

'No, I don't, I promise.' Alva laughed. What she *felt* was envy, of their presumptuous love and the simple feeling of rightness and simplicity about their relationship. She told them so. 'You feel very *right* to me,' she said.

She left them soon after, engrossed and happy and exclusive, and went in search of Juno's suckling pig. It was grotesque and it was ready, turning slowly on the spit where it was being sliced at and piled onto plates by a semi-barbaric crowd.

'Glad to see you joining the real party.' Juno shoved a plate into Alva's hands. 'Help yourself to some salad too.' She cocked her head to one side. 'You look very, *very* . . .' she thought, then grinned, 'desirable's the word I'm looking for. Any man's fancy, Alva, that's you. Why don't you mingle, do something about it?'

'Thanks for the pig,' Alva piled salad onto her plate, 'and for the advice.'

She grinned, stepped back from the heat of the fire, began to mingle as she nibbled the pork. Juno's compliment was the kind she'd wanted to hear. Desirable was how she wanted to look in the midnight-blue crushed velvet she'd chosen for the night, was what she'd hoped for when she'd piled her hair and threaded silvery beads through it. After six weeks of jeans, shirts and sweatshirts she'd needed the boost of a bit of desirability and glamour.

'Hi, babe, how're you doin'? Why don't you and me step the light fantastic? Show this lot how to really move?'

The arm which draped, then dangled its hand casually over her breast, belonged to a technician she recognized but had never spoken to. He was skinny, with a grey ponytail and red braces, and he wasn't what she'd had in mind when she'd wanted to be desired. But he danced well, loose-limbed and rhythmically to Van Morrison coming from speakers somewhere by the stables. It lasted all of three minutes before, with a groan, he draped himself around her shoulders again.

'I'm bolloxed,' he said. 'Why don't you and me sit this one out in a dark corner?'

His tongue, quick and darting, moved under her hair and into her ear. Alva, with a small yelp, jumped back.

'Thanks, but no thanks.' She slipped nimbly out of his uncertain grasp. 'Been there, done that and didn't like it much.'

'What *do* you like, babe?' He closed one eye and focused blearily with the other. 'You into other babes, maybe? Or is it old men?' He guffawed and Alva moved off. He followed, stopping her with a hand around her waist. 'We'd a bet going you were frigid, me and some of the lads. Want a little help in that area? Tonight could be your lucky night . . .'

'Joke's over, Charlie.' Luke O'Hanlon stepped between them and put a finger on the other man's chest. It was not a friendly gesture. 'Make tonight *your* lucky night, and piss of out of here. *Now.*'

'Jesus, Luke, I was only—'

'I know. And it's a party. And it's all good, clean fun.' This time the finger jabbed, hard, against the man's bony ribcage. 'Move it, Charlie. Go fast and go somewhere I won't have to see you for the rest of the night.'

Charlie went.

Luke took Alva's arm. Gently, as if afraid she might run. 'Sorry you had to put up with that sort of yob behaviour,' he said.

'He's not your responsibility,' Alva shrugged, 'and, as you said yourself, it's a party.'

'Yeah.' He frowned. 'Only Charlie's a bit long in the tooth for adolescent passes. He's one of the best sparks in the business but he's a clown. A burnt-out sixties hippie still looking for the action . . .'

'Relax, Luke,' Alva laughed, 'the chivalry's appreciated but I can deal with creeps like him.'

'Glad to hear it.' He picked a piece of crackling from her plate. 'Tastes like more. Why don't we get me a helping of that and find a quiet place to eat? I've got something I want to show you.'

Alva followed him back to Juno and the pig, considerably pared down by this time. Even under the polychrome lights strung about the yard, probably the work of Charlie the Sparks, Luke looked strained. He was wearing the tweed jacket and jeans he'd worn for working in that day but had changed his T-shirt. His hair tonight was a relatively tidy arrangement on his head. Juno kissed him effusively before packing his plate and pointing to where champagne bottles sat on ice.

'Help yourselves,' she said, 'I'm out of here. I've a little private partying to do.'

'Enjoy,' Luke laughed and Juno, as she moved off, pointed at Alva.

'Don't you think our chatelaine looks desirable tonight, Luke?'

'Yeah.' Luke looked at Alva, grinning. 'And not just tonight.'

'You're carrying this chivalry thing a bit far.' Alva, smiling, balanced a glass of champagne on her plate and found them a stable doorstep to sit on. It was a tight squeeze for both of them and she didn't look at him as they sat down. 'What is it you want to show me? Have you heard from Eric again?'

He nodded, put his plate on the ground between his feet and took a postcard from his pocket.

'This one's a bit more specific.' He handed it to her and wolfed down some food as she studied it. The picture this time was of a mountain peak with a pathway winding through terrifyingly beautiful high green plateaux which turned to slate blue as they disappeared into low-lying cloud. At the almost dead centre of the clouds an X had been marked in biro. Above it was written the word *Infiesto*. Alva turned the card over. There was a small drawing of a stick man with curly hair and, beside him, the words *el ultimo pueblito.*

'The last village,' she read aloud in English. 'That's what it says, Luke.' She looked at the picture again. 'Looks as if he's up there in a village called Infiesto.'

'That's what Marcia thinks. She phoned yesterday, says the place exists, that it's known as a sort of last frontier.' He paused. 'She says again that I should stop worrying. That he'll come down in his own time.'

'He's not her brother,' Alva said. 'You can't delay post-production, even by a few weeks?'

'We've discussed it. Kelly's threatened to hand over to someone else if I so much as cut a day. There's not a lot I can do about it.' He gave a wry grin. 'In fact there's fuck all I can do about it.'

'I'd have thought the Oscar fiasco would have weakened his stranglehold,' Alva said. 'Can't you beat him over the head with any of that? Figuratively speaking, of course.'

He gave a small laugh. 'In the world of film-making Oscar's behaviour is everyday. Dishonest and shitty, but basically your everyday, parochial corruption.' He looked thoughtful. 'Now if old Jack the Lad were to misbehave on a more global scale, mess about with funds in a way that could endanger the whole project, well . . .' He took a deep breath, 'That might give me a bit of leverage all right. But he's unlikely to take the risk. Or at any rate unlikely to get caught.' He put his plate down and turned to her to finish what he was saying. They were very close, thighs touching and now, when he turned, their faces were less than an inch apart. His eyes, staring into hers, were very dark. 'You know, I got you all wrong, Alva, at first. I thought you were a beautiful, cool user. Someone who knew what she wanted and had her eye on the main chance. A match for Kelly, in fact.'

'And now?' her voice was husky. She held her plate in her lap like a shield. He didn't touch her but the space between them had closed until they were inches apart. He wore a half smile, his eyes following the lines of her face as he spoke.

'Now I don't know what you are, except that the only one of those things you are is beautiful. I want to know you and all about you, what you want to do with your life and what you've done with it in the past. And I want to know', he did touch her then, putting a hand lightly on her hair, tracing the silver beads with a finger, 'what you do for love and if there's a lover in the background, waiting.'

'No lover.' Alva looked away. Her voice sounded all right to her, reasonably free of the frenzied confusion she was feeling inside.

'Do you like me, Alva?'

She looked back at him, startled. He was smiling broadly now, waiting for an answer. Just the smallest move and he could have kissed her.

She wanted him to.

'I like you, Luke. I like you a lot.'

'That's good. That's a beginning.' He made the move at last and put his mouth against hers. It was a long kiss and it was going somewhere, becoming more insistent, when a voice, hoarse and giggling and right beside them, interrupted.

'What's this then? The innkeeper and the director? Nice work, Luke.' Nick Hunt, swaying and wobbly-limbed, loomed over them. 'Hardly love's young dream, though, are you darlings?' He giggled again and almost fell on top of them. Luke pulled Alva to her feet and neatly sidestepped the actor.

'It's past your bedtime, Nick.' He held Alva's arm tightly and began across the yard.

'But I've no one to tuck me in.' Nick's wail was followed immediately by his footsteps after them. 'I need a woman, a *real* woman.' He caught up and staggered alongside. 'My mother didn't love me, you know. Can you believe,' his voice rose again, 'she actually said I was a wretched, demanding child and that I wore her out? Those were her very words. She was always leaving me on my own to go off to work or to a party or somewhere.' He swung in front of them, blocking their way. He lowered his voice confidentially, handsome face full of drunken cunning. 'I've been thinking, Luke, that maybe Clara would understand me. She's been around the track, as they say. I know she's getting on but she's still some dish. An older woman's what I want. How's about you put in a word for me?'

'Oh, I don't think you need me to do that, Nick.' Luke was offhand. 'Clara'd much prefer to hear it from you yourself.'

'You think so?' Eagerly.

'Absolutely.' Flatly.

'Thanks, Luke, you're a mate.' For several perilous seconds Nick looked dangerously close to embracing Luke. But then, tears of gratitude in his eyes, he lurched away.

'She'll chew him up and spit him out,' Alva observed.

'That's exactly what she'll do. He deserves it. His timing's lousy.' They were close to the kitchen door, open and emitting blasts of noise and heat. Luke moved his arm to circle Alva's shoulder. 'Hell's curse on Nick Hunt.' He gave a wry smile. 'God knows when I'll get you to myself again in all this . . .' he paused, '. . . unless you'd like to slip away?' He nodded towards the front of the house, the avenue and escape. Alva, not at all sure why, shook her head.

'I don't think I should leave the party,' she said. 'Theo and Ellen—'

'Aren't here,' Luke said.

'They are, in a way. And I'm sure Ellen at least will make an appearance. Plus, I brought all this here.' She waved a hand. 'It would be like a betrayal to go now.'

He tightened his arm around her shoulder and pulled her slightly towards him. He spoke into her hair. 'I go to London tomorrow morning, for a week. Maybe we could meet when I get back?'

'I'd like that,' Alva said.

The party wound down, slowly. People paired off and sloped into the night, others pleaded exhaustion and fell asleep and woke and went home. Luke left, saying he had to get up at six for a flight and Alva, watching him go, felt oddly bereft.

She was right about Ellen making an appearance, though she didn't know it until later. What she hadn't expected was Theo, in a woolly dressing gown wandering from room to room at three in the morning.

'Love the party gear, Theo,' she laughed, deciding against a display of surprise at seeing him. 'Most original outfit of the night.'

'I'm looking for that silly old woman.' Theo grumbled, 'heard her leave her room an hour ago. She didn't come back up.'

'Oh?' They were in the drawing room, empty and due to be restored to its De Novo Hotel self the following day. 'I haven't seen her. Why don't we look around together?'

They did, first in the downstairs part of the house and then the light-dazzling courtyard. Alva told Theo about Bernie's plans to marry Jasper as they went.

'The child needed a father,' he said. 'What's he like, this man she's chosen? Reliable type, is he?'

'Very. Nice too,' Alva said.

'I've never put much store by women's judgement of men.' Theo cast a prejudiced eye over a young continuity girl who was draped round a much older, bit-part actor. 'But since they can't be put off it's always best to encourage marriage and the like. The continuation of the race makes it necessary.'

'What about men's judgement of women?' Alva asked. 'Was there ever anyone you felt encouraged to marry?'

'I'd have been a poor bargain for any woman.' Theo was gruff and glaring. Alva refused to be put off.

'Oh, I don't know about that,' she looked him over, 'there's a certain *je ne sais quoi* about you . . .'

'You can save that sort of flattery for a man who can give you what you need, my girl.' Theo's big hands hung by his sides and his eyes searched still for Ellen. 'Only don't save it too long. You're not getting any younger.'

Alva decided to ignore the barb and followed him round the side of the house towards the gardens. They'd skirted the cars parked in the front and were deciding where in the garden to begin looking when a young set-worker, a shy boy who'd always seemed to Alva hesitant about embracing manhood, came running up the avenue.

'Alva! Mr Donovan!' He charged straight in their direction then stopped, breathless and mouth open and looking from one to the other.

'Well, what is it you want to say?' Theo's agitation made him snappier than usual.

'It's the old woman, Miss Donovan. She's down at the gates and she's dancing. I don't think she's very well. Or maybe she's just drunk but—'

Ellen was dancing all right. She'd found herself a spotlight between the fire-sticks positioned by the gate to show people the way in. She was moving slowly, her arms waving in graceful arcs above her head, her thin legs making uncertain glides across the stony ground. Her eyes were closed and she was humming to herself, something tuneless and uncertain. She was wearing a nightdress, calf-length and in red satin. Her hair was stringy-loose to her shoulders.

'She never did have a note in her head.' Theo briskly approached his sister. 'Come inside, Ellen, it's too cold for you to be out here dressed like that. Come on now...'

Ellen's voice rose an octave. She didn't stop.

Alva started towards her but Theo, gently, signalled that she should stay where she was as he quietly doused first one and then the other of the fire-sticks. In the darkness Ellen's dance came slowly to a halt.

'You put out the lights, Theo,' Ellen said.

'I did,' Theo agreed and took her arm. 'Come on, now, back to your room.' She went with him, unresisting and tired. 'You need a rest,' Theo told her.

Chapter Twenty

'Genuinely and truly amazing!' Bernie, completing a tour of the house, gave a couple of low whistles. 'It really *is* as if they'd never been. Just like they promised.'

'Don't exaggerate, woman,' Theo said, 'the place smells.'

But even Theo, smell of paint apart, had to concede that the film company had returned De Novo House uncannily to as it had been. The redecorated rooms were bright again and the heavy, dull, borrowed Victoriana had been returned whence it had come. Alva's comfortable squashy armchairs were back in place and her pastel curtains allowed light once again through the windows. There was added cheer in the flowers everywhere, a gesture from the set-workers.

Alva touched a carnation bud. It was a short half-hour since the last set-worker had departed and it was, as Bernie had said, as though nothing of the last six weeks had ever been.

Or very nearly. The mood in the house was subtly different. The departure of the company had left De Novo feeling lonely in a way it might well have been before but had never seemed to be.

'Place feels empty.' Alva heard her voice echo in the hallway.

'That's because it *is* empty.' Bernie was brisk. 'I need people to feed, Alva, where are they?'

'Reaching for their telephones, I hope,' Alva looked at their silent instrument, 'or at the very least planning to. God knows I've advertised enough. Half the country should know we're reopening for Hallowe'en.'

Filming, in the end, had finished in the last week in October. In the three days it had taken to remake De Novo Alva had thrown herself into a frenzy of promotional activity. She'd had a fun, blood-curdling radio ad broadcast and had ordered the hotel brochure to be redesigned for wide distribution. She'd made countless phone calls and sent stills of filming at De Novo to every publication, local and national, she could think of. The well of her optimism had been so high she'd re-engaged the hotel's casual weekend staff for Hallowe'en. Bernie had drawn up menus for 'authentic Victorian suppers' and together they'd made some atmospheric changes to the dining room – a few tassels here, sets of dark candles there, darker tablecloths.

Hallowe'en was two days away and there was not a thing left to do but wait hopefully. And try to ignore the empty feeling. It wasn't just the general exodus which made the place seem vacant. Jasper, an almost live-in guest for the last ten days of filming, had left for England to put his affairs in order. And Clara had gone back to New York. Alva hadn't been at all prepared for how much she would miss the actress's sardonic, but oddly warm and sympathetic company. Living with Theo and Ellen again was going to take some getting used to.

The day was foul, a cold, rolling mist obliterating the bay and heavy damp air pressing round the house outside. Alva decided to shake herself up.

'I'm going for a run,' she said. 'I need to get myself back into my hustling-hotelier mode.'

When she got back the phone was ringing.

The first booking since early September was for six people, all of them taking up De Novo's dinner, bed and breakfast offer.

'A flush of enthusiasm,' Theo said on Friday when the weekend bookings became too many. 'It may be that we're facing a period of success in the hotel business.'

'Why, Theo, you sound positively encouraging,' Alva said drily. They were breakfasting in the kitchen and it was another misty, cold day. 'Have you considered that De Novo might even make money?'

'Haven't carried my enthusiasm quite that far.' Theo got up and made for the door. 'Other things on my mind; a lot of old weeds to hoe out and the apple trees need a major pruning.'

Ellen appeared down the stairs a couple of hours later. Alva was working out a combination of bookings at the davenport in the hall and looked up to see her dressed for outside in the lynx and with an extravagant mauve feathered hat on. Her face was carefully and elaborately made up and she looked wonderfully, exotically over-the-top. Alva told her so.

'We try.' Ellen's tone was regal. Her breath smelled of Pernod. 'I am off to take my daily constitutional.'

'In those shoes?' Alva looked doubtfully at Ellen's satin-covered two-inch heels.

'I have always been well shod.' Ellen looked down at the shoes and then haughtily at Alva. 'Just as I have always tried to live beautifully and gracefully. There is no other life, really. You may not think so now, since you are young and don't appear to think at all. But you will remember what I have said, in the future and as you grow older. And older still. As you become like me.'

She went then, with much briskness of purpose and greatly to Alva's relief. She wished, for something like the ten thousandth time, that Ellen would make peace with herself and settle for a comfortable, quiet existence helping around De Novo. When she got up to close the door after the old woman she caught a last sighting of her quickly moving figure disappearing down the avenue into the chill swirls of mist.

Afterwards, Alva would wonder at how completely she had lacked any premonition, at how easily and callously she had dismissed Ellen from her thoughts and got on with the business of dinner reservations and bed night figures and hiring a plumber to look at the water pressure in one of the bedrooms. She had even become absorbed enough to rough out the projected heating, lighting and food costs for the winter ahead. It had all taken less than an hour.

And in that same hour Ellen, standing just outside the gates of De Novo, had waited for a suitably speeding car before stepping out into its path. There was no doubt, either then or in later, tortured analysis, that her action had been a deliberate and premeditated suicide. A dramatic, risky way of ending a life gone sour.

Death was not instantaneous. The distraught driver, using his car phone, had called for the police and an ambulance before kneeling with Ellen who, with a dignity and resignation which denied the pain she was so obviously suffering, waited for what must come. She was in the ambulance and on her way to hospital before her identity was established and the gardaí arrived looking for Theo.

Ellen took twelve hours to die. For all of that time Theo, becoming older by the minute, sat by her bedside and watched her with eyes which looked only to the past. Alva watched too and saw in the old woman's unconscious face how the lines and deep wrinkles softened until her skin became smoother, less aged. She'd seen the same thing happen to her mother's dying face. It was, she knew, the peace of death approaching.

'She had beautiful skin,' Theo said once, 'pale and satiny like the petal on a magnolia bloom.'

'I can see that,' Alva said and left them alone for a while.

When she came back, a couple of hours later, Theo said, 'She always marched to her own tune, even from a small child. I don't think she *ever* heard any tune but her own. Once, as a child, on a day when the rain was beating across the garden, she announced she wanted to take her doll for a walk. Our mother, exhausted by her demands, let her go, out into the garden and into the weather with the doll. She thought Ellen would tire of it and come back inside. She didn't, of course. She walked that doll all over the garden in the rain until my father arrived and carried her inside.' He sighed. 'She got pneumonia and the doll was ruined, a sodden thing that never dried out.'

'What do you think she wanted from life?' Alva asked.

'To be twenty for ever.' Theo gently pushed a strand of hair back from his sister's high, white forehead.

Alva wasn't there when Ellen died. She'd gone back to the hotel to cancel bookings and tell the extra staff not to come in. Losing the Hallowe'en custom wasn't going to make things easier but, in the circumstances, there was really no choice but to close for the week.

And so it was Theo's big hand which held Ellen's while, with a couple of small shudders, she slipped away from life. She had regained consciousness for a few minutes only.

'She asked me if I thought she'd rot in hell,' Theo told Alva later, when it was all over and Ellen was in the morgue. 'Then she said that there, at least, she'd be in company she knew. They'd given her something for the pain and she was smiling. She'd no regrets, nothing at all like that.' The thought seemed to give him comfort.

The funeral was five days later, delayed by the need

for an autopsy. Alva put a notice in the paper and phoned a few people. One of them was Oscar Duggan. Ellen would most certainly have wanted him at her funeral. He'd heard, of course, but was nonetheless grateful to Alva for phoning. His shock seemed to her genuine. It even moved him to offer a home to Thomas.

'Thomas is gone,' Alva said and realized just how long Ellen had been planning things.

'Ellen was frightened.' He sounded very sober. 'She frightened the hell out of me but I think she frightened herself too, a lot of the time.'

'Frightened herself?'

'By her inability to feel anything. There's boredom and boredom, my dear Alva.' She could hear him give a long sigh. 'See you at the funeral,' he said.

Alva was surprised at the numbers who turned up for the funeral. Quite a few of the film people came, as well as most customers from McNally's pub, friends from around the neighbourhood and some old people, men mostly, who Alva presumed were from Ellen's past. The Wicklow sisters, Lucille and Angeline Fogarty, came and cried together, large noisy tears, as Ellen's coffin was lowered into the ground. Theo, with enormous dignity, accepted sympathies at the graveside.

'She endured,' he assured a handsome, white-haired old man. 'She endured for as long as she could bear to.'

Clara phoned from New York. Luke, she said, had

rung to tell her what had happened. She was saddened, and apologetic that she couldn't be there, but would be in Dublin in December with her sons and would see Alva and Theo then. She was very Clara on the phone, throaty and philosophical. 'The end crowns all, as the Bard said – and since Ellen lived as she chose why shouldn't she have died as she chose, too?'

'No reason,' Alva said, 'no reason at all.'

Luke, just back from post-production work in London, came to the funeral and was apologetic he hadn't been on hand earlier in the troubled week.

'There was nothing to do, anyway,' Alva said sadly, 'except get through it. Theo's been worryingly quiet but he seems fine today.' They were in the sitting room at De Novo. Bernie had laid on snack food and a waiter served drinks. Quite a few people had come back after the burial.

'Just you and Theo now,' the director said. He was pale, Alva thought, as if he hadn't been outdoors for days. 'Could be a lonely winter,' he said. 'Think you could handle a bit of company from time to time?'

'I'm hoping for a busy winter, once we reopen again,' she smiled. 'But yes, I think I could handle company.' He was wearing a black polo jumper under his inevitable tweed jacket. Out of nowhere came a memory of Ellen calling him 'perilously attractive but hungry-looking'. Alva widened her eyes to stop quick tears from falling.

'I hope that our being here didn't . . .' He paused. '. . . Had nothing to do with Ellen's . . .'

'No,' Alva shook her head, 'Ellen was unhappy long before the company came to De Novo. Who's to say what tipped the balance?'

Oscar, with a tray on which there were three glasses of wine, appeared beside them. His expression was untypically humble. 'It would have amused her to think of us three drinking together,' he said. 'So, please, will you join me?'

They drank and spoke together a little, sadly, of Ellen and of the manner of her death. Oscar's face was puffier than usual and Alva had difficulty keeping her mind off Ellen's many cruel, but often hilarious, jibes at its expense. Watching him, she wondered if he'd perhaps shed a tear or two. She abandoned the thought when he drained his wine and grabbed a gin and tonic from a passing tray. He was still, obviously, hell bent on his own, slow form of suicide.

'Any post-production problems?' With an arch look Luke's way Oscar changed the subject.

'None. So far. Should there be?' Luke was cool.

'Wouldn't be surprised if there were.' Oscar's expression was bland. 'Our man doesn't give up easily, you know.'

'What the hell does *that* mean?' Luke's voice took on an edge, and he glared. Oscar's bland expression didn't change as he gazed back. Alva watched them both.

'It means that Kelly's not finished interfering with *Death Diminishes*.' Oscar shrugged, spilled some gin on the charcoal linen of his jacket and mopped it with a yellow handkerchief.

'I didn't think he was,' Luke said, 'but it *did* seem to me that his opportunities for interfering are severely limited at this stage.'

'You'd think so, wouldn't you?'

'Listen, Oscar,' Luke took a step closer to the other man, 'if you've got something to say, then say it. If not, stop pissing around.'

'Well, actually, I *do* feel somewhat driven to tell you a thing or two I think you should know.' Oscar studied the wedge of lemon in his glass. 'You're not the only one with principles, Luke.' He gave a small giggle, a strangled sound which seemed to end in his nose.

Luke turned away. 'I should be going.' He touched Alva's arm. 'I'm up against it at the moment. Can I ring you later?'

'You'll want to know this, Luke.' Oscar lurched between them. 'No need to be so almightily snotty about brushing me off. It's about Jack and what he's been doing with the money he was syphoning off—'

'Syphoning off?' Luke shot the question at him and Oscar, having got his attention, smirked.

'That's what I said.' He signalled the waiter for another drink.

'That's a very serious charge, Oscar.' Luke spoke slowly. 'Are you sure you can back it up?'

'I may be a drunk,' Oscar spoke with some dignity, and a little sadly, 'but I haven't lost my reason. Yet. In fact I'm having what you could call one of my finer moments.' The waiter arrived with his drink. 'So here's the story. Jack's real interest in the Millennium Project had to do with the Czech film. Not just because of his mother coming from that country, though I gather she's some act. He says it's the sexy one, the best of the lot, the picture that's going to put bums on seats the world over. Maybe he's right. He's pretty certain, anyway, because he's got himself in on a personal slice of the action there. Which was why he started syphoning off money from *Death Diminishes*, and, I suspect, the British film too, and putting it into the Czech effort. It was like this: you got your period carriage, Luke – on paper, anyway. The money went elsewhere. And those days that were cut? You got those too, on paper. There's more, but you can get Gray to sort out the rest. I gather he's got wind of some of it anyway and is nosing around.' He stopped, turned to Alva. 'Another thing, Alva my pet, you can forget about owing Seona. I looked after her when she set this place up for me. There's no reason for you to arrange those interviews for her.' He heaved an enormous sigh. 'And that, folks, is my conscience cleared.'

'Does this mean you intend returning my £10,000?' Alva raised a caustic eyebrow.

'That, I'm afraid, will not be possible.' Oscar shook a mournful head. 'My need was great, my creditors many . . .'

'It was just a thought,' Alva said.

Luke was looking thoughtfully at Oscar. 'Can you prove any of this?' he asked.

'I don't have it in writing, if that's what you mean. But the proof's there, if Gray looks hard enough. Or at least enough to cook Mr Kelly's goose.' Oscar mopped himself with the yellow hanky. 'Obviously, and before you ask, my motives in telling you are less than pure. The bastard owes me money and he's just seen to it that I don't get work on another production coming on stream. Also,' he gave a shrug which was really a roll of his shoulders, 'I felt that in the spirit of the woman we're mourning I should seek revenge. She would have approved.'

'Thank you, Oscar, I'm much obliged.' Luke looked as if he meant it. 'Wish you'd been moved to revenge yourself before this, though.' He checked his watch and turned to Alva. 'Felim's in London. He sends his sympathies and apologies. I need to talk to him before he leaves his office there. I'll have to go. I'm sorry.' He held her arm and squeezed it. 'I'll phone.' He hesitated, looking at her. Then he gave a sort of hopeless shrug and was gone.

Others were leaving too. Many of the mourners were elderly, and a sense of their own mortality had descended like a slow, inevitable weight on proceedings. They moved off, in ones and twos, subdued, reflecting on Ellen and their youth, on what might have been and on what was. Just four hours after the burial De Novo House was silent as the grave in which Ellen had been laid.

In the days which followed it became, if anything, quieter. Bernie, with the hotel closed for a week and no meals to prepare, took time to get her own life in order. Theo, displaying an obvious preference for his own company, spent all of the shortening daylight hours in the garden and the rest of the time in his room. Alva missed Ellen, her presence and even her vitriol.

And she hated the solitude in De Novo. It was as if, and the thought frightened her, she had stepped back in time to the house in Churchtown. De Novo had taken on the tight, compartmentalized, no-feel, no-touch life she had lived there with her parents. She remembered what Clara had said – that in taking on De Novo she had retreated from life, gone back to her childhood existence. She'd dismissed the idea as non-sense. Now she thought there might be something, not a lot but certainly something, in what the actress had said.

Luke didn't ring for three days. She was more upset than she cared to admit and when he did finally call she was more relieved than she cared to admit too. He wanted to see her, he said; could he come out?

'No,' Alva said quickly, 'I'd prefer to meet you in town. I need to get out of here.' He named a pub, a quiet place off Grafton Street, and she pulled on a warm jumper over her jeans and left immediately.

He was waiting for her in a corner, a half-finished pint of Guinness in front of him.

'I'll have a half-one.' She slipped into the bench seat beside him.

He emptied his glass in two gulps. 'Haven't eaten all day. That was my breakfast,' he said. 'I'll have another and that'll have to be my dinner.' He called for a second pint and for Alva's half-one. The barman, who knew him, pulled the drinks quickly and brought them over.

Luke paid with a twenty-punt note. 'The last of my Irish money.' He slipped the change into his pocket as they sipped their drinks. 'I leave for London tomorrow and go on from there to Colombia in about two weeks.' He put down his drink, studied its frothy top and was quiet.

Alva gave herself several seconds to absorb what he'd said before she spoke. 'That's great, Luke. But how did you manage it? What changed things?'

He drew a smiling face in the creamy froth and sucked his finger. 'Oscar's revelatory burst at Ellen's funeral was what swung it. Remember all that stuff about Jack's wheeler-dealing, taking money from one film's budget to promote another? Well, it all had to do with his own personal struggle for more control of the whole Millennium Project.'

'I remember Oscar saying something about Jack syphoning funds from *Death Diminishes* to put into the Czech film . . .'

'Right. Only *Death Diminishes* wasn't the only victim, so to speak. I passed on Oscar's titbits to Felim and he's come up with a few very interesting facts. Jack's been a very bad lad. But a clever one too.'

'Not clever enough, by the sound of things,' Alva said, 'since it looks like you've got your time off to go to Colombia. Or are you just taking it?'

'Both,' he grinned. 'I've told Jack I'm taking it and there's not a lot he can do about it, under the circumstances. Felim's got enough proof to cause him extreme difficulties, though not enough to hang the bastard, unfortunately. Still, a guy like Jack makes a lot of enemies and he's more than keen to bring Felim's investigative trawlings to a halt. I've got a month's stay on post-production. I do a couple of weeks now, in London, then head off to Colombia around twentieth November.' He hesitated. 'That's if I haven't heard from Eric by then.'

'Do you think there's a chance you will?'

'Frankly, no.'

'So – what you're telling me is that you blackmailed Jack Kelly?'

'What a prosaic mind you have,' Luke grinned. 'I prefer to think I put up a persuasive argument. My point to him was that if he wanted to maintain his altruistic interest in the Czech film he'd better leave me in charge of the post-production of *Death Diminishes.* He saw my point.'

'Put like that he would, wouldn't he?' Alva laughed, then became silent. What she felt like saying seemed inappropriate, selfish even, in the circumstances, a litany of self-interest. He would be gone six weeks. She would miss him. She would worry about him. She'd been reading about Colombia and its problems. He would have to be very careful . . .

He wouldn't want to hear any of it, wouldn't want to cross half the world in search of a missing brother with the burden of her need hanging about him. Instead she asked, very carefully, 'Will you be home for Christmas?'

'I hope so.' He spoke, she noticed, with equal care. He lifted her hand where she'd laid it on the table, traced the fingers thoughtfully with his before turning it palm up. He turned and looked at her, his eyes serious and dark in the dim pub lighting.

'My timing's probably lousy,' he said, 'given that you've got your hotel to get up and going again and I've got all this other stuff to look after.' His fingers tightened around hers and he smiled. 'Relax, my love, I'm not going to ask you to sign anything in blood. I just want to ask you to think about me while I'm gone. Good thoughts, if you can manage them. Because, when I get back, I'm going to woo you and I want you to be in receptive mood. I'm going to be the chivalric knight of old and . . .' he paused, 'hope for the best. Think you can do that – think about me positively, I mean?'

'Oh, I think I can manage that.' Alva smiled what she hoped was an easy, confident smile. Of course she would think about him. He was what she thought about a lot of the time these days.

'I feel vastly reassured.' He gave a short laugh and lifted his glass. 'To tomorrow, to the future.'

They talked on for a while, of desultory things, both of them aware of the looming separation, of the futility of saying anything that would be a commitment, a promise.

'I'll write, or at any rate send a card,' Luke said.

'Clara's coming, in December, with her sons,' Alva said.

'I know.'

'Of course you know. It was thoughtful of you to phone and tell her about Ellen.'

'I'm a thoughtful fella. Be nice to her when she gets here. It's the first time for her boys.'

'Of course I'll be nice to her. I'm a nice person.'

They walked to Alva's car, parked in Dawson Street. She opened the door quickly and turned to him. His hands were in his pockets and he was smiling, cool.

'Be seeing you,' he said and gave her forehead a chaste brush with his lips. He had turned the corner into Anne Street when she was taken with a fierce urge to give him a hug, a fierce kiss goodbye. But the urge didn't bring with it the courage to run after him and she ducked into the car, turned on the ignition and drove away quickly.

In bed that night she had a dream. She was in the old house in Churchtown and all the doors were locked and though she tried and tried, frenziedly running from one to the other, pushing and pulling and searching for keys, she couldn't get out. She woke up in a cold sweat.

Chapter Twenty-One

The hotel reopened amid rumour and speculation.

'We heard there was a *tragic* death at your gates just after they finished filming here. What happened exactly?' The young blonde with the avid expression and vermeil nails spoke in a theatrical whisper as Alva took her order. Her elderly companion looked up from a study of the menu with a frown.

'I asked you, Orla,' he was severe as only a father could be, 'to refrain from ghoulish behaviour for the night. That was the deal if we came to this place.' He nibbled on Bernie's lemon sugar wafers.

'I'm not being ghoulish,' Orla pouted, 'just naturally curious. A murder film followed by a tragic death – you have to admit it's not every day.' She tried a winning smile on Alva. 'I'm sure you've had lots of people asking about the . . . coincidence.'

'A few,' Alva admitted drily, 'and really, that's all it was. A coincidence. A road accident. Can I recommend the prawns? They're particularly good tonight.'

'Tell me about the filming.' The girl giggled. 'Is it true that Nick Hunt needed a life-support machine to help him act?'

'I'll try the prawns,' the father interrupted, his expression resigned. 'And an oil-free salad. My daughter will have the same. And no wine unless she shuts up.' He glared and the girl sighed into silence and asked for a Sancerre.

Giving the order in the kitchen Alva sat for a minute. 'What happens', she asked Bernie, 'when our infamy dies the death and we become just another very good eating place?'

'We could start throwing in the odd murder for dessert,' Bernie said. 'Or arrange to have Ellen haunt the place.'

Alva gave a small, protesting yelp. 'That's just a *bit* tasteless, Bernie,' she said.

'Yes, but Ellen would have enjoyed it,' Bernie said placidly, 'you know she would. And she may very well come back to haunt the place, for all that.'

Since reopening four weeks before, the restaurant, on the four nights of the week it operated, had been turning customers away. Saturday and Sunday lunch-times were bringing prowling, curious and always hungry family groups. De Novo House Hotel was, for the moment, *the* place to eat and see.

Jasper and Bernie planned a January wedding. Alva planned no further than the next day's menus, the next night's staying guests – though there weren't many of them. She worked at everything, keeping staff at a minimum and falling exhausted into bed each night. It gave her no time and less energy to worry about the fact that she hadn't had a card from Luke O'Hanlon. When she did stop, did allow herself to think, it was to look across the grey dazzle of the wintry bay and wish and wish that she had said more, *given* more for God's sake, on that last day in the pub. He'd called her his love. He wasn't extravagant in the usual way that film people were. He didn't throw endearments around. Maybe he meant that she was . . .

So why didn't he get in touch? Where was the card he'd promised? She worked harder still, doing jobs which weren't hers to do, reminding herself that Clara would arrive in a couple of weeks and have news, surely.

She almost didn't notice what was happening to Theo.

It hadn't been a severe winter, so far. Rainy dark days followed one another but there was no frost, no real hardship to the garden. Theo was nevertheless very busy, covering every exposed inch of soil with leafmould. It occurred to Alva, on a day when several lorries of bought-in leafmould arrived, that he was using enough of the stuff to protect the gardens from a couple of years of monsoons. The white wintry sun and crisp, biting air drew her outside to ask him about it.

'You seem to be using a lot of leafmould,' she said, but carefully. He'd been notoriously sensitive since Ellen's death.

'Protecting the soil structure,' he said. 'Has to be done.'

'Yes, I know. Just seemed to me you were lashing on more than usual. You expecting an especially bad winter?'

'Best to leave it all protected, just to be sure.' He checked the sky, then his watch. 'I'll have to be getting on with things. Days are short enough and I've to get on now with cutting back dead flowerheads.' He tried to push past her with the wheelbarrow but Alva stood in his path.

'What do you mean, leave it all protected? Are you going somewhere, Theo?'

'Might be.' He didn't put the barrow down.

'That's not an answer.' Alva felt herself getting angry. She deserved better than this. They were supposed to be partners in De Novo, after all. 'Are you taking a holiday, or what?'

'You can see I'm busy,' he said and neatly manoeuvred the wheelbarrow sideways past her and downhill to where he'd completely dug up and replanted part of the herb garden. Alva followed and stood beside him as he began to work, muttering to himself. 'I'll have to lift and split some of my mints. Can't have the roots going rampant when I'm not here . . .'

'This is not fair, Theo.' Alva spoke quietly. 'I deserve to know what your plans are, what it is you intend doing. I certainly need to know if you're taking off for any length of time. We're partners, remember?'

'And *I* should be left to the peace of my thoughts. In my own garden at least.' Theo raised a shooing arm at her but Alva stood her ground.

'You're doing more than thinking, Theo. You're acting. You're preparing to leave and I want to know for how long. I do *not* mean to invade your peace or privacy – but if you're making decisions that are going to affect De Novo then I need to know.'

Theo got up slowly from where he'd been hoeing

the ground. He stood leaning on the handle, looking out to sea, his brows together in a frown above his glasses. 'The mistake was mine,' he said, 'and I apologize. I should never have brought you here. I should have sold this damn place and put Ellen in a home where she would have been looked after.'

He turned to Alva and on his face was an expression so bleak it shocked her. Shocked her in a way that even Ellen's death hadn't managed to do. For all his taciturn behaviour she had always thought of Theo as being for life and optimism what Ellen had been to despair and cynicism. She waited for him to go on, feeling a chill that went to her very bones, and leaden in a way that nothing – not the bright day, not the smell of wood fires in the air – could lighten.

'I've done a disservice to the two of you, to you and Ellen both,' Theo said. 'I wanted to hold on to the garden and I wanted to have Ellen where I could keep an eye on her. I had doubts about bringing you here, but I ignored them. I guessed you were running away from something, a man I supposed, and wondered if a lonely old house was the best place for you to run to. I felt having the film crowd here would make the reality of her age and mortality too harsh for Ellen to handle and still I agreed to let you bring them in. I have been wrong, wrong, wrong. And now it's all ended.'

He stopped, looked at her briefly and sadly before, with a resigned shrug of his shoulders, he began to hoe at some weeds. Alva watched him, resisting a desire to take the instrument and put her hands in his and comfort him. He would be embarrassed and would resist and, worse, he might retreat into silence again.

She waited for him to go on. After several minutes he did so, looking down and talking to his beloved earth.

'There was some point to it all while she was alive. Now that she's gone I don't see the why of it any more. She was nothing but trouble all of her days but she was my flesh and blood and we spent our unhurried youth together in this place. We spent our old age in it too, even if she never admitted to an old age. But it's time for me to go now.'

He began to put the garden implements into the wheelbarrow, one by one and slowly. Alva stood, appalled by her own insensitivity; that she had not understood things better. De Novo had existed for Theo as a home only while Ellen lived. He'd needed her to need him. Alva could have wept, only Theo wouldn't have liked that either.

But there was the garden. She couldn't accept that the garden had ended for Theo too. The garden was a living, growing thing, his creation, nurtured and brought to mature fruition by him. How could he think about leaving the garden?

It was grief talking. She would change his mind. He couldn't abandon her and the hotel now, not now that it was beginning to take off. She knew she would be appealing to the wilderness of his lonely logic but she had to try. She was too desperate not to.

'The garden's a reason to stay, Theo. This garden is *you*. How can you leave it, trust it to someone else while you're still alive?' He didn't answer immediately, looking across the walks, the grey and brown wintry hues of the stark stems and bare trees. In the end he shook his head, smiling a little.

'Gardens always find someone to care for them – much more easily than people do. Gardens give back what you put into them. Man, as a species, is much less reliable.'

'But what about me, Theo? What about our agreement?' Alva was aware she sounded desperate but didn't care. 'I trusted you. I invested my money and my life in De Novo because of you . . .'

'No you didn't, Alva.' Theo looked at her and his expression was infinitely sad, infinitely regretful. 'You did it because the opportunity came at a time when you needed an escape, to change your life. And you did it too because you liked the old place. Anyway, I'm not planning to take any of that away from you.'

'What *are* you planning to do?' Alva asked the question quietly, knowing there was nothing more she could say, nothing which could change Theo's mind about whatever it was he planned. He lifted the wheelbarrow and, with him wheeling it, they walked together slowly back towards the house.

'You've been running the place without me,' he said. 'Despite me, you could say. You've got it working now and you don't need me.' Alva started to interrupt and he threw her a quick, silencing glare. He didn't stop wheeling the barrow. 'Listen to me, or we'll be debating all evening and I haven't the patience for that. Here's what I've decided to do. I'm leaving here, going to allow you to run the place on your own and as you will. I don't want you to give me my share of the place in money, nothing like that. If you could pay me an allowance each month that would be grand; not a lot, because I've got the pension. I'll be dead long before what you pay me adds up to my share in the place, so you're getting a bargain. I'll be leaving you the place in my will anyway. If you want to sell at some point, then that's all right with me too.'

'It's not what we agreed,' Alva said shakily. She felt as if everything secure and knowable had been whipped away from her. True, Theo hadn't helped much. Not at all, if she was really honest. But he'd been *there*. This way she would be alone, completely in control. Completely responsible.

'You're right. It's not what we agreed and I'm sorry,' Theo said, 'but it'll be better for you this way.' They'd arrived at the house and he began around the side with the barrow.

'But where will you *go*?' Alva asked him.

'Go?' He looked at her in surprise. 'I'll go down to the Fogarty girls in Wicklow, of course. The garden there's a disgrace. In need of care and imagination. The girls have none, you know. Never did have a scrap of imagination between them. I'll pay for my keep and get it in shape for them before the summer.' He smiled, a reassuring Theo smile with a touch of his old arrogance. 'They'll be glad to have me.'

'I'm sure they will,' Alva said.

Chapter Twenty-Two

On December 18th Clara Butler, arriving at Dublin Airport, was caught immediately in a blaze of publicity. With Christmas looming there was the inevitable newspaper and TV hype about the seasonal return of the nation's diaspora. Even had she wanted to, it would have been impossible for her to slip unnoticed through the throngs of returning sons and daughters. Glamorous and glowing and clinging to her lively sons as she emerged into the arrival hall, she was ideal camera fodder. A TV news crew spotted her in seconds.

'Of course we're glad to be here,' she smiled at the reporter. 'I haven't had a Christmas at home in Dublin for years.'

A few rudimentary questions about *Death Diminishes* were got quickly out of the way and the reporter shoved the microphone towards Clara's sons.

'This is Frederick,' Clara, introducing her red-headed younger son, quickly took control of the situation, 'and this is Danny.' The dark-eyed older boy nodded, the younger one fidgeted and pulled at his mother impatiently. Both were tall and already on the way to being handsome.

'How do the two of you feel about being in Dublin for Christmas?' The reporter, vague memories coming back to her of summertime newspaper stories about Clara's childhood, dug in for something more than the usual home-for-Christmas story.

'It's cool,' said Danny.

'We haven't seen anything yet,' Frederick said, reasonably. 'This is our first time.'

'Oh? You mean it's your first Christmas in Dublin?'

'No. Our first time in Ireland,' Frederick said and the reporter, scenting a yuletide family reunion, or better still, a family sundered, stepped with the microphone between Clara and her sons.

'Why is it that you've never come before?' She beamed the question at Frederick, the obvious candidate for an indiscretion.

'Just didn't.' He shrugged and looked at his mother who, with another huge and dazzling smile, explained.

'The three months I spent filming here earlier in the year decided me it was time. And the boys are just full of impatience to see the city and meet their uncles.' Waving, she called a bright 'Happy Christmas' into the cameras, took a son on each arm and forged through the milling crowds. They parted for her good-humouredly, then closed ranks so that the reporter and her microphone were swallowed into the jaws of a fresh rush of arrivals. The pictures in the papers were of the emerging Clara, smiling as she burst through the crowds, a grinning son on either side. The TV snippet begged questions it didn't answer but gushed on about how just about everyone wanted to be in Dublin for Christmas.

Alva, watching the TV news, waited impatiently for

Clara to ring. She did so within an hour, almost as soon as they'd settled into their hotel.

'You made your usual quiet entrance,' Alva laughed, 'unsung and unnoticed. Where are you? You could have stayed here, you know.'

'Believe me, I'd have liked nothing better,' Clara said, 'but the publicity people have decided I must sing for my supper, and they pay the piper. I'm at the Newgrange. Can you come visit me tonight?'

'Not tonight.' Alva was regretful. 'We're very busy. How does tomorrow afternoon sound?'

'Great. How's Theo doing?'

'Hard to tell. I'll explain when I see you. You'll be coming out to see him?'

'God, yes. Day after tomorrow, if that's all right with him. And you. And Bernie. Can't wait in fact – and nor can the boys after all I've told them about the place. See you here tomorrow then? About three?'

'Yes. And Clara—' But the phone had gone dead. Alva stared at it a while, wondering if she should ring back and deciding against it. She would ask tomorrow if she'd heard from Luke. Another night of not knowing wouldn't make that much difference. Another, she checked her watch, twenty hours or so . . .

The Newgrange, close to Stephen's Green and the south city's explosive air of festivity, was in full seasonal flight, all gold and silver and with brightly lit miniature fir trees everywhere. It was a lot more flamboyant than anything De Novo had laid on for Christmas; there

377

Alva had gone for lots of ivy, a modicum of holly and one big, overdressed, Victorian-style tree.

Theo's imminent departure – he had arranged with the Fogartys to move early in January – had flattened her enthusiasm for a more robust decorating job. Guests, in any event, said they liked it.

Clara appeared as soon as Alva announced herself, swooping down the staircase like a green and red advertisement for designer elegance at Christmastime. All trace of Constance Moore had gone and she was well and truly into the role of visiting star, friend and mother.

'God, it's good to see you Alva.' Her embrace was smothering. She held Alva away and looked at her, hard. 'You know, in the six weeks since we finished filming I've thought of you and Theo and Bernie and De Novo almost every day. And Ellen.' She tucked Alva's arm into hers and led them to a quiet corner of the upstairs tea terrace. They ordered and for a while talked of Ellen and then Theo. Clara was less surprised than Alva had expected her to be by Theo's decision.

'He hated the idea of the old place being used as anything but a home,' she said, 'you could see that. With Ellen gone his family's gone and it's simply and solely an hotel. As far as he's concerned anyway.'

'That's a large part of it,' Alva agreed and took a deep breath.

'Clara, have you heard—'

The question went unasked as Clara the mother

stood and, with more pride than was decent, said, 'Alva, I want you to meet my sons.'

They were taller than they'd looked on the television, but younger-looking too. On the news snippet they had seemed precociously New York and collected. Standing in front of Alva, shaking her hand, murmuring greetings and being impatiently, obediently polite, they were a couple of nice-looking, very typical eleven- and thirteen-year-olds.

'Mom told us about your house.' Frederick – who said he was never called Fred or Freddie and didn't want to be – elected himself spokesman as they sat down. 'Sounds cool.'

'It's pretty cool,' Alva agreed. 'But you can see for yourself tomorrow. You're all coming to visit?' They nodded. 'Sammy will be there and Bernie's doing something special.' She looked at Clara.

'Sure. But there's no need to go to all that trouble.'

'We want to,' Alva said. A time was arranged and Danny and Frederick, to Alva's guilty relief, took themselves off to watch a video in their room.

'Clara,' she leaned forward, her hands locked around her knees, 'tell me you've heard from Luke. Please . . .'

'I haven't. Not a word. You haven't either?' Clara's face was serious. She broke a biscuit in half, then broke it again and made crumbles of it. 'I kept telling myself you'd have heard.'

'Likewise.' They sat and stared at one another, tinkles of glass and laughter all around them and, from the street, the floating harmony of a well-rehearsed carol-singing group.

'He's been in Colombia a month now.' Alva broke the silence. 'Oh, God, I'm so worried . . .'

Clara leaned forward and covered her hand. 'Let's think this thing through.' She paused. 'He could be in the mountains, no way of sending a card. He could be . . . Oh, I don't know. He said he'd be a month, didn't he? Maybe he's on his way back.'

'He's not. There's something wrong.'

'Is this instinct talking? Or the panic of someone worried about a man they could be in love with?'

'Oh, Clara, please shut up with the psychobabble.' Alva gave a gulp and a sort of smile. Clara said nothing. Behind them two small children stood at a Christmas tree with their father, their creamy hair shining under the lights. The smallest of them reached and curled her fingers towards a hanging reindeer. She had grabbed it before her father could do anything.

'You could be right,' Alva said. 'I could be in love with him.'

'Thought you cared quite a lot for him,' Clara said. 'Thought it the night I made dinner for you both.'

'The night you made dessert,' Alva corrected. 'You set us up that night, didn't you?'

'Yup.' Clara was brisk. 'Wasn't so hard to do, either. Willing victims, both of you.'

'I suppose we were . . .' Alva paused. 'The worst of it is that I let him go to the other side of the world without a word of love or . . . anything.'

'That is most certainly *not* the worst of it.' Clara became all at once practical. 'Though it *was* rather mean and self-protecting of you. The worst of it is that we don't know where he is or what's happened to him . . .' She hesitated. 'You might as well know, Alva, that I called Marcia Tulins. She met him when he arrived but since then, nothing.'

'I'm going to do something.' Alva's panic made her voice jerky. 'It's gone on for long enough. I'll get the Foreign Affairs people onto it . . .'

'I think you should. And I'll get things moving in New York. I go back on December 23rd. Christmas is a big thing with the rest of Larry's family since he died. I can't not be there.' She signalled a waiter. 'Look, Alva, Luke's a big boy and he's been in tight corners before. Why don't I get you a proper, reviving Christmas drink? Luke'll probably roll into De Novo one of these days, Eric in one hand and a whopper of an emerald in the other. Did you know Colombia is famous for its emeralds?'

Clara was meeting her twin brothers that evening, so Alva left soon after. She'd already met them briefly the night before but this was also to be a meeting with the wife and baby of the married twin, John.

The following day, from an under-thirteen point of view, was a howling success. Sammy strutted and showed off De Novo as if to the manner born and, as soon as adult backs were turned, disappeared with Clara's boys to the beach with a football. Bernie's pizzas had to wait but it gave Clara time to have a quiet walk in the garden with Theo. And a less quiet talk with Alva and Bernie about her brothers. And about Theo.

'Do you think he can be persuaded to stay on here?' Alva asked, without much hope. Clara's influence with Theo was not negligible.

'No. He's decided and I think he's right. He's lost heart for this place. It's *his* life, Alva, let him be. Reassure him a little – he's worried about you.'

'Not worried enough to stay,' Alva sighed. 'All right, Clara, I'll help him pack his bags.'

'Tell us about your brothers.' Bernie was all curiosity. 'Has the season of goodwill brought you close?'

'It *has* worked some of its spirit on things,' Clara admitted. 'The twins really opened up. A lot of it was thanks to the woman John married. She's a real honey, and very funny too. The best thing ever to happen to *both* of them, I'd say. Anyway, they talked and talked and talked. Memories until three in the morning, real floodgate stuff. It was as if they'd been saving it all up . . .'

'How was it for you?' Alva asked.

'Fine, really fine. They wanted me to tell them about Danny, his death, what our father was like. They're a lot younger than me, you know, and their memories of it all are hazier.' She pulled a face. 'They've arranged an outing to Danny's and our father's grave. Our mother's too. And they've rattled up some cousins who haven't wanted to know for years. All good therapeutic stuff.'

Bernie's meal was inspired: enough pizza and chocolate cake to satisfy appetites made ravenous by the sea air, and a braised shoulder of lamb with walnut stuffing for the older, but not much less controlled, appetites. Theo, more animated than Alva had seen him in a long time, captivated the boys with unlikely, and probably untrue, stories of De Novo's nefarious past.

Before they left Alva went with Clara to her old room.

'I loved living here.' Clara walked slowly about, touching a picture, the ornate woodwork on the wardrobe door, the bedside lamp. She adjusted her perfectly all right hair in the mirror and sat on the bed. Alva sat facing her from the stool by the dressing table.

'I'm having a problem imagining the place without Theo,' Alva admitted. 'He's got me someone who'll do the garden, though I'll have to let part of it grow wild. Theo hasn't been able to keep up with it for years and it would need an army of gardeners anyway to keep it in really top shape . . .'

'I hadn't thought about it like that.' Clara looked perturbed. 'But of course you're right. He told me about the deal you and he've worked out together . . .'

'The deal *Theo* has worked out.' Alva paused. 'It's feasible, of course. But there are other things I should perhaps do as well . . .'

'What do you mean?' Clara was suddenly very alert.

'I've thought a lot about what you said about my burying myself here. Theo said much the same thing, said I was running away. Both of you are only partly right. De Novo's been both a refuge and a challenge.'

'I can accept that.' Clara was magnanimous, and so

off-hand that Alva knew she was more than ordinarily interested in the conversation. 'So – you've obviously got something in mind to do.' Clara got up and walked to the window. Seeing her stand there, looking out across the darkened bay, Alva was reminded of the last day's shooting, of how well and meticulously Clara had played her role. And of how well and meticulously she'd been directed by Luke O'Hanlon.

'I have.' Alva paused, then spoke in a rush to Clara's back. 'I've decided, if Luke doesn't show up by Christmas, that I'll go to Colombia in the new year and find out for myself what the hell's going on. The idea's been festering and I've been putting it away, but last night, once I knew that you hadn't heard from him either, I decided I would close De Novo down for the month and go. January is a slack month and Bernie's getting married and will be away for two weeks.'

'You make it sound like you're going on vacation, nothing more.' Clara was sharp. 'Colombia is not the same as a couple of weeks in Ballyferriter. Things happen—'

'Which is why I'm going.' Alva got up and stood beside Clara at the window. The darkness outside was punctuated by the ring of the city's lights around the bay. There was something hopeful-looking about it. 'When I took a chance on De Novo it was on something knowable, something I couldn't really lose on.' She smiled. 'I think it's time I took a look at the unknown. Going out there, to Luke, is something I really want to do. If it's just that he's found himself a Colombian lover, then so be it. At least I'll know. And De Novo will be here, waiting, when I get back.'

'Far be it from me to dissuade you.' Clara put an arm through Alva's. 'In fact, in your place I'd probably take the road to the Andes too.' She took a deep breath and turned Alva to face her. 'I've also got a plan. Like yours it came to me last night. And it needs your agreement. Tell me, Alva, how would you feel if this place wasn't here for you when you get back from Colombia?'

'What do you mean?' Alva frowned.

'This', Clara said, 'is what I mean . . .'

It took her ten minutes to outline what she proposed. By the time she finished speaking Alva was feeling utterly liberated and utterly confused. But the confusion didn't mean she wasn't sure about what she wanted to do. About that she was absolutely certain.

Chapter Twenty-Three

Even at three in the morning the *Transito* lounge at the airport in Puerto Rico teemed. And sweltered. The heat was like nothing Alva had ever imagined, air so still and heavy it had been like walking into a wall when first she'd got off the plane. But after three hours in this drab, melting, low-ceilinged room she was getting used to it.

Just as well, since the airline had announced a further delay of an hour. Refuelling, the voice said. No apology, no elaboration – and not a murmur of complaint from the 395 passengers taken off their Boeing flight from Madrid to Bogotá. Alva hadn't complained either. Lassitude filled the air as densely as the heat.

Her flight route, booked at short notice because she'd waited until the last minute hoping to hear from Luke, was of necessity complicated. She'd first had to fly to London and from there to Madrid to pick up the Lima flight which would take her to Bogotá – and whose refuelling stop at San Juan in Puerto Rico now looked like going on until the Caribbean sun rose.

Which sun she would not see, if things up to now were anything to go by. The fabled romance of the Caribbean, its starry skies and waving coconut palms,

were somewhere out there, within reach but unseen.
All she'd been aware of so far was the dead air and
endless phlegm-coloured corridors, all of them leading
with nightmarish inevitability to this room. There
wasn't a whiff of bougainvillaea, not an orchid in sight,
nor a rolling tropical wave to be heard.

Up until yesterday, when she'd left Dublin, no one
who knew him had heard from Luke. Not Clara in
New York, not anyone she'd contacted from the film
crew, not Felim Gray – who'd been away and whose
concern when he got back was as great as Alva's own.
And not Marcia Tulins, whose Bogotá number Alva
had got from Clara. She'd been away from Bogotá for
Christmas but Alva had finally managed to make
contact with her two days ago. Alva had introduced
herself as a friend of Luke's and said she was coming
out to Colombia. Marcia Tulins had been lazily
reassuring.

'Come if it'll make you feel better,' she'd said, 'but
I think myself the brothers O'Hanlon will roll down
from the mountains any day now. Luke went off to the
village Eric mentioned in his last postcard, Infiesto,
about a week after getting here. I'd say they're holed
up there, doing whatever it is brothers do when they
get together after a long absence.'

'You may be right,' Alva said, 'but it's strange he
didn't send me a card.'

'Is it? In my experience it's odd when men *do* send
cards. Out of sight out of mind with most of them.'
Alva could have sworn the other woman yawned. 'Also,
they invariably show up, all of them, when it suits.'

'His brother Eric hasn't shown up. He's been gone ten months . . .'

'Yeah, well, he will. Look, I gotta go. Sorry. It's midday here, hour of the lizard they call it, but some of us gotta work anyway. Give me a call when you get here.'

Alva had had a bad Christmas, worrying about and imagining all sorts of horrors befalling Luke. Her nights had been filled with dreams in which his lifeless body lay at the bottom of a ravine, or, a Christmas Eve special, the discovery of a Christmas tree on a rocky outpost dripping red with his blood. It was easier now she was on her way, now she was doing something. There was also, in spite of everything, an excitement about crossing time zones, oceans and continents, being part of the world's cavalcade of travellers.

She got up for a third cup of the weak, lukewarm orange juice donated by the airline for the comfort of its passengers. It came in styrofoam cups, handed out by a small fat man in a pale grey, perspiration-soaked shirt. Alva's smile seemed to make him more miserable than before. A baby whimpered as she sipped the orange juice and the sound filled the air with a momentary vitality. Alva knew she wouldn't sleep. She'd tried. She leaned instead against the wall and studied some of her fellow passengers. African faces, Indian faces, white and Spanish faces: they all had a place in the teeming hotbed of Latin America. She brushed aside a chilling doubt about what exactly her place was and sipped again at the orange juice. It tasted weaker but was strangely soothing. Maybe they'd put something in it.

Moving into the corridor she leaned against the wall there, hoping for cool and finding none, and thought about Colombia. Everything she read focused on the country's *mala fama* – the lawlessness, corruption, poverty and political insecurity which had its roots in drug trafficking and the powerful and terrifying control wielded by the drug barons. None of it was reassuring.

Two hours later they took off for Bogotá. In the plane sheer exhaustion helped her sleep. She woke as they came down over the Andes and, thirty hours after leaving Dublin, began at last to loop over green valleys and darker green jungle into Bogotá.

Bogotá's El Dorado was another teeming airport, much noisier than San Juan. She found a taxi and gave the driver, a gentle man with a completely bald golden pate, the address of her hotel.

The hotel, in a northern suburb of the city, was small, single-storeyed and welcoming. It was set back off a wide, curiously North American-looking street with trimmed gardens and Chevrolets in the driveways of three of the houses.

The door was opened by a large, bluntly handsome woman in a blue overall. She was Estella, she said. Alva was late and must be tired. She took the suitcase and Alva followed her broad, straight back to a large low room at the back of the house. Once there Estella started a bath running, then left, to return almost immediately with warm milk. Alva had them together, the milk in the bath, and afterwards lay on the bed and watched fast clouds scud across the sky. Clouds and the chill in the air had never figured in her imaginings about Colombia. It was 8.30 a.m. She had been travelling for thirty-five hours.

She woke six hours later and was immediately filled with panic about time lost. This increased when she got a hurried, hassled-sounding Marcia Tulins on the phone and found the journalist couldn't see her until six o'clock. She would walk there, Alva decided, see the city and fill in time that way.

But Estella was adamant. Alva must not walk. Not only that; while travelling alone she must take off her rings, the chain from around her neck, her watch. Where there was hunger and want, she said, people took what they needed to survive. Also, Alva should keep to herself. Or, as the Bogotá saying went, *zapatero, a tus zapatos* – cobbler, mind your last. 'Mind your own business,' she warned as Alva, just after three and much too early, set off in a taxi.

Bogotá was not beautiful. There were beautiful things about it – the way the Cordillera Oriental range of the Andes rose like sheltering arms round about and the small, refreshing breezes that puffed through the street and never let you forget you were nine thousand feet above sea level.

There was beauty in the old tile-roofed houses and Spanish colonial churches – but there were also the concrete tower blocks which smothered the tile-roofed houses, the wide slashes of new roadways cutting across old streets, fast-food joints and shops made of plasterboard, shopping centres for the rich with machine-gun guards patrolling their flat rooftops.

And, around every corner, there was the relentless reality of a poverty without dignity and with no limits. It stripped and left no emotion save a vicious determination to survive. Its face was menacing. There was no expectation amongst the poor and the maimed Alva saw in Bogotá that day; no joy or hope or compassionate fellow feeling. The eyes which stared into the taxi had the cold, calculating look of the desperately starving, the barely surviving; images which would stay with her for ever.

Contradicting this there were the proud, overdressed beauties on the expensive streets, the men in dark suits and vain, closed-in, handsome faces.

Even after an obliging detour by the taxi driver she was an hour early arriving at Marcia Tulins's apartment. To hell with it, she thought, I've come too far to be put off now.

The block was no different to its equivalent in any other city, an unadorned and unpainted concrete tower. It was fourteen storeys high and Marcia Tulins lived on the tenth floor. Alva took her shoes off and leaned against the glass of the front entrance. There were no balconies, no ledges anywhere on the sheer sides of the building. Anyone falling from a window would plummet unimpeded.

She found and rang Marcia Tulins's bell.

'Who is it?' The voice was tinny-sounding on the intercom.

'It's Alva Joyce. I know I'm a bit early, but could I come up to see you now?' There was a pause, long enough for Alva to wonder if the person on the other end had gone away. She was about to try again when the voice came back.

'Tenth floor,' it said, 'push the door when you hear the buzzer.'

The apartment door wasn't open and Alva had to ring the bell there too. Marcia Tulins took a full three minutes to answer.

'Hi!' She was a heavy blonde, about thirty years old. 'You caught me having a catnap. I was working until near dawn.' Her voice now was the strong, reassuring one of the telephone.

'Oh. I'm sorry.' Alva stood awkwardly, waiting to be asked inside, while the other woman, looking indeed as if she'd just got out of bed, leaned against the door jamb. She was wearing an orange kaftan and her hair was a dishevelled halo.

'If you want to work I'll sit and wait ...' Alva was polite, refusing to be unnerved by the other woman's silent assessment. 'Do you think I could come inside?'

'Hey, I'm sorry,' Marcia Tulins said, 'come on in.'

The apartment was curiously unlived-in, as if someone worked and occasionally slept there. Which was probably exactly how Marcia Tulins operated. Most of the space was given over to a large, square living room with brown leatherette settee, a wall covered with maps, another lined with filing cabinets and the entire rest of the room filled by a desk, computer terminal, printer, fax machine and telephone. The windows were uncurtained and a fluorescent tube was the only lighting.

'I've never had time to make a home of this place.' Marcia Tulins looked around. Alva guessed she offered the same explanation to all guests; that it was an attempt at small talk which, along with home-making and social courtesies, was something she wasn't much interested in. Alva had met people like her in journalism before; work obsessed and without much of a life outside it. No wonder her relationship with Eric O'Hanlon had foundered. The miracle was it had ever got off the ground in the first place.

'Please don't feel you have to explain how you live to me.' Alva sank onto the brown settee and rubbed her tired feet. 'I was a journalist for a while myself. I'm just glad to meet you at last.'

'You were a journalist?' Marcia perked up. 'I didn't know that. Is that how you met Luke?'

'No. I met him when he was filming the hotel I . . .' She hesitated. She was going to say own but, given the changes about to happen, the verb seemed wrong. 'The hotel I run,' she said.

'Oh. So that's what De Novo House is.' Marcia, having apparently exhausted her store of small talk, crossed to the fax machine and gave it an impatient thump on the side. 'Damn message is late,' she said, 'should've been here three hours ago.' She turned, undisguisedly impatient and looking at her watch. 'Look, Alva, I gotta go soon. What is it you want to know about Luke O'Hanlon?'

'Everything *you* know.' Alva sat forward.

'You got that already.' Marcia frowned down at the fax machine. 'He arrived here, spent a week sussing things out, then headed for the hills and his brother. Look,' she turned, 'you want to go after him, I'll give you directions and advice. I think you're crazy but since you've come this far you may as well go on up there, see some of the rest of the country. It's truly spectacular. You able to look after yourself?'

'Yes.'

'Good. I'll get you a map.'

She gave the fax machine another angry thump, harder this time. 'Goddamn New York! They never send when they say they will. Outta sight, outta mind, especially when you're down here. Sons of bitches promised me two o'clock, latest.' She turned to Alva. 'I need a drink. Want one?'

'I'd love one. What've you—'

'Bourbon, nothing else I'm afraid. I'll be right back.' With a swish of the kaftan she left the room, into what was apparently a kitchenette. Alva, sticky after her walk, stood and looked around for the bathroom. It had to be through the bedroom, just behind her. She headed in there.

A couple of suitcases lay half-packed on the bed and gave the bedroom an even less lived-in look than the rest of the apartment. It was entirely bland – except

394

for a wall of photographs. Alva moved closer. They were mostly black and white, some of them in colour, all of them telling, in the faces of victims and tormentors alike, the sad, bitter story of the lives lived by the disadvantaged in Latin America. Here was a group of children, none of them more than ten years old, their glazed, hollow eyes turned towards the camera as they paused in their drug-taking. Here was an imbecilic-looking stick man, foraging in a garbage tip. In the picture next to him a child lay in pain, stomach torn open, mouth stretched in screaming appeal to the heedless legs of passers-by.

'Not pretty, are they?' Marcia Tulins's voice behind her was off-hand. 'Plenty more where they came from, but nobody wants to know.' She shrugged, handed Alva a tumbler of bourbon. 'It's all old hat according to the newsdesks in New York and Washington. Get us something new, they say. A different angle. So I try.' Her finger stabbed at a picture. 'Look at that for an angle – couple of transvestites fighting with knives. Or how about this one,' the finger stabbed again, 'hooked hookers. And here. That boy was fifteen years old when he was shot to pieces and then knifed for good measure. What more can I do? I've given them the entrails of this goddamned country and it's not enough. It's not enough that more people die of gunshot wounds in Colombia than any other place on earth. They want drug baron stories, money stories, political stories. Nothing else, and fuck all even on those. No one wants anything on what drugs and money and politics are doing to the poor who have to live here. But that's the way it is in this part of the world. Sometimes you win but mostly you lose.'

Her voice, as she said all of this, was a flat monotone. Alva, turning to look at her, was shocked by the cold, hopeless anger on her face as she looked at the photographs.

'I didn't know you were a photographer.' She couldn't think of another thing to say.

'A good one.' Marcia continued to look at the wall of photographs. Her face, in the light from the window, could have been lovely given a little care. As it was it was prematurely aged, her skin blotchy. 'I take pictures like this, and words are what they want. Words and words and more words. So I give them words and I make a living. And I manage to stay here.'

'This is where you want to be?' Alva sipped the bourbon. It was neat.

'South and Central America, yeah. It's where I want to be. And don't ask me why.'

'Why?'

'Shit, Alva, I said . . .' The other woman shrugged. 'Because it's real and the people are the greatest on earth. How's that for pure sentimentality from one of the hardest-bitten pros in the business?'

Alva looked again at the pictures, slowly. 'Sounds like a good enough reason,' she said. 'I'm sorry.'

'Sorry? What're you sorry about?' Marcia topped up her own drink from a bottle left by one of the suitcases. She didn't offer to top up Alva's.

'About your pictures. About your not being able to sell them. They deserve a showing.'

'Yeah. Well, as it happens, I have sold them.' Marcia took a long gulp. 'A lot of them anyway. Had to write a goddamn book to do it but I sold them.'

'As illustrations for a book?'

'Yeah. Look, I hate to hurry you and you're real nice and all that but I've got a job to finish. Come in the other room and I'll show you how to get to Infiesto.'

Following her out of the bedroom Alva nodded at the suitcases. 'You off somewhere?'

'Yup. Movin' on. Story of my life.'

'Where are you moving to?'

'Nicaragua. Elections coming up there. Trouble, strife, work for Marcia. I've been here long enough anyway. Place gets to you after a while. Lucky for you I haven't packed the essentials yet.' She grinned and nodded to the bourbon bottle. 'Help yourself.'

It had darkened outside and she flicked on the fluorescent lighting before spreading a map on the floor and treating Alva to a fast barrage of advice on how to get to Infiesto in three days, two if she was lucky with flights.

'You can do the first leg of the journey by plane from El Dorado to a town called Pereira. Pretty place. Make your way from there – take a taxi, they're cheap and safe around there – to a town called San Mateo. It's the last biggish place en route to Infiesto. To get from San Mateo to Infiesto you're going to have to use local transport, a bus or truck. And for Christ's sake get a money belt and bring the minimum of everything with you.'

'Are you telling me I should leave my lurex number behind?' Alva's laugh was the nervous kind.

Marcia folded the map and shrugged. 'Good luck,' she said. 'And I'd definitely leave the lurex behind. You'll meet nothing but the greatest of people up there, but no club life. I'd go with you myself if I wasn't leaving tomorrow.'

'Tomorrow? So you won't be here when we get back?'

''Fraid not. Keep the map. Enjoy the mountains. Tell the O'Hanlon boys hi for me.'

Alva, aware she was not being encouraged to stay, folded the map and stood up. 'Can you call me a taxi? I don't fancy walking.'

The fax machine, silent so long, came to life with a sound like an irritable cough. Marcia jumped, crossed the room in two strides and grunted in satisfaction as the message spilled onto the desk. Alva, reluctant to leave without ordering a taxi, stood ignored in the middle of the room. The message was a long one and the phone, she saw, was on the desk by the fax machine. She moved closer, intending to call the taxi number Estella had insisted on giving her, but found her way blocked by a quick, subtle move on Marcia's part.

She thought at first that the other woman didn't want her to use her phone but quickly realized the move was more insulting than that. Marcia Tulins was deliberately blocking her view of the emerging document; so work-obsessed she thought Alva was trying to steal whatever story she was working on.

Alva tapped her on the shoulder. 'Thanks for your help,' she said, 'I'll see myself out.'

She found a taxi quite easily. The streets she'd walked earlier were now lit up, but the softening glow did nothing to minimize the wasted look on the face of a boy of about eight, an infant strapped to his back, who ran begging alongside the taxi. The driver cursed him and speeded up. Alva closed her eyes. When she opened them the child and his pleading face had gone from the window.

She took her dinner, chicken and rice delicately seasoned, on a tray in her hotel room. She needed to think and Estella's very friendly other guests would make that difficult.

She wanted to focus on Marcia Tulins, on something about her which hadn't rung true. Some of it had to do with small, but specific, things she'd said, but most of it had to do with intuition which, half the world away from everything she knew and a whole world away from everything she understood, had in Alva's case gone into top gear.

Intuition was screaming at her that all was not as it seemed with Marcia Tulins. And that whatever she was up to had something to do with Eric and Luke O'Hanlon.

The lies were little, none of them important on the

face of it. But why should Marcia bother? She wasn't the kind of person who did things without a reason, least of all lie. The reason was what bothered Alva.

In the first place she hadn't been sleeping when Alva had arrived at the door. Not with two half-packed suitcases on the bed and a vital fax two hours late. She had, in any case, told Alva beforehand she would be working until six o'clock. Her dishevelled state was simply her natural style.

Then there was the fact of her mentioning De Novo by name, right after evincing surprise that Alva ran a hotel. There could be a perfectly good reason for this, such as Luke having said something about it. But it was still one of the things which hadn't sounded quite right. On a different level, she'd contradicted herself in her anxiety to get rid of Alva – on the one hand saying she had a job to finish urgently, on the other that she needed to rush off somewhere.

Marcia wanted to go all right, and in a great hurry. She hadn't really wanted Alva to know about her departure, either. She'd probably planned to have her cases packed and hidden by six, the time Alva had arranged to arrive. Her destination might very well be Nicaragua, but the really interesting thing was that Marcia, unless Alva's instinct was betraying her completely, wanted to be long gone before the O'Hanlons got back to Bogotá. The plus side was that Marcia's anxious haste had convinced Alva that they were indeed in the village of Infiesto.

Lastly there was the fact that Marcia, a woman of some passion as was obvious from her feelings about her photographs, had been too cool by half about the disappearance of a man she'd once cared for and too keen by half to put his brother off coming to Colombia in search of him.

And now that the inevitable had happened and two people coming in search of him made Eric's return imminent, she couldn't wait to get away ...

None of it made enough sense to be the whole story.

Hit all at once by jet lag, Alva lay back on the bed. It was three a.m. when a melodious gurgle followed by a great belch from the hotel's plumbing system woke her.

Sometime in her sleep an idea, half-formed when she lay down, had hardened into resolve. She would go back to Marcia Tulins's apartment, catch her before she left for Nicaragua. It would be crazy to journey into the Andes without first knowing exactly what was going on on the ground in Bogotá.

She set her alarm for five and drifted back into a fitful sleep.

Chapter Twenty-Four

It was just getting bright when Alva got to Marcia Tulins's apartment block. Very few of its windows were lit up and she stood back and counted, working out which set belonged to the journalist's apartment. Her lights were on. Alva had thought they might be. Marcia had seemed intent on getting away early. Alva had no plan beyond talking to her again, hoping the surprise element of her visit and the threat of delay would shock the journalist into revealing something closer to the truth.

In the chill dawn she waited just outside the glass porch for the first, early rising inhabitant of the block to appear, praying it wouldn't be Marcia. If their meeting happened here, and if Alva was right and Marcia was getting out of town fast and with something to hide, she would be unlikely to hang around to talk. If Alva could get in and up to the tenth floor she would make it a lot harder for Marcia to walk away.

She didn't have to wait long. Her quarry, when he appeared, was a small, moustachioed man with tired brown eyes. Alva flashed him a look at her journalist's card – out-of-date, but he wasn't checking – muttered, 'Señorita Tulins', slipped past him and inside. He didn't even register surprise.

The lift was old, something she hoped would be a help in getting her time with Marcia. She got in and pressed the button for the ninth floor.

When it stopped she jammed the door open with her foot while she carefully and strategically inserted a credit card to see that it stayed open while she went on foot to the next floor. It was a trick she'd seen used by an ambitious photographer and should ensure that the lift was out of action for a while, at least.

On the tenth floor she stood outside Marcia's door, waiting again. There was nothing else to do. This was Bogotá and Marcia wasn't going to open her door to someone arriving unannounced. But she *did* have to come out. That this would happen sooner rather than later was Alva's guess.

She waited twenty-five cold minutes in the gloomy, windowless corridor. It was long enough to give her doubts about what she was doing, and to begin to worry about the outside chance of a maintenance man appearing. When the door opened Marcia obligingly pulled it wide.

''Morning, Marcia.' Alva slipped past her startled face and into the packed-up living room. She'd been busy: equipment, maps and everything relevant to a journalist on the move had been stored in boxes to await collection.

'What the hell do you think you're doing?' The other woman recovered fast and spun into the room after Alva.

'Couldn't get you out of my mind, Marcia.' Alva continued to look around. The two suitcases stood just inside the door, along with a large bag. Marcia was definitely going to need the lift. 'So I decided to pay you another visit.' She took a deep breath. 'I want you to tell me what's really going on.' She moved to the centre of the room and stood facing the other woman.

'I don't believe this.' Marcia Tulins ground her teeth. 'You come barging into my place just as I'm rushing to—'

'And if you want to continue rushing, and get your flight, all you have to do is be straight with me. Because you weren't straight yesterday.'

For a moment, her stomach contracting with fear, Alva thought Marcia was going to hit her. Her eyes were wild and her hands in tight fists by her sides. She was wearing jeans and a denim jacket, and without the cover-all properties of the day before's kaftan was a *very* big woman. Alva forced herself to stand her ground. Marcia had to know she meant business and was not going to be put off.

'What sort of nut *are* you?' Her New York accent sounded a lot harsher and more nasal than the day before. 'I'm becoming seriously pissed off with you people. First Eric, then Luke and now you taking up my time. Why don't you get off my back!' She picked up the bag, slung it across her shoulder, grabbed a suitcase in each hand. 'I'm outta here. You can entertain your fantasies alone.'

Alva watched her struggle through the door with the luggage. She timed things and got Marcia's squawking discovery of the jammed lift right to the second. What sounded like kicks to the cage were followed by loud and voluble swearing. Alva walked to the door of the apartment and leaned there. It was important to give the impression that she, at least, had all the time in the world.

'I'm willing to do a deal, Marcia,' she smiled. 'You tell me the truth about what's going on and I'll get the lift working for you. I'll even help you down with your luggage.'

Marcia continued to swear. Proving herself someone who believed in coming to terms with a language in all its uses she threw several words not in the Spanish dictionary Alva's way. Her face had gone bluish, and Alva had started to worry about her heart, when the intercom buzzed on the wall beside her. She picked it up. It was the taxi driver for Señorita Tulins.

'Sorry,' Alva told him, 'Señorita Tulins is delayed. Please wait.' She cut him off and looked thoughtfully at the instrument in her hand. Marcia, silent now and staring by the lift, gave a screech of protest as Alva ripped the cord from the wall.

'He'll wait about ten minutes, I'd say.' Alva was sweetly reasonable. 'But he won't be coming up ten flights to help you with your bags. So – what about a deal, Marcia? You could be on your way in five or six minutes if you talk fast.'

Marcia Tulins was not a survivor by accident. She took several, cooled-down seconds to assess her situation. The sudden wail of a siren in the street below seemed to help make up her mind.

'Possession is nine-tenths of the law,' she almost grinned, 'so I can't see what harm telling you will do at this stage. Deed's done. This is just hassle, aggravation. Nothing more.'

'Fine,' Alva snapped, 'you can get on with telling me the truth then.'

Marcia Tulins, a study in demented urgency, jammed her hands into the pockets of her denim jacket and began to pace in front of the lift. Frizzy curls had escaped from the tight bunch she'd made of her hair and she gnawed on her bottom lip. Alva tapped her foot, hoping to add to the other's frenzy, and Marcia began to talk at speed.

'You have to understand that my job is all I have,' her mouth twisted a little, 'is all I'm ever likely to have.'

'I'm not interested in your self-justification or in self-pity.' Alva was curt.

''Course you're not.' Marcia threw her a look of pure dislike. 'Christ, but the righteous are a pain in the butt. What do you know about anything? You probably spent a few years in a newspaper office, all regular with salary and pension, and thought yourself a journalist. Well, this is the real world. Here we're talking dog eat dog and the devil take the hindmost. We're talking too about me breaking my ass getting my agency pictures – but we've been through that and you don't want to hear. Well, the story is this. One night just over nine months ago, my old friend Eric O'Hanlon turns up with pages and pages of words stuffed into a backpack. Turns out it's a book he's writing about Colombia, faction-style – real events mixed with fiction. It's good. Very good in fact. And I'm sickened. It's not enough Eric dumps me in New York.

He turns up on my patch with a fucking good book, the book I should've been writing myself, if I could.'

She stopped pacing and looked at her watch, flexing her fingers. They were strong, square fingers and Alva tensed herself against the door. But the other woman's voice was calm when she went on. It was as if, once started, she wanted to continue, to tell all.

'I offered him a deal. My pictures and his words, together, in a package to a publisher. Something different and exciting.' She paused. 'But he said no. He wasn't writing that kind of book, he said, he wasn't interested only in Colombia's *mala fama*. He wanted to show the good too.' She paused again and her expression became briefly bleak. 'He didn't use the word exploitative about my idea but it was what he meant. He always managed to make me feel ... unworthy. Another from the ranks of the self-righteous. Must be something to do with the climate in Ireland. Or the lack of reality.' She tightened her lips and began to pace again. 'But one thing holier-than-thou Eric didn't have was professionalism. Which is where crude old Marcia Tulins had the edge. He'd done the research all right, moving around to Cartagena and Barranquilla on the Caribbean and up into the Indian territories of the Sierra Nevada. He'd already written his first chapters and he gave them to me with the draft—'

'He gave them to you?' Alva interrupted. 'Why?'

'Because he's an idiot,' Marcia was pitying, 'and because he was going back up to Infiesto, where he'd been already, to finish the book. He asked me to put it all in a bank deposit box, same bank he said there would be money coming into from a screenplay he'd written.' She shook her head. 'A group of villagers come down to Bogotá every six weeks or so and Eric arranged for them to bring me down what he'd written each time they came. The idea was that I'd read and send comments back. I was also supposed to put the chapters in the bank box and send him up money from his account. Oh, and I was to send the bulk of the money to a project he'd been working on.' There was a puzzled frown between her eyes. 'I've never been able to decide whether Eric is an arrogant shit or a naïve fool. He really thought I'd do all of that for old times' sake, no problem . . .'

'Doesn't seem a huge thing to ask,' Alva said. 'Read a couple of chapters of a book and visit the bank every six weeks.'

Marcia looked at her irritably. 'It was inconvenient and there was nothing in it for me. It was fucking insensitive of him too. He'd already given me the heave in New York. He seemed to think we could still be friends and that he could turn up here and screw me up all over again.'

'So you didn't take out the money?' Alva knew she hadn't. So far the story was ringing true.

Marcia shrugged and kicked the wall, but tiredly. 'I sent him money of my own, enough to keep him up there. You could say I've paid for the book, that I deserve it. Plus his own money's still in the bank for when he comes down.'

'And the project money?'

'Told him I'd sent it on to them.' Marcia gave a tight smile. 'Even sent him regular reports on how things were going. Trick of the trade – I can be quite inventive with facts when I have to.' Something in Alva's expression made her fleetingly defensive. 'They'll get their money,' she was sour, 'it's just a delay as far as they're concerned. Everything's *mañana* in this country anyway.'

'So you held on to the chapters as they were brought down?' Alva wanted to be clear how things had happened.

'Jesus, woman, haven't you understood a thing I've been saying to you?' Marcia shook her head and went on, with infinite patience. 'Look – he turns down the deal I offer for the book and then expects me to help him with it, act as a mentor and banker. Of course I held on to them. I had plans.' She dragged up a deep breath. 'Only then, out of the blue, Luke starts getting in touch, worrying about his brother. I didn't want him out here before things were tied up so I sent him a couple of postcards, reassured him.'

'You didn't do a marvellous job,' Alva said drily. 'If it hadn't been for the film he was working on he'd have been here months ago. What did you do with Eric's book?'

'You *know* what I did with the book, Alva, don't play dumb.' Marcia's voice was angry again. 'I rewrote parts of it, remoulded it nearer to my heart's desire as the poet once said, and then I sold it, along with my pictures, to a publisher in New York. I signed the contract over Christmas. It's done, a *fait accompli.*

There's nothing you or anyone else can do about it. The final tees were crossed in that fax you saw coming through last night.'

'You put your name to Eric O'Hanlon's book?'

'*My* book. I *made* it mine. I did the corrections. I wrote the end. He hasn't sent that down yet and I couldn't afford to wait any longer, not after Luke arrived.' She closed her eyes and rubbed a hand across them. For moments she looked old and hollow and Alva had a flash of how she would be in a few more years of living the way she did. When she opened her eyes again they were sharp, impatient.

'Now you know and I want to go. We had a deal.' She nodded towards the lift.

'Just one last thing . . .'

'We had a deal.' Marcia Tulins shook her head. Her voice was tight.

'The deal was for the whole story. Why don't I go down in the lift with you and you can fill me in on a few points?'

'Sure,' Marcia said. '*As* we go down.'

'Wait here,' Alva said, 'I'll send it up to you.'

On the ninth floor she deftly removed the credit card, stepped into the lift and pressed the start button. Nothing happened. She pressed it again and with a slow grinding the lift moved slowly upwards. On the tenth floor she held the door open for Marcia to load her suitcases and bag.

'What did you tell Luke?' Alva demanded as they moved down. 'You obviously diverted him. I just don't believe he's been up in that village for five weeks.'

410

'If I miss my plane – if my cabbie's gone . . .' Marcia, watching the floor numbers as they passed, punched a fist into the palm of her other hand.

'Does Luke know the full story?' Alva persisted. 'When did he go up to Infiesto?'

The lift stopped on the ground floor. 'Why don't you just piss off to Infiesto and find out for yourself?' Marcia Tulins gave a mirthless laugh and dragged her luggage out. Alva didn't try to stop her. She didn't help either. On the forecourt outside the glass entrance a grey taxi waited. The driver was asleep at the wheel.

'The devil looks after his own,' Alva said. Marcia Tulins, yelling at the man through his window, ignored her. She didn't look back as the taxi disappeared into traffic.

Alva walked slowly in search of a taxi for herself. That was it, then. A simple, everyday story of frustrated love, greed and ambition. None of what had happened, not Eric's disappearance, nor Luke's, nor the sick panic which had brought her here herself, had anything to do with this beautiful country and the baleful twosome controlling it, *la droga y la muerte*, drugs and death.

It had everything to do, though, with exploiting Colombia's tragedy and with one rather sad woman's ego and desperate need.

Chapter Twenty-Five

The plane to Pereira took Alva back out over the mountains, down along the valley of the Magdalena river and up again, across ever-higher, snowcapped Andean peaks. The volcanic tip of a mountain poked through the clouds and a child behind her asked his mother if it was dead. Alva wished he hadn't. It *looked* defunct. But if she'd learned anything from life in recent years it was that things were rarely as they seemed.

What she hadn't known was that she had a taste for travel. Under different circumstances she would have revelled in the changing scenes and lusty life she found herself a part of. Her only fear, as she moved higher and deeper into the mountains, was of what she might find at the end of her journey. For herself she felt no trepidation at all.

She was travelling light, in jeans and a jacket, one small bag with necessities, a change of clothing and a jumper for the cold nights. Everything else she'd left with Estella until she returned with Luke and his brother in a week or so. She was refusing to consider any other scenario.

Pereira was a shock and a delight; a place of tropical foliage, bright flowers, smiling people, and where the air was soft and warm against the skin. As darkness began to fall she found a taxi and headed, through mountainy plantations of coffee shrubs, for San Mateo. The town was coming awake for the night as they got there and, after a quick shower in her very basic hotel, she watched from the window the strolling men, boys, children and dogs in the streets. The absence of women was notable. Sleep, when she went to bed, came slowly and was fitful.

She was up early. Life was a seamless business in San Mateo, daytime activities taking over from those of the night without a break. At reception she discovered a regular bus left at ten for Almonte, the next village up, and that from there another went twice a week, thunderstorms permitting, to Infiesto. With an hour to kill she decided to walk to the bus depot.

The streets, at first, were carnival-like; huge, skinned pineapples in makeshift barrows sat row upon row beside sliced coconuts and mangoes. She bought some to eat as she went along, then stopped to have a *tinto* in a bar filled with men playing board games. It was insipid and the waiter apologetic.

'The best coffee is exported.' He shrugged. 'In Colombia we are left with the dust. And with *la blanca*.' *La blanca*. Cocaine. Always drugs. She left and began walking again.

At the edge of town she found that instead of the bus depot she had arrived at a sprawling shanty town. As she stood, undecided, a small boy approached. One hand held a long, dirty rag tied to a sad-looking dog. He shoved the other hand at her.

'Money,' he demanded. 'Give me money.'

Alva held up a note. 'For you if you take me to the bus station.'

He gave a quick nod, grabbed the money and with a jerk of his head led the way along the side of the shanty town. She knew he could be taking her anywhere, trusted him not to – but was relieved when the bus station came quickly into view. At the ticket desk he turned to her, tapping the side of his head.

'You must be careful in Colombia, señora.' His expression was pitying. 'And you must be clever.'

Alva looked at him, an eight-year-old going on four hundred, and gently ruffled his black curls. 'I am neither so unwise nor so naïve as I seem,' she spoke gently, knowing he would understand, 'and I am very determined to get where I am going.'

He understood. 'I think you will get there, señora,' he said. He waited with her until the bus arrived. His name, he said, was Alvarito; his dog's name was Julio, and they lived together on the streets of San Mateo. Marvelling at how similar their names were, Alva, smiling, said she hoped he would be lucky for her. He nodded. The day got warmer and from the shanty town there arose the sweet, stifling smell of urine.

When the bus came Alva would have hugged Alvarito but he moved away too quickly for that. Sitting in her seat she watched him leave the depot, a small figure whose shadow was already lengthening in the sun.

In Almonte the driver found her a room in a

boarding house and told her where to get the bus two days later for Infiesto.

The time spent in Almonte was oddly peaceful. The mood in the village was lethargic and Alva took life at its pace, ignored for the most part as a strange *gringuita* who liked her own company.

In the bright, late afternoon of the second day she walked to the edge of the village. A white-haired man on horseback picked a slow way across the valley below. He brought Theo to mind – and brought to mind too that long ago, sunny day in May when Seona's phone call had started the chain of events which had led her here. Watching the blue-green mountain peaks and almost clear sky, Alva wondered if there had been some sort of cosmic design at work that day. Here, in this place, anything seemed possible.

Theo had been more himself than he'd been for a long time when she'd left, happy about Clara's proposal and De Novo's future. Thinking about things now, all this distance away, Alva felt more than ever sure that her decision to sell to Clara had been the right one. Clara loved De Novo and she loved the gardens. She had children, who would bring life and energy to the place – who were in fact the reason Clara wanted to buy.

'I want to get them out of New York for their teen years,' she'd explained, 'send them to school here. And I want to have a base in Ireland for myself. Sell to me, Alva; give Theo his freedom and take your own.'

'But Bernie . . .'

'Work something out with Bernie. She'll be fine. She's doing something with her life. You should do the same. It's time you acted, Alva,' she'd grinned. 'Life's not a dress rehearsal.'

She was right. De Novo was Alva's past, not her future. She agreed to sell to Clara and knew that the first act of the rest of her life had happened.

This, her journey to find Luke, was act two, and was a lot less certain.

The bus for Infiesto left earlier than scheduled next morning. Alva was having a coffee in the sun when the driver arrived to round up his passengers.

'Storm coming.' He was young and very handsome. 'We go now we get there before it strikes. We go later, someone else can drive.' He held up the keys. There were no takers.

His bus was a vividly painted rattle-trap. The journey, a constant climb, would take three hours.

Alva, an hour into their slow, lurching ascent, felt unaccountably tired. The altitude getting to her, she supposed, and abandoned both the awesome views and thoughts of Luke for sleep.

She awoke from a confused dream to a muttering disquiet in the bus. It was crawling along a stony, red-clay road from where, outside her window, a deep gorge fell away into a valley. Across the mountaintops storm clouds had massed, and as she looked the first ricochet of thunder rattled in the distance. A series of quick thuds against the window announced rain and the woman beside her produced a string of rosary beads. In seconds the rain had become a torrenting downpour. The driver's storm had arrived.

The red clay of the road turned to a watery mud which loosened and carried stones and rocks past and under the wheels of the bus. Small rivers poured through cracks in the chassis. They inched forward, going nowhere until, without warning, the bus swerved, skidded and, to a low, collective moan from the passengers, slid to a stop horizontally across the road.

Alva closed her eyes tight, but an image of the wheels hanging over the gorge persisted anyway. With it came flashing memories of newspaper stories about tropical storms and busloads of people crashing to their deaths in ravines like the one below them. She opened her eyes and focused on the driver. His mirror was hung with Christmas tinsel and through it she could just see his eyes, black and intense as he straightened the bus and began to inch forward again. All of the women were now praying, some of the men too.

No one told the driver what to do, no one suggested stopping or getting off. They came to a bend and the valley, hundreds of feet below, was again and sickeningly in view. The praying became louder and then they were around the bend, moving forward on a relatively straight stretch of road.

As suddenly as it had started the rain eased and then stopped. Half an hour later they reached the outskirts of Infiesto.

Numb, only half-believing they were safe, Alva watched the village take shape as they began to pass houses. The first few were low, boxes almost. Most had only one window. To the back of them, like tentacles bearing down, there were giant palm trees. They passed bigger houses and then, all at once, were in the main square. On the church, colonial and rather grand, a triangle of Christmas lights had been lit to welcome the bus. Villagers came from everywhere, calling and laughing and waving their relief that the bus had made it.

Slowly, with infinite courtesy to one another, the passengers filed off. Alva stopped in the door. Below her a sea of waiting faces looked up. She scanned them, daring to hope, and saw him. He was at the back of the crowd, wearing an expression of shock so complete it was laughable. She waved and smiled and went to meet Luke.

There were no words, not for the moment. He held her against him, crushingly tight, running his hands over her as if to convince himself she was whole, complete and really there.

'Don't you have a home you can take me to?' She raised her head.

'In a minute,' he said and kissed her. As kisses went it was more than satisfactory; long, deeply probing, very promising.

'Come on.' He took her bag and then her hand and they half-ran, holding tight onto one another, up a narrow sidestreet. When they came to a low white house he led her inside, still moving fast, through a kitchen and into a small bedroom with a high narrow window and a bed covered with a bright Peruvian blanket. Alva thought it a most beautiful room.

Luke kicked a chair into place under the door handle and they fell together onto the bed. For a long while they held one another, whispering and laughing and reassuring themselves. Then they kissed again and Alva's only thoughts were that she wanted Luke O'Hanlon, all of him, now. It was her only thought for a long while.

Afterwards, lying in the small, but very adequate bed, she told him she loved him.

'I know.' He grinned and lifted her fingers, kissed them one by one. 'But I'm glad you mentioned it anyway.'

'Do you?'

'Do I what?' He brushed damp hair from her forehead.

'Do you love me, Luke?'

'O, ye of little faith,' he grinned again, 'you know that I love you. I love you now and I always will love you. You're lovely and I've missed you, every day since that last day in the pub.'

'Why didn't you send a card? It's been six weeks.'

'I did. I sent several. All of them through Marcia.' He paused. 'It's only since meeting up with Eric that nastily suspicious thoughts have presented themselves. Why do I feel, Alva my own, that you have the answers to the puzzle Eric and I have been putting together?' He pulled her against him. 'Tell me everything you know or I'll—'

419

'You'll what?' She laughed softly against the mat of brown hair on his chest.

'Later,' he promised. 'Tell me first.'

So she did, beginning at the end and the news of how Marcia had stolen Eric's book, working back to how she'd discovered this and so all the way to the beginning and how not getting a postcard had driven her crazy but made everything wonderfully and ridiculously clear to her.

'You could say that coming here to find you and discover what had happened became an obsession. And you'd be right.' She held his hand in hers and absently watched a golden ladder of street light filter down from the window. 'I had to know for myself.' She grinned. 'I knew that if I found you we'd work something out.'

'Foolish woman,' he kissed her, 'I'd have been home to you in a couple of weeks.'

'I wasn't to know that.'

'No. And now I know why. I gave Marcia the cards to send you because they don't have a postal service in Bogotá jails.'

'Jail . . .' Alva sat upright. Away from his body heat the room was cold so she flopped down beside him again. 'Bogotá jails,' she repeated.

'I spent a month in jail and now I know why.' He was very sober. 'Your story's filled in a few things.'

'Tell me,' Alva commanded quietly.

'She's good, our Marcia, I'll give her that. Knows how to be ruthless enough to get what she wants. When I arrived she convinced me she'd heard again from

Eric, that he'd moved on and that it would save time if she made the enquiries. Well, I swallowed that, and for a week she gave me the run-around. That's hindsight speaking, by the way. At the time I thought she was helping. Then I began to nose around myself. I must have been going to the right places; either that or I was getting on her nerves, because one night, for reasons I still can't fathom, I found myself in a fight in a bar. It ended with me in jail and a Bogotá policeman claiming he'd found cocaine on me.'

'Oh, my God.'

'Wasn't so bad,' Luke grinned. 'An experience I'll be able to use in my masterpiece film some day. Thing is, this is a country where anything can be arranged. I knew someone was stitching me up and I figured it had to do with Eric. I was too busy looking at the bright side – machete gangs do a brisk trade in getting rid of people in Bogotá, so I felt reasonably safe in jail. Marcia busied herself playing the role of saviour, pulling strings to get me out. God, but she was good at it.' He gave a short laugh. 'She really must have had to work at keeping me in there while she got the book together and wound things up in New York. Christ knows what favours she called in, what promises she made. She got me out when she got back from New York and sent me on my way up here.'

'Eric!' Alva sat up again. 'He *is* here?'

'He's here,' Luke pulled her back against him, 'and he's fine. You can meet him later, but not just yet . . .' He moved her hair away from her neck, began to kiss her.

'He'll have to move quickly,' Alva shook herself free, 'if he wants to salvage anything of his book. Marcia really seems to have things sewn up.'

'She may find there are a few complications.' Luke's voice was lazy, his mouth very close. 'Eric didn't quite tell Marcia everything. Seems that about four months ago he sent a few revised chapters and an outline on how it would work as a film to a mate in New York. Wanted to do it on his own this time, without big brother's help. It looks like he's done it, too. There's a lot of interest, a contract's being drawn up . . .'

'Complications.' Alva gave a small laugh. 'What lovely sounding complications . . .'

'Nothing to do with us, nothing to do with now . . .' He kissed her. 'We've got other things to think about.'

'And do,' Alva said.

It really was a most beautiful room.